HIS RIGHT HAND

Also by Mette Ivie Harrison
The Bishop's Wife

HIS

RIGHT

HAND

Mette Ivie Harrison

Published by Soho Press, Inc.
853 Broadway
New York, NY 10003

Library of Congress Cataloging-in-Publication Data

Harrison, Mette Ivie, 1970–
His right hand / Mette Ivie Harrison.

ISBN 978-1-61695-763-6
eISBN 978-1-61695-611-0
I. Title.
PS3608.A783578H57 2015
813'.6—dc23 2015019898

Interior design by Janine Agro, Soho Press, Inc.

Printed in the United States of America

10 9 8 7 6 5 4 3 2 1

To Neca, David, and Grayson,
who invited me along on their journey

HIS RIGHT HAND

CHAPTER 1

One Friday night in May, in lieu of our regular couple's date, my husband, Kurt, and I were going to the annual bishopric dinner. Kurt was the bishop of our Mormon ward in Draper, Utah—it was the second year of his five-year calling, so this was the second annual dinner I'd attended.

I wished that I were looking forward to the dinner more, but it was just another one of the tasks of being a bishop's wife. Tasks like playing Mrs. Claus at the annual Christmas dinner, coming up with excuses for Kurt when he was constantly late for family functions, and keeping a vigilant eye out for problems in the ward so I could alert Kurt to them. This dinner was going to be a little awkward no matter what. Kurt and his counselors would probably hint at all kinds of church matters that the wives didn't and couldn't know about, and we women would be left trying to make small talk.

There would be six of us coming to dinner: the first counselor, Tom deRyke, who was in charge of the adults and the Primary, and his wife, Verity; the second counselor, Carl Ashby, in charge of the Young Men and Young Women and the Primary, and his wife, Emma; and of course, Kurt, the bishop, and myself. We were going to Texas Roadhouse to celebrate surviving another year of performing the hardest jobs in the Mormon church—jobs which, I should mention, are completely unpaid, since we Mormons have a lay clergy. Kurt, Tom, and Carl served in the bishopric because they had been called to do so, and they performed their duties in addition to working full-time jobs to support their families financially.

As a bishop, Kurt was in charge of making sure that the whole ward was staffed, officiating at funerals and weddings, organizing the finances of the ward, conducting annual spiritual wellness interviews for all the youth, and holding church courts for discipline issues. He did a thousand other things, but those were the ones that he couldn't delegate to his counselors. Tom deRyke and Carl Ashby handled a lot of the oversight of meetings, extending callings, girls and boys camp visits, dealing with tithing donations and missionary interviews, among other things. Without them, the job of bishop would have overwhelmed Kurt. They were his right hand in more than one way.

"Ready?" asked Kurt, poking his head into our bedroom.

I was wearing a nice blouse and slacks. "Do you want me to change into a dress?"

Kurt was wearing his standard button-down plaid shirt with khakis. He had told the other members of the bishopric that tonight was to be "business casual," but the problem was, they didn't always listen.

"No, you're fine," he said.

I slid into the passenger seat of Kurt's truck and he drove down the mountain, past the temple and onto the freeway. I thought about the strange juxtaposition of the state prison on the western side of Draper, across the freeway, and the temple on the mountain by our neighborhood. The temple is the symbol for eternity for Mormons. It is where we are sealed forever as couples and as families. I was sealed to Kurt and our children there.

Kurt and I were unexpectedly early, and as he paced and sent text messages to the counselors who were probably driving and shouldn't be reading them, I observed the families waiting to be seated—husbands and wives with small children who would have been happier at home with macaroni and cheese. But it was so difficult to find babysitters these days. And this might be their only night out. The parents were tense with each other, and their body language showed anger rather than love and caring. Being in an eternal family was supposed to bring more joy to everyday chores, but sometimes it just added more stress.

The deRykes arrived next, and Kurt and I stood to greet them. Verity and I gave each other hugs. The men shook hands. I thought how beautiful Verity was, at nearly seventy. Her hair was perfectly white, and she wore it long, nearly to her waist. She had strong cheekbones that seemed to get better with age. Tom was slightly shorter than she was, which always struck me as unusual.

The waitress came over shortly after six and asked if we wanted to be seated and order appetizers or drinks. Kurt said that we would wait until the rest of the party arrived. He texted Carl Ashby again, then tried him on the phone. No response. We chatted with Tom and Verity about their landscaping project. They were redoing their entire front lawn, adding in rocks and bushes around the edges, and taking out a huge tree in the middle that had died on one side when it was hit by lightning. Ten minutes passed and Kurt tried Carl again.

Finally, I got up and went outside. I said I was going to stretch my legs, but what I really did was call Emma separately to see if I could get her to answer. It worked.

"Hello?"

"Emma, this is Linda Wallheim. We're at Texas Roadhouse, waiting. Are you on your way?" I tried to be as pleasant as possible, making sure not to make her feel guilty about putting the rest of us out, though that was precisely what she was doing.

"Yes, we're on our way," she said in a tight voice. "I'm sorry we're running a little late."

I heard a loud beep, as if Emma had pressed a button on her phone. When I heard Carl's distant voice in the background, I realized Emma probably thought she had hung up already. Carl was saying, "There are some decisions that are simply mine to make as a man and as a husband, and if you're not going to respect my authority in that role, then I wonder why we ever married in the first place."

"Oh, God," Emma said. I suspected she had just realized I was still on the phone. "I'm so sorry about that, Linda," Emma said in embarrassment. "Carl and I will be there as soon as we can." Then she hung up.

I felt my chest go heavy. I couldn't imagine what Carl and Emma had been arguing about, but the tiny snippet I'd heard made me worry that this wasn't just a throw-away spat. This dinner was going to be even more difficult than I'd expected.

CHAPTER 2

I went back inside the restaurant, and in another ten minutes the Ashbys had arrived and we were seated in a separate, small room, away from the noise of the families in the main area. It was dimly lit and decorated with oversized caricatures of celebrities I probably should have recognized but didn't.

I was watching the Ashbys carefully. Emma was a few years younger than I was, blonde and very petite, which made Carl, who was more average in height, look quite tall. Emma didn't look like she worked out, but was one of those women who fidgeted their way to increased metabolism. Carl had thick, dark eyebrows to match his thick, curly hair, and a square chin, clean shaven now that he'd been called in to the bishopric. He looked like he did work out considerably. Even in his forties, he was very attractive.

I hadn't known either of them before Kurt was called to be bishop, but Kurt had worked with Carl in the Young Men's Presidency and had been impressed at his devotion to the church. Carl was always there, doing whatever he was asked, even the least-liked jobs like the midnight cannery cleanup. He was a passionate speaker when it came to doctrine, although his opinions were a little black and white for my tastes, and I sometimes felt sorry for Emma, though I'd never noticed her struggling with their relationship before now. They both struck me as rather reserved, to the point of being cold. There was nothing wrong with taking a long time to warm up to other people, but I'd always felt they were holding something back, even with us, their good friends.

After the waitress left us with our menus, Kurt had decided to add a spiritual note to the event by asking each of us to read a scripture. I wished sometimes we could just put aside the church and be friends, but Kurt and his current counselors didn't seem to think that was possible.

Kurt had chosen a passage from the Book of Mormon about the zealous Nephite missionary Ammon (also known for cutting off the arms of those who were trying to steal the king's sheep), who had been visited by an angel and told to repent for his early life full of terrible sins. As a sign of repentance, Ammon and the other sons of Mosiah were called to preach to the Lamanites, a difficult mission since Lamanites were so antagonistic toward the Nephites because of a history of abuses between the two.

Kurt read to us from Alma 17, when Ammon tells King Lamoni, *"Yea, I desire to dwell among this people for a time; yea, and perhaps until the day I die."* When the king offers Ammon one of his daughters to wife, Ammon says, *"Nay, but I will be thy servant."* The message was obvious here, that Kurt and his counselors were servants to the other members of the ward, not above them in any way.

I read part of 1 Corinthians 13: *"For now we see through a glass, darkly; but then face to face. Now I know in part; but then shall I know even as also I am known."* I said I liked it because I felt like sometimes we thought we understood everything about this life and the next one, but in my opinion, we were still unable to really comprehend God or heaven or even the true nature of the gospel.

Tom and Verity both quoted from Joseph Smith—History in the Pearl of Great Price. Tom chose to discuss how Joseph Smith said he saw that in many religions the seemingly good feelings of people preaching *"were entirely lost in a strife of words and a contest about opinions."* Tom added, "I sincerely hope that we are not like this, that we keep disagreements out of our meetings, and remember to have the Spirit of God with us always." Verity quoted the much-used scripture in James that had sent Joseph Smith to the Sacred Grove to pray to know which church to join, which had led to a vision of God and Jesus Christ: *"If any of you lack wisdom, let him ask of God, that giveth to all men liberally and upbraideth not and it shall be given him."* She added that she believed God gave to all of us, men and women, black and white. We had only to ask and the revelation would come. I agreed with her, though I wished sometimes that understanding personal revelation didn't leave so much up to interpretation.

Then Carl read from the Family Proclamation, which he had loaded on his phone's screen: *"All human beings—male and female—are created in the image of God. Each is a beloved spirit son or daughter of heavenly parents, and, as such, each has a divine nature and destiny. Gender is an essential charac-teristic of individual premortal, mortal, and eternal identity and purpose...*

"The first commandment that God gave to Adam and Eve pertained to their potential for parenthood as husband and

wife. We declare that God's commandment for His children to multiply and replenish the earth remains in force. We further declare that God has commanded that the sacred powers of procreation are to be employed only between man and woman, lawfully wedded as husband and wife."

The Family Proclamation had been given by the First Presidency of the church when Gordon B. Hinckley was the prophet in 1995. It had quickly become the most commonly quoted piece of Mormon doctrine, as it supposedly explained why gay marriage was impossible in the Mormon temple. God doesn't so much give us our gender as affirm it is real and not a social construct. It is part of our spirit, which was created at the beginning of the universe and will continue to exist in one form or another for the rest of eternity.

It didn't surprise me that Carl had chosen to read the Family Proclamation, however often we had all heard it already. Carl Ashby was a TBM, a True Blue Mormon. The church was everything in his life.

"And Emma?" asked Kurt, since she was silent for a long while after Carl spoke.

Emma's lips thinned and she shook her head. "I just feel a little wrung out today. If you don't mind, I'll just listen and learn."

"Of course," said Kurt. "I hope that you feel better soon." He looked at me, clearly meaning that I should add Emma Ashby to my list of people who would need a friendly, informal "bishop's wife" visit in the future. Kurt didn't know yet that I'd already added Emma to my list, after having overheard that telephone conversation.

After this exchange of spiritual thoughts, the waitress came and we ordered. I got the small Dallas filet, the same thing I always ordered. You can't beat a good, tender filet, and I liked the one here medium rare.

After all the orders were taken, Kurt began a conversation with Tom and Carl about an upcoming service project and which people in the ward he thought could use help in their yards. That left me to make conversation with the wives. I asked Verity about any suggestions she had for dealing with an empty nest. She and Tom already had grandchildren who were starting college at this point, and had plenty of advice.

"Do you ever feel like you have nothing to do?" I asked.

"Never," said Verity. "That's the wonderful thing about children. Just when you think you're finished raising them, they come back. Or they need you desperately. Don't worry about that part. They don't ever really fully leave you."

That was not reassuring to me. I had enjoyed being a stay-at-home mother, but that didn't mean I wanted my children to remain dependent on me forever. "You never considered getting a job or going back to school?" I asked, thinking back to the waiting college application on my computer.

"Not really. I had plenty of things to fill my time," said Verity.

"What about you, Emma?" I asked. "Your two kids are teens now, too. You must be thinking about what you'll do when they're gone."

But Emma didn't have a chance to answer, because Carl cut in, "A woman's proper place is in the home, whatever her stage in life." He had turned away from the bishopric to speak to us women.

I could see Kurt close his eyes briefly. He was worried where this was headed—he knew I wasn't good at biting my tongue when I disagreed with someone.

"Maybe women should decide for themselves where they belong," I said, "once they've taken care of their responsibilities."

Carl was silent for a long moment. "We don't decide for ourselves what is right and wrong," he said finally. "We look to God for that, surely. Isn't that what religion is?"

"Of course," Kurt intervened, "but there is always individual revelation. Not every woman's path will follow the same route." There was an apology in the hand patting my shoulder.

"I think women's paths diverge less often than men's, though," said Carl. "Women are meant to be the compensation for a difficult day at work, a comfort after the battle against Satan and the world itself, the softness when everything else is hard."

Compensation? I looked at the other two women. Verity had a faint, condescending smile on her face. Emma, on the other hand, seemed about ready to explode. I didn't blame her one bit.

"Am I not soft enough for you, then?" asked Emma. Her voice was hardly audible above the background noises of the restaurant.

"We could all do with improvement," said Carl, looking at his wife as though he was about to give her a more complete list of the ways in which she could do better.

Kurt said, "Perhaps now is not the time for this." I could see his discomfort with the situation. Clearly Carl and Emma were still engaged in whatever fight they had been having before they arrived. What did you do in a bishopric when the leaders were the ones who needed the counseling?

But Carl Ashby wasn't done. *"By divine design,"* he

persevered, *"fathers are to preside over their families in love and righteousness and are responsible to provide the necessities of life and protection for their families."* He was quoting from the Proclamation again. *"Mothers are primarily responsible for the nurture of their children.* That is their sacred duty," he spat, staring his wife in the eye. "Fathers provide and mothers nurture."

It sounded like he was saying that Emma was not doing her divinely appointed job, that she was an unnurturing mother. I was too stunned at this open criticism to say anything. Kurt also seemed unable to speak.

"It must be a comfort to you to know that there is always a scripture you can quote to prove your mastery of any situation," said Verity deRyke after a moment. I could hear the sharp sarcasm in her tone. Her husband was shaking his head slowly, though he didn't say a word.

"Wow, look at this dessert menu they have here," said Kurt, picking up the plastic standing menu advertising giant sundaes. What a ham-fisted attempt to change the subject. "Carl, which one do you want?"

Kurt could have done better. He could have called Carl out, told him to apologize to his wife. He could have gone further and asked for him to repent his arrogance and told him to stop using the scriptures as weapons to launch at other people's hearts. But he'd taken the coward's way out, and it made me angry.

I wasn't going to let Carl off so easily. "We're all God's children, here to do His work to serve each other," I said to him. "The form that service takes surely matters less than the fact that we have a joint purpose." I watched Emma nod once and set her hands on the table, folded.

But Carl didn't let it go. "We may have a joint purpose, but our roles are entirely different. Women have one path to follow and men have another. We can only find true perfection in fulfilling our roles completely, and accepting that God is the one who chooses who is to have one role and who is to have the other."

I could see Kurt opening his mouth to say something, but it was too late. Emma Ashby was already standing up, placing the cloth napkin carefully on her empty plate.

"Wait!" said Kurt.

She turned to face him. "Excuse me, Bishop," she said.

"Emma," said Carl. "Please sit back down." He sounded calmer now, but he would have needed to act a lot more contrite to convince me he'd be a pleasant dinner companion for the next hour—and Emma had had to listen to him on the car ride down here.

"I can't stay here. I have to go home," Emma called, already on her way to the door.

If she took their car, that would leave Carl to ride with one of us. He had one moment to decide what to do; as far as I could tell, he seemed most likely to just watch her flee.

Kurt finally spoke up. "Go after her, Carl! Take her home and we'll deal with things here."

Carl blinked once, and then did what Kurt suggested.

He took long strides to catch up with her. I caught a glimpse of a flush of red on his face before the door closed behind him, and thought that at last he had figured out he was in the wrong.

"I apologize," said Kurt. "To all of you. This was not the celebration I intended it to be." Verity and Tom were making noises about it not being his fault, but Kurt was looking specifically at me. He knew I held him responsible for not intervening sooner.

But was it really his fault? I was the one who had overheard their conversation on the phone earlier. I could have warned Kurt there were problems to begin with.

CHAPTER 3

The waitress brought out our food, including what the Ashbys had ordered, hesitating before putting them down at the spots that Kurt indicated.

"We'll box it up and take it over after," he said. "Then we can see if there's still something wrong."

I raised my eyebrows at him. Did he think an argument like that could be fixed in a matter of minutes? I had no such optimism. Carl criticizing his wife in public like that wasn't going to be easily repaired. You couldn't apologize enough for something that arrogant and obnoxious.

As I thought more about it, I realized it wasn't the first time I had heard Carl take a reactionary position on gender roles. I remembered how unhappy Carl Ashby had been when Kurt had volunteered the bishopric to cook at the Christmas breakfast last year, the first year they were all in the bishopric together. "I don't know how to cook," he had said. "I'll make a mess out of it."

"That's half the fun," said Kurt, and he insisted on it. Carl had refused to wear the apron that Kurt had brought, however, and had, as promised, made a mess of the pancakes. I had wondered if anyone could really be so inept as to ruin pancakes, or if he had done it on purpose to make a point.

Clearly, gender roles were a strict law for Carl Ashby. And something Emma had done had tweaked him about it.

"Has he mentioned any problems in their marriage before?" I asked. This wasn't gossip. It was an attempt to help.

"No, nothing," said Kurt. I could sense his reluctance to speak about a private topic here. I hoped he and Tom would have a discussion with Carl later on, when they had their next meeting.

"I'm sure they'll work things out," said Tom. "Marriage is the most important thing in the world for all of us."

Did he mean for Mormons, who believe marriage is a necessary ordinance to get into the highest level of heaven, the celestial kingdom? Or did he mean the bishopric specifically?

For all the problems that I have with the church as a patriarchal institution, women have power in unexpected ways, and one of them is as a wife of a member of the bishopric. Men in the Mormon church have to be married in the temple in order to serve in the highest orders of the church. It isn't a man alone who holds the highest priesthood, it is a man-woman unit, a marriage. That is why a wife is always asked if she accepts the calling of her husband into the bishopric. It is one of the few cases in which her vote truly matters. If she is against it, or if the marriage is unsteady, most of the time the calling will be withdrawn. And a divorce for a serving member of the bishopric almost always means an immediate release from the calling.

We ate in silence for a while. Kurt eventually tried to talk about football, a safe topic. But when he noticed me looking at him balefully, he switched the conversation back to Fourth of July preparations, a topic more likely to involve Verity and me.

It was all a façade, though, and we knew it. There wasn't any real bishopric bonding going on, now that Carl and Emma had left in that state. We were just trying to make it to the end.

Kurt asked me if I wanted dessert, but I declined and excused myself to go to the ladies' room. Verity followed me.

We were the only two women in the ladies' room. I felt old looking at myself in the mirror. There were lines in my face that were recent, and my hair was going salt-and-pepper gray. I knew I shouldn't be vain about it, but I was.

Verity paused in front of the mirror as well. She caught my eye in the glass. "When I see women like Emma Ashby, I think it's too bad we don't know more about Heavenly Mother," she said. "We need a model for how women are to be womanly and still strong, how they use power in a righteous way, even when their husbands are being unrighteous."

If my eyebrows could have flown off my forehead, I think they would have. I'd heard feminists within the church agitate about discussing Heavenly Mother more, even praying to her, but Verity deRyke was not the kind of Mormon I would have thought interested in the topic. "I suppose you're right," I said, wondering if she would say anything else. But she didn't.

After an awkward moment, we each used a stall, then washed our hands and went back out to sit with the men.

As Verity and I sat down again, I was relieved to realize the men were talking about Carl and Emma, which meant they were taking the matter seriously. "Something is deeply bothering Carl," said Tom deRyke, taking a bite of a giant brownie sundae that had arrived while we were gone. "He wouldn't be acting like this otherwise."

"I'll pray about it," Kurt offered.

"I will, too," said Tom, nodding gravely. "Maybe add a fast."

I wasn't happy with this. It wasn't that I thought that fasting and praying for someone couldn't possibly help; I just didn't think that was a cure-all.

WHEN WE GOT home that night, I checked in the living room to find that Samuel had fallen asleep studying for finals. I got him tucked into bed upstairs, then walked over to the Ashbys' place and knocked on the door lightly. The porch light came on first, making me blink rapidly. I held out the food from the restaurant in the takeout boxes, stone cold now. I wondered who would appear on the other side of the door.

I waited for a long minute before Emma opened the door. I looked her over quickly, searching for some sign of abuse, but the only thing I could see was puffy, reddened eyes.

Emma took the leftovers. "I'm sorry about ruining the bishopric dinner," she said hoarsely.

Where was Carl? Was he going to apologize, too, or was he going to act as if it had never happened? I realized Carl reminded me a little of my father, long gone now, and long forgiven, too. But how it used to bother me that the man could never apologize for anything or admit he had done anything wrong. I remembered, when I was a child, my father knocking over a glass of milk and then blaming me for it, forcing me to clean it up. I had struggled so much in my relationship with him, love combined with resentment.

"You don't need to apologize," I told Emma. "I just want to know if I can do something to help."

"We're fine. Really." Her eyes flickered, and I realized that

Carl must be standing behind her. My skin crawled. Had he been there the whole time?

"We'll talk later, in private," I told Emma. "You know, everyone has problems. There's nothing wrong with admitting that and asking for help."

"No, no. It was just a fuss I made over nothing. I'm embarrassed about it now." Her cheeks flushed bright red.

"You're sure you're fine? You could come over to our house for the night, if you'd like." I really had a hard time believing she was in any danger from the stuffy, sometimes punctilious Carl, but I could be wrong. I had been wrong before. Too often, when it came to judging marriages in the ward.

"No, that's not necessary." She tried to laugh. "Thank you for coming by, though. And thank you for the food. We both appreciate it so much." Then she closed the door.

I had the feeling she wasn't very grateful to me at all. She thought I was being nosy, and maybe I was.

CHAPTER 4

On Saturday, when I finally had a chance, I talked to Kurt about the conversation I'd overheard on the phone. "Carl sounded so controlling and critical. Do you think there's any possibility he's abusing Emma?"

Kurt seemed thoughtful. "I don't know if abuse is the problem. Last night was the first time I'd seen Carl try to exercise any authority. You don't know how many times Emma has called him during a meeting at church and demanded that he come home for some trivial thing."

Kurt thought it was trivial, but clearly Emma did not. I was certainly not going to condemn another woman for being jealous of the time her husband spent in church service. It left a heavy burden for the wife, and Emma's children were younger than mine were. I sympathized with a woman who felt she needed the father of her children at home rather than serving the children of other people in the ward.

"Do you think you should release him?" I asked.

"I can't release a member of the bishopric. The stake president would have to do that. But ask to have him released? I suppose, if he came to me and explained why he needed that. But he isn't asking, Linda. And Emma hasn't asked, either. We really don't know what is going on between them. And unless they tell us, we shouldn't leap to conclusions. That phone conversation could have been about almost anything."

I figured I would wait and see, and church on Sunday went without a hitch. Carl Ashby was on the stand for sacrament meeting, sitting to Kurt's right. Emma was in Relief Society. I meant to go talk to her afterward, but she hurried out early and must have taken her children with her, because I didn't see them when I walked by the youth rooms.

I thought about Alice and William, who were both in high school. They had been adopted as infants. Emma and Carl both seemed rather strict as parents, filling the children's lives with long lists of rules.

Would either Alice or William know what was going on with their parents? They were in high school, certainly old enough to have observed the tension. Of course, it would be completely inappropriate for me to go to them for information just to satisfy my own curiosity.

Late on Thursday night, Emma called Kurt's cell phone and asked to speak to me.

"Hello?" I said.

"Linda? Is that you?" she asked, her voice tired.

"It's me. What's wrong?" I was suddenly afraid that Carl had escalated from demeaning her in public to hitting her. I suppose I had become ready to expect the worst of men.

"Kurt answered the phone," she said.

"Yes," I said, confused as to why that mattered. I glanced up and saw Kurt in the doorway of our bedroom, unsure if he should stay or go.

"I thought there was a meeting at the church until late tonight," said Emma. "For the whole bishopric."

"Not that I know of," I said. I held my hand over the receiver and asked Kurt, "Was there a bishopric meeting at the church tonight?"

"No," he said.

I let my hand fall from the phone. "Kurt says no meeting," I told Emma.

"But Carl said he had to go to the church. He said the meeting would run late and that I shouldn't wait up for him."

What kind of a meeting could Carl have been talking about? "Kurt could call the stake president and ask if it was something on that end," I offered.

Emma hesitated a long moment. "Carl left just after six and he isn't answering his cell phone. He's never this late getting home." There was a banked panic in her voice.

"We can go over and check on him." I looked at Kurt, and he nodded. He was still dressed, but I would have to change.

"Thank you," said Emma. This time it sounded like she meant it.

I hung up the phone.

"He really shouldn't be at the church this late," said Kurt as we got into the truck. "I can't imagine what he's doing. If this had been something to do with the stake, I would have known about it."

What I couldn't imagine was what we would tell Emma if he wasn't there. Where would we look next? What if Carl was involved in an affair, or some other lifestyle secret he was hiding from his wife, drinking or gambling or drugs?

In the church parking lot, Kurt pointed at a brand-new silver Lexus. "There's his car." I had to admit whenever I saw Mormons, especially ones as sanctimonious as Carl Ashby, driving cars like that, it bothered me. The money spent on that car could have paid for ten missionaries. Or a whole lot of food in a shelter. We talk so much about modesty in terms of clothing in the church, less about modesty when it comes to giant houses, cars, or television sets.

"So he's here," I said, and got out my phone.

Kurt put a hand on my arm. "Wait until we've seen him," he said.

He parked and we got out. It was one of those late summer nights when the weather was perfect, warm with hardly even a breeze. I noticed there wasn't another car in the church parking lot, so he wasn't here with anyone else. I felt relief briefly as I dismissed the idea of him being involved in anything sexually illicit. I should have known better when it came to staid Carl Ashby.

So what was he doing here? Praying in a quiet space away from home? Playing basketball all by himself in the gym? Doing genealogy on the computer in the library? Or just avoiding his wife?

Kurt pulled on one of the main glass doors. "It's unlocked," he said. I followed him in. He checked the bishop's office first. It was locked and dark. We went through the rest of the chapel, room by room, until we found him. He was in one of the small classrooms on the east side, in his usual suit and tie.

He was dead.

It was obvious as soon as we saw him. His face was a mottled reddish gray and he was completely motionless. I gasped at the sight and put a hand to my chest. My heart seemed to have dropped into my stomach.

Carl was sitting on a chair alone in the center of the room with a woman's pink silk scarf on the floor underneath his feet. His hands were at his sides, and he looked almost as if he were waiting for someone to arrive. My nose wrinkled as I recognized the smell in the room. Feces. His clothes were stained with it, but I couldn't tell without getting closer if the carpet was covered as well. The advantage of multicolored, low-pile church carpeting was that it hid so many problems.

I let out a sound. At least, I think it came from me and not from Kurt. I'd never seen an actual dead body up close like this, not before it was cleaned up by a mortuary, anyway. Kurt reached for me and pulled me to his chest.

I could hear the beat of his heart against my ear. It was thundering.

I felt a wave of guilt. I had been so angry with Carl the last time I saw him, it felt like I'd had something to do with his death. Did God want me to do something here? If so, what? I tried to pray, but felt a heaviness that made it impossible to reach for the heavens.

Kurt released me and took a step forward to lean over the body, putting his hand to the neck to check for a pulse. Why hadn't I thought to do that immediately? But Kurt looked up at me and shook his head.

"How? Why?" I asked, the words bubbling up without conscious effort.

"Choked to death, it looks like," said Kurt, his voice hoarse. He motioned to the line of red around Carl's throat, right above his white shirt collar.

Right. And the scarf on the floor—was that the murder weapon? If Carl had been murdered, then who had done it? How long ago? Were we in danger? The church doors had been open when we walked in. Had the murderer escaped already or was he still here? I wished Kurt and I could hurry out and pretend we hadn't seen any of this. But of course, we couldn't.

I said, "We should call the police."

"Yes," said Kurt. As bishop, he had perfected the gift of sounding normal no matter what the circumstances. "Maybe it was a break-in. Someone trying to steal something and Carl caught them."

I held tight to Kurt again, then let go as I realized that the other possibility was that the murderer was someone we knew, someone from our ward. Again.

I cleared my throat to make my voice sound more normal. "But why was Carl here in the first place?" The more I thought about this, the less sense it made. I stared at the room, the table and chairs all in place. Surely there would have been some kind of struggle. And why leave the scarf? Was that really what he had been killed with?

Kurt stepped into the hallway to make the call, out of respect for the dead, I suppose. I heard his steady voice through the open door, explaining to an emergency dispatcher what we had found. He had to repeat himself several times.

I wanted desperately to step out with him, but I found myself staring at Carl's body. He did not deserve to be left alone here. I felt like the last thing I could do for him now was to stay with him for a few moments. Kurt came back in. "One of us needs to call Emma," he said. "She needs to know about this. She can't just sit and wait all night." Kurt's voice sounded just slightly different to me, as if he had a cold. Or was it just that my ears weren't hearing normally?

I forced myself to think of Emma and her needs. "Not over the phone. I should go over to her place myself," I said. I glanced at the body, still reluctant to leave it.

But Kurt shook his head. "We can't leave before the police arrive. I think you should go ahead and call her. It may be hours before either of us is free to go over and talk to her in person."

He was the bishop. But the fact that he was asking me to do this difficult job for him meant something. It was the only sign of his distress in all of this. He was shirking his responsibility, and Kurt never did that.

"All right. I'll do it." I got out my cell phone, took a deep breath, and stared at Carl's body. Kurt was with him, though, so I didn't have to stay in the room. I moved to the hallway and called Emma's number.

"Hello? Linda, is that you? Did you find him?" asked Emma immediately, her voice eager.

"Yes, Emma. I found him," I said. My voice sounded strange in my own ears, tinny and uncertain.

"Is he on his way home?" said Emma.

"No, Emma. He's not."

"Oh. When will he be on his way, then? Did he give you an estimate?"

"Emma, he's dead," I said. It was so blunt, but how else could I say it?

"What?" Her voice was stunned and confused.

"I don't know what happened," I said. Somehow, though I'd been able to tell her he was dead, I couldn't bring myself to offer any details, like the fact that he must have been murdered. "We're at the church and we found his—him. Kurt called the police and we're waiting on them."

"But—I don't understand. How could this have happened?" said Emma, now bewildered and childlike.

"I don't know, Emma. I'm so sorry. I'll be over as soon as I can. In the meantime, who are your visiting teachers? I'll call them up right now and make sure they come over and sit with you." I couldn't think what else to do. I didn't think Emma would be sleeping any time soon and it seemed cruel to tell her she should try.

"But what about my children? What about Alice and William?" she asked. "They're already in bed."

"You'll have to talk to them in the morning," I said.

"Are you sure you're not mistaken? Maybe it's not him. Maybe it just looks like him," said Emma. She was starting to ramble in that way people do when they have stopped being able to think rationally.

"His car is here, Emma. And Kurt and I both know him quite well. It's him."

"But—why? How could God do this to me? To us?" said Emma. "It's not fair. We don't deserve this."

As if only people who were evil had anything bad happen to them.

"Emma, it's not that either of you did anything wrong," I said. "Please, you have to believe that. This is just a terrible thing that has happened." But I didn't know that. I had no idea what Carl had been doing here at the church on a Thursday night, alone. Maybe he *had* done something wrong.

Emma started to cry. "I'll come over as soon as I can, Emma," I said, and hung up the phone. I felt like a monster. Maybe I should have insisted Kurt make the call, after all. Maybe, since he was a bishop, God would have given him the right words to say.

But I focused on the other call I had to make. It wasn't going to be any more pleasant. I dialed Sheri Tate, the Relief Society president, who had a special spiritual stewardship over all the women in the ward. She was as much of a straight arrow as Carl Ashby had been.

The phone rang and then voice mail suggested I leave a message. I called again.

The third time, she answered in a sleepy voice, "This is Sheri."

I explained to her briefly that Carl was dead and that Emma Ashby needed someone to be with her right now. "I don't know who her visiting teachers are, but can you make sure she isn't alone?" I asked.

"I'll do it," said Sheri.

I hung up feeling calmer. Emma was in Sheri Tate's capable hands. We might have our disagreements, but Sheri was always there when you needed hands on deck.

I sagged against Kurt in the hallway. We waited for the police.

It was a long night. Uniformed police officers came and took statements. They ran crime scene tape all over the church. A police investigation van arrived on scene. Detectives would come later, presumably.

Outside the church, Kurt and I said the same thing over and over again. The words always felt the same. And they didn't matter. Carl was dead.

When the coroner took the body away, Kurt spoke briefly with one of the uniforms. "They say we can go now," he told me.

I checked my watch and saw that it was 3:30 A.M. "We have to go see Emma, now," I said dully. It was the last thing I wanted to do.

We walked over to the Ashby house because it was so close. It was still warm, and the moon was up, full and bright. It seemed unfair that there could be such a beautiful sky on a night like this one.

I knocked on the door and Sheri Tate answered with a finger to her mouth. "She's finally gone to sleep," she said, her eyes taking in both me and Kurt on the doorstep.

"Then I'll come back tomorrow," I said, relieved. "I can answer her questions then." But could I? I could tell her that her husband had been strangled, but not by whom or why. I had none of the important answers, and the only details I could share were gruesome and likely to cause more hurt than help.

"Some detectives were here already. It seemed like mostly a formality, to set up a time for her to identify the body. But they didn't say anything about what happened. How did he die? A heart attack?"

Sheri didn't seem to realize that a heart attack wouldn't involve the police. That probably meant that Emma didn't realize it, either.

"We need to get home to bed, too," said Kurt. "We'll talk in the morning."

"Of course," said Sheri, and closed the door.

It was only a ten-minute walk back to our house, but it felt very long. Kurt's truck was still at the church. He said he would walk over and get it in the morning.

"I keep thinking about all the things he might have done to cause this," I whispered to Kurt as we lay in bed together, neither of us with enough energy to change into bedclothes. We had taken off our shoes and that was all. "I'm blaming him for being a murder victim and I know I shouldn't." I wasn't used to thinking of men as victims.

"Carl was a good man," said Kurt stiffly. "I know that he

was sometimes dogmatic and inflexible, but I felt privileged to work with him. I don't know how I will ever replace him."

Of course he couldn't. And of course he would have to anyway. A bishopric couldn't function with only two counselors. While Kurt was mourning, he would have to be quietly interviewing new people for Carl's job. How horrible for him. But the longer he put it off, the more work he would create for himself. And he was already being crushed by the bishop's responsibilities. He and I both.

"How will his family be financially?" I asked. It seemed a crude thing to wonder about it, but it was practical, too. "What was his business, anyway?" I realized I'd never heard him talk about it, which was a little strange.

"He did stock trading, I think," said Kurt.

"You think?" It was one thing for me not to know, but how could Kurt not either?

"He seemed uncomfortable talking about it. I think he was quite wealthy. Work he'd done before ever moving to the ward."

"Do you think that might've had something to do with his death?" I asked, my mind swirling with darker possibilities. If Carl had been murdered because of some secret from his past, it seemed somehow better to me than if the murder had to do with our ward. Or his family.

"No. I think it was an invention of some kind," said Kurt tiredly.

"What did he invent?" I asked.

Kurt shrugged. "He never would tell me. He seemed embarrassed about the money."

But not embarrassed enough to stop himself from buying that silver Lexus. I thought about Emma and Alice and

William. At least they would have a nice nest egg to take care of them while they were dealing with grief. I couldn't imagine quiet, petite Emma trying to go out and get a job as some mothers were forced to do in difficult circumstances.

"I hope she can forgive him, whatever rancor there was between them." I tried to imagine losing someone with whom I was intimate and still angry. I had plenty of things I would have liked to resolve with Carl, but I was not his wife. I was not bound to him eternally through temple covenants. Emma and his children were.

I waited for an answer, but Kurt was already snoring softly.

CHAPTER 5

I went over to the Ashbys' house to relieve Sheri Tate Friday morning at about 7 A.M. "Is Emma awake?"

"Not yet," whispered Sheri as she let me in the front door. It was clear from the blanket spread across the couch that she had tried to get some sleep herself. I didn't blame her. "But Alice and William are up. They're getting ready for school."

It seemed ridiculous for the children to go to school just hours after their father had died. "What have they been told?" I asked, wondering if Sheri had left the bad news to me.

"They know that their father died last night. I told them when they woke up."

I shouldn't have underestimated her, I thought. And if she hadn't said it was murder, that was only because she didn't know. "Thank you. You've done so much," I said.

"In a situation like this, it never feels like enough. But I'll keep checking in to see what the family needs. And I'll be sending over her visiting teachers as soon as they can manage. But if you or the bishop think we need a whole schedule of people to stay with Emma, let me know and I can make sure the compassionate service leader has people signed up for every time slot, even through the night."

"I'll ask him," I said, thinking how strange it was that she referred to Kurt with his title only.

"I assume you talked to the police already?" Sheri asked.

"Of course. Last night Kurt and I talked to them for hours."

"Ah. Well, I guess it's my turn." She held up her phone and waved it at me. "They want me to come in this afternoon."

I was surprised at this and tried to remember how well Sheri and Carl had known each other. In Mormon wards, men and women who aren't married to each other are cautioned not to spend time alone together, no matter what their callings are. I sometimes thought it was silly, but Kurt always followed the rules, and so had Carl.

"They probably just want to ask you background information about Carl's relationships to other people in the ward." I hoped they weren't compiling a list of suspects from the ward.

"That must be it," said Sheri. "I'm nervous about going in, but I know I shouldn't be."

"No reason for that," I said. I wondered who else in the ward the police were going to talk to about Carl. Had I seen or heard something that would indicate animosity toward Carl? I had thought I was getting better at noticing deeper problems in people's lives, but it seemed I still wasn't doing a good enough job at being the bishop's wife.

On the other hand, Kurt could still be right. It might have had nothing to do with our ward. It could have been a random burglary, or something related to Carl's business dealings. Some part of me hoped that was true.

After a quick, sisterly hug, Sheri left, and I went into the kitchen, where Alice and William were eating breakfast. Cold cereal seemed a terrible start to the day. I should have gotten up early enough to make them something hot and fresh like pancakes or waffles. They were very quiet, though William seemed to be eating heartily.

I tried to recall what I knew of them from my days in the Primary Presidency a few years ago. Alice was the older of the two, a junior in high school, seventeen. If I remembered correctly, William was a freshman and on the younger end, with a late birthday that put him in a church class with junior high kids. He still looked like a kid, with a buzz cut that only made him look smaller and a little naked. This morning, he wore a gray hoodie.

Like many Mormon girls who were bombarded by messages about the virtues of modesty in an evil world, Alice was dressed in white capris (not shorts) and a long-sleeved floral tunic over a white shirt. Her eyes looked huge, like wounds throbbing in the center of her face.

"How are you two holding up?" I asked. The kitchen was a little messy. There were a lot of appliances on the countertops, and the counters themselves were splattered with food, especially around the stove.

"We're fine," said Alice, poking at her cereal.

William said nothing, pouring a big second bowl as if he were trying to make the football team. Or force himself not to think about anything but eating.

"Are you sure you're up to going to school today? I'm worried that your mother may want you here when she wakes up, as moral support." I wasn't trying to make them feel guilty about Emma, but I did want to give them an excuse.

"Dad would have wanted us to go to school," said Alice. She sounded congested. From crying, or trying not to cry? "He would have wanted us to keep following the rules. Rules are there to protect us, and to keep us happy."

"Of course they are," I said gently. "But there are times for the rules to be suspended, too."

"He would have said that school is our job and there is no excuse not to do our job every day," said William. "Some days it's harder than others, but you always do it anyway." He looked like he was going to disappear into that sweatshirt of his. He was trying so hard to be grown-up.

Kurt had told me since becoming bishop that he was surprised at how often he gave very basic advice to people: don't be unfaithful to your spouse, don't spend more than you earn, go to work even if you don't feel like it, do your church job even if you have doubts. But this wasn't one of those cases where people just needed to suck it up and do what had to be done. These were kids who were hurting and needed time to process what had just happened.

Still, now was not the time to tell these children their father was wrong. "Do you want to talk to someone? After school, if you don't want to miss school? The bishop has names of professional therapists who are also church members. The ward would pay for it."

William shrugged. "Dad always said people didn't need that kind of stuff. Saying a prayer and reading scriptures can fix anything." His voice, which was still changing, squeaked.

I avoided rolling my eyes, and tried to think of a scripture verse that would have some meaning in this situation, but I was blank. I wanted answers to questions from God, and I realized I felt more than a little angry. I felt especially so for William, because I had always known that my sons needed their father more than they needed me.

"Can I do anything?" I asked hoarsely.

William scooped a last spoonful out of the bowl, then stood to put his dish in the dishwasher.

So well trained, I thought. But he was trying so hard to avoid me and my searching eyes.

"I think Mom is the one who needs the most help," said Alice, licking the milk off her spoon and standing up to mimic her brother. I realized she was right, and that it might be useful for Emma to have the kids out of the house, at least for today. "Don't worry about us. We're tough." Alice closed the dishwasher with more force than was necessary, and then put her hand to it, as if trying to erase that motion.

I wanted to give them a hug, but they were so clearly making an effort to keep themselves away from me. Alice had one arm crossed over her chest and William was standing behind her, as if for protection. I felt so useless.

"Well, anything you need, call me." I rattled off my cell phone number, and Alice at least pretended to put it in her phone. William didn't even bother with that.

Did they feel close to their youth leaders in the ward? Did they have friends they'd call and talk to? Teachers at school? Grief could be so lonely. No one understood and no one wanted to be close to that conflagration of anger and fear and pain. "I'll be here for your mom, and if you change your mind about school—if things get to be too much for you—I'll come down and pick you up, anytime. It's no trouble. All right?"

"Sure," said Alice.

William mumbled something and went to get his backpack and school books.

Despite the temptation to procrastinate by cleaning the kitchen, I went upstairs to check on Emma. She was lying curled into a corner of a king-size bed. I wondered who in the world had chosen that. Neither Carl nor Emma were tall enough to require a king, and it looked to me like they would get lost in it.

"Emma?" I said softly. She didn't stir.

A part of me wanted to let her sleep, but I was afraid that if the kids were gone when she woke up, she would be even more upset.

I moved closer and shook her shoulder gently. "Emma? Your kids are getting ready to head off to school. Do you want to say goodbye to them?"

Emma opened her eyes and then started awake, launching herself out of the bed and into a standing position. "Carl," she said.

I grabbed one of her hands to anchor her. "I know this is hard. I just thought you'd want to help Alice and William get out the door. They're very insistent that they're going to school today. They think it's what Carl would want them to do."

She looked down self-consciously, brushed at her night-gown, and went to the closet to put on a robe. She tied the robe tightly, and I saw her face change from sleepy and confused to wrecked and gray.

I followed her downstairs, refusing to offer any platitudes. Everything was not going to be all right. I did not believe that this was God's will. I didn't know that something good would come out of this. I knew people said that it was in circumstances like this that you should pray most fervently, but I couldn't feel any connection to God at the moment.

In the living room by the door, Emma hugged Alice and kissed the top of her head. Then she stood by William and held out her hand. It was the strangest thing. Instead of hugging him, she shook his hand and then told him she loved him and hoped he had a good day at school. After that, the two teenagers went out the door to walk down to the bus stop.

"Is he uncomfortable with you hugging him?" I asked, though I knew it was an insignificant thing to talk about at a time like this. I had hugged and kissed all five of my sons before school every day, all through high school, whether they wanted it or not. I'm sure there had been days when they wished that I wouldn't, but I had ignored that completely. Boys needed physical affection just as much as girls did.

"He's too old for that kind of thing," Emma said. "Carl had me stop hugging or kissing William when he turned twelve. Carl said that once William was a deacon, he needed to start learning to be a man. Carl . . ." Her lower lip started to shake, and then she collapsed on the floor, right there in front of me.

I tried to get her back to her feet, thinking to at least help her to the couch in the front room. But despite her size, Emma was quite capable of resisting me. Apparently determined to weep where she was, she wrapped herself into a ball. All I could do was fold one arm around her. I did not want her to feel alone. Sobs ripped through Emma, her whole body convulsing.

"I'm here," was all I said to her. I didn't know if I was making anything better. I felt obliged to stay but found my thoughts wandering as she cried and cried. Did Emma have any idea who might have wanted to murder her husband? I wanted to make a list of suspects, but I didn't know where to start. What could Emma tell me about Carl's business life? But she would surely not want to talk about that now. She didn't even know he had been murdered yet.

Finally, Emma got to her knees and I was able to pull her to the kitchen table. I started on some hot oatmeal with cinnamon and raisins, and served her some hot cocoa as it was cooking.

"I still can't believe he isn't going to come through the door any minute and tell me all of this is a big mistake." Emma stared down at the liquid in the mug.

"I'm sorry. I know it's hard, but he isn't coming back, Emma." Maybe once she'd seen the body and identified it, that would help her mind to stop playing tricks on her.

"I know. He's gone and I have to get used to living my life without him."

"It might be time for you to think about what would be appropriate for the funeral," I said. If I could get her to think about something other than her own sadness, it might be good for her.

"No. Not yet. I can't do that right now." She put out a stricken hand and I immediately regretted the suggestion. I was pushing her too hard, which was not what I was here for.

"Kurt can take care of it, of course." How many funerals was Kurt going to preside over during his term as bishop? Too many.

"William should speak. Carl would have wanted that." Her voice was strained but sure now.

"If he's up to it, I'm sure that will be fine with Kurt. But you needn't put pressure on him. I'm sure Kurt will be able to speak personally about Carl. He and Tom deRyke both knew him very well."

"William was his son," she said firmly, straightening so she could look me in the eye.

"Of course. I'll tell Kurt and see what he thinks." As the bishop of the ward, Kurt wasn't obliged to do exactly what the family asked of him if the funeral was held in the chapel of our meeting house, where he presided. But of course he would want to be conscious of their wishes. If William was up to speaking, I suspected Kurt would encourage him to do so.

There was a long silence as I tried to think what else I could do to offer comfort to Emma. How was it possible that there had been so much violence and tragedy in our ward in one year? Was it a sign of some sin or just random reality? Violence could happen anywhere. Why not here?

"Is it terrible of me?" asked Emma, looking down at her hands.

"Is what terrible?" I focused on her once more, as she sat at the island that bordered the dining room, turning the mug in her hands again and again.

"I feel sad, but I also feel relieved. I don't think he ever loved me as much as I loved him. He hurt me so many times. He didn't even know he was hurting me."

I was a little startled, and I couldn't just let her comment pass. "Did he hit you, Emma?" I asked.

"What? No. No! I didn't mean that." She waved the thought away. "He would never have done that. You don't know Carl at all if you could think that. He would never strike a woman. You should have heard him talk to William about that, ever since William was two years old. He was never allowed to strike his sister."

Yes, and there were men who did not practice what they preached.

"He never hit me, Linda. Never." She had risen to her feet, and I worried I had upset her, but she was reaching for a washcloth and began to wipe down the counters.

"Here, Emma, let me." I tried to take it from her, but she evaded me by going around to the other side of the island. "I only meant that Carl had expectations," she said, eyes on the

Formica she was scrubbing. "Sometimes they were hard for me to live up to. Everything had to be done in a particular way. He followed every commandment, every rule set by the church, every suggestion by the prophets. We read scriptures every morning before the children went to school, even if he was ill, or I was. We said family prayers morning and night. If that meant we had to stay up late for the kids to get home, we stayed up late.

"We always had a year's supply of food. If I used some of it, I had to replace it immediately. That same day. We had Family Home Evening every Monday night. We went to church together every Sunday. We went to every extra service project and stake supplemental meeting, and weekly temple service. We never went on vacation because it would have interrupted our church service."

"Oh," I said. "I see." Did I? Was this a case of taking commandments too far? Or was there something more going on here? Mental illness, perhaps?

"He was so much more than I was." Emma had put down the washcloth and was chewing at a fingernail. "How will I cope when I'm alone? I'm not strong enough. And if anything happens with the children, if they leave the church or face any problems, I will always think it was my fault, because I was less diligent than Carl was. He's gone and it's because I didn't deserve him anymore. It's a test."

"It's not a test. God doesn't make tests like that." If He did, He wouldn't be God. At least not the kind of God that I could worship.

"And I'm relieved," she choked out. "A part of me is glad that I will never have to iron his shirt with starch in the morning before church, that I'll never have to polish his shoes. I will get more sleep, I will worry less, and be able to spend time watching movies he would never have let me watch. That's the kind of person I am. That's why God punished me by taking him away from me." She let go of the washcloth and tears streamed down her face.

I slammed a hand onto the counter. It made her jump, but I needed her to pay attention to me. It was important. "No, Emma. He didn't punish you. Something terrible happened and you're out of sorts. I don't know how you will feel about Carl when this is all over, but now is the worst time to decide. Your mind is still reeling. Give yourself some time. Be kind to yourself, Emma. You're a good person. You're innocent in all of this."

She nodded, still looking startled, and picked up the washcloth again. I wasn't sure she'd really processed what I said.

An hour later, one of Emma's visiting teachers, Karen Behring, came to relieve me, and I went home. I still hadn't told Emma that Carl had been murdered.

That evening, Kurt spent a couple of hours on the phone with the stake president, who had some pull with the police and city government. President Frost had insisted that Emma Ashby was not to be asked to identify her husband's body in her current fragile state. He felt strongly that it was the duty of the priesthood of our ward to do such a difficult job to protect the more delicate sensibilities of the women.

I could tell that Kurt was upset about the stake president's interference, and he tried several times to point out that it was better to allow the police to do their job unimpeded, but President Frost demanded to know how Kurt would feel if after he died the priesthood members left behind in his ward were not taking good care of his wife in his place.

So Kurt ended up spending a couple of hours down at the police station, identifying Carl Ashby's body himself. He came home late, tight-lipped, and went into his office. He didn't come to bed until nearly dawn, and he slept in until ten o'clock the next morning, which was a rarity for Kurt, even on a weekend.

CHAPTER 6

On Sunday morning, Kurt came home from church only a few minutes after he'd left, which was about 7 A.M. He was dressed in his suit, white shirt, and tie. His hair, thinning on the top, still glistened from his recent shower. I noticed it was getting a little long. I hoped that he had simply gotten too busy for a haircut and that this wasn't his new look. I had no intention of being married to a man with a comb-over.

"What is it? Forget something?" I asked.

He shook his head. "The police haven't finished with the building yet. I didn't even think to ask about that, which was stupid of me. They've had it closed up for nearly three days. But I went over today to open up and there were officers stationed at the doors around the building, telling people they couldn't go in. When I finally demanded to talk to someone, they told me they hadn't finished processing the scene. There were so many samples to collect because of all the people that have been in and out of the church."

"So what are you going to do?" I asked. Three wards met in that church building every Sunday, with roughly five hundred people in each ward. It was going to be hard to find anyplace else to shift us to.

"I called President Frost, in case the other bishops didn't know about the problem already."

"I guess he might have to just cancel church for everyone," I said. I tried to remember the last time that had happened and couldn't. Even when we'd had a terrible windstorm a few years ago, the wards up north, where it had been particularly bad, still had sacrament meeting—although they then dispersed to take care of the storm wreckage. The massive hierarchy of the Mormon church is very capable in emergency situations. There are phone trees, and everyone is assigned someone to look after them and report back to a higher authority. We had lists of lists, not just for the dead to be baptized and counted, but for the living, too.

"I'd hate to cancel," Kurt said. "I don't want rumors to fly about danger in the neighborhood. We should all go about our regular schedules and stay calm."

"Maybe we could meet in the bowery?" I suggested. The bowery was an outdoor venue with picnic tables and a pavilion. It was noisy as well as rather public, but we could probably manage one meeting there, in a pinch.

Kurt's eyes lit up. "That's a very good idea. I'll go call the stake president again. You can go back to sleep." He bustled out of the room.

But I couldn't, in fact, go back to sleep. I tried for a while, then sighed and got up to take a shower and get dressed for church.

Kurt joined me in the kitchen to eat some of the eggs I scrambled up for breakfast.

"So?" I said.

He took a bite and shook his head. "President Frost called the chief of police and he thinks that they should have everything they need by noon. So the plan is now to have shortened meetings in our own ward building in the afternoon. We'll be starting first."

I wondered about President Frost's relationship with the police. Was it a good thing or not? In emergency situations, Mormons have a tendency to call ward members in authority rather than the police. I'd heard that Elizabeth Smart's parents had done that when she was kidnapped, which had made it far more difficult for the police to find clues; the DNA evidence at the scene of the kidnapping had been contaminated by several dozen members of the priesthood quorums. This sort of thing happened over and over again—in robberies, kidnappings, and rape cases. No one intended to circumvent the law, but Mormons trusted other Mormons in their community more than they trusted government authorities.

"It sounds like it's all settled," I said. "But you still look worried."

"I just hope that it goes smoothly. If the police are late, it will make the schedule difficult. And we can't have any of our other meetings with the leadership today."

"I'm sure you'll manage. You know how to run things. It isn't as if you're a new bishopric." As soon as I said the words, I regretted them because I realized that there wasn't a full bishopric anymore, not without Carl. "What are you going to do about your second counselor?"

"President Frost told me to pray about who to replace Carl with, because he says I need to have a full bishopric up and running again soon. But I've prayed and prayed and I just don't have a feeling about anyone yet," Kurt said, shaking his head. "I have to wait on that. When God tells me who the right man is, I'll listen. But for now, I guess we all have to accept being in mourning."

Had he prayed to find out who the murderer was? No, probably not. He wouldn't feel that was his stewardship, and it probably wasn't.

"You and Tom can manage for as long as it takes, I'm sure," I said, trying to sound supportive. It would mean more time that he was gone from home, but I was getting used to that by now.

"For a while," he said. He only ate half a piece of toast, then returned to his office. I checked on him an hour later and found him staring vacantly at the wall.

"Are you all right?" I asked.

"Not really," he said.

For Kurt to admit that he was struggling was pretty big. He had been very close to Carl, closer than he was to anyone else in the ward, probably. He had lost a dear friend, and even if he was good at soldiering on, at some point he was going to have to stop and simply mourn. "Is there anything I can do for you?" I asked.

"Come sit with me?" he said.

So I pulled a folding chair up to his desk and held his hand in silence for a while.

He let out a long breath, and then nodded. "Thank you, Linda."

It was my cue to go, I guess. As I left, I could hear him getting down on the floor to kneel. More prayer. I hoped he got the answers he needed. He headed out for church about fifteen minutes before I did.

By the time I arrived on foot a few minutes before noon, there was no sign of the police. Instead of going straight to the chapel, I made for the room where we had found Carl's body and opened the door. I wrinkled my nose at the faint antiseptic smell and ran a finger along the walls. It was very clean. No hint of feces. No scent of death. The chairs were folded against the wall. I pulled one out and sat on it.

I should be in the chapel with everyone else, if for no other reason than for Kurt to see that I was there. But I needed to do my own mourning, I suppose. It felt right to come back here, to say a few final words to Carl. Carl had been a friend, even if he hadn't been a close one. I was going to miss him.

I took a breath and let my mind settle. I closed my eyes. Then I said softly the only words that came to me: "I'm so sorry."

A moment later, I felt it. A hand on my shoulder. Or—not a hand, really. A warmth.

"Carl?" I said, eyes still closed.

My whole body went all pins and needles. I wanted to leave and I wanted to stay, both at the same time.

I thought about when I had been an atheist, how I would have explained this feeling. Just a physical response to fear. Some aftereffect of being so close to a dead person. I wanted him to be here, and so he was here.

"Help," I heard in my ear. It wasn't a normal voice. It was like a strange, belled instrument. It felt crazy for me to believe that Carl could actually speak to me from beyond the grave. Was this just what I wanted to believe was possible? Nonetheless, I responded as if it were him.

"Carl? Help who?" Emma? His children? Carl himself? I felt no answer, and the room suddenly seemed cold. Was this just reality setting in, or was this what it felt like when a spirit left a space?

I shook myself. I had to act rationally, as if nothing had happened. And really, even if that had been Carl's voice I'd heard, what did it mean? It wasn't as if he'd told me anything useful. I'd never felt a spirit speak to me before. I wasn't sure how I felt about it. Unnerved, mostly.

Eventually, I stumbled into the chapel and somehow managed to make it through the meeting despite feeling weak and trembly. Had it really been Carl's spirit in that room talking to me? And if it was, what could I do to help?

Mormons believe that spirit prison and spirit paradise (the way stations before resurrection) are right here on this earth, but invisible to us. So we believe strongly in contact with the spirits of the dead. There are several prophets who have been visited by spirits of the dead to tell them what they should do. The most famous was when Wilford Woodruff had a Charles Dickens-esque visitation by the spirits of the signers of the Declaration of Independence and some other early presidents of the United States who were annoyed that Mormon temple work had not yet been done for them, and demanded that it be carried out forthwith.

But it happened to normal people, too, not just prophets. Many Mormons feel they have dreams or other visitations by their own dead ancestors, asking for temple work like baptisms for the dead to be done. When my daughter, Georgia, died, I was counseled to go to the temple in hopes of seeing her and knowing that she was still living on the other side. I tried, but never had any distinct impression of her.

Why, then, did I feel Carl Ashby? Why would he feel more need to contact me than she did? Or why would I be more receptive to him than I was to her?

CHAPTER 7

Kurt got a phone call Monday night, and I knew as I watched his face that it was about Carl Ashby. He put his hand on the counter in the kitchen, as if to hold himself up. Then he swore under his breath. Kurt does not swear often, and to my memory, he hadn't ever used that particular word before. Finally, he hung up the phone and turned to me.

"What is it? What did they find out?"

"That was President Frost. The coroner's office just called him."

Again, I noticed the odd confluence of spiritual and secular authority here. Why would the coroner's office call the stake president before the wife of the deceased? Did they think Emma Ashby was too fragile to hear the truth without Kurt being on hand to tell her? Was that ethical? "What did they say?"

Kurt shook his head. He kept shaking it.

"Kurt?" I had never seen him like this before, so distraught. He looked like someone had just proven to him that Jesus Christ had never walked the earth, that it was all a myth.

"He—Carl Ashby—the person we found in the church building—"

"It wasn't Carl?" I said, astonished. We had both been so

sure it was. And the spirit who had called to me had felt like him as well.

"The person who was killed wasn't a man," Kurt got out at last.

There was a long silence as I tried to let in what he had said. *Not a man.* But then—? But what—? But how—?

"Carl Ashby—he wasn't Carl. He was born Carla Thompson. They have the birth certificate. They had his fingerprints on file. Some minor arrest in his youth. Her youth," Kurt said, shaking his head again. "I don't even know what pronoun to use anymore."

What? This was impossible. How could we have been fooled all this time?

I conjured up an image of Carl Ashby in my head. He had been maybe five foot six or seven, but he had been muscular. He'd had a strong jaw and a wide nose. He'd seemed so masculine, at least to my eye.

"He never filed any paperwork to change his gender. Which means he couldn't have legally been married to Emma. I don't know if he used a false birth certificate or had someone marry them without the proper documentation," Kurt was saying, gesticulating erratically.

I felt sick at the idea that Emma had been lied to like this. Had she ever doubted the legality of her marriage? Probably not. How often did I go look at my marriage certificate? Carl had probably told her that everything was fine, and she had believed him. She must have simply trusted him to handle it whenever anything legal came up.

"He had a hysterectomy some years ago, as well as surgery to remove breasts, and he was taking testosterone regularly, had been for some time. But they think he—she—was pregnant in the past, because there are signs those pelvic bones delivered a child. Somewhere, there is a child out there. Unless it died." Kurt glanced at me, perhaps to gauge my reaction.

I would never have guessed Carl Ashby was born a woman. All his posturing, his black-and-white view of gender—had that all been a blind of some sort, a way to keep anyone from suspecting the truth? I found my sympathy shifting from Emma to Carl.

"Maybe God wanted the truth to come out, and this was the only way it could happen?" said Kurt shakily.

"God isn't like that," I said. I didn't believe in the punishing God of the Old Testament. I couldn't. Not when I had so much to be punished for.

"But how could God look on someone like *that* with any degree of acceptance? How could He allow Carl to remain in the bishopric? How could He have let me feel that I should ask Carl to serve with me?"

Because God loves us all, no matter how disgusting we are to others. God looks on the heart, not on the appearance. Surely God would have seen the man Carl was trying to be, not the woman he had been born as.

"What about Emma?" I asked suddenly. She and Carl had been married twenty years. He'd converted to the church because of her. Or at least that's what he had always said. I wasn't sure we could believe anything he'd said now.

"She has to have known. How could she not know? They adopted children together, though it must not have been through any official agency," said Kurt. "You can't hide something like this if anyone had done a proper background check."

But there were adoptions done without those checks all

the time in Utah, family to family, trying to avoid anything public. It meant that the children might not be legally Emma's now, either. Would there be any kind of ramifications for that?

And as for Emma's not knowing much about male body parts, I thought that Kurt might be underestimating how sheltered some Mormon women are when they marry. With a rush of sympathy, I began to wonder how much Emma had known about Carl when they were sealed.

There had been so much I hadn't known going into my first marriage, problems I could have prevented if I hadn't been taught so little about human sexuality. That failed marriage was one of the darkest times of my life; sometimes I am still violently angry at the social structure of my church for tricking me and my ex-husband into thinking that marriage was a good idea, and that everything would be fine if only we made vows in the temple.

Some Mormon women from very conservative families come to marriage ignorant of even the basics of sex. One major goal of the Mormon youth program was to prevent premarital sex, even for engaged couples. It is not unheard of, even now, for young girls to be excused from sexual education classes in schools because of parental objection. I'd heard stories of young women getting pregnant without realizing that what they were doing was sex. If a young woman could be tricked into having sex without knowing what it was, could an older woman be tricked into believing she'd had sex when she hadn't? William's and Alice's adoptions might be relevant to the marriage problems as well.

Kurt pulled at the hair on the top of his head, which made me wonder if that was what had caused it to thin there—he had only picked up the habit since he'd been made bishop.

"How could I not have known? He was in the bishopric all this time and I never once suspected. He—I have no idea what to do next. President Frost is incensed. He says that we have to make a list of every ordinance he participated in and have them redone, since Carl's ordination to the priesthood is void. Which is completely impossible, and he must know it."

Only men can have priesthood callings in the Mormon church. But what happens when someone like Carl comes into the mix? An ordinance performed by a woman would be void. It isn't about whether women have the capacity to communicate with God or to fill leadership positions competently. It's all about the order God ordained within in the church, and that order is gendered. Women and men have separate roles, and the role of men is presiding with the priesthood; the role of women is to nurture children, just as Carl had said when he'd read from the Family Proclamation.

"Every ordinance?" I said. In the last year, Carl Ashby could have been involved in a hundred or more ordinances, counting temple ordinance work, and ordaining young men in the ward to the priesthood or baptizing people into the ward. "But surely it doesn't matter who did the ordinance work. God's power works through any hands, even if they are unworthy." Redoing ordinances like this wasn't done even in excommunication cases for men who were pedophiles or criminals.

"President Frost kept talking about how this was Satan's work and how we would all be tainted until there was a cleansing of some kind."

"Kurt, are you sure you understood him properly?" This just seemed so outrageous. I had no idea what President

Frost might mean by a "cleansing." A priesthood blessing of the church itself? Some kind of laying on of hands for every member?

Kurt nodded. "Oh, I understood, all right. He's going to hold a disciplinary court postmortem of some kind, or try to get permission from the First Presidency for it." He looked shattered. "So Carl's records can be removed from the church and his temple sealings to his wife and children canceled."

Usually, canceling sealings was reserved for men who betrayed their priesthood power, seminary teachers who had affairs with teenage girls, or Boy Scout leaders who sexually abused young boys. Or church members who directly rebelled against church authorities and created their own new doctrines. But it was rarely done after death. In fact, I couldn't recall that happening in any case I had ever heard of.

"An abomination. That's what President Frost called Carl." Kurt was shaking now. "The man I thought of as one of my dearest friends. I don't understand it. How could this have happened? How could I have been so betrayed?"

Poor Kurt. I was shocked by this news, but it must have been so much worse for him. He came from such a conservative family that something like this would never have even been talked about, let alone tolerated.

More than that, Kurt and Carl had been as close as brothers this last year, and Mormon men depend on their fellowship with other men for identity. Kurt didn't have any coworkers at his accounting business, and he didn't have any hobbies outside of church work and being a father. His deepest friendships had always happened within the church. And to have that taken away like this must have made him feel like he was floundering, unsure of anything anymore. I was still trying to find the right words when he went on, "All that time, he was pretending to be someone he wasn't," said Kurt. "I feel so . . . deceived."

Kurt hated being fooled. He had never been a man who liked practical jokes. It wasn't that he didn't have a sense of humor; he simply didn't like lies, for any reason. He had never allowed a surprise party for any of our children, because he wouldn't lie to them. He wanted them to always trust him. He wouldn't let us pretend to them about Santa Claus, either.

I was no expert on transgender people, but I suspected that deceiving or fooling other people wasn't the right way to look at it. I tried to think of Carl's perspective. If he had believed he was meant to be male, then perhaps he hadn't thought of it as deceit at all. Perhaps that was why he was so adamant about gender roles; he must have been adamant about his own gender identity to have made the change, especially years ago, before transgenderism had become more visible.

I said, "Just because he never told you all the details of his DNA, that doesn't mean he wasn't really the man he said he was. Or at least, the man he was trying to be." And wasn't that what all of us were doing? Trying to be the best version of ourselves that we could? Trying to show the parts of ourselves that were good and that we believed were most true?

"He was—all that time I was with him, alone in a room together—all those moments when I thought I was talking to my brother in the gospel—" Kurt couldn't finish a single sentence.

"But if God didn't tell you anything was wrong, what does that mean? Did you ever feel like Carl was evil or malicious in his intentions?" I decided right then I was going to keep calling him Carl and using a male pronoun. That was what he had chosen in his life. If we respected him at all, we had to respect that choice first and foremost.

Kurt shook his head. "Never malicious. I never felt a sense of evil around him." He seemed to be calming down a little now.

"So you never felt that he was using his power for his own purposes? That he was hurting people with untruths or false doctrine?"

"No," Kurt said again. "Maybe all that means is that there's something wrong with me, too. If I couldn't see through this, what am I doing as bishop?"

"Maybe you're doing everything right. Maybe God meant it to happen this way," I said. Even if we couldn't understand how. Maybe it was time for people to start seeing things differently in terms of gender, and our ward had been chosen to lead the way. Could God have decided that Kurt was the kind of man who could be trusted to do something this difficult?

"President Frost may well decide to have the whole bishopric released in this cleansing," said Kurt dourly. "We've shown we can't possibly see God's true will. It's probably just as well we're all released. If this gets out, we'll be a laughingstock."

I tried not to feel selfish relief at the thought of having my husband back, as he'd been before he was called as bishop. But I knew that if Kurt was released because of this, he would never recover from it. I didn't want that. I wanted things to be the way they had been before, but not at that price.

"Why does anyone have to know?" I asked.

"Gossip like that? Of course it will come out sooner or later," said Kurt.

"Not if the police are careful in their investigation." If this had something to do with Carl's murder, they'd want to see who knew and who didn't, wouldn't they? That couldn't happen if they let that information loose. "Look, someone has to talk this through with Emma." I hoped it could be done without humiliating her further. "She has to be able to prepare in case word starts to get around. Think about how this could affect his children in our strict community." I didn't call it closed-minded, though sometimes I thought it was that, too. "Do you really think they should have to carry this burden when they're teenagers and at their most vulnerable?"

"You don't think they have a right to know that he might have used his priesthood wrongly?" he asked.

"There you go again. His priesthood." I waved my hands. "It didn't belong to Carl any more than it belongs to you. God chooses whether or not to grant his power, not us."

Kurt pressed his lips tightly together. "This isn't about protecting children. This is about the truth, and about proper channels of authority. That's what the whole church was founded on. Joseph Smith couldn't join any of the other churches because they didn't have the authority. He had to be confirmed by the resurrected Peter, James, and John, and all authority goes back to them. They had the keys. If they didn't, then we don't. If we don't, then what makes us any different from any other church?"

I knew that. I had seen Kurt's line of authority on the wall in his office, a list of names going back to his father, and his grandfather, and so on, until it came from Joseph Smith himself, and from Peter the apostle, who just got it from Christ. Every man who was ordained to the priesthood had a line of authority that went back to Christ Himself.

Kurt put his head down and I saw his shoulders shaking. I put a hand on his back. I wanted to draw him into my arms, but I didn't think he would let me. He already felt weak, and that would only make it worse for him.

"I never guessed," said Kurt after a long time, his voice still muffled by the countertop.

I felt like we were getting at the heart of this. It wasn't as much about betrayal as it was about confidence. "Carl thought of himself as a man. Why shouldn't you think of him the same way?" I asked.

Kurt didn't acknowledge my question. He seemed to be talking to himself at the moment. "I never thought it strange that he wasn't interested in his own family's genealogy. He never helped when we had activities about FamilySearch. He said that he had been rejected by his whole family, but he never said why. I assumed it was because he joined the church. He said that he would do the work when his parents were dead and they stopped interfering with him. But all of that was a lie. He must not have wanted us to see his birth certificate and realize the truth. He must not have wanted any of us to talk to his parents."

What would I do if one of my sons announced that he thought he had been born into the wrong body? I didn't think there was an official church policy on those who were transgender, though I'd heard that gender reassignment surgery could lead to excommunication. But that was a generation ago. Was it still the case? If it could lead to excommunication, did it always?

I also wondered about Carl's childhood and family. Had his parents rejected him as a man? Or had he decided that he couldn't bear to be with them because they continued to treat him as a woman and use the wrong name for him? I didn't know if his parents were Mormons or not, but there are bigots everywhere. Did I feel an obligation to find them and tell them about Carl's death? Would they want to be at the funeral? Would they want to know Emma and the children?

It seemed like Carl had gone to a good deal of trouble to avoid any connection to them. Would we ignore all that his life had been and send him to the grave as Carla Thompson instead of Carl Ashby? Who was the one betraying a brother in the gospel then?

"The signs were all there," Kurt was saying. "He never took his shirt off while swimming at scout camp. I thought he was modest, and maybe a little self-conscious about his height. But I never thought he was concealing surgical scars."

I felt a bit voyeuristic, imagining what Carl had looked like without his shirt on.

"Is our body the truest self we have?" I asked. "Don't we Mormons believe that the body is often flawed, that it will be made perfect later? Children who have disabilities are told that they will be resurrected into a perfect body. Why shouldn't Carl have believed the same thing?"

Kurt stood up, holding his hands rigidly at his sides. "Because that's not about making something right again. It's about changing it. It's like a tattoo. You won't see those on a perfected body."

"How do you know?" I asked. "Maybe you'll be surprised when you get to the celestial kingdom and see who's there and who isn't. And what they all look like."

Kurt shook his head, his chin jutting out more prominently than ever. "I don't want to argue with you about this. You have this agenda you press on everything that comes along. This isn't about the place of women in the church. This is about someone who wanted something and couldn't have it. So she figured out a way to get it at any cost."

The way Kurt used "she" made me wince, as if it were a knife and he were stabbing at the fabric of Carl Ashby's life with it.

"She stole something from me. And I will never get it back. How will I ever trust another man in the church again? I can't demand they all drop their pants."

"Why not?" I said, deadpan. If he was going to be a jerk, then he should be a jerk all the way. "You and President Frost can do it together. Every priesthood worthiness interview. Include a dick check."

Kurt stomped off to our bedroom.

I tried to cool my temper. I knew Kurt was suffering and I wanted to help him through that, but the arrogance of the man! To think that in the process of creating bodies, God could make people blind, deaf, autistic, psychopathic, sociopathic, schizophrenic—he even made Hitler. But that God would allow a person to be born in the wrong gendered body—no, that was impossible! God would never do that.

I felt faint for a moment as I heard Carl's voice in my mind, quoting the Family Proclamation as he had at the bishopric dinner. He had been diligent in his church service to the point of obsession. He had not wanted Emma to kiss their son for fear that it would make him weak, or turn him feminine. And yet he—

What was he? Who was he?

What made a man a man? Was it a body part? If that was so, then what about the men who were injured in war? Were they no longer men? I was sure Kurt would say they still were able to hold the priesthood, that he would not be ashamed of serving in a bishopric with such men.

If it was genetics, that elusive Y chromosome, then what about people who were born with unusual combinations? What about those who were XXY, or XYY, or triple X, or fragile X? What about genetic females who developed as males because of some drug their mothers took in the womb? Or genetic males who developed as females because they weren't sensitive to testosterone? What about people who thought they were female until they took genetic testing to figure out why they were sterile? What about young males who were physically damaged in early childhood and were raised as females?

There were so many ways in which gender could be confused. Kurt wanted a world where at least this one thing could not be questioned, but it wasn't so.

Maybe I had it easier because I had given up the idea that questions were the opposite of faith. I believed in God because I wanted to, not because He had proven Himself to me, not because it was logical, not because it was right. I needed God, and I needed Him to make mistakes, like I did.

And Carl? The real question here was whether he had been killed for being born Carla and refusing to continue to live as her or if he had been killed for something in the life he had achieved as a man. God would sort all the rest out, I had to believe. But it seemed my job was to sort out this death.

CHAPTER 8

There were reasons that I knew more about LGBT people than Kurt or other Mormons did, and they weren't only because of my personal beliefs that people should be allowed to be different. My children and almost everyone else believed that Kurt was my first and only husband. It wasn't true. On August 16, 1981, years before I ever met Kurt, I married my first husband, Ben Tookey. I was twenty years old. We were both students at Brigham Young University, the church-owned college in Provo, Utah.

I had grown up in Utah, but Ben seemed so much more sophisticated and well traveled. He had been an army brat, and had lived in Japan, Germany, and South Korea. He'd spent a year traveling the United States before he'd applied to college. He was six years older than I was, and I thought he was so confident and assured about what he wanted in life because he'd spent several years working before going back to college.

He was majoring in engineering, because, he said, he wanted to build up cities all over the world and put his mark on them. He was tall and thin, with curly blond hair that he grew as long as he was allowed according to the BYU dress code—and sometimes a little longer, enough that he wasn't allowed to go to the testing center until he went and got it cut, or put it into a ponytail and hid it under a hat.

We met at the BYU bowling alley at a ward activity. He wasn't in my ward, but he had come with a male friend who was in my ward. I still remember how it felt when Ben tried to show me how to throw a ball properly. His warm breath against the back of my neck, his hand touching the small of my back, the weight of his fingers on top of mine, pressed against the cool stone of the ball.

I'd fallen hard, and so quickly that my roommates teased me about it endlessly. I was supposed to be the sensible one, the one who was voted most likely to finish college without an "MRS degree." I worried that I wasn't pretty enough for Ben, who was movie-star handsome. But he always made me feel like I was the only person in the room. He'd look at me with his brown eyes and I'd melt.

We spent every minute together from the day we met until the day I went home that summer to talk to my parents about getting married. They were in the midst of arranging the reception for my oldest brother Trent's marriage, after years of waiting for him to find the "right one."

Telling my father that Ben was not a returned missionary was difficult. I knew he would be disappointed. I had been taught all my life not to settle for anything less.

"We're getting married in the temple," I remember explaining to my father that first night home. "Ben already has a reservation for a sealing room. In the Provo Temple," I said again, for emphasis, because my parents had always insisted on a temple wedding. Provo would be a bit of a drive for them, from all the way north in Logan, but it wasn't as if we were asking them to drive out of state.

"He hasn't even asked me for your hand officially," my father complained.

I flushed because I knew that was what he expected. "Dad, I love him and he loves me. We're both active members of the church. What's wrong with that?"

"What's wrong with it is that he doesn't have the courage to come up here and announce it with you. Why is he hiding behind your skirts?" At least that's what I remember him saying.

I retorted, "He's not hiding anywhere. I thought you'd rather meet him already knowing who he is to me."

I'd worked so hard to ease the tension between them after I introduced Ben, but it had never worked. Dad disliked Ben, and he made me cry several times in the weeks leading up to the wedding. I thought I would never forgive my father for what he did, both before and after the marriage. It was only when he got sick a few years later that I finally felt all my long-held anger drift away. To this day I still find it difficult to talk to my brothers, and my mother died before I could really have an open conversation with her. My stubbornness in marrying Ben had only made her and my father distant and unsympathetic when I had problems in the years following the marriage.

During our engagement, Ben was so sexy; I was always eager to touch him. When he took off his shirt, I would look at him and think how lucky I was. I tingled all over. I longed for him to touch me, even if only accidentally, because it gave me a jolt of feverish sexuality. I had dreams about our sex life, and I thought everything was normal between us.

After a date night, Ben would kiss me dutifully, but only on the cheek, or a peck that didn't land quite squarely on my lips.

He hugged me, but his hands didn't roam anywhere and I didn't sense that he was bursting with anticipation the way that I was.

A few days before our wedding, I was concerned enough about this behavior to talk to the friend who had brought him to that ward party. I was hugely embarrassed, but I worried that we would be incompatible in some way when we were married, because I was so attracted to Ben and he didn't seem to feel the same urgency toward me. I thought this meant that even though he said he thought I was beautiful, he wasn't very attracted to me and maybe we shouldn't be getting married if that was how he felt.

"You're kidding, right?" said Charlie. "He adores you. He talks about you all the time."

"But what does he say?" I asked. We were just in the other room while Ben went to get us some Cokes and chips, so I was keeping my voice down. There hadn't been any other chances to talk to him because Ben and I were always together.

"He talks about your figure. About your wedding night and how much he's looking forward to it. He's a red-blooded guy like the rest of us," Charlie assured me.

I felt stupid for questioning Ben's love for me, and even stupider for how embarrassed I felt when Charlie reported Ben's lascivious-sounding talk with the boys. "Then why doesn't he ever really kiss me? Or touch me? I mean, even pull me hard against him when we hug?" I was struggling to put my feelings into words, but they seemed to fail me, though I had always depended on them before.

"You're worried about nothing. He's just holding himself back. He knows that if he started kissing you like he really wants to, you'd both end up in bed and you wouldn't be able to get that temple wedding you're so set on," said Charlie.

Ben came back then, so I couldn't ask any follow-up questions, like why Charlie thought I was the one set on the temple wedding and not Ben. Wasn't it equally important for both of us?

We went through the temple to receive our endowments together the day before the wedding. Most men would have gone through the temple ritual for adulthood before they went on missions, but a lot of women only went before they got married. We had little colored paper tags pinned to our clothing to mark us as first-timers, so people could help us and make sure we didn't make any mistakes in the ritual words or motions and handshakes.

I felt rattled by the ceremony, despite the fact that my mother was right at my side throughout. My father was a temple worker and he helped Ben bring me through the veil, since Ben was so nervous about it after just having gone through himself. Going through the veil is the final part of the ritual, where each person taking out their endowment speaks through a curtain with holes in it to someone representing God on the other side, offering names and tokens to prove worthiness. After the veil, we were allowed to go into the beautiful, open space of the "celestial room," which was meant to be like going to the highest part of heaven. The furnishings are always in white or beige colors, and there is a big chandelier overhead, and though you are allowed to talk, the room feels nearly silent because mostly people sit and try to feel the Spirit of God and His love there.

That first time, I felt so confused and wanted to ask questions, but my father refused to answer. I had made so many promises, and tried to learn so many things. When would the promises come up again? What would happen when I came back to the temple without people escorting me and whispering the answers to me throughout?

Ben hugged me more tightly that evening than he ever had before, and the kiss on my dormroom step was the closest to a passionate one as we had ever shared. I wanted to pour myself into him through our mouths, be one with him in some way beyond the spiritual pledge we would make in the morning.

"I love you," said Ben. He was teary eyed. His hair had been buzzed short the day before and I reached a hand to touch it. It had been his attempt to appeal to my father, to try to look more the part of the Mormon missionary, even if he wasn't one. I missed the curls, but I figured he could always grow them back.

The next morning was all a rush of getting dressed, making sure I had everything I'd need for the sealing in the temple. I was so nervous I didn't bother with breakfast. Ben's parents were coming into town for the wedding itself, and we had plans to go out with them for a luncheon, but I'd be meeting them for the first time at the temple.

Looking back, I see the signs that there was something wrong with everything that Ben did leading up to the wedding. He made sure I didn't meet his parents until I was committed; he knew they would have even more reservations than my parents did. But it wasn't until the wedding night that I realized something was gravely wrong. Until then, I'd kept telling myself that we were just nervous.

My dad had offered to pay for us to stay one night at a hotel in Park City before we drove to California for a week-long honeymoon at a beach house that Ben's parents were paying for. In the hotel room, I kept waiting for Ben to kiss me. Instead, he held my hand casually as we sat on the bed and looked at a list of restaurants that we could go to that evening. There was no kissing, no scrambling for clothes. No desperate release of pent-up sexual feelings.

"We could go shopping at the outlets after dinner. I think they're open pretty late. And there's a midnight show at the theater. What do you think?" Ben asked me.

"Don't you—? Isn't it—?" I choked out.

"It will be fun," said Ben. He must have known what I wanted, and he ignored it.

When we finally got home, I was so exhausted that I fell asleep easily. I wore the fancy white negligee my roommates from college had bought with me, a giggling shopping trip I remembered with equal portions of humiliation and hilarity. There were dozens of tiny buttons and bows he would have to undo to get it off. That had been the point of it, to make things difficult. But in the end, the only one it made things difficult for was me.

In the morning, we woke up on opposite sides of the huge bed and went to the hotel breakfast.

"We'll have to hurry," said Ben. "They close at nine. And we want to get a head start on our drive to California." He went into the bathroom, locked the door, and stepped out again twenty minutes later, fully dressed.

I showered too, feeling dejected and exhausted. We drove in near silence for ten hours, then collapsed again after a fast food dinner into the lumpy bed of the beach house.

By the next morning, I was sure that I must be hideous. I wished I had brought clothes that hid me better, with long sleeves. I refused to get into my swimsuit, sure that Ben was embarrassed to be with me. What other reason could there be for his lack of sexual interest? He liked me. He enjoyed my company. I made him laugh. That was all clear. But why he would marry someone whose body made him want to run away, I couldn't figure out.

I spent another month sure that it was all my fault.

Then I decided to take matters into my own hands. I lay on the bed completely naked one night. Ben turned off the light, rolled to his side in his flannel pajamas, and made no comment. I tried to massage him, but he pushed me away once I moved below his waistline. I turned on a pornographic movie that was recommended by a clerk in the adult section at a video store. Nothing worked.

That was when I started going to the library, listening to talk shows about sexual problems, and asking questions of my friends. For the first time, I heard about homosexuality, something that truly had never been on my radar before. If Ben was gay—if he was only sexually attracted to men, and not to women—it would explain his behavior toward me.

Once I hit upon this possibility, I became convinced that that must be the secret Ben was hiding. But at the time, Mormons described homosexuality as some kind of sinful and debauched choice, probably caused by watching too many naked guys in the locker room or by being abused by an older man as a child. I felt horribly sorry for what I thought Ben must have gone through, and more determined than ever to love him no matter what.

Because there were explanations of "reparative" techniques, I kept thinking that I could help "cure" Ben, or that he could get treatment at a hospital or from a clinic doctor.

But Ben refused. "I don't have a problem," he said to me.

"How are we ever going to have children?" I asked, trying to get him to see past what I thought was his embarrassment.

"We'll figure it out eventually," Ben said vaguely.

"Sex isn't a bad thing, you know. It's supposed to draw couples together. Even if you're not trying to have kids, it's a good thing." That was a line from one of the books I'd read, about people who lived Christian lives and had spent too much time hearing about how sex was bad, so they struggled in their marriages to enjoy sex.

"I don't want to right now," Ben said. "If you want sex so much, don't you think that's a problem you should deal with on your own?"

He always reflected it back onto me. He didn't tell me I was ugly or unattractive, just suggested once that I was a nymphomaniac. I looked that up at the library, too, trying to figure out if Ben was right and the problem was mine. Was wanting to have sex in the first six months of marriage that unusual? How often did normal couples have sex? Did it take them a long time to figure out how to do it?

I bought some books and taught myself about my own body and figured out some tricks to give me sexual release, but I felt guilty about it, even though I was married. Ben refused to look at anything I tried to show him, and started telling me that I needed to talk to our new bishop to repent. I tried to do that once, but the bishop wouldn't listen to me. He said that men always want sex more than women do, that I must just be misunderstanding the situation. He said I should pray and ask God how to proceed, and then stood up and walked me to the door.

I was terrified to talk to anyone else in the ward about my sexual problems, and I doubt any of the other women would have known what to tell me, anyway.

I felt as low as I ever had in my life, but it wasn't as if Ben were doing fine, either. He'd lost the job we'd moved to California for and basically sat around all day in his pajamas. I was working full-time, but having trouble coming up with enough money to pay rent and for food for both of us. I finally called my father.

In tears, I poured out everything over the phone. I was hoping my father would be able to give me some magic fix for everything. But he told me that I was married now, that I had to "cleave unto your husband" and not go running to my father with every problem. He said I'd chosen Ben against his objections, and now I was going to have to live with that choice eternally.

After Dad turned me down, I tried going to my newly married brother Trent for help. But Trent wouldn't listen to me at all. He told me that this was a chance for me to learn a lesson, though he didn't tell me exactly what that lesson was. I didn't bother going to my second brother Garrett.

I decided to get a divorce three months after that, and didn't tell my parents until it was final, when I wrote them a short letter. My father sent me a letter in reply telling me how disappointed he was in my selfishness. My mother never spoke to me about it at all, and acted like it hadn't happened, going so far as to continue addressing my mail to my married name and asking me if Ben would be coming to a family Christmas party that year.

I tried to go to a singles ward in our same area, but the bishop told everyone I was divorced and the reaction of everyone at church seemed to be that I had committed a great sin in asking for a divorce from someone who wasn't a murderer. My home teachers called me to repentance constantly, and I was asked not to attend the Gospel Doctrine class because I was a bad influence. So I stopped attending church completely.

Eventually, I went back to school at the University of Utah because by then I had become an atheist and could not get back into BYU. I simply couldn't believe that all of the bad things that happened to me were my fault, no matter how many people told me that I needed to repent to be good with God again. It was the darkest period of my life, up until the death of my only daughter, Georgia.

I didn't see any of my family at all for a couple of years, and things were strained between us all the way up until my dad's death.

Ben was furious with me, too. Getting a divorce wasn't what he had wanted, despite the fact that he'd done nothing to keep our marriage together. He started bad-mouthing me to any friends we had in common, but by then I was so depressed that I didn't care. I felt disconnected from everyone.

It took me years of living as an atheist and doing all the things I'd been told were wrong before I realized I was unhappy. Psychically lonely, actually. I decided I wanted to believe in God again, and returned to the Mormon church. Almost immediately, I met Kurt and could tell he was seriously interested in me. But I was pretty reluctant to date again, and it took me a long time to learn to trust Kurt. I think I will always love him for the tenderness and patience he showed me then, even before he knew the whole story about Ben.

Kurt told me over and over again that I shouldn't blame

myself for my failed marriage, because God didn't. He also made sure to kiss me passionately, though I think he might have preferred to hold back more. I was needy and weepy for a long time while we were engaged, and I broke things off twice. But he waited for me to change my mind both times, gave me the time and space I needed, and insisted that he would always love me, in every way. My past is one of the reasons that Kurt has had a chip on his shoulder about gay men in the church, so perhaps there was a part of him that put transgender people like Carl into the same category.

It might seem strange to say I sympathized with the plight of Carl, a transgender man, because I had been married to a man I believed was gay. After so much study, I had learned that gay and transgender identities are very different, that sexuality and gender are not the same thing. But the Mormon church is so unaccepting of both groups, along with several others, that it meant in some ways Carl and Ben must have had similar challenges and problems in their attempts to assimilate into Mormon culture. Ben's secrecy, his insistence that everything was normal, his refusal to talk about his real sexual feelings—it all came back to me now when I thought of Carl Ashby.

I had been nearly destroyed by Ben Tookey, but I didn't hate him. My love for him had remained an open wound for a long time, and then it had closed over, leaving an unexpected sweetness behind. A part of me still loved him, and I had tried to expand myself to understand him. After all, he had been hurting, too. He had loved me in his own way, I believe that, though he had not known how to make our marriage work.

When I wanted to be married to Kurt in the temple, I'd had to get a letter from Ben to send to the First Presidency along with my own letter about why our marriage had ended. I'm pretty sure we sent very different letters, because when I talked to Ben on the phone, he'd insisted any problem in the marriage was mine, and he certainly rejected the label "gay." But whether or not anyone believed he was gay, there was no decision on a cancellation of sealing made in time for my marriage to Kurt, which was why Kurt and I had ended up being married in the church building instead of the temple. Then we'd had to wait a year for our official sealing.

Carl's bombastic tirade about the Family Proclamation should have rung that chime for me last Friday at the bishopric dinner—should have reminded me of Ben and his defensiveness forged by years of pretending to be someone he wasn't. If I'd made the connection, could I have done something to help him? To help Emma or their family? To help Kurt when he came to the realization that things were not what they seemed to be, even with the man he considered to be his best friend in the ward? I had failed them, and all I was left with was the hope that I could find out who had done this to Carl—and why. Maybe that was all his spirit had been trying to ask me to do, when I felt his presence in the classroom at church. To help not just his family, but the whole ward, maybe even the whole church.

I will try, I thought to Carl, though I no longer felt his spirit anywhere near me. *I swear to all angels listening, I will do my best.*

CHAPTER 9

Tuesday morning after school had started for the kids, Kurt and I prepared to go talk to Emma so she had a chance to react before the police came to follow up on the investigation. Sheri Tate had made sure that Emma knew about Carl's death, but as far as I knew, she still hadn't seen her husband's body.

"Will President Frost start any disciplinary action against Emma if it turns out she did know about Carl being transgender?" I asked. It didn't seem to me at all likely that she had, given her personality, but I couldn't know for sure.

"I don't know," said Kurt. "I don't think so."

Because she was a woman? It was true that far more men were excommunicated than women—one of the few bonuses to being born female and Mormon.

As we pulled into the driveway, Kurt shook his head and hesitated a long moment, bowing into the steering wheel. "I just don't know how to do this," he said.

I stared at my husband and wondered what had happened to him. "I thought being called as bishop cured you of cowardice," I said.

"Ha!" Kurt said without any amusement. "I just—I don't

think I'm going to have the words for it. How to tell her about President Frost's sealing cancellation and everything else. She might not have been legally married. She might not have legal custody of her own children."

"Don't tell her any of that," I said. "That would be cruel." I kept to myself the hope that President Frost would be set down by higher levels of authority once they knew what he was doing. And if no one came to demand the adopted children back, there was no reason that would be a problem, either. As for the marriage being legal, I hoped that the life insurance company would have to give the money to Emma because she had been specified by name, not because she was legally Carl's wife. She had thought she was, in any case.

"But she'll want me to counsel her about Carl's eternal salvation. She'll want to feel secure about her children being hers forever."

And was that possible if her marriage was void and they had no father? As far as I knew, she wasn't the first woman whose husband was excommunicated. The temple sealing was still valid on her side, if she remained worthy. Whether she would be expected to find another husband in this life or the next, I didn't know.

"Just tell her that you don't know."

"Over and over again?" asked Kurt.

"Yes." I was surprised he was so uncomfortable with that answer. I had been saying "I don't know" for a long time, to a lot of things. In my experience, as soon as you find one answer, a thousand new questions spring up. It's like a hydra. Whatever you do, don't answer questions. You just make more of them.

Kurt finally opened the truck door and we headed inside.

Sheri Tate passed us on the way out the door, since she was apparently still staying over at night. "She's doing better. A lot better," she said.

Well, Kurt and I were about to change all that.

Emma Ashby had us sit down in her front room, side by side on one of two small couches that faced each other. Emma was an expert quilter, both hand quilting and machine quilting. She'd led group lessons for Relief Society weekday meetings, and I'd seen her handiwork before.

There were three beautiful pieces hanging on the walls of the living room—a tree of life, a Noah's Ark, and an empty tomb. As we sat with her, she worked on one that had Adam and Eve (in abstract geometric cutouts) with a tree of apples between them and a snake that twisted up the trunk. The colors were jewel-like and amazing. It was detailed work, though, and I was surprised she had the attention span for it.

"How are your children?" I asked, trying to begin with a safe, or at least expected, topic.

"Alice is very upset, but somehow I worry more about William." Emma glanced at the empty spot on the couch next to her, as if consulting with the absent Carl, who would never again sit beside her there. "He won't say a word about his father and I think he's holding it all inside. I was hoping that you might talk to him, Kurt. I think he feels lost."

She was looking at Kurt with a beseeching face that made me a little nervous. I had seen plenty of women gravitate to Kurt after he became bishop. It was easy to let him take over the part of the male authority figure in their lives, and divorced or widowed women calling on Kurt for help with car repairs or home maintenance had become normal. I was sharing my husband with other women all the time. But the way Emma Ashby looked at Kurt made me tense up and want to sit beside him, an arm wrapped around him to mark him my territory.

Which was ridiculous, of course. Emma was no threat to my relationship to Kurt. She was just needy at a time like this, and that was perfectly normal.

"Of course, I'll do whatever I can for William," said Kurt. "I was blessed to serve with—" Kurt hesitated. "Carl," he finally said, leaving out any pronoun.

Emma's tears dripped into the quilting piece and she put it aside with a sigh of exasperation. "I feel so helpless. I just need to know what happened to Carl to move on, I think. I need to know there will be justice, and the world will make sense again soon. You understand, don't you, Bishop?" asked Emma.

"Of course," said Kurt.

"Do you know anything about the investigation by the police?" Emma asked, leaning forward. "Do they have any leads? Is that why you're here right now?"

Her hand brushed Kurt's knee, and he subtly moved away from her. I wondered how often he had to do that with other women. I had never seen him do it before, but maybe I just hadn't noticed.

"No," he said. There was a long pause.

"Kurt had some troubling news about Carl himself," I said finally.

But Emma acted as if Kurt was the one who had spoken. Her eyes were riveted to him. "What is it?" she asked. She seemed very tense, her head upright, the tendons of her neck so tight I thought they might snap. "I had begun to wonder if something was wrong, because he was acting strangely the last few weeks."

That was something I wanted to hear more about. Was the scene at the restaurant one example of his change in behavior? But I bit my tongue, hoping Kurt would speak up.

"I have some information from the coroner's office that I'm afraid will be very upsetting to you," said Kurt at last.

"Oh, please tell me. I'm sure if you're here with me, it won't be too bad," said Emma.

Kurt glanced at me, took a deep breath. "I can't think of any way to put this delicately, Emma. The coroner has revealed that Carl was—well, he was not biologically male," he got out at last.

Emma's eyes went wide. "What do you mean?"

I could see Kurt's face go dark with color. "He was born a female. But he had some surgery done to—uh—look outwardly male, at least. And he had been taking hormone injections fairly regularly. Do you know anything about that?"

She didn't answer. She just stared at Kurt.

Kurt continued. "There is a birth certificate. He—she—was born Carla Thompson." He was making a mess of this, I thought.

"But that—that's impossible," Emma croaked. Her face had gone very pale. I thought again of how fragile and small she was.

One thing I was fairly sure of was that this was an authentic reaction. Somehow, even after twenty years of marriage, she had truly been that innocent, that naïve.

"I'm afraid there's no question about it," Kurt said. "Carla even had an old arrest record, from the time before you knew her. Him." Kurt was confusing us all now with his pronouns. "He graduated from high school as Carla. It wasn't until later that she changed her name, and uh—her persona. Around the time he—she—he met you and joined the church."

Kurt didn't mention anything about the possibility that Carl had delivered a child before he transitioned to being a man. Where was the child? Dead? Stillborn, as Georgia had been? Given up for adoption? Did this child know anything about Carl at all? I couldn't help but spin off a dozen questions in my mind. But it wasn't our business, really, what Carl had done before we knew him. Whatever had happened to that child, Carl's family was Emma and Alice and William.

"But he—we—" said Emma. Tears were spilling down her face as she reached for Kurt's hand.

I moved to sit by her and took her hands in mine. I hoped she would think of it as a kind gesture, though I knew very well it was a territorial one on my part. I found myself making all sorts of guesses about what kind of sex she and Carl had had, things that were none of my business.

"Can you tell me how you two met?" I asked, trying to distract us both from the details of her married sex life. "You and Carl?"

There was no wedding photograph in the front room, I had noticed. Not every couple had one, of course, but I didn't see any photos of Carl at all. There were some of the children with Emma. She hadn't already taken down the ones with Carl, had she? Had he simply been camera shy?

"Oh, nothing special about that, really," said Emma, her voice unsteady. "Carl was in one of my classes in college at the University of Utah. A ballroom dance class. He was so commanding on the dance floor, so smooth in all his movements." She lifted her hand as if she was about to dance with him again, then dropped it. "I don't know why he picked me as his partner. He could have had anyone. I'd taken high school dance classes, but I felt so intimidated there. Until he came along, that is."

I thought about Carl's quotes about a woman's place. Had Emma at one point in the past found comfort in his commanding presence? It was hard for me to fathom, since my relationship with Kurt was so different.

Emma went on, "He asked me to marry him before the end of that semester. It was very romantic. He took me on a balloon ride and proposed before we landed. I was clinging to him the whole time, terrified." She was half smiling.

After a moment of silence, Kurt brought the conversation back to the topic at hand. "If you would prefer that the truth about Carl not be made public, I can speak to the police on your behalf. I don't know what their response would be, but sometimes they take the well-being of the family into consideration when drafting press releases."

"Please—" said Emma, bowing her head.

I thought of President Frost and his need to redo all of Carl's ordinances. Would he be able to keep the truth from people if he insisted on that? Did he want to make our whole stake hit the national newspapers? Again? Surely not.

"I can talk to William, if you'd like. Try to explain it," said Kurt.

"No, no," said Emma. "He misses his father so much. He can't deal with anything else." Was it William who couldn't handle the truth, or Emma herself?

"But if Carl was killed because of his other life, the police might need to ask rather pointed questions to find leads to his murderer," Kurt said, trying to reason with her.

"His other life? What other life?" asked Emma, bewildered.

"His previous life as a woman might have bled into the present. Was he frequently gone without explaining where he was?"

"He did a lot of business with the bishopric," Emma said. "Or at least he said that's what he was doing. I don't know how I would know for certain if he was or wasn't anymore. I trusted him. I always trusted him. He was my everything." And for her, that seemed to mean that she couldn't accept that he had ever been a woman. It would simply destroy her worldview too completely.

"Of course. Carl was a good man," said Kurt softly.

I stared at him as he said this, and realized that he believed it finally. If the only thing that came out of this conversation was Kurt seeing that, it was a good use of time, I thought.

"But you said that he had changed recently. Can you say in what way?" asked Kurt.

"Oh, that. Well, he and William fought a lot the last few weeks, and about nothing that seemed important to me. I felt that Carl was almost picking the fights. It was the same with Grant Rhodes."

I perked up at this. I hadn't heard about any problems between Carl and Grant Rhodes, the rogue Mormon who had been kicked out of his previous ward and had asked Kurt's permission to attend ours. Considering Grant's refusal to let certain perfect depictions of church history to go unchallenged in Gospel Doctrine class, though, it made sense. That had to have bothered Carl. But why more recently?

Emma continued, her words faint: "But he had never been like that before. Carl had always been slow to anger. It was one of the reasons I always felt safe around him."

"Is it possible that someone discovered his secret?" I asked, feeling sick at the idea of someone threatening Carl.

But Emma again refused to address the question. She simply shook her head and looked away from me.

"Was he getting any mysterious phone calls? Had any money gone missing from your joint accounts?" I asked bluntly, though Kurt was shaking his head at me. But the questions were surely ones the police would get to as soon as President Frost stopped shielding Emma from interviews.

"Just think calmly for a moment. I'm sure something will come to you, Emma," Kurt said, and this time he was the one to lean over and take her hand.

"There might have been one or two phone calls with numbers I didn't recognize," she said. "But I thought they had to do with the church, with the bishopric."

"Anything else?" said Kurt.

Emma shook her head. "You must think I'm useless," she said. "I was so used to Carl doing so many things. I feel like I've been thrown into an ocean and I'm drowning. There's too much for me to do, to think about. I married Carl when I was very young, and I never thought something like this could happen to me."

There was a part of me that was judging her for her weakness now, perhaps too harshly. She was a mother. She had children to take care of. She couldn't act the part of the damsel in distress. But it seemed that was what Carl had encouraged her to do for most of their life together.

"I'll talk to your home teachers," said Kurt, withdrawing his hand from Emma's at last. Home teachers are the male version of the visiting teachers. "It's their responsibility to step into your husband's shoes in a situation like this. If they're not up to the task, I'll see to it you have different ones assigned."

"Oh, there's no need for that, I'm sure," said Emma, waving a hand. "I don't want to be trouble to anyone."

"It's no trouble. It's our privilege to act as God's hands in this case," said Kurt. "I'm here to help you, and that's why I came by. I want to make sure that you're prepared for what's ahead with the police."

"The police? I don't know how I could possibly help them," said Emma. "I know Sheri said it was murder, but it doesn't make any sense to me."

"If you want Carl's killer caught, tell the police the full truth about everything, even if it's embarrassing. As I said, I'll do my best to make sure the details aren't tossed about publicly."

"Of course. Thank you, Bishop," said Emma, smiling tremulously.

Kurt stood up and motioned for me to do the same.

"About the funeral—" Kurt began, realizing he had one last thing to talk about.

"Sheri Tate said she would take care of the details for me," said Emma, seeming eager to relinquish such tasks to others. "Whenever they release the—the—" Her voice broke off.

IN THE CAR after we left, Kurt said he had wanted to warn her that Carl might not be buried in any temple clothes at all, and certainly not in male ones. "I suppose I'll have to decide on my own, unless President Frost insists."

I knew what he thought President Frost would insist on, and it felt like a travesty to me.

"Have you prayed about what God would want for Carl's burial dress?" I asked.

"I've tried," said Kurt. "But the words won't come out. I don't know what to say."

"Try harder," I told him.

CHAPTER 10

My friend Anna Torstensen and I went walking three times a week. We usually went in the mornings after breakfast, but on occasion we woke early and walked in the pink dawn, and sometimes we headed out late as the mountains melted into the sunset.

She called Thursday that week and asked me if I wanted to walk. Anna had radar for when I needed company. I hoped that I did the same for her, but I think I tended to be easier to read. I didn't hide things. But then again, I hadn't spent twenty years of a marriage with a man who had kept terrible secrets from his past. Needless to say, Anna was more used to reading people's nonverbal signals than I was.

It was a beautiful late summer morning, the sky already bright blue, no clouds in sight. Utah is a desert, and we were in a long drought, so we should probably have been happier to spot a cloud, but I couldn't help but enjoy the heat as it pricked at me.

We started off walking through the ward, the main artery with the older, more modest homes, and then turned right into the newer neighborhood with homes so large they didn't seem to have any yard. You could jump from one house's window through another without much effort, going right over the pro forma fence. All this opulence squashed together, despite the constant talks we heard repeated from General Conference about the need to keep our finances in order, to live without debt, along with a three-month supply of food.

"You're angry with Kurt, aren't you?" Anna said after we'd settled into a rhythm. Anna wasn't one to hold back. I think she had gotten tired of being patient with her husband. It hadn't gotten her anywhere, so she had given it up.

Despite his apparent softening toward Carl, I was still mad. "I really don't want to talk about it," I said.

"Maybe not, but unless you want to end your marriage by saying something you can never take back, you need to talk to me before you start yelling at Kurt. So what has he done now?"

"You heard about Carl Ashby's death?" I asked, trying to skirt on the edge of what I was allowed to say.

"Of course," Anna said.

"Kurt found something out about Carl that makes him see the man completely differently."

"And that's what made you mad? Carl Ashby? I thought you didn't like him much anyway."

"That's not the point," I said. How had she guessed that? I had never expressed my feelings about Carl aloud to her, had I?

"Then what is the point?"

"The point is that Kurt is sitting in judgment over this other person, and even though it hurts him to think he didn't know his friend, he doesn't think the problem is his. He feels justified in pointing a finger."

"And you never sit in judgment," said Anna mildly.

"I don't!" I said. I was huffing and puffing on the street's incline.

"You are constantly looking at people in the ward who are doing something obviously wrong and you want to lecture them about it, don't you? Come on, if I asked you to name the five most annoying people in our ward, you could do it easily."

She was right. I knew I was judgmental, especially when people were so stupid. And judgmental. I sighed to myself. I had a mental list. They were people I tried to avoid as much as possible at every church activity. I had created routes to get out of sacrament meeting via the south doors so I could avoid meeting them in the parking lot.

"That's not the same," I protested.

Anna raised her eyebrows. "You think you're so open-minded, but you absolutely draw lines between right and wrong. They may be in different places, but they're just as hard and dark a color.'"

I tried to get out a couple of words to contradict her, but I was breathing too hard. After all these walks with Anna in the past couple of months, you'd think I'd be in better shape. Maybe I should break down and get a gym membership. But a big group of the women I disliked at church were the ones who spent all their time chattering about their latest workout and then complaining about how their bodies weren't quite perfect enough.

Anna continued, "It's why you're a member of the Mormon church. You want someone to tell you what to do so you can argue with them and have an excuse to articulate for yourself what the real right and wrong are." Anna handed me a water bottle she'd been carrying with a carabiner on her belt loop.

This was a habit she'd picked up from her friend Richard Abayo. He always carried water with him when he exercised.

I drank nearly half of the bottle and handed it back to her. There might have been some spit in there. And some backwash, too.

Anna stared at the bottle and put it away without taking a drink herself.

We were stopped at the top of the hill, which gave an incredible view of the valley below. In pioneer times, there would have been farms below us, and cattle. Now there were only houses, roads and freeways, and the carefully combed Kentucky bluegrass brought west to make it look like we still lived in the east, and which required elaborate sprinkling systems to keep alive here. There were few trees except in the oldest parts of town, and very little of the original scrub oak or sagebrush that was authentic to this climate. Anna's husband Tobias would have had plenty to say about that, but he was gone now, his complaints about bad gardening silenced forever.

"Let's talk about a hypothetical situation," I said, finally able to breathe and talk at the same time. I didn't feel like it was my place to openly out Carl at this point.

"Okay," said Anna.

"Imagine you felt you were a man, in your deepest heart, in your very soul. How do you think Richard would take that?"

She stared at me for a long moment. "I don't think he would like it. At all. He likes me as a woman. I like me as a woman."

"Imagine you didn't. Imagine that the only way for you to be happy is to be treated as a man, to live as a man. And Richard, who loves you most in the world, wants for you to be happy and wants you to be who you feel you truly are."

"Then I guess I would start living as a man," said Anna, clearly confused. "What's the problem here? Because I don't believe either you or Kurt want to change genders."

"The problem is that everyone else in the ward would be disturbed by the choice. They'd never accept it. They'd act like it was all about cross-dressing. They'd say it was degenerate, a sign of the end of days when Satan has power over the hearts of men. They'd say it was unnatural and somehow it would be all about kinky sex." Mormons might have finally accepted that gay people existed and didn't simply choose to feel same-sex attraction because they were evil, but we were still a long way from accepting anything other than sex between straight, married people as normal.

"Is this really about you and Kurt?" asked Anna. She stared at the Draper temple just north of us, shining brightly in the dim morning light.

"Yes," I said. It was, if in a roundabout way.

"Hmm," said Anna.

"For Kurt, it's all about the rules. You're born and you spend your life doing what is right and expected of you by God and by the community of the church. Your life is a list of rules and you do them, whether you like it or not, because it's what the world needs."

And really, I had benefited enormously from this, because I had a husband who had always made sure that he worked enough hours that we lived comfortably, that he got repairs done around the house and did yard work regularly. And he'd benefited, too, from having a wife who took care of the children even when she was sick, who ran errands, did household chores, and made sure there was always breakfast, lunch, and dinner waiting when he was hungry.

"What if being who people expect you to be is killing you? What if you feel that God Himself knows that you are meant to be someone else? What if you feel like you have to be more authentic and put on a role that other people think doesn't belong to you?" I felt a rush of understanding for Carl Ashby as I spoke.

"Are you that unhappy with your life?" Anna asked.

"No. Of course not. I'm not talking about me," I said quickly.

"Aren't you?" said Anna. I sped ahead of her for a few steps. I just didn't see why people couldn't accept that Carl had been trying to be more authentic, and make his body show what he must have felt his soul had always been.

Anna paused for a moment, then said, "Have you considered how threatening the idea of a woman wanting to be a man may be for Kurt?" She turned to me and looked me in the eye.

"How could that threaten him?" I asked. "It's not his identity in question."

We started walking again, heading back down the hill.

"Let me tell you a story. When Liam was little, he used to sit and watch me paint my fingernails," Anna said. "It was this ritual of ours. I redid my nails maybe twice a week; when he smelled the polish, he would run up to my bathroom and sit cross-legged on the floor and just stare at me. Later, I got used to it, so I would call him when I started. It made me feel like I was really connecting with him. And then about six months after I started doing this, Liam asked if I would paint his nails, too."

Anna was walking backward in front of me as she talked, quite a trick. "I thought it was so cute that I painted his nails for him. All the same color as mine. He loved it. He was so excited to show his dad when he got home from work."

"I'm guessing that Tobias wasn't thrilled," I said.

"No. In fact, he told Liam to go clean his fingernails right away. And then he chastised me for it, too. He wouldn't sleep in our bedroom for a week, he was so angry with me." She shrugged. "I still remember we had to get every bit of color off before Tobias was satisfied, and then Liam's cuticles bled because they'd been so abused. I expected that Tobias would at some point relent and realize that he was being silly, that it was just a little boy who wanted some color on his nails, that he wanted to be like me, and that it was a good thing."

"But that never happened," I said. I could imagine Kurt in the same situation. None of my boys had ever had the opportunity because I didn't paint my nails.

"It never did," said Anna. "What happened was that a couple of years later, I caught Tomas at about the same age Liam had been, in my bathroom, putting nail polish on himself. And everywhere else—the carpet, the cupboards. And when I walked in, Liam was yelling at him. His tone was exactly the same as his father's had been. So strident and angry, and maybe a little afraid.

"So I helped Tomas clean himself up, and then while I worked on the rest of the house, I asked Liam if he could have a little compassion for his brother, since he had done the same thing himself. But Liam refused to believe it. He absolutely denied that he had ever put fingernail polish on. He said that I was making things up and he threatened that he would tell Tobias that I was lying about him. He was so vehement that I stopped talking about it. I brought it up once, years later, and Liam was just as adamant that it wasn't true."

"You're saying boys can't bear to remember a time when they weren't masculine?" I asked. What did this have to do with Carl? Or Kurt?

"I'm saying masculinity is a fragile thing. It can be taken away, do you see? For a woman, it isn't the same," said Anna. "We have everything else, all the other interests in the world that aren't the limited ones marked as masculine."

"All the ones that are denigrated," I complained. "No matter what we choose, we're always seen as lesser. We're the ones who are always being abused. We're the ones without power."

"Are we? I had power over Liam and Tomas, both of them."

"As their mother, yes," I said.

"And I had power over Tobias, too. Do you think that if I had laughed at him, mocked his masculinity, he wouldn't have been hurt?"

I thought about that. Was that what I had done to Kurt? Mocked his masculinity? Made him feel insecure because I told him that he should accept Carl Ashby's masculinity as the same as his own? "You sound like Freud, all that talk about women destroying the phallus. Wasn't that repudiated decades ago?"

We had reached the bottom of the hill again. My knees ached from the descent, from all that middle-aged weight coming down on them with every step. "Sometimes I think that you tell me what some part of me has been trying to get me to hear all along," I said.

"That's what a true friend does," she said. She waved and left me at my door.

I wondered if I should ask her in for a snack. But I didn't. I needed to be alone, and she knew me well enough not to be offended by that.

VERITY DERYKE STOPPED by that evening.

"Linda, how are you holding up?" she asked when I opened the front door.

I led her into the front room. "I'm fine," I said as I sat down next to her. "How about you and Tom?"

"He's disgusted," said Verity, shivering a little. "Finding out about that creature. How can you trust anyone after something like that?"

I tried to be calm about this, and to think about Verity's age and the generation she had grown up with. Transgenderism was even less talked about then than it was now. I had thought she was more modern with her ideas about women, but apparently I'd assumed too much.

"I think once they've thought about it, Tom and Kurt will see that Carl deserves to be treated as God must have seen him in his soul. After all, we always talk about how important it is for God to look on the heart, and not on the outward appearance." I put in a little scripture mastery verse in there, something that was quoted fairly often in church.

"But they all thought he was one of them. He might have seen them when they were—you know," said Verity, waving a hand and blushing.

Were we talking about genitalia again? "I'm pretty sure that Mormon bishoprics spend relatively little time staring at each other naked," I said. Did people really think that was the reason behind transgenderism? Some voyeuristic desire to become intimate with the opposite gender? There were plenty of better ways to do that, surely.

"He was using the men's bathroom, at church and everywhere else," said Verity. "For years. What was he doing in there?"

"Relieving his bladder?" I said blandly. It had sounded from the autopsy report that Carl hadn't had full gender reassignment surgery, so perhaps he had never used a urinal, and only a stall. But really what business was any of this of ours? What did it have to do with Christ or even the priesthood?

"Well, I just think it's sick and wrong for a woman to wear men's clothing all the time," said Verity. "After all, God made women for a reason. He wanted us to become mothers and have children, didn't He?"

"Not all women can have children," I pointed out. "Do you think they aren't serving their purpose to God? Are they useless?"

"Of course not," said Verity hotly. Tears started in her eyes and I wondered if I'd touched a sore spot there. Was one of her daughters infertile? I remembered that someone may have told me something about that.

"I think we have to continue thinking of Carl as a man, not as a woman pretending to be a man," I said.

"So people should just be allowed to be whatever gender they want? What if people switch back and forth, man one day and woman the next? Like putting on new clothes? Don't you think that's wrong?" said Verity.

I thought she was exaggerating the idea of transgenderism to the point of absurdity.

"I don't know. This is one of those things that I think we just have to leave to God," I said, trying to be conciliatory.

Verity didn't seem to be happy with this. She became more animated. "But—what if other women decide they want to do what he did? Just stop being women and become men instead? There will be an epidemic. Everyone will want to be a man."

I was very quiet. She had just revealed a lot about how she felt as a Mormon woman.

"Anyway, it seems to me that he was sick," said Verity.

She still referred to Carl as a "he," I noticed. I considered that a small victory.

"Maybe I should pray for him, so that he'll be able to cross over from spirit prison to spirit paradise, once he's repented of what he did here."

I didn't say anything, but I couldn't believe that God would require such a sacrifice to enter heaven. It wouldn't be heaven then, would it? Not for me, and not for Carl.

CHAPTER 11

On Saturday, the police went to interview Emma Ashby. In the midst of it, she called me in hysterics, and I rushed over. When I got to the Ashbys', a detective I didn't know, an African-American woman who looked to be in her early thirties, was sitting with Emma in the kitchen. Other officers were searching the family room, bedrooms, and offices.

"Hello. I'm Detective Gore." The officer waved to a chair for me to sit in next to Emma. "I suggested that Mrs. Ashby might like to have a family friend with her, or perhaps even a lawyer. She chose you."

I looked at Emma. She squirmed in the chair, and her hands were cold as ice when I touched them briefly to reassure her. "I'm here. I'll be right here for all of this," I said.

"Thank you," Emma managed. She had broken out in some kind of stress rash. There were patches of red, scaly skin peeling off her forehead and cheeks and nose.

"We have reason to believe that the person who murdered Mr. Ashby a week ago was a woman," said Detective Gore.

"And what reason is this?" I asked, turning to the detective.

"I'm afraid that I can't give out details about the investigation at this time."

But they were searching the house. I thought of the pink scarf I'd seen on the floor near his dead body, the scarf I'd assumed he'd been strangled with. Was that why they thought it was a woman? Did it have some connection to Emma?

I looked at the trembling woman next to me, the woman who had made me jealous over Kurt the last time we were here, who had said she was helpless without her husband. It seemed impossible to believe that she could have found the strength to strangle anyone, let alone the husband she needed so desperately.

"We would like to know if you have an alibi for the time of the murder, Mrs. Ashby," said Detective Gore. She had a spiral-bound notebook and a ballpoint pen out.

"I was home all evening," said Emma. She looked at me and rubbed at her face. The scales were shedding and drifting in the air like lint.

"Was anyone here with you between the hours of six P.M. and eight P.M.?"

"My—William was here until six. Then he went out with friends. And Alice was here until seven, I think," said Emma.

I noticed the kitchen was perfectly clean now. The countertops were wiped, the dishes put away. All the appliances were shining. I wondered what had driven Emma to do that.

"So you have no alibi from seven P.M. until what time?"

Emma looked at me again. "I called Linda at about midnight," she said.

I nodded at the detective. "That's true. She called to tell me she was worried about Carl." And why would she have been worried about him if she had killed him herself?

"We would like to take your fingerprints, if you don't mind.

To rule you out as a possible suspect, of course," said the detective.

"But her fingerprints might have been on Carl anyway," I said. "She might have been in that room in the church recently enough to leave other evidence, too." I was defending her because I didn't want her upset over nothing. Besides, it was a waste of everyone's time.

The detective glanced up at me, then returned her attention to Emma. "If you choose to decline, we will have to wait until we can force your compliance."

Emma would never have been good in a poker game. "No, no. I don't want you to have to do that. I don't have anything to hide," she said. She laid her hands on the wooden table. "Whatever you need me to do, I'll do it."

"Good. I'll have the kit brought in."

Emma was being so cooperative. She always was, it seemed.

"Are you going to tell us what you are searching for?" I asked. "Isn't it required for you to state what it is in the warrant?"

The detective spread her hands expansively. "Mrs. Ashby gave us permission to search the house without a warrant," she said. I had the impression that she wasn't waiting with bated breath on the results of the search. Why? Was it because she thought Emma was innocent, as I did?

Emma looked at me nervously. "Should I not have done that? The detective said the sooner they rule me out, the sooner they can go on to investigate other suspects and find the real murderer."

"I'm sure it will be fine," I said dubiously. I glanced back at Detective Gore. She was watching me closely now, and it made me acutely uncomfortable.

I could hear footsteps overhead and drawers opening and closing. What had they found up there?

"Can you tell us the name of anyone who had a grudge against Carl? Anyone you'd heard him argue with recently?" asked Detective Gore. I wondered how many murder cases she'd investigated.

"I don't know of anyone who had a grudge against Carl. He was a kind and upright man," said Emma. "As for arguing, I suppose he argued with Linda sometimes. He disagreed with her about things like the role of women in the Mormon church. Last Friday, for example, the week before Carl died, we both left a dinner with Linda and her husband because she and Carl argued."

I stared at Emma in shock. That was the way she remembered the bishopric dinner? That I was the one who had argued with Carl? I didn't contradict her, but it was odd.

"But I'm sure Linda, as a righteous Mormon bishop's wife, would never have sunk to such violence as this," said Detective Gore with a faint note of sarcasm, turning to me. "Even so, I suppose I'll ask where you were the night of Carl Ashby's death."

"I was at home," I said coldly.

"Alone?"

"My husband was there some of the time," I said.

"Hmm," said the detective. "I would have thought you and your husband would be together every hour you could manage. Perfectly devoted and eternally married couple and all."

I felt myself grow hot at the mockery. So, she wasn't Mormon. Did that mean she had no respect for the institution of marriage?

"Carl had views about men and women that I disagreed with," I said.

When I said nothing else, Gore turned back to Emma. "Mrs. Ashby, did you notice any changes in your husband lately?"

I was extremely relieved that the focus was back on Emma.

Emma chewed at her lower lip. "No, none at all. He was the same loving man that he had always been, at least to me and the children."

What? "I thought you said that Carl was more irritable lately," I said. When Emma had talked to Kurt and me some days after the murder, she'd unmistakably hinted that Carl had been unhappy about more than the argument at the bishopric dinner. She'd said he argued with William, and with Grant Rhodes.

Now Emma shook her head and seemed so completely confused that I wanted to text Kurt and ask him if I'd misremembered completely. "You're the only one he was irritable with, Linda. You picked a fight. You do that sometimes." Emma ducked her head shyly, as if embarrassed to accuse me, and then let Detective Gore take over.

I couldn't believe that Emma was doing this on purpose. She had to simply be confused. And I wasn't going to point a finger at her with the detective in the room. Besides, I was very well schooled at biting my tongue.

"So Carl didn't mention any problems at work or worries about anyone he worked with in the church?" Gore asked.

Emma shook her head. "He was a perfect husband and father and we all miss him so much already. I don't know how we're going to get through this."

"He was a businessman, I understand?" said Gore.

"He was in stock trading," said Emma. "He worked for himself."

"And did he do well?"

"Very well," said Emma. "We have plenty of money. And of course, he had his nest egg to rely on as well."

"Nest egg?" said Gore, leaning forward, pen on paper.

"He invented a medical device some years ago."

"What was it?" asked Gore, scribbling away.

"Oh, I don't know," said Emma, her hands held out innocently. "He didn't tell me the technical details. He just made sure that I knew it would keep us financially secure no matter what happened. Something about copyright or patent laws."

I could believe Emma was this naïve, but I didn't know if Detective Gore did.

"Is there someplace I can find that information?" asked Gore.

"It's probably in his files somewhere," said Emma.

"Of course. We'll look at those files. But there were no financial problems currently? No one angry at him for owing money? No one he was suing? Anything like that?" When Emma just shook her head without elaborating, Gore added, "I'm just trying to see if there were any red flags in his life that might help point us toward the murderer."

But before Emma could respond, there was a drumroll of feet coming down the stairs. Three white, male uniformed officers appeared in the kitchen. "Ma'am," said one of them to Gore, and shook his head. "We did find these, in the basement." Another man held up a bag containing a half-dozen medical syringes.

Gore nodded as if she had expected those.

I guessed that this was the testosterone that Carl had been giving himself to look more masculine, with facial hair and vocal changes. Did he have a doctor prescribing those for him somewhere, or had he found a black-market source for them?

"All right, then," said Detective Gore to Emma. "We'll get the fingerprinting kit from the car and we'll be out of your hair." She nodded to one of the uniformed policemen, and in a few minutes, he came back with the fingerprinting kit. "I hope you accept my condolences for your loss, Mrs. Ashby. And of course my apologies for this intrusion."

I watched the fingerprinting procedure, feeling guilty I hadn't encouraged Emma to talk to her lawyer first about it.

Detective Gore and her team had finished taking Emma's prints and were packing up to be on their way when the back door slammed loud enough to make me jump. It was William, and he was scowling.

"What's going on here?" he demanded of the police officers. "What are you doing with my mother?"

"It's okay, William." Emma shot up from her seat. "You don't need to worry about this. They're just trying to find out what happened to your father."

"Mom, you can't be that stupid," William said. "They're taking your fingerprints because they're going to accuse you of killing him."

"But I didn't, William. So there's no need to worry about that." Utterly calm.

William threw up his hands. "And since when did that stop the police? They go for the easiest target and then close the case."

I thought William might possibly have been watching too many TV murder shows. Or did he know something the rest of us didn't? Was there any possibility that William could have killed his father? Emma had already admitted he wasn't at home.

William wasn't very muscular, but he was taller than Carl.

Could he have strangled his father and then come home to fall asleep that night, leaving his mother to deal with everything? He had been strangely insistent on going to school the morning after his father's death.

"I assure you, Mr. Ashby, we are going to find out the truth here," said Detective Gore forcefully. She was taller than William was, and weighed a good deal more. She held her head high, right in William's personal space.

"Well, then, do whatever. Just stay out of my life," said William, and he disappeared upstairs.

"I apologize for my son," Emma said to Gore as the detective followed her colleagues out. "He's had a very difficult week."

But my thoughts were still spinning on the possibility that William might have killed his father. It seemed so far-fetched, but my gut reaction was that something here was wrong. Had William discovered his father's secret?

As the police vehicles pulled out, I wished I could do more for Emma. But I left her with a casserole the Relief Society had brought in, and the promise that she could call me if she needed anything.

At home, I told Kurt what had happened.

"That sounds like they're looking at Emma as a suspect," he said.

"Either her or William."

"That's ridiculous. They're the victims in this case, and anyone who knows them should see that immediately. I'm going to call President Frost."

I thought for a moment about Kurt's initial assessment that Carl was a liar and deserved to have his sealings canceled, and his assumption that a teenage boy and his mother couldn't possibly be murderers. Was I falling prey to the same assumptions?

"You don't feel that President Frost interfering in this case is, well, wrong?" I asked, thinking that the quick cleanup on the Sunday after the murder must have been partly due to President Frost's intervention as well.

"Not if Emma Ashby is innocent," said Kurt. "And I'm sure President Frost will pray about it before he does anything."

I wasn't convinced praying about it was a pass to use arm-twisting or Mormon connections to influence the outcome of a police investigation.

CHAPTER 12

We had our regular family dinner that Sunday night. All five of my boys (Adam, Joseph, Zachary, Kenneth, and Samuel) and my two daughters-in-law drove over to our house in Draper for the evening. Willow, Joseph's wife, was noticeably pregnant now. I think I was as excited about the new baby as either of the prospective parents. However, I was surprised that Joseph was the one who was having the first grandchild, and not Adam, who was older. But Adam had gone on a mission and Joseph hadn't, so Joseph had actually been married for longer.

Samuel, the only one of my sons who still lived with us, was late since he was coming from work. Kurt disliked the fact that the summer job Samuel had found was at the local movie theater, which meant he had to work every other Sunday. I was pretty sure that Samuel had taken the job at least in part to avoid church and not just to save money for college.

"Let me go change!" Samuel called as he went up the stairs two at a time. "Be right back!"

"That's one kid who is desperate to go to college," said Adam, nodding fondly after his little brother.

"Just wait until he's there. He'll have so many girls chasing him, he'll ask to come home on the weekends just to get away from them," said Kenneth.

Samuel was a good kid. More than that, he was the most empathetic of all my sons. He hurt when others hurt, and he was the kind of teenage boy whose shoulder the girls of his group would cry on when they had been mistreated by others. I had always assumed that he would do something extraordinary with his life, including marrying a woman who was his equal in tender kindness and deep thought.

Shortly afterward, Samuel came back downstairs in jeans and a T-shirt advertising one of the new Mormon music groups I didn't know. Kurt was vaguely suspicious of them all, assuming any group that became successful outside of Utah must have lowered their religious standards. Samuel's jeans were very tight. He had bought them himself with money he had earned from his job.

Maybe Kenneth was right about girls chasing him at college, after all.

I handed Samuel a plate and he piled it high with food, then dug in while the talk around him resumed. Joseph helped Willow move to the couch so she would be more comfortable. Marie joined them, chatting about baby things, despite the fact that she and Adam had shown no interest in getting pregnant. But that was their business, not mine.

At the table, Kenneth mentioned his new business venture, laundromats. He suggested that Samuel could get a job there that would pay better than the movie theater. "As soon as I'm up and going, which will be in a couple of months' time," he said, "you can work part-time through college."

Adam started clearing his side of the table, working around Kurt, Kenneth, and Samuel. I helped myself to a second serving of salad, partly just to have an excuse to stay and listen. Zachary made a snide comment about me turning into a rabbit, which I and everyone else ignored. Zachary often tried to derail fraught conversations with laughter.

"And you'd make sure he didn't have to work Sundays, wouldn't you?" said Kurt.

"Well," Kenneth said, "a lot of people do their laundry on Sundays. I have to stay open then."

"But can't you find other people to work on Sundays?" Kurt persisted.

"Are you suggesting that I ask my employees to do something I'm not willing to do myself?" asked Kenneth.

"Well, aren't you hiring some non-Mormons?" Kurt said, his tone strident. "It's not against their religion to work on the Sabbath."

"Isn't it? You know nothing about any religion but your own," said Kenneth.

I tensed, sure a full-blown argument was imminent. Kenneth had served a mission unhappily and had already expressed grave doubts to me privately about the Mormon church. I suspected that Kenneth might be gay, that that might be the explanation behind his anger, but I hadn't talked to either Kurt or Kenneth about it.

Adam tried to hand Kenneth his plate to encourage him to move toward the dishwasher, but Kenneth ignored the hint.

"And I wonder where I went wrong teaching you your own religion," said Kurt.

"Maybe you taught it to me just fine. I just didn't like it," Kenneth shot back.

"The décor is pretty awful," Zachary quipped, trying to

break the tension. "I think we should have an official calling of Church Decorator, and it should be voted on."

But Kurt and Kenneth didn't even seem to hear. They were still glowering at each other.

Samuel put his glass down loudly, stood up between Kurt and Kenneth, and said, "I have an important announcement to make. I'd like everyone to pay attention, please."

Kurt looked away from Kenneth and toward Samuel. For months now, Kurt had been hoping that Samuel would announce that he planned to leave on a mission next year instead of going straight to college. He had been accepted to BYU and had a half-tuition scholarship there. But BYU, which is Mormon owned, would be understanding if Samuel wanted to defer his admission until after he served as a full-time missionary.

Joseph drifted back from the living room, and in a moment Willow was at his side, leaning her bulk against him.

"This is hard for me, so if you'd allow me a few minutes . . . " Samuel said. "If I have to stop, just let there be silence for a bit. And please don't ask me questions until I get to the end. I'll tell you when I'm finished, and then I'll try to answer whatever nosy questions you guys throw at me." He sent me a faint smile, but there was a strange sadness in it.

I knew in that moment that he was not going to announce he was ready to go on a mission. And in fact, I felt a whisper in my mind that my life was about to change, and I needed to brace myself for it.

In the long pause, I wanted to be closer to Samuel, to put an arm around him. All my sons were all about the same height, a little over six feet, but Samuel was the thinnest and most fragile looking of them.

"I'm not going to BYU," Samuel said.

"What?" said Kurt, jumping to his feet.

Samuel put up a hand. "Give me some time," he said. "Remember?" His voice cracked and I could see he was fighting back tears. Was he upset because he was disappointing his father? All the other boys had gone to BYU. It was a family tradition.

Kurt sat back down, as if defeated. I wished he could just accept the wonderful sons we had, instead of trying to force them into a mold.

"I was accepted at BYU, but I turned it down a month ago. I know I should have told you then, but I was waiting for the right time." He shook his head, then put a hand to his heart. "Waiting to gather enough courage, really. I decided to accept the University of Utah's offer, and I know that isn't exactly what any of you wanted."

Kenneth clapped slowly several times in the silence, but he said nothing.

Samuel didn't look particularly pleased with the attempt at solidarity. "The U is offering me full tuition, which is nice, but that's not the real reason I decided to go there. In the end, I feel like I don't really belong at BYU." Samuel was staring down at the table. "I know that it's a great school, Dad. I know they have a great football team, though I suppose I will now be obliged to cheer for the opposing team." He raised a fist and grinned at this, but the expression faded quickly. "The U also has a great medical school, and I think I eventually want to go to that. But all of that is only part of the reason I chose it, and none of the reason that I've kept this secret from all of you."

Samuel took a deep breath, looked straight into Kurt's eyes, and then said, "Dad, I'm gay."

I felt poleaxed. Samuel was the one who was gay? How had I been confused about that? I thought we were so close. I thought I had understood him better than any of my sons.

There was absolute silence in the kitchen, as if we were in the celestial room at the temple. But the feeling was all wrong.

I glanced over and noticed that Kenneth was the only one in the room who didn't seem surprised by the announcement. Samuel took a deep breath, and Kenneth put a hand on his brother's shoulder. "Any time you want to talk about it more, know that I'm here for you."

Kurt opened his mouth once, but only a hoarse frog-like croak came out.

"How did you—that is, when?" Joseph sputtered.

"Dude, if I'd known, I could have embarrassed you way more the last few years. So unfair," said Zachary.

No one laughed.

Samuel seemed to hold himself a little taller and said, "I always knew I was different from the rest of you. I didn't have a name for it for a long time. And then last year, when I was supposed to be thinking about preparing for a mission, and I felt all this pressure to go on dates one last time, to make sure I had memories to carry with me—I knew. It was who I was, and always had been.

"But I didn't tell any of you because I was afraid of how you would react. I didn't want to take the chance that my family would reject me, and I thought maybe I could keep it to myself. I didn't think of it as hiding who I was or lying to you. I just thought of it as making peace." He looked at Kurt beseechingly.

I could hear Kurt take a deep, shuddering breath as he prepared to respond.

Mormon doctrine on the cause of homosexuality has changed only very recently, since the website www.mormonsandgays.org had launched. But a lot of Mormons didn't know about it, or ignored it for their own reasons. No longer were gay people told that being gay was evil and that they should go through electroshock therapy to get rid of gay thoughts—or marry and hope that heterosexual sex would change them. Instead, the new message was that people are born gay and can't change that. They are also told that God loves them and made them the way that they are—though it is still wrong for them to act on homosexual love. They are basically asked to be celibate for the rest of their lives.

My Samuel, as giving and loving as he was, would never be allowed to express romantic love openly, in the way that comes naturally to humans, if he wanted to stay a Mormon in good standing, able to attend the temple. How could he bear that? How could I?

Once again, Samuel took a deep breath. "But at the end of school this year, I realized that I had to stop hiding. I had to let you show yourselves to be the awesome people that I know you can be." Samuel smiled, but there were tears running down his face.

"Okay, I'm done now. You can ask questions if you want," he said, after wiping his nose in his T-shirt, which made me look around for tissues. But there weren't any in the room and I wasn't going to leave to get them.

"You have to know we love you just the same," I said. It wasn't a question, but it needed to be said.

Then Kurt asked, "So you're not planning to go on a mission?"

"I don't see how I can," said Samuel.

"But you can serve and be gay. There's no problem with that," said Kurt.

That was all Kurt had to say? He was pressuring Samuel to go on a mission, even now?

"All right. I guess I'll think about it, maybe after I've had a year to figure things out," said Samuel.

"And talk to the bishop in your college ward," Kurt added.

Samuel nodded.

"Hey, more girls for the rest of us. You're better looking than I am anyway. Yes for getting rid of the competition," Zachary joked. "Someone will have to marry me now, right?" Everyone laughed at that, except for Kurt.

"Time for cake!" I announced, and hurried over to finish clearing the last plates from the table.

Kurt and I would talk about this later. If he couldn't celebrate Samuel's openness, at least he could pretend. Because I was not about to allow his attitude to ruin our family. We had married to create this bond of unity, and nothing was going to tear us apart. Not Georgia's death, not Kenneth's doubts about the church, and not Samuel's truth.

CHAPTER 13

Kurt and I did not speak that night about Samuel's announcement. We both went straight to bed, and we didn't speak about it in the morning, either. I was angry at Kurt for not being more immediately understanding and loving, but I knew I should give him the time and space he needed to adjust to what was obviously a huge change in his expectations for Samuel. Kurt wasn't perfect, but that didn't mean he wouldn't rise to the challenge.

But as soon as I heard the garage door close Monday morning, I did what I needed to do for myself. I went upstairs and looked through my old handwritten address book from college days. I thumbed through the pages until I stopped at *Tookey, Ben*.

There were six different addresses listed. I had updated his listing until about six years ago, when I had given up trying to keep track of Ben. It wasn't as if he wanted to keep contact with me. I had always had to get his new address or phone number from someone else—one of his old friends, or his sister, whom I kept in touch with occasionally. She told me he had gone back to college, had gotten a PhD in engineering, and was teaching at a university in Kansas, or

Nebraska. Somewhere as far into the middle of nowhere as he could get.

Kurt had suffered a lot because of Ben Tookey. It wasn't Kurt's fault we couldn't initially be married in the temple, or that I was damaged in so many ways. Kurt had always been angry any time Ben came up, which hadn't been often lately. But what Kurt didn't know was that I had sent Ben a couple of Christmas cards. Ben had never replied. I had never received a letter from him, not even a photo.

I took out my cell phone and punched in the most recent number I had in the book.

It had been disconnected.

Damn!

I tried the number for Ben's sister Emily. It wasn't disconnected, but the woman who answered it was not Emily. It had been two years since she had this number, she informed me, and she had no idea who had had it before.

I had left all of this until it was too late. I should have called Ben long before now. I should have told him I forgave him for everything that happened in our marriage, and even for the nasty letter he had written when Kurt and I wanted to marry in the temple. I should have asked if we could be friends. I should have told him about my life, asked him about his own. He might not have told me anything, but at least I would have had contact with him. I would have tried, and felt some satisfaction in that.

I had been so angry when I filed for divorce thirty years ago. It had all been his fault. He ruined my life. He was a liar. He had told me he loved me, and clearly he never had.

But my life hadn't been ruined, not permanently anyway. And I had always hoped that Ben had gone on to find some

kind of peace, and maybe even love in his life. I never would
have guessed that one day I would be calling him to ask if he
could talk to my son. Was it stupid to think that one gay Mormon man would have anything to say that would help another
gay Mormon man? Things were different in the church now
in some ways, but the old prejudices against people who were
different were still there. I thought that at this point, Ben must
have come to terms with who he was, and that he would be
able to offer some advice as someone who had lived with the
worst possible things that Samuel could be imagining might
come in the future.

I opened my computer and went on Facebook. I searched
for Ben Tookeys in Utah, Kansas, and Nebraska. Nothing. So
I expanded and looked for Benjamin Tookeys in the United
States. There were four of them. I squinted at grainy photographs and clipped biographies, read through recent posts,
and narrowed the search to three.

I tried to message all of them.

One responded with a lewd comment about sex and Mormonism.

One did not respond at all.

The last responded a few hours later, after I'd finished my
lunch.

"It's been a long time," Ben—I was sure it was him—wrote.
"I hope we've put a lot of hard and sad things behind us. Sometimes I miss you, but I've always been afraid to reach out. I
know you have a new life now, without room for me in it."

That was all. No phone number. No mention of where he
had been and what he had done with his life. I really had no
right to ask for more from him, and I knew it. But that didn't
stop me from hoping for something.

I read as much as I could about his life online. There were photographs of him with women and men, but never of him in a couple. He had no children that I could see. He did not list a committed relationship. He lived in Chicago and taught at a university there. I could see a few of his journal publications, all very academic.

I wrote only, "I am sorry for all I did to you. I hope you are happy now," and left it at that.

I realized I needed to tell my boys about my first marriage. For years, Kurt and I had talked about the best way to tell them, the best time to tell them. We'd decided we should wait until even Samuel was old enough to understand, perhaps eleven or twelve. But by the time Samuel had hit that age, Joseph and Adam were out of the house and it was never the right time. It was ancient history. Why bring it up with them now? It had nothing to do with them, or even with me and Kurt. Not really. Not anymore.

Now I thought about Emma Ashby. She was the woman I might have been if I had stayed with Ben. And that woman would not have been a happy one. She would have made the best of a difficult situation. She might have adopted children. And she would have told herself every day that this was what she was destined to do, that this was what God wanted of her. But inside, she would have died a little more each day.

I didn't regret becoming an atheist—without that, I wouldn't be who I was today. And then Kurt had come along and I'd been given a whole new life, one I was convinced God had wanted for me all along.

All those old scars from my past. What about Carl and Emma Ashby's past? What secrets had they hidden, and how many of those did we not yet know?

CHAPTER 14

On Monday evening, Kurt had eaten quickly, answering questions in monosyllables with a distant look on his face, and then muttered something about needing to do church work and headed to his office. That left me and Samuel together for what was supposed to be Family Home Evening on Monday night.

All Mormon church activities are scheduled for days other than Monday in order to allow parents to spend one evening just with their children. Some communities even try to expand the effort to get sports activities, school events, and government meetings moved to different nights of the week as well. The Mormon church has Family Home Evening resources online, but we had an old manual printed from when the boys were younger with short lessons for all ages, scripture references, and sometimes illustrations for smaller children, along with ideas for fun activities and treats. The point is to build family bonds.

I could not remember the last time that Kurt had skipped a Family Home Evening.

"I feel like I should say I'm sorry, but I'm not," said Samuel, as he and I sat still at the kitchen table.

"You're not the one who should be sorry," I said, glowering at the closed door of Kurt's office.

"I could have brought it up privately with Dad first, I guess," said Samuel, head low. "Or maybe hinted at it somehow."

It made me angry that my son was hurting, and I had to defend him, even against Kurt. I was sure that Kurt had his own side to this that made sense to him, but I couldn't imagine what it was at the moment. "We're the ones who should be saying we're sorry. The fact that we never noticed or asked you about the issue—that shows we were blind and probably completely wrapped up in ourselves rather than thinking about you."

Now that Samuel had come out, it seemed so clear to me how uncomfortable he had always been with the idea of dating women. He had never had crushes on girls. If I had been paying more attention, I would have seen the signs of the crushes he must have had on some of his guy friends.

There were several stories on the Internet in recent years of Mormon men who openly admitted their homosexuality but committed to marriages with women so they could be considered worthy priesthood holders with temple blessings. But the church didn't officially encourage that strategy anymore, thank goodness. With my history, I couldn't abide the idea of Samuel trying anything like that.

"I wondered if Dad knew," Samuel said. "There were a couple of times when he seemed like he was about to ask me directly, and then he veered off in another direction."

"He never said anything to me, if he did," I said. Would he have?

"Is it really such a horrific thing? Why can't he just sit and talk to me about it? If he has questions, can't he just ask them?"

I thought about how many times in my life important conversations had happened right here, in this kitchen, while I
was doing the dishes. Joseph had confessed he was about to
ask Willow to marry him. To me, not to Kurt. And Adam had
told me he was interested in his best friend's girlfriend, who
turned out to be Marie. I'd given him the best advice I could
about how to manage the situation, which was to be honest
with everyone involved. He had ended up being estranged
from his best friend temporarily, but once Hank got engaged
to someone else, everything was good between them again.

"I think it's just hard for him to adjust," I said. "He's trying
to adjust his expectations for the future."

"But I'm the same person I was before. I just—needed to
be open about this."

"I know what you mean, I think," I said, and debated
whether to go on before adding, "Would it bother you to know
something about me that I've kept secret for a long time?"

Samuel stared at me for a moment with wide eyes. Then
he smiled. "You, Mom? A secret?"

I felt like my chest was about to burst. This is what Samuel
had felt like on Sunday, I reminded myself. Breathless and
unsure if he should do it, but then realizing that he had been
lying for too long, even if it had seemed to be for a good reason
at the time. I would have to tell all of the boys at some point,
but right now it seemed fair to share this with only Samuel.

"I was married before I married your father," I said softly.

Samuel's head jerked up. "What?"

I nodded. "It was only for eighteen months, and it was a
disaster from the first night. I left the church for a few years
afterward because of it. I felt so angry that God had allowed
me to be so hurt."

"Did he hit you?" Samuel asked. His hands were tightly clenched, and so was his jaw.

I laughed gently. "No, Samuel. It wasn't anything like that."

Samuel relaxed. "Then what? How was it a disaster?"

I had always been more comfortable talking to Samuel about personal things than the other boys, but this was difficult even with him. "To be honest, I think Ben was gay. He never used that word, but he was never—uh—interested in me sexually, and that was devastating. At first all I could think was that there was something wrong with me, that I didn't dress right, or that I'd said something wrong." I was rushing through the words, and tried to force myself to slow down. "It took me most of those eighteen months to realize it wasn't me, it was him."

"Ben? That's his name? Do you still keep in touch with him?" asked Samuel.

I didn't mention the Facebook search or the brief message Ben had sent. That was not keeping touch. "Not really."

"Maybe he wasn't gay," Samuel said. "Maybe he was asexual. I've been studying up on different kinds of sexualities, and apparently that's real. People who just aren't interested in a physical relationship. Ever."

"I hadn't heard about that," I said, and considered the idea now.

I remembered the day I'd tried to catch Ben's interest by wearing a sexy swimsuit, but instead I had only caught the change in his expression when he looked at another man at the pool. The heat in Ben's eyes—he must have been gay.

"I guess we should ultimately let people define themselves, but my best guess was that he was gay," I said.

"And you actually left the church because of how your

marriage ended? That seems pretty extreme," said Samuel. He was looking down at his hands on the counter now.

It felt like admitting to failure, even still. "I really felt like I had been guided to marry Ben. And when I divorced Ben, it was like I was divorcing God, too."

"Do you think that you did the wrong thing and now God is making you go through it all over again? With me?" asked Samuel, moving to stand up.

"No!" I pulled him back to his seat, and held his face in my hands so he could see the truth in my eyes. I hadn't meant anything like that.

"You think this guy being gay almost destroyed your spiritual life," Samuel said. "So what does that say about me?"

I took a moment to think this time before I opened my big mouth. "It says that you aren't Ben Tookey. And the church isn't telling you to get married no matter how you feel. It says that you being open about who you are is brave and right."

"So if I tried to find a woman who would marry me anyway, you'd tell me it was the wrong thing?" Samuel dug his hands into the soft skin around his neck, until I pulled them away.

Why was he even considering that? Was this what he thought Kurt would want him to do? "Yes, I would say I thought it was the wrong thing. But I would also try to listen to you and let you make your own choices. So long as you were honest about who you are, and so long as I believed that she was a good person, I'd ultimately have to trust you to be guided by the spirit in your own way."

Samuel shook his head. "That's not my plan at the moment."

My chest expanded in relief. "Okay," I said.

"Right now, I'm not sure I have much of a life plan. Except going to the U and studying biology."

I glanced again at the door to Kurt's office.

What more of a future could Samuel look forward to, in Mormonism? What did it mean, really, if God made some people gay in a world where we were all supposed to be getting married and having eternal families? If you could only get to the highest order of heaven through marriage, and marriage was only heterosexual, that only left the idea that gay people would somehow be made heterosexual in the next life. I was sure that we all had parts of us we didn't realize were wrong and needed to be fixed, but I couldn't bring myself to tell Samuel that this part of him was fundamentally a barrier to getting to heaven and living with God again. Or that God had made him this way on purpose, knowing that he would forever be disallowed from having a family and children, which were the sweetest blessings of life to heterosexual couples, and the way that we understood God's divine love for us most clearly.

"I love you, Samuel," I said, because the rest was too big for words.

Then we left the dishes and went out for ice cream for our own private Family Home Evening. For the time being, we didn't talk any further about Samuel coming out, and it felt right.

When I came back, the dishes were done but Kurt was still in his office. I went to bed alone.

CHAPTER 15

The home phone rang at 3 A.M. Tuesday morning. I nudged Kurt to get it, and he heaved himself up to stumble across the room for the portable home line.

I heard Kurt say "Hello?" as he reached the door of the bedroom. He normally took bishop calls down in his office for privacy, and he was probably headed there, but he stopped. "Oh. Yes, she's here," he said. And he came to stand by my side of the bed. "It's for you, Linda."

For me? My heart thumped hard in my chest, like a fist punching me awake. I sat up, sure that this had to be bad news.

"It's Alice Ashby," Kurt added.

Alice Ashby? Why would she want me instead of the bishop? I sat up and took the phone. "Hello?" I said.

"William is gone," said Alice's trembling voice. She sounded like she was five years old, her tone was so high-pitched.

"Gone where?" I said.

"I don't know where he went. He was upset last night and Mom thought she'd calmed him down. But I was worried about him and I kept waking up to check on him. The first two times, he was in his room. But now he's not."

"Does he have a cell phone?" I asked.

"Yes, but he didn't take it."

"Maybe he just went for a walk to clear his head," I suggested.

"It's been an hour, and he didn't take his diabetes kit," said Alice.

I hadn't known he had diabetes. "Does the bag have his insulin, too?" I asked. That was all I knew about diabetes.

"Yes, it has insulin, but that's for when his blood sugar is high. High blood sugar isn't likely to kill him and he has a pump that mostly takes care of that," said Alice. "The bag is more in case he goes low and needs glucose to avoid a diabetic coma."

I wondered how likely it was that he would go low if he had a pump and had been treating his diabetes properly. "Diabetic coma" sounded pretty serious. "Right." I yawned. "Sorry. I'm just having trouble waking up. I'll be right over."

"Okay, but be quiet. I don't want to wake up my mom."

Of course she didn't. She could have called her home teacher, her Young Women's leaders, any of her church friends. But she had called me instead. "I'll be over in ten minutes. Wait at the door and let me in so I don't have to ring the bell." I hung up.

"Do you want me to deal with it?" Kurt asked.

I shook my head, wondering if this was really a crisis or not.

"Do you want to tell me what's going on?"

"William is missing without his diabetes kit and Alice is freaked out about it," I said succinctly.

"Ah," said Kurt. "Carl would have been furious. He had very strict rules for those kids."

"Stricter than your rules?" I asked. I'd always thought Kurt was hard on our sons. Fair, but he accepted no half measures.

"My rules? Compared to my father, I'm a pushover," said Kurt.

He was right about that, I was sure, but that didn't mean that he hadn't been strict for our generation.

Wondering if Kurt would go back to bed, I threw on some yoga pants. From our bedroom window, I could see lights on all over the valley.

I could have taken a car, but I was afraid that the engine would wake up Emma, so I walked over.

As I headed up the front steps, the door opened, and I saw Alice's face peek out.

Instead of sitting on the couch in the front room, I led her back into the kitchen, and then downstairs into the family room. I'd had time to think on the way over. "What aren't you telling me about William?" I asked in a hushed tone.

Alice folded her arms across her chest in a typical teenage defensive gesture. "I don't know what you're talking about. I thought you were going to help me find him."

"Why would you keep checking on William all night? Why would you call me as soon as he was gone? What are you so nervous about?" Not waking her mother wasn't just about protecting her from further worry, either.

"I told you, I was worried about him." Alice shrugged. "Since Dad died, he's been really weird." She shrugged again.

I thought of the way William had acted with the police, and my inkling that they might suspect him in his father's murder. "But it's more than that, isn't it?"

Alice studied me for a long moment. She should have called

someone else if she didn't want questions. Finally, she said, "He's been talking about stuff lately."

"What kind of stuff?" I sat down on the couch, but she remained standing, agitated.

"He's been mad. And he wants to do something about it."

"Mad?" I said, and waited.

She let out a long breath. "He thinks he knows who killed Dad," she said.

Now we were getting somewhere. "Who does he think did it?" Although it proved nothing conclusively, it was a relief to me to realize that Alice, at least, did not believe her brother had killed their father.

She hesitated, then said, "Brother Rhodes."

I was baffled. "Why?" Emma had mentioned an argument between Carl and Grant, but Grant Rhodes seemed so unlikely to ever become violent.

"They had been having arguments about church stuff," said Alice.

"And William thinks that was a reason to kill? I don't think you should worry about that."

"William has Brother Rhodes's keys from mowing his lawn," Alice added breathlessly. "He said he was going to use them to get inside and deal with him."

No one had mentioned William doing lawn mowing for Grant Rhodes. But this meant that William couldn't have murdered his father if he believed someone else had. I tried to remember where exactly Brother Rhodes lived. It wasn't within our ward boundaries, but it was fairly close by. "I'll go see if I can find him over there," I said. "You stay here in case your mother wakes up."

Alice nodded, and I realized she had the same habit as her

mother of chewing on her lower lip. She might not be bio-logically related to Emma, but she still looked like her. "Thank you," she whispered.

I walked out of the house wondering if I should call the police instead of going over to investigate myself. But if William was there, doing what Alice thought he was doing, he could end up with a criminal record. I was annoyed with the boy for being reckless, especially when I had a hunch the police sus-pected him in his father's murder, but I didn't think he deserved permanent damage to his life plans.

I checked the stake directory for the exact address of Grant Rhodes's house. It was about a mile from the Ashbys' and I wished now that I had taken the car, but it would take longer to walk back home and get it. I also knew that if I went home, Kurt would likely insist on going with me, and I didn't want him involved as bishop.

The fifteen-minute walk took me through utterly silent streets, past dark houses and not a single moving vehicle. I let my thoughts circle around Grant Rhodes. He wasn't mar-ried, and I couldn't remember if he ever had been in the past. But why would a single man buy a house in a family neighbor-hood like this one? There had been a rumor a year or so ago that he was gay, but Kurt refused to call him in for an inter-view on that topic based on rumors.

When I got to the right house at last, I saw that the lights were on in the garage, and I feared I had gotten there too late. Had Grant Rhodes already found William there?

Then, as I watched, the garage door opened and a car lurched out, one I had never seen in the church parking lot. It was a classic show car that had been meticulously restored. It was painted cherry red and looked like a gangster car from the movies. William's head was visible over the steering wheel.

"William, stop!" I shouted. I leapt into the road in front of him and waved my hands. It was a stupid thing to do, on many levels.

William pulled sharply to the side to avoid me. The car made a terrible screeching sound and I turned in time to see it jump the curb on the other side of the road, then crash into the brick mailbox, leaving a nasty scar on the beautiful red paint job.

"William!" I shouted again.

I stumbled toward the car, feeling distinctly nauseous with guilt. I'd been trying to save him from doing something stupid, and instead I had caused him to crash. At his age, he shouldn't have been driving any car, let alone one that expensive. Had he crashed on purpose or by accident?

Lights had started to go on all over the cul-de-sac. There was movement in the car. Did that mean William was okay?

The driver's side door of the car opened and I rushed forward to help William out. He looked pale and sweaty, and his eyes shimmied around, unfocused, but he was cursing under his breath. Air bags weren't standard when this car had been built, and William had a bad cut on his head. I pulled him toward the curb and he leaned against me as he breathed heavily. A part of me worried that the car was going to blow up. I had no idea where the gas tank was or if it had been punctured. I also remembered that William had diabetes and Alice had been worried he might go into a coma. Would I be able to tell if that was what had happened? Did I have anything sugary in my purse to put under his tongue and bring his blood sugar back up? Was that even the right thing to do?

"What were you doing in that car?" I asked, staring into William's eyes. Was one pupil larger than the other?

"Had to—make him—pay," William got out.

Grant Rhodes, presumably. "By stealing his car?"

"Wrecking it," said William, thumping his hand on the ground.

Well, he had succeeded at that. I let go of him and scrambled to my feet. What lesson was he going to take from this? That reckless behavior paid off?

Grant Rhodes came out of his house then, dressed in a robe and a T-shirt that had a photograph of Buffy the Vampire Slayer printed on it. "Oh my God!" he shouted, and ran toward the car. He put a hand out and touched it. Then he glanced up at William and me. "What in the name of Jesus Christ happened here?" he asked. I had never heard him swear like this before.

"It was an accident," I said, though I knew it wasn't.

Grant Rhodes had pulled his phone out and was dialing.

"We need an ambulance more than we need the police," I said.

Grant Rhodes's mouth was tight with an expression that was severely at odds with the goofy T-shirt he wore. "This car is insured. Even an accident has to be reported to the police for me to collect," he said.

"But after we deal with more important things," I said. "Like getting William to a hospital." I waited a moment, but Grant didn't contradict me. So I got out my own phone and called an ambulance. Grant Rhodes and I sat with William until it came.

I called Kurt and explained the situation as briefly as possible. Kurt promised he would drive over to break the news to Emma Ashby so she could meet William at the hospital.

When the paramedics came, I weighed my options and decided to let William go to the hospital alone. His family would meet him there, after all, and I wanted to see what Grant Rhodes would do next. As soon as the ambulance was out of sight, he called the police.

"There's been an incident," he said, watching me watch him. "My car has been damaged and I need an official police report."

I was relieved he hadn't mentioned William's name. At least, he hadn't yet. Maybe Grant Rhodes would be inspired to be merciful to this angry, suffering kid. I prayed for that and tried to feel peace that I had done as much as I could.

The police said they were already en route because of the ambulance call, but they hadn't arrived yet by the time Kurt came to pick me up. The sun was already dawning and I felt completely exhausted.

"It's going to be a long day," said Kurt, shaking his head at the sight of the wrecked car and Grant Rhodes's mournful expression. He wasn't wrong.

CHAPTER 16

William Ashby had three broken ribs and a concussion, and his right arm was broken in three places. Kurt gave me the report that afternoon on the phone. I had just woken up from a long nap, feeling groggy and unattached to my own body.

"So he'll be in the hospital for a while?" I had made my way downstairs to the kitchen, trying to drum up an appetite.

"A few days, at least," Kurt said. "I've asked Sheri Tate to arrange for the Relief Society to send meals to the Ashbys for another few weeks."

"And you want me to do something as well." It was obvious from the tone in his voice.

"If you could pick up Alice from school and drive her to the hospital to see her brother, that would be helpful."

"Of course," I said. I thought about our conversation in the middle of the night and wondered if she would think it was her fault that this had happened. I felt it was mine.

If I had gotten there earlier . . . If I had reached out to William when I had first thought he was troubled . . . If I had thought to call Grant Rhodes before I went over to his house . . . If I hadn't been in the way and startled William into crashing . . . If, if, if . . . It was a dangerous cycle of blame, as I knew very well. But having been through it before did not inoculate me from going through it again.

"Has Brother Rhodes already made his statement on the official report?" I asked.

"As far as I know from President Frost, all the police did was write up a few of the damages. Grant hemmed and hawed about who was driving, and the police think it was his own fault. They didn't take a statement. Grant said that he wasn't up to giving one because he was too upset."

I felt relieved, but was surprised that President Frost had intervened yet again in this case.

"I was hoping that Grant might be willing to let William work for him and earn enough money to pay for the repairs," said Kurt.

I raised my eyebrows, though Kurt couldn't see that. "Let me guess. Brother Rhodes was not enthusiastic about that plan."

Kurt sighed. "He said that there was no reason for him to believe that he could trust William after what had happened, and what sort of work would be useful for him if he couldn't be sure of the person doing it?"

Which was a sensible response, if not a particularly compassionate one.

"I am still hoping that when the immediate emotions pass, he may be willing to reconsider, but at the moment, he says he is going to make a full report to the insurance company, and at that point, Emma Ashby may be liable for more than forty thousand dollars."

"What if I tried to talk to Grant Rhodes?" I suggested.

Kurt paused. "I don't think that's a good idea," he said at last. "You could just make him angrier, you know."

But I had to try something. After all, this already involved me. Grant could change his mind and name William as the driver. He could ask me to testify since I was a witness. I didn't think I could bring myself to lie either to the police or in court, if it came to that. So I needed to do what I could to prevent such a situation.

Before hanging up, Kurt reminded me that I had promised to pick up Alice at school, and suggested that my talents might be better used calming her and her mother. I checked my watch and realized I didn't have much time, so I hung up and got into the shower.

When I arrived in the high school parking area, I was late and Alice was the only student left. She got in the backseat and put on her seat belt, saying nothing while I apologized. She looked paler than she had the night before, and I itched to brush her hair. It seemed to be sticking out all over the place, but I wasn't sure if that was an intentional style.

"I'm supposed to be taking you to the hospital to see William. Is that what you really want?" I asked, craning my neck to look at her. I wished she had chosen to sit in front with me, but I didn't want to pressure her.

Alice shrugged. After raising five sons, I'd become fluent in teenage body language. This was not an "I don't care" shrug. It was an "I have no words for all the feels I am feeling" shrug.

"I can take you home instead, if you'd rather," I offered.

"Yeah?" She looked at me, staring into my eyes.

"I can do whatever you need me to do. I'll take you to get some ice cream if you want, then drop you off at home. Whatever you want." I could go over and see how William was doing on my own, make excuses for Alice.

"Because you think I'm an idiot," she said flatly.

"No." I could just barely reach her knee around the seat with my hand, so I touched it gently. "Because I think you're a hero. You love your brother and you did everything you could for him last night."

"And that's why he's in the hospital," she said bitterly, looking out the window to the lake and the mountains to the west.

"No. He's in the hospital because even God can't stop other people from making stupid mistakes." Apparently. "So why should you think that you can? Do you think you're more powerful than God?"

"No," said Alice, but there was no strength in the word. She was defeated.

"Then tell me where to take you. I think you have just proven how adult you are, and you deserve to be treated like you can make your own good decisions in your life." Unlike her brother.

"Let's go to the hospital. I want to see him," Alice said, sounding slightly more energetic. "I didn't get to see him this morning. Is he really all right?"

I listed his injuries for her. "He's not going to look good, but he's alive. I think you get some credit for that."

"Hmm," she said, and we didn't talk much the rest of the short drive over.

When I parked in the Lone Peak Hospital visitors' lot, Alice took off her seat belt but didn't get out of the car. I waited with my hand on the door for her to say what she had been thinking about for so long.

The sun was so bright I put up a hand to block it. The mountains were behind the hospital building, completely stripped of snow at this time of year. They looked green and young and hopeful.

"William gets all the attention," Alice said finally. "He's always been like this. He goes off and does something stupid and then the rest of us have to fix it. He was like that even before Dad—"

She didn't finish. She was biting at her lower lip again, and I was sure I could read her mind. She was angry at William, and feeling guilty for being angry, and angry at feeling guilty that she felt angry.

I didn't think that William had tried to hurt himself, but he had been reckless. "Can I give you some advice?" I said, letting the sun pouring in through the windshield soak into my skin.

"Okay."

"Be as kind to yourself as you would be to someone else." I turned to face her.

"That's it?" she said.

"That's it," I said.

I walked into the faceless stone of the hospital with her then, thinking about the amazing things I'd seen people do while grief stricken. But I'd also seen people become cruel and rude. We always said that you found out who people really were when they were under stress, but I wasn't sure it was true. All you found out about people under stress was how people acted when they were under stress. Was that more real than when they weren't under stress?

William's room was in the intensive care unit. As non-family, I wasn't allowed in, so I passed Alice off to Emma and paced around the industrial seats of the waiting area. Feeling the need to clear my mind of anything too serious for a moment, I got out my phone, played a game on it, and when I got bored with that, downloaded a book. I didn't have my glasses, which meant I could get about ten words on the screen at once in the font size I needed, but at least it was something.

An hour later, Emma and Alice both came out. "Visiting hours are over," said Emma, whose eyes were bright red from crying and whose hands were shaking. "And Alice needs to get home to do her homework."

"Would you like me to drive her? Do you need to stay here?" I wasn't sure Emma should drive anywhere at the moment. This family did not need another tragedy.

"I need to get some rest, and William is sleeping in any case." Emma tried to smile, but it started her crying again.

"I'll walk out with you," I said.

"Thank you so much for just being here," Emma said, when we got to her car. She leaned on my arm and took a long, deep breath. "You were there at the right time, for both of my children. You know that, as a mother, I will never forget that."

"Of course," I said. I should have been grateful she wasn't angry at my part in all of this, but I noticed instead how easy it was for Emma to once again let someone else take over. I wanted to help the struggling Ashby family, but at this point, I really thought that Emma needed more than just a friendly neighbor. Like maybe therapy. And possibly a vacation from her kids and everything here. When fasting and prayers didn't work, that was when it was time to call LDS Family Services, a whole menu of therapy choices for those who were in serious need.

Alice had gotten in the car, but Emma's hands were trembling so much, she kept fumbling with the car door handle. She looked back at me. "Kurt asked me about money this morning, and I'm afraid I was too scattered to answer him properly. But would you tell him that I don't need the church to help with house payments or groceries or anything like that? I'm fine."

"Are you sure?" I asked.

"I have Carl's stocks, as well as that nest egg from Carl's invention. Do you think Brother Rhodes would be willing to take—" Her voice squeaked and she swallowed before trying again. "Take a cash settlement rather than going through the police to press charges against William?"

Kurt had just told me not to do this. "Just leave it to me. I'll talk to him about a settlement of some kind," I said anyway.

"You can offer him up to a hundred and fifty thousand dollars," she said.

I was stunned. That was far more of a nest egg than I had imagined. "You should leave yourself a cushion, you know," I said. She seemed to be acting out of desperation, not rationality. "Is that really how much you can afford to offer him?"

"I don't know. I think so. What do you think?" she asked. "Less than that? A hundred thousand dollars? Would that work?"

"How about if I offer him about a third of that amount and see what he says," I suggested.

"You don't know how much it means to me that you have stepped in like this. You are a true friend. The only woman I have ever really been able to trust." Emma embraced me and I could feel the trembling all through her body.

After a moment, she waved goodbye and closed her car door.

Once she was gone, I thought of how hot and cold she seemed to be. Pointing at me when the police asked if anyone had a grudge against Carl, her over-attentiveness to Kurt when he came to comfort her, and now this overflowing gratitude toward me. What were her real feelings toward me—if she had any besides what was convenient for her to express in the moment?

Shaking my head, I put my judgment of the woman out of my head and tried to think of the best way to approach someone like Grant Rhodes. I decided I would resort to the age-old Mormon woman's trick: winning his heart through his stomach.

CHAPTER 17

I waited until Kurt had left the next morning for work and Samuel was out looking at apartments near the U. Then I called Grant Rhodes as a batch of fresh banana bread lay cooling on the stove. I didn't think he had a strict schedule with his job at the university. If I recalled correctly, he wasn't a full-time employee. But when I called his house the first time, there was no answer. An hour later, I called again, and after about ten rings he finally picked up.

"Hello, Brother Rhodes. This is Linda Wallheim. I have a little extra banana bread and I was wondering if I could bring it over today. I don't want it to go to waste, and I'm afraid that with my boys mostly gone, I sometimes make too big a batch." In fact, Kurt and Samuel could have finished off all four loaves without a problem. But the secret to all negotiations, I had learned, was to make it sound as if the person was doing you a favor by accepting what you offered them. If this tactic didn't work, I had a history-related question about the church that I could ask him to explain to me at length.

"Well, I'm heading to the library in an hour—" Grant Rhodes began.

"I'll be right over then. I don't want to delay you," I said, and hung up the phone before he could object.

I wrapped a cooled loaf in plastic, put a ribbon on it to make it look pretty and feminine, and drove over to Grant Rhodes's house.

William Ashby thought—or at least, according to Alice, said he thought—that Grant Rhodes might have killed his father. I was headed, alone, to the house of someone whom at least one person suspected capable of violent crime, and I was doing so in order to offer him a monetary bribe to not be fully truthful with the police. Maybe I should have felt more nervous than I did, but a strange sense of calm washed over me.

I knocked on the door, and when he opened it, I held the loaf of bread out. "After all that excitement last night, I thought you could use a little pampering," I said. "Here, let me put this directly on the kitchen table. It's still warm and I wouldn't want it to crumble on you." I walked straight into the kitchen without waiting for an invitation.

"Well, thank you for thinking of me," he said stiffly. He had followed me into the kitchen but kept his distance. "But I really do need to get to the library this evening. I have some significant research to do before my lecture next week."

I realized he was uncomfortable having a woman in his house. And no wonder. The kitchen looked like it hadn't been used in a decade, except for the microwave, which was filthy, and the garbage can, which was full of cardboard boxes from the freezer section of the grocery store. I wondered if the man ever ate fresh fruit or vegetables.

"Of course," I said. "I'll be off in just a minute. I wouldn't want to interrupt your work." It was time to launch into plan

B, flattering my way into his confidence. "I can't even fathom all the reading you must do. I mean, with your reputation as such a respected historian . . . " I smiled. Was that spreading it on a little too thick? I'd worried about it beforehand, as I rehearsed the scene in my head. "I'm just a mother, after all."

"Don't say 'just a mother,'" Grant Rhodes said quickly. Oh, what a relief. He was eating it up. "A mother is one of the most important roles in the building up of the kingdom."

"Do you really think that?" I asked. "Sometimes it seems like all the things I do make no difference." I decided to entrench myself with physical labor, and reached for a washcloth to wipe down counters. He seemed happy to let me do it.

"The prophets of every age come from the hands of attentive mothers. I would never have become an academic if my mother hadn't read to me tirelessly when I was little." He leaned against the wall, watching me with an air of distracted memory. "I was in all the remedial classes through elementary school, but my mother had confidence in my abilities. She never gave up on me, and it is to her that I owe my current success."

"How proud she must be of you today," I said, continuing to wipe and organize.

"That looks so good," he said, nodding to the banana bread, and I knew I had broken him. "We should share a slice."

"What a good idea," I said, and found some plates.

Grant Rhodes slathered his piece with butter, then took a few bites. "Mmm, delicious," he said. He was making a mess of the bread, crumbs everywhere, but I took it as a compliment.

It was time for me to cut to the chase. "I am so sorry about what happened yesterday. That a boy would act so recklessly—such a shame." I shook my head and tried to look stern and sad.

Grant Rhodes licked his fingers, and picked at the crumbs on his plate. "I spent fifteen years restoring that car," he said. "And that's not including the time it took me to find the pieces." He seemed more peeved than angry now, which I counted a good thing. It was hard to be angry with a bellyful of banana bread, I'd found.

"What a labor of love," I said. I cut another slice of banana bread and put it on his plate.

"That car is built with blood, sweat, and tears as much as it is with steel," he said.

"What a wonderful talent you have. I'm sure that you are grateful to God for it," I said. After a moment's hesitation, I added, "Such a blessing must make you want to bless the lives of God's other struggling children, in turn."

This time I'd gone too far. Grant put down the bread and shook crumbs off his hands onto the floor. "I am not interested in blessing the life of William Ashby, if that's what you're here for."

"I can't believe that. You're a thoughtful, kind man, Brother Rhodes. You had a mother who saw the best in you, even when you were at your worst. And as a mother myself, when I look at William Ashby, who has just lost his father, I can't help but wonder what would happen to our Samuel if Kurt were suddenly gone. You knew Carl, didn't you?"

I watched carefully to see his reaction, and I was sure he flinched.

"I knew Carl a little, yes," said Grant Rhodes, wrapping the plastic around the remaining loaf. His tone was tense. He was hiding something, I was sure of it.

"I heard from William that you and his father had frequent—discussions—about the gospel and its history."

Grant stared out the window and his hands rubbed down the sides of his pants. "I called Carl the day he died," he said, surprising me. "But it wasn't anything important, no matter what the police think. It was just about a reference for a lesson he was teaching."

The police had talked to Grant Rhodes about a phone call on the day Carl Ashby had died? "Then you know how difficult it is to deal with the police," I said. "And you're a grown man, not a young boy."

Grant Rhodes looked at me with a wry, knowing look. "It sounds like you're trying to make sure that I don't name William as the driver during the accident," he said, making air quotes around the word "accident."

I put up my hands. "Well, I would never tell you to do anything contrary to your own conscience. I'm sure you would pray about it and consider seriously what a boy like William Ashby would most be helped by, after the devastation of his father's murder. And perhaps if you had compensation for the damages, that would make it easier to be compassionate?"

"How can you compensate me for fifteen years of my life?" he demanded.

I held out my hands in a submissive gesture. "Not for your time, but for materials. And if you need to hire help in the future, for repairs."

"I don't need help to repair my own car. I know every inch of its engine and chassis, inside and out. I put every piece of it together with my own hands."

"But there must be something that could be done to help

you," I said. "Perhaps thirty thousand dollars to defray the cost of any new parts you have to buy? Or new tools?"

"Thirty thousand dollars?" he asked, his head tilted to the side. "And no guarantee that I not press charges?"

"Of course not. That's between you and God. Though I'm sure that you aren't a vengeful person. No true Mormon could say that he was." No lightning struck me where I stood, which meant something, I hoped.

"And what about justice? I knew Carl Ashby well enough to know that he wouldn't want his children raised to ignore justice." I heard tenderness in his voice. I had no idea what it meant, but I figured I should exploit it.

"What is justice without mercy?" I asked, putting a hand on his arm.

There was a long moment of silence. As it drew on, I decided I would make Brother Rhodes's decision for him. I stood up. "Thank you so much for agreeing with me about William. I am going to go straight to Sister Ashby and tell her that you accept her offer for money and a sincere apology. I will leave it to William himself to show his humility and repentance, but I am sure that you will be satisfied." I turned and took a step toward the front door.

"Wait! I didn't say anything about not pressing charges," he said.

I turned back around. "I know that. But I also know that you are a worldly man. None of this is about money, is it? It's about all of us working together as a ward family to make it back to God, isn't it?"

Grant Rhodes sighed. "Emma needs to get that boy therapy. Or medication. Or something."

I smiled warmly. "I knew you would be like this, Brother

Rhodes. Concerned for William's welfare rather than your car's damage. I've always admired you as a scholar, but I've never seen before how much you live your life as a true Christian." I leaned forward and kissed him on the cheek.

He reddened like a little boy who had been kissed in kindergarten by his first girlfriend. I had played the right part here, but I still had other parts to play.

As I left, I felt I had made progress. I had, I hoped, prevented William Ashby from facing police charges, and had done so without squandering Emma's entire nest egg. I'd also learned that Grant Rhodes was hiding something about that phone call with Carl.

CHAPTER 18

Kurt invited Tom deRyke over on Thursday night after temple-recommend interviews at the church, and they spent a couple of hours closeted in Kurt's office. They were probably discussing who to put into the second counselor position, but I suspected they wouldn't be able to avoid talking about the fallout of Carl's gender revelation. I wondered if Kurt would confide in Tom about Samuel. I figured that might be a good thing, since he and I certainly weren't talking about it.

I came downstairs to say goodbye to Tom when I heard him step out into the foyer. "How is Verity?" I asked.

"Sad about all of this," said Tom, rubbing his chin.

"And how are you holding up?" I asked.

"Well enough," said Tom, and headed out.

"How about you?" I asked, turning to Kurt after I closed the front door.

Kurt let out a long sigh. "Tom deRyke and I have made a list of the ordinances we may have to redo. It could be more than thirty. I don't know how we're going to find time to do it unless I take a good week off work. But that's assuming that people will be willing to take their own time off work or school to have it done. And I don't know how to explain to them why we're doing it without telling them all far too much about Carl and Emma's private life."

The whole undertaking seemed so ridiculous to me. "I'm sorry," I said, as sympathetically as I could.

"It may well take a month of trying to catch people on Sundays and evenings before it's all finished."

And of course Kurt would have to stop all the other work he was doing: counseling members in need, thinking about new callings and how to fill them, working with the youth. The ward would notice that, too. It would hurt us all. Did President Frost really think it would be worth the cost?

"I feel so spent, so useless," said Kurt. "And underneath it all is just this sadness that Carl is gone. After all that I could blame him for, I guess I'm surprised that it's the only thing that I really feel."

I felt a rising swell of love for Kurt. "Do you really think this is necessary? Can't you tell President Frost that he's wrong and that you know what's best for your own ward? Aren't you supposed to be the only person who gets revelation for us all?"

Kurt shook his head. "You know that's not the way it works. First of all, he's the stake president. That means he's authorized to make decisions regarding any wards in the stake. And he's in authority above me. If I tried to tell him what to do, he'd rebuke me heartily—at the very least."

The unspoken threat here was that he would release Kurt.

"What about your Area Authority? Can't you appeal to him? Or to the Quorum of the Seventy? Or someone?"

"I'm not going to go over President Frost's head. And he said that he was writing to the First Presidency anyway," said Kurt.

He said? Did that mean Kurt doubted whether he had done it? Even if he had, it might be months before we heard back, and by then it wouldn't matter anymore. Sometimes it was frustrating that the Mormon church had gotten so large and unwieldy. In the days of Joseph Smith, you'd just walk over and ask the prophet his opinion directly.

"And what about Carl's records? His marriage? His sealing to his children?" I asked.

"That really does have to go through the First Presidency," said Kurt. "So nothing's going to happen right now."

"What about the burial?" I asked, wondering if Carl would be allowed to wear temple clothing.

"We're not making a decision on that. President Frost says the police aren't going to release the body until the murderer is charged, so we have some time," said Kurt.

I squinted at him. "Seriously? I've never heard of anything like that before in a murder case." I wasn't an expert, but I'd read lots of mysteries and seen plenty of crime shows. The body was always released to the family after the autopsy was complete. I had been so busy thinking about other things that it hadn't occurred to me how odd it was that we weren't already talking about the funeral plans.

"You think President Frost is stepping in there, too?" Kurt asked.

I just looked at him.

"Right," he said, and nodded. But he didn't suggest that he was ready to call the First Presidency himself. I guess I should give him a break. I didn't know everything that he'd been given when he became bishop, but I was pretty sure there was no Bat Signal to the First Presidency and no red telephone in the Church Office Building or in the top rooms of the Salt Lake Temple where the First Presidency met every week.

"This is just prejudice," I said. "President Frost is sticking himself in where he doesn't belong because he's angry about Carl being transgender." The man was clearly transphobic, and it made me wonder what other phobias were lurking in his psyche. I was glad that Samuel was going to be interviewing with a different bishop and stake president rather than the ones here in his current ward. Leadership roulette was a real problem when it came to discipline. The prophet and apostles left most decisions up to the local leaders, and there was no clear doctrine on transgenderism.

"You're talking about a man I admire and believe is inspired by God," said Kurt defensively.

"And what about Carl? Do you now think that all those times you felt God speaking to you or to him, you were wrong?"

Kurt was silent for a long moment, then shook his head. I decided that it was time to talk to him about Samuel, now that he'd finally gotten around to admitting he was wrong.

"You know that Samuel will end up meeting more people like President Frost. His own mission president might think that he doesn't belong in the church at all, at least not if he's openly gay. How do you expect him to deal with all the prejudice he's already about to face, even before going out on a mission?"

"It might not be that bad," said Kurt softly.

"But it probably will be." I had no reason to believe there were fewer bigots in the Mormon church than anywhere else; there were plenty right in our own ward.

"I think it would be a difficult journey, but he could do a lot of good by showing people the courage it takes to admit to a problem and carry on with the best life possible even so," said Kurt.

I tensed at the word "problem." Did that mean Kurt thought there was a "solution"?

"Linda, you know that I love him," Kurt added. "I would do anything for him, just as I would for any of our sons."

Yes, I did know that. If Samuel were in danger, Kurt would stand in front of a train to protect him. If Samuel needed money, Kurt would give him every last cent we had. If Samuel were hungry, Kurt would starve to feed him. Wasn't that love? Hadn't he always wanted what was best for him? I sagged into Kurt and could feel him press a kiss into the hair at the top of my head.

"Samuel is a great kid. He's going to have a wonderful life," I said. Somehow.

As we headed to bed, I thought about Carl Ashby and his decision to become a man twenty some-odd years ago. He had said that he was a convert, and that his parents rejected him when he joined the Mormon church. But I now suspected that was all part of the lie, an attempt to reinvent himself. What he must have given up to become a man—I could hardly imagine it. And yet, it must have been necessary, or he wouldn't have done it. What was it like to feel so rejected that you were compelled to walk away from every part of your life and begin entirely anew? Samuel would never have to face that, I vowed to myself. No matter what I had to do to get Kurt to move past this.

ON FRIDAY, EMMA Ashby called me around midday. "I need you to come over, Linda. As soon as possible. Before the children are home from school."

"Is it about the car accident? Did Grant Rhodes contact you?" I asked, sure that I had fixed everything there.

"No, nothing about that," she said dismissively. "This is important. This is about Carl's murder."

"All right," I said. "I'll be right there."

I hung up the phone and realized that I wasn't leaving anything at home that needed me. All my life, being needed had made me feel important. Having children who relied on me had made me feel important. Would the rest of my life be answering calls from neighbors who needed me as desperately as my children had? Because that would make me feel important?

I drove over to the house, and didn't have to knock. Emma was waiting for me and ushered me inside. "Upstairs," she said, and led me to the master bedroom. There were envelopes and unfolded papers scattered all over the unmade bed and the floor. It was a cluttered space to begin with, too much furniture, the closets bulging, shoe racks stacked knee-high.

"I found these today when I was searching through Carl's drawers." Emma's face was pinched; I sensed that her self-control was crumbling.

"What are they?"

"Love letters," Emma squeaked.

From her? No, obviously not. "From an old girlfriend?"

"Just look at them!" She pushed me forward.

I was reluctant for some reason, but I picked up one of the letters. There was no name listed at the top, just a term of endearment: *Darling.*

I didn't read much of it. It contained some rather explicit descriptions of sexual acts. I was no prude, and Kurt and I had consulted a few books over the years to help enliven our sex life, but we hadn't used language like this to describe things.

I looked up at Emma. "This must be very upsetting to you," I said. Had the police found these letters? If they had, why hadn't they taken them? Was it because they already knew who was guilty and these letters had nothing to do with it?

"What if the children had found these?" Emma asked. "I could never have believed this of Carl. He was such a strict man. That he could do this . . ."

I flipped through several letters, resisting reading too closely. They weren't dated, but the paper was yellowing, so they were clearly quite old. All of the letters were from a woman about what she wanted done to her, and what she wanted to do to a man's body. They were all signed *Your lover* or *Your soul mate*. Could Carl have written them before he transitioned? Could this be a clue to the child he'd given birth to?

The best hope of information was surely from Emma herself. "Do you have any idea who might have written them?"

"Of course I don't know!" Emma's face had gone from pinched and pale to bright red.

I thought about the argument the night of the bishopric dinner. "Do you think that Carl might have been—dissatisfied in your marriage?" I asked, as delicately as possible.

Emma collapsed onto the floor and began moaning. She thrashed this way and that until I caught her and held her in my arms, trying to calm her down. "It's all right," I kept saying, though I wasn't at all sure that it was. She was still grieving the loss of her husband, I knew that. But her reaction wasn't merely sad. It seemed unhinged somehow. Her world had crashed in on her, and now that she was no longer able to moor herself against it, she seemed to be drowning.

"I told him that night. I told him, and he said he understood. He said that he would love me no matter what. He always said that."

"Of course he did," I said, unsure of what she was driving at.

"But he didn't. I know he didn't. Men don't love women who don't—who can't—"

I could feel the hairs rise on the back of my neck. What was she trying to say?

"He must have thought he would change my mind, but he didn't ever ask me or pressure me after the first night." She was sobbing the words. "He would lie next to me at night sometimes. I could feel his breath in my ear. But he never did more than that. He said that he would wait forever, if that was what it took. Until we were both perfected in our resurrected bodies. He said his love for me was eternal, and that it didn't matter what we did here, because we were bound forever."

I had never wanted to know the details of her sex life with Carl, but was she telling me that she had forbidden Carl from touching her sexually on her wedding night? And that she had never changed her mind?

I'd heard the word "frigid" thrown around before to describe women who had some sexual abhorrence or malfunction, sometimes because they had been abused. I'd wondered if "frigid" could refer to women who were merely ignorant of sex and what it entailed. I wasn't sure which category Emma Ashby would fit into.

"Were you ever abused?" I asked, unable to think of another way to put it.

"No! No!" shouted Emma, pushing me away from her and getting to her feet. She seemed steadier now, but her face was a fiery red and her eyes were blazing with anger. "I am pure. I was always pure! That's what women are supposed to be. That's what I wanted to be."

Was she saying she had never had any sexual contact, after twenty years of marriage? If that was the case, the wedding night itself might have seemed a godsend to Carl. He wouldn't have had to explain anything to Emma about his body. But for the next twenty years, he must have gone over that decision again and again, trying to decide if he should reopen it or let it lie. How could he live for so long in a marriage with no sexual intimacy? Had he felt forced to go outside of his marriage for that? Was that safer than wrecking it by telling the truth and having to deal with the consequences?

"Emma—" I felt horrible even thinking about the intimate details of her relationship with Carl.

"Don't look at me like that." She glared at me as if I had accused her of something. The tears had evaporated and now there was only defensive anger. "We were happy. Just the way we were. There was nothing wrong. Except that Carl had these urges. Some people have them, and they don't know what to do with them. Even women."

Did she mean sexual urges? Did she think only some people had those? Or was she talking about affairs? Prostitutes? Pornography, masturbation? It would probably be impossible to get her to distinguish between them, with her level of ignorance combined with my attempts at delicacy.

"So what did you do?" I asked.

"He told me sometimes that he needed to repent. But he never said about what." She was wringing her hands, and now

I could see signs that she had run her sharp fingernails up her arms, probably before I had come. Those lines might scar.

"Emma, whatever happened between you, I'm sure Carl loved you. You have to believe in that. You're married eternally."

Emma shook her head again and again. "I know there were women in the ward who looked at him lustfully."

I stopped myself from asking which women. I was not going to encourage her jealous fantasies now.

Emma started gathering up the letters, crumpling them into a ball rather than placing them back in their individual envelopes. "Just take them, please! Burn them! I never want to see them again."

"Of course," I said. "That's a fine plan." And if they were evidence in the murder? If they might lead the police to the right suspect? I would deal with that myself.

When I had all the letters collected, I looked around the bedroom. "Is there anything else here you want me to take? Should I help you go through Carl's things, before I leave?"

It was one of the most difficult parts of dealing with a death. I'd come home from the hospital after Georgia was born, only to see the crib and all the pink baby things I'd bought for her in the months I was pregnant, so excited for the girl I thought was coming. I boxed them all up and Kurt did something with them. He never told me what. I never asked. It was too painful to reopen.

"No," said Emma, the word bursting out of her with force. "I'm not ready for that yet. I need to keep his things here for now. It's all I have left."

"All right. If that is what you want."

She took a breath, shook herself, and seemed to calm down.

"I'll leave now and let you have some peace," I said, tucking the letters under one arm.

"Promise me you'll burn the letters," Emma said. "I can't bear the thought of anyone seeing them. Especially Kurt."

"I'll burn them," I lied, and took a breath of relief when I stepped out of the house.

WHEN I GOT home, I put the letters in a dresser drawer before I decided what to do with them. Why had Emma called me to ask me to burn the letters for her? Was she helpless again or was it an act? If it was an act, what was the point of it? My head spun with theories that made no sense, and I decided to wait to do anything.

Samuel was in his room, so I went to check on him. He was reading scriptures.

"How are you doing?" I asked.

"Meh," he said. He had tucked his arms closer to his sides, as if he were afraid of what I was going to say to him. It hurt me to see him like this.

"Have you and your father talked again?"

Samuel shook his head.

"He just needs some time to readjust." I sat down on his bed and put a hand on his ankle. I wanted to wrap him in my arms and rock him to sleep, but obviously that wasn't going to work at this point.

"I wish he would just talk to me, and see I'm the same person I always was. I'm still trying to be good. I'm still trying to do what Jesus would have me do." He nodded to the scriptures. "I pray every morning and every night."

I wanted to cry. "I don't think I can push him about this," I said. "It wouldn't help." Neither would pushing Samuel into saying he'd go on a mission to please Kurt.

"No, I know. We'll work it out. I don't want you to do anything. It's just hard waiting sometimes."

"Can I hug you?" I asked. We hugged for a long while, and then I tiptoed out and let him get back to his reading.

This would work out. It had to. The people involved were too good for it not to. I was just impatient about the time frame. I always was.

I went into my room and read scriptures, too. Unfortunately, one of the first was the story of the Prodigal Son, which made me cry. I didn't want Samuel forced to live with pigs before he came home and his father realized how much he had been missed.

When Kurt got home, I told him, "I think we need to watch Emma Ashby carefully." That was all that had come out of my trying to figure out what to do about the letters. I didn't bring up Samuel, and I thought I deserved an award for that. Closed Mouth of the Year.

"We are already watching Emma carefully. Everyone in the ward."

"I know, but I'm worried about her. That she might do something . . ."

"Like what?" asked Kurt, his eyes crinkling in real concern.

"I don't know. Something terrible."

"You think she's suicidal? Did she say something to you today about that?"

I shook my head. "Not like that. But she's—brittle. I don't know how good of a mother she can be to her children in this state." After the condition I'd found her in at her house that day, I worried about all of them.

"But she needs them. And they need her. Surely the worst thing for the family would be to be separated at a time like this. They are all hurting right now. We can't just tell them they're not doing it right." This was a gentle reminder of what I had been like after Georgia had died. I'd been able to handle mundane tasks, like doing the dishes and keeping the house tidy. But I'd had trouble speaking to anyone about anything real. My anger, my grief, my thoughts about Georgia. For years, I spoke only about schedules with the kids. Had I been a good mother then? No. Likely I had forgotten plenty of things, too. I had been in a fog of pain and sorrow.

I thought about the letters, but I didn't feel like I could talk about them to Kurt. "She thinks Carl wasn't who he was pretending to be," I said.

Kurt laughed harshly at that, and I realized why. But I had not been referring to his transgenderism. I saw Carl as a man and Emma as a woman, and the problems in their marriage as typical between the two sexes.

CHAPTER 19

Kurt and Samuel came down for waffles on Saturday morning, and for a few minutes, things seemed like they were back to normal between them, each teasing the other about the amount of syrup he used. But then Samuel announced he had to go to work, and Kurt said he had to mow the lawn, which had been Samuel's job for years. I think Samuel was offended, and he left without another word. Kurt didn't give me a chance to say anything to him. He spent all day on the yard.

On Sunday, I looked around for Emma Ashby during Relief Society, but I didn't see her. The Relief Society lesson was about chastity. I was glad that Emma wasn't there for that.

In Sunday School, Grant Rhodes was unusually quiet, especially considering the fact that the lesson was about the final days of Joseph Smith's life before the martyrdom at Carthage. The teacher, Brad Ferris, was standing up in front of everyone with all the printed materials for the lessons in his hands, trying to be as orthodox as possible.

The official story was that Joseph Smith was a righteous prophet and that Nauvoo had become so successful a city that those living in surrounding areas were jealous and determined to kill Joseph. I'd heard Grant Rhodes insist that it all had to do with Joseph's secret polygamous teachings coming to light and the mob attacking him because of a sense of moral righteousness.

Near the end of the lesson, we had a second hymn, unusual in Sunday School, "Praise to the Man," and then read at the end from Doctrine and Covenants 135, about the fact that Joseph Smith "has done more, save Jesus only, for the salvation of men in this world, than any other man that ever lived in it" because his work had brought back the true church, the true priesthood, and temple work, and had translated the Book of Mormon.

But Brad's lesson was virtually uninterrupted. The only time members raised their hands to speak was to read scriptures he asked for or to share their own testimonies about Joseph Smith and the Book of Mormon. We opened by singing the song "A Poor Wayfaring Man of Grief," which was the prophet's favorite hymn and which Hyrum, his brother, had sung the morning of the martydom at the jail.

Mormons don't worship Joseph Smith, as some outsiders think or claim, but sometimes the admiration of him skirts close to worship.

As soon as sacrament meeting started, I noticed the entire Stake Presidency on the stand to Kurt's right. We sang "We Thank Thee, O God, for a Prophet," had an opening prayer, and then, when it was time to make announcements, President Frost stood and said that he had some changes to make in our bishopric.

I had known this would happen at some point, but I admit I was surprised they had come to a decision so soon.

"You all have heard of the tragic loss of our beloved Carl

Ashby in the bishopric." President Frost was a very large man, over six feet in height and probably more than three hundred pounds. His face was fleshy but kind. "He was a worthy priesthood holder and we can all feel a measure of happiness in the surety that he will be waiting for his family in heaven and watching over and protecting them though he is unseen."

I'd had no idea that President Frost was so good an actor. If I hadn't known how he felt about the man, I would have believed his every word. But I noticed the way that he avoided looking at me or Verity deRyke—the two people in the audience who knew the truth. I also noticed Kurt shift uncomfortably in his seat, though Tom deRyke seemed less bothered.

President Frost said a few more words about how God means for His work to proceed, and that everything was always in place to make sure the work itself did not stop, because it was a great work meant to bless the lives of all of the children of men.

Nothing to explain the reordinations that Kurt had said they would have to do. But as far as I knew, he hadn't done any yet. Was Kurt delaying to show just the tiniest bit of rebellion? Or was President Frost not following up because he had the smallest sense that he was wrong?

"After much prayer and fasting, and consultation with the leaders, a new member of the bishopric has been chosen. He named Brad Ferris and then asked the congregation to sustain him. And we'd like to ask Brother Ferris now to come up and bear his testimony to the ward. We would also ask his wife to come to the stand and share a brief testimony as well, if she is up to it."

I was somewhat surprised but pleased when Brad Ferris was then called to take Carl Ashby's place in the bishopric. He had done a good job for the past few months as the adult Sunday School teacher, but he was only in his twenties, and still had to be made a high priest before he could be added to the bishopric.

There are several levels of priesthood within the Mormon church. Young men receive the Aaronic priesthood at age twelve, and move up through the offices of that priesthood—deacon, teacher, and finally priest—until age eighteen. Those with the Aaronic Priesthood are allowed to bless and pass the sacrament in our Sunday meetings, to collect offerings from church members, and as priests to baptize. Then, at age eighteen or nineteen, if they are worthy, they are given the Melchizedek priesthood, which has its own series of offices, from elder, which is what Brad Ferris was, to high priest, and patriarch.

Brad Ferris was a man I had been very impressed with in the last year. By getting to know his wife, Gwen, I had learned a bit about Brad and about their marriage, and from what I had heard, I couldn't imagine a better man to be in a position of leadership. My eyes grew moist as I watched Brad and Gwen walk together to the podium. They held hands, and it seemed to me that Gwen Ferris shone, holding her chin high.

Brad was not a tall or imposing man, but as he stood at the podium, there was a force in him. His voice commanded the whole room. "I am humbled and honored by this calling. I know that God wants me to accept it and that He expects great things of me. I hope that I am worthy of doing what needs to be done."

Brad bowed his head for a moment, then continued with some passion, "I know that Christ lives and that He stands with us through every trial in this life. He knows us as His brothers and sisters. He whispers to us when we need whispers and He nudges us when we need a nudge. Sometimes He might even push us, though he never forces us. He waits patiently, and sometimes He weeps with us when we face the consequences of a wrong choice. But He is always with us and wants the best for us." Brad took a shuddering breath and looked across at President Frost.

"I know the Book of Mormon is true, and I know that Joseph Smith restored the only true church on this earth. I know that Thomas S. Monson is now the prophet and mouthpiece of God and that he holds all the keys of the priesthood which can bless our lives."

He swallowed hard and sniffled. Though there was a box of Kleenex by the podium every Sunday, I rarely saw men reach for it. Women often did.

"I thank my wife, Gwen, for all that she has taught me, both by example and by her words. Without her, I would never have known God's love, because her love for me is as pure and true as His. And I say these things in the name of Jesus Christ. Amen."

He sat down, but I could tell by the looks between Kurt and President Frost that he had not taken as much time as they'd expected. Well, good for him for being concise. I thought he had said everything that needed to be said, nothing that shouldn't be said, and had bared his soul. Could anyone doubt that he was going to be a stalwart member of the bishopric?

As Gwen Ferris took the stand, there was a scuffling

sound in the back of the chapel. I turned and saw that Emma Ashby was walking out, her head bowed, her feet moving swiftly.

I regretted not hearing Gwen's testimony, but I felt it was more important to go after Emma, whom I hadn't even realized was there. I hurried down the hallway, past the restrooms and the Primary room where another ward was starting their meetings, then out the back doors.

"Emma?" I caught her arm at her car.

"I need to go home," she said.

"This doesn't mean Carl won't be missed," I said.

"I know."

"But we needed someone in that position."

"I know," she said again.

"Please, don't be hurt by this."

"I miss him," she said. "So much." Her face was a curtain of tears.

"Do you want me to bring William and Alice home after sacrament meeting is over?" I asked, assuming they were still inside, though I hadn't seen them.

"They wouldn't come to church today," she said. "I threatened them with no allowance for a year, and told William that his father would be ashamed of him. But they said they were too tired and too sad. Can you imagine how Carl would feel? Everything he taught them, and they're at home when they should be at church."

I thought that maybe they were wiser than Emma was, coming when she was this emotionally distraught. "Just give them a chance to grieve," I said.

"They should grieve here. They know where they belong."

Did they? Did she?

I reached to put my arms around her, but she shook her head and got into the car.

I watched her drive off, and wished I had been able to do something more. I would have to work harder, for her sake, and for the whole ward. We all needed the healing of knowing what had happened, and why.

CHAPTER 20

Monday morning at about 10 A.M., Detective Gore appeared on my doorstep.

"What can I do for you?" I asked, a bit taken aback.

"I'd like to come in and talk to you about Mrs. Ashby," she said.

I felt like I had stepped into a retelling of "The Tell-Tale Heart." Mine was thumping furiously and I was sure that Detective Gore must have heard it. It was all I could do not to run immediately to the letters and hand them over.

"Come in," I said, opening the door wide.

"I'm sure this must be difficult for you. A murder in your own neighborhood," she said as she came inside and followed me to the front room. I led her to the couch by the piano and sat opposite her, under the window.

There was a bitter undertone in her voice that made me wonder how she felt about living in Utah, where Mormons had for so long deliberately excluded African-Americans from our religion. The church had stopped conversion efforts of the whole race in the 1800s under the direction of Brigham Young. Because of his racism, it had become entrenched as part of the doctrine that "Negroes" could not enjoy the full blessings of church membership, including temple work and priesthood, until the 1978 revelation changing the long-held practice. Some said that it was because they had been the least valiant in the war in heaven between Lucifer and Jesus Christ, though that theory had recently been publicly rejected by the highest levels of the church.

"There was another murder in our neighborhood not long ago," I said. "Carrie Helm. Do you remember that?"

"Carrie Helm was here?" said Detective Gore, eyes widening. "I've been following that case." In fact, the sentencing portion of the trial wasn't finished, though the guilty verdict was. "I hadn't realized it was so close. I wasn't in Draper then. I was up in Salt Lake City until last month."

I decided it would be arrogant of me to say that I was the one who had solved the case for the police. That hadn't been publicized and I wasn't eager for the spotlight now. Besides, the more I thought about what I had done then, the less I thought of myself as a hero. I had been stupid. Untrained, blundering, and ignorant.

Which was possibly just as true of me now. Maybe I was just nosy at heart, and had nothing else to do with my time but muck around in other people's business.

"Carrie lived just down the street," I said, gesturing out the window behind me. "Though her husband and daughter have moved now." Because of me and how badly I handled things with them.

"Did you know her husband and her parents?" she asked me.

I felt pinned like a butterfly on a board. Was she silently accusing me, as I had so often accused myself, of being utterly blind when it came to the true character of those surrounding Carrie? Well, no one could think worse of me than I thought of myself. "Not her parents, but obviously, I wished I had known more about her relationship with her husband," I admitted. "And her past."

Gore waited for something else, but I had no intention of making excuses. "If I'd known about Carrie Helm being in this ward, well—maybe I would have treated this case differently from the first."

"Oh? How?" I asked.

But she shook her head, refusing to elaborate. "I shouldn't have said that. What I meant to say was that I came to you because I've seen how the women in your ward look up to you, how you're the behind-the-scenes leader while your husband is the public one."

I blushed a little at this. "I don't know about that," I said. There were plenty of women in the ward who probably thought of me as the last person they would reveal their problems to. But I'd made a little headway. With Sheri Tate and Emma Ashby, for instance. And Anna, of course.

"I was hoping that you might have a deeper perspective on the inner workings of the minds of the women in the ward." She took in a breath and smiled at me. She had a wide, winning smile. She had certainly never shown it to me before.

"Do you mind if I ask you some questions about the Ashbys?" she said.

I tensed. "I can tell you what I know," I said, "though I admit that I am surprised to realize how little that seems to be, in retrospect."

"You didn't know that Carl Ashby was masquerading as a man?" she asked bluntly.

"I never guessed he was transgender, no," I said, annoyed at her phrasing. It sounded all too much like Kurt.

"But he—she—"

"He," I said.

"He, then." I felt like the butterfly again, the way she scrutinized my discomfort so scientifically. "He didn't officially change his gender on court documents," she added.

Official government documents didn't matter much to me. "He'd been living as a man for twenty years. You can hardly call it masquerading. It was his real life," I said.

"Then you accept him as a man?" I was amazed at how stoic she could make her expression. She was waiting for my reaction, not at all giving me hers.

"Of course I accept that he was a man," I said. "I didn't know he was transgender, but it isn't for me to tell other people who they are or aren't."

"And what about his wife? She never had any doubts about his identity that you know of?"

"Not that I know of," I said after careful hesitation. What was she trying to get at here? "But I don't know that I can say absolutely what Emma knew or didn't know."

"Are you not friends with her?" asked Detective Gore.

"Of course we are friends. But that doesn't mean I know everything about her."

"Do you know if Carl and Emma Ashby were struggling in their marriage?" she asked, as if it were a completely innocuous question.

I still didn't know what the argument at the bishopric dinner was about, and I certainly wasn't going to tell Detective Gore anything that she might see as a motive for Emma to kill her husband. "They seemed fine, from my perspective. But as I said, it was a limited perspective."

Nor did I bring up the letters. Emma hadn't found those

until after Carl's death. I was sure about that. Though I wondered again why the police hadn't found them when they'd searched the house. Maybe they hadn't been looking for them?

"And what is your impression of Emma Ashby's relationship to others in the neighborhood?"

"Everyone admires her," I said, perhaps kindly more than honestly. "She is a devoted mother, a loving wife, and a good member of the church. She gives much of her time to her family, but what time there is left, she gives to her service. She quilts as a hobby, but she gives away many of her finished products to the Church Humanitarian Service to send abroad or to use in disaster relief efforts locally.'" I'd heard Emma talk about how it comforted her to imagine that people who had lost everything had at least one of her beautiful handmade quilts to cling to while they waited in shelters as a storm passed.

Detective Gore wasn't writing anything down now; she was simply watching me. I wondered what my body language was communicating. My hands were in my lap and I knew I was fidgeting. I was uncomfortable.

"And does she have any more intimate friends we could speak with?" asked Detective Gore.

I realized I couldn't think of any good friends of Emma's. But that is simply what frequently happens in Mormondom— people focus on their own forever families, not on others'.

"She was in the Primary Presidency a couple of years ago," I said. "I think she worked with Grace Wong and Carolyn Lieber."

Detective Gore nodded. "Thanks. I will talk to them." But she didn't log the names into her phone or ask for numbers, which made me wonder if she really cared.

Why was she really here?

"And does Emma Ashby have any close relationships with any men in the neighborhood?"

What was Gore getting at now? "No," I said flatly.

"I'm talking about platonic friendships, nothing untoward," said the detective, giving me half of that winning smile.

But I saw she was playing a game now, and I didn't like it. "Emma would never cheat on her husband. She wouldn't even do anything that appeared to be cheating," I said.

"But you said that you two aren't close. How can you be sure?" asked the detective.

"Because—well, I suppose I can't be sure. But she doesn't seem the sort of woman who would have an affair." That sounded lame, I knew. I was trying too hard not to talk about the letters. Or the very personal information Emma had shared with me about the lack of sex in her marriage.

"And what sort of woman is that?"

"A woman who is looking for more. Adventurous, maybe. Rebellious." I answered too quickly, and I knew it. I was the subject of this interview, far more than Emma was, it seemed.

"You don't think that Emma Ashby has ever wanted more from her husband, who was pretending to be a man?"

I was tired of talking about the difference between being transgender and pretending. I let it go. "I think that she was happily married, and that she honored her marriage covenants." The Ashbys' marriage hadn't been anything like mine. But who was I to judge?

"You don't think that a woman who is sexually frustrated might ever be tempted to stray?" asked Detective Gore. That same stoic look.

"I don't think Emma was sexually frustrated," I said.

If she only knew the truth here, Detective Gore would be amused at the idea of Emma Ashby going to someone else for sexual satisfaction. Emma might very well be sexually frustrated, but I didn't think she would have looked for relief in the way that Detective Gore was suggesting.

Detective Gore raised her eyebrows. "Did she tell you that she was satisfied, then?"

How much of the truth was I giving away? I kept my hands folded together in my lap and answered her with eyes firmly focused on her face. No obvious prevarications. "No. But she said that Carl was the perfect husband."

"Is it possible that one of the women in the ward might have had . . . more than a close friendship with Emma Ashby?" asked Detective Gore next.

I clenched my teeth, took a deep breath, and tried to fight the flush I knew was on my cheeks.

"Emma Ashby has not been engaged in a lesbian love affair behind her husband's back, if that is what you mean," I said tartly.

"Do you find lesbians disgusting?"

I realized I might have stepped into something here. "No, not at all," I said, glancing at her briefly. I'd always told the boys they couldn't tell someone's sexual orientation just by looking at him or her, and now here I was doing it myself. It didn't matter if she was lesbian, anyway.

"But you aren't a lesbian?" she asked.

"No. And I don't believe Emma Ashby is, either."

Detective Gore silently stared at me for a long moment. It was unnerving. I wondered if I could duplicate that stare.

"Can you think of anyone in the neighborhood who might have had a reason to wish Carl Ashby ill?" asked the detective.

"No," I said honestly. "I really can't." I was afraid to feel too relieved that she'd moved on to another topic of questioning. She could move back at any time. "He was a good man, a good neighbor, a good friend," I added.

"It's likely the murderer was someone he knew, given the circumstances of his death and the staging of the body," said Detective Gore, her eyes narrowing.

"You're sure it wasn't a break-in?" I asked, although I knew the answer.

"There's no sign of any door being forced open, or any window," she said. "We didn't find any DNA samples or fingerprints from anyone outside the ward in the room or anywhere else in the building we checked. And nothing was taken."

"Do you have any leads?" I asked. Was there any way I could convince her to think of someone other than Emma without throwing out suggestions of suspects in the ward myself?

Gore gave me a long, guarded look. "What about you, Mrs. Wallheim? Is there anyone you suspect?"

I forced myself to look at her, no matter how much I wanted to evade her gaze. "It has been more than two weeks, and it would be good to know when there will be closure. That's all. Our ward has been very disturbed by all of this." This was her problem, not mine. Her failure, not mine.

"Closure is difficult to offer when people want something other than the truth," Gore said, though she didn't elaborate.

Leaving me with her card and the instructions to call her if I had any "sudden inspiration," as she put it, Gore very briefly examined what she could see of the rest of my house, and walked out the door. I looked at what I could see of the kitchen and the living room and wondered what the homey look had revealed to her.

One thing I was sure of was that Detective Gore knew more than she was letting on. I was beginning to wonder if we, in our ward, really wanted to know the truth about what happened to Carl. But I had never been one to hide behind palatable lies, and I wasn't going to start now.

CHAPTER 21

Wednesday morning, the police picked up Grant Rhodes for questioning. The news spread quickly through the ward, and as soon as it reached me, I called Kurt.

"If this is about Grant Rhodes, I've already heard," he said.

"Do you think he might be guilty?" I asked.

"I don't know. I thought they believed it was a woman," said Kurt.

We had both thought the police had Emma Ashby in their sights. But why bring Grant in if they thought that? Had Detective Gore changed her mind after talking to me on Monday?

I tried to restrain myself for a couple of hours, but eventually called Emma and asked her if I could come over. I didn't tell her why. She sounded too tired to say no to anything, and I decided to take advantage of that.

"How are you doing today?" I asked politely when I got there.

She looked terrible. I wondered if she had eaten a full meal since Carl had died. She was thinner than ever, and she had dark shadows under her eyes. Her nose was red and raw, and every movement she made seemed startled, like that of a wild animal.

"I got a call from the life insurance company," she said as she let me inside.

"Oh." I said noncommittaly, hoping desperately they weren't calling to tell her that her marriage with Carl had never been legal and that they were arguing fraud to deny her the money. I followed her to the kitchen, where she sat holding a cup of water I never saw her drink from.

"They said that their internal reporting structure requires an investigation on any suspicious death unless there is a finished police investigation that clearly identifies the perpetrator of the crime." She didn't look at me, as if doing so would make her more likely to burst into tears.

I was suspicious of this explanation. It sounded like a delaying tactic. Clearly, there was a political battle being waged here, and I could only see part of it. Kurt said President Frost was friends with the chief of police and had asked him to keep certain things from the media. Was he also keeping them from arresting Emma? Was that why I'd had that bizarre conversation with Detective Gore on Monday?

"I'm so sorry," I said, still unable to see Emma as a murderer. Those tiny arms, those small hands, choking Carl with a pink scarf? And then calling me and Kurt not long after, with innocence and terror in her voice? It made no sense.

"I want to know what you think of me calling a lawyer. Someone who can defend me against the terrible things that are being implied." Her voice wavered, and I felt protective of her again.

"A lawyer sounds like a good idea to me at this point," I said. I wondered if a lawyer would instantly see all the legal problems here, and get to work on them without telling Emma. I hoped so.

"You don't think it will make me look bad to the insurance company?" She was back to her pleading uncertainty.

What would be worse, looking bad or being arrested? But she didn't seem capable of seeing the big picture right now. "Emma, you need to make sure your children have what Carl would have wanted them to have," I said.

"The insurance company said that I could refuse the investigation and forfeit the claim to begin with," she said. Her voice was all over the place: scratchy, high-pitched, and then a hoarse whisper. I had to listen carefully to catch what she was saying.

"Why would you do that?" I was appalled.

"They said that in my financial situation, I'm not desperate for money, and so it might be easier for me to avoid the scrutiny."

"That sounds like a threat," I said. I hated big corporations who seemed to care nothing about honoring their contracts and everything about the bottom line. A man had died. His family was suffering, whatever the legalities were. Didn't that matter more than a profit statement to shareholders? Apparently not. "What do you want to do?" I asked.

Emma was shaking again. "I just want to bury Carl. I want the police to release his body and let us get on with the funeral so that we can start healing. I feel like we're stuck in this place and we'll never get out of it."

"Full healing will take a long time, Emma," I said as honestly as I could. I remembered people telling me when Georgia had died that I would never get over it. I'd hated that. I had wanted to believe that I just had to hang on for a few more weeks, maybe a few months, and I would be fine again.

"William needs there to be a funeral. He needs to see his

father's body resting in a coffin," Emma said. "He needs to hear people talk about Carl's life. He's so confused right now, I think he might explode."

Did she think that I could do something to make the funeral happen more quickly? Kurt was my husband, not my puppet. I had no control over his actions as bishop, and even if I had, President Frost was the one who had stopped the release of the body, not Kurt. But I suppose Emma didn't know that.

"Do you think a lawyer could make the police release his body?" she asked.

"Emma, you need to be careful here," I said. "I think you should just be patient for now." What she didn't seem to see was that the longer the police spent investigating this, the more likely they were to find the right person. And stop looking at the easy solution of the wife murdering her husband.

"Thank you," said Emma, her voice very faint. She looked up at me, wide-eyed and hopeful. "Linda, I've always felt that you and I—that we had nothing in common. I've been afraid to talk to you for fear that you would look down on me. You're so smart and articulate, and I've never felt up to your level."

"But I—that's—" I tried to protest, but she kept going.

"You have been a dear friend through all this, better than I could have hoped for. I guess you don't really find out who your friends are until you are in trouble. So, thank you." She put her hands in mine, and I could feel how small and cold they were.

"You're welcome," I said, because there was no other way I could respond.

AFTER A LIGHT lunch, I headed over to Anna's for one of our walks. At her doorstep, I paused to look at the valley

below us—so many houses, so many different cities that had
grown out of the one original settlement. The pioneers in
the 1800s had only seen the mountains and the desertscape,
and must have had no idea how much the buildings would
spread. I could see the different sections of Draper city, the
older parts with the larger acreages, and houses added onto
again and again, and then the smaller homes of the 1950s
and '60s made of brick, and up the hill to where we lived,
amidst the tall homes on small pieces of land that looked
like unending rows.

It was a brilliant, hot day, not a cloud in the sky. As usual
in June, we hadn't had a drop of rain, and if there was any
wind at all, I'd be seeing dirt being blown around the lower
sections of the valley. Brigham Young had said that Mormons
as a people would make the desert "blossom like a rose," and
I suppose we had. Looking out over the whole of it, I was able
to let go of all my pressing concerns for just a moment, and
feel amazed that I was part of this enormous project. I might
struggle with parts of Mormonism, but I was proud of the
grand, historical sweep of our church history.

"What happened?" asked Anna.

"Does something have to happen for me to want to go on
a walk?" I asked.

"Generally, yes," said Anna. "But you have the kind of life
with all your boys where there's always something exciting
going on."

I told her what Emma had said. "Am I intimidating? I want
you to tell me honestly."

"You are who you are," Anna said with a faint smile.

"What does that mean?" It sounded like something Kurt
would say to me, and I hadn't gone to Kurt with this

conversation for some very specific reasons. I didn't want vague, Kurt-like answers intended to spare my feelings.

"It means that other people aren't who they really are—they aren't true to themselves. So it can be intimidating to see someone who is. But it can also be inspiring, Linda. I hope you don't think you should change."

"But I don't want people to think that I believe I'm above them somehow. I don't want them to feel like they can't talk to me."

Anna didn't say anything for a while as we walked up the steep hill. Once again, I wished I had brought water with me. I was already dripping with sweat.

I wished the air were cleaner as I pulled it into my lungs with heaving gasps. We reached the top of the hill and stopped to catch our breath. "Linda," Anna said finally, "the reason people don't want to talk to you is because you are honest. Brutally, unflinchingly honest. You force people to face their own failures and weaknesses, and that can be painful."

Directly below us was the temple. I wished I could believe all my answers were in that building, but I didn't. "I face my own failures and weaknesses. I can make long lists of them. Do you think it would help if I brought that up more?"

Anna laughed and we started back down the hill again. "No, I don't think so."

So I was stuck with who I was and how people reacted to me, it seemed. I had Anna as a friend, though. Maybe that wasn't so bad.

CHAPTER 22

That afternoon, I was elbow deep in sweet roll dough when the phone rang. This time, it was Grant Rhodes. He sounded stiff and angry.

"Sister Wallheim, I am wondering if you would be willing to come and pick me up at the police station. They've finished questioning me and are letting me go, but they aren't driving me home." His voice was a little slurred with exhaustion.

If they were letting him go, they must not have been planning to arrest him. At least not immediately. "If you're sure you want me to get you," I said, "I'll be there as soon as I can."

"You're the only person who has treated me like a human being in the last two weeks," said Grant. "I just want to relax and feel safe again."

"All right," I said. I was dying to ask him what was going on. I hung up and put the roll dough in the refrigerator. It would keep until I got back.

But before I left for the station, I called Kurt to tell him where I was going.

"I don't know if that's a good idea," he said. "Isn't he a murder suspect?"

"I'll be fine," I said. I'd talked to the man dozens of times before. "I brought him banana bread."

"And that's like a shield of virtue to protect you against any evil intention?" said Kurt. "Linda, I could ask someone else to go pick him up. One of the retired high priests in the ward. Or I could find someone who can take time off work."

I considered it for one brief moment. Should I be warier here? But I shook off any fear. "Kurt, I'd much prefer he think of me as a friend than an enemy. That's surely the best thing for the whole ward in the long run, if we're ever going to heal."

"We do need to heal," Kurt agreed.

"And the police are releasing him. That means they don't think he's guilty, right?" Then again, it also meant that the murderer was still out there, somewhere in our ward. Possibly at church every Sunday.

Kurt was silent for a moment. "You're itching to ask him about why the police called him in, aren't you?"

I was a little embarrassed about that, but it was true. Kurt knew me too well. "I'll talk to you tonight?" I said.

"Yes. Take notes. I want to hear it all." His tone was more amused than worried.

I drove down to the police station and waited for a few minutes. Grant Rhodes was filling out some final paperwork at the front desk, and he waved to me when he heard the door open.

Hunched over the papers, he looked different than I'd ever seen him. Diminished, somehow. The skin of his face seemed paper thin, and his jowls hung down limply. His protruding skull appeared small and fragile. Here was Grant Rhodes as he would look when he was dead, I thought.

"Thank you for coming," he said.

"You're welcome," I replied, and led him out to my car.

He got into the passenger side, but I had to remind him to put his seat belt on before I pulled out.

I didn't know what to say to him. I'd imagined asking him questions, but considering his state, that seemed utterly inappropriate, so I waited for him to speak.

He started to weep when I was only a block away from the station. Not quiet sobs, but great, loud waves of pain.

I pulled over and put a hand on the top of his shoulder to comfort him. He threw himself toward me, his arms outstretched, and I felt trapped for a moment. But he rocked back and forth and once I got into the rhythm of his grief, I felt less constrained. I patted his back and said, "Grant, Grant, it's okay, I'm here," over and over again.

Several times, I thought he was finished, but then he'd break down uncontrollably again.

About a half hour later, Kurt texted to see why I hadn't told him I was home. I texted back quickly—LATER—just so he wouldn't call in the cavalry.

"Do you want to talk about it?" I asked, when Grant was winding down a fourth time and I finally thought it might be for real.

He took in a shuddering breath. "They wanted to know where I was on Friday night. When he was killed. Carl."

"Where were you?" I asked. "Home?" That would make it difficult for him in terms of an alibi.

He shook his head. "I was out. On a date."

That was a surprise to me. "With a woman?" I said before I could stop myself.

But he didn't seem to notice the implication of my surprise. "Her name is Jenny. Jenny Rue. She's a car enthusiast," he said. "I met her at a vintage show a few months ago."

"Oh. How lovely," I said.

"They wanted her name, her cell phone number, everything about her. How often we had dated, who had introduced us, what we had done that night. Every detail."

Well, at least it was clear the police were looking beyond Emma.

"I feel so humiliated," Grant went on. "They said they would call her and ask her to come in and verify everything. They said that if she disagreed with me in any substantive way, they would have to ask me to come in again and account for myself."

"I'm sure everything will be fine," I said, hoping I was right.

"I haven't talked to her since that night," said Grant. "I'm afraid she'll be angry at me and that she might—well—not tell the truth." He pulled back so he could look me in the eye. "Do you think she might hate me enough to lie to the police?"

"Did something happen on the date that would make you think that? Did it end badly in some way?"

He shook his head. "But what do I know? It's been so long since I last went on a date that I'm not sure I could tell."

How hard could it be to tell if a woman had been unhappy on a date? To someone like Grant, maybe very hard. "What did she say to you at the end? Did she ask you to call her? Did she get out of your car quickly without saying goodnight?"

"She was polite," he said. "She didn't ask me to call her again, though. She said, 'Thank you.'"

"Ah," I said. Well, it didn't sound like she'd been angry at him. Just not interested.

"I don't understand women. They make no sense to me at all." His mouth twitched. "I'm sorry. I shouldn't be saying that to you."

"No, it's fine," I said. He was just being honest. Though I have always been confused by the way some men seem to think that women are alien creatures who need to be explored scientifically. We are much more like men than we are different from them.

"Do you think I could drive you home now?" I asked.

For the first time, Grant seemed to notice that I had pulled over to the side of the road. "Oh, of course. You must be wanting to get back to your own life. I am sorry to have taken up so much of your time."

But what life was there for me back home except for roll dough? Samuel wasn't home; he had found an apartment and was signing the lease for it today. He would graduate at the end of the week, but he'd skipped classes all of last month, not caring if he got bad grades. In his mind, he was off to college.

Kurt and I were already empty nesters in every way that counted, and I guess this case had come up conveniently as an excuse for me to deal with something other than the emotional implications of everything going on at home.

"I only meant that you might be more comfortable at home," I said, feeling like I had somehow eased into the role of Grant Rhodes's mother figure. The banana bread had worked almost too well.

"Yes," he said. He sighed and nodded.

I started driving again. He tried to pull himself together, wiping at his eyes and taking deep breaths. It took a good ten minutes.

"Carl Ashby's death affected me more than I thought it would," he confessed when we were almost at his house.

"Oh?" I said nonchalantly, hoping that would keep him talking.

"It made me think of how easily we all could die. Just one moment alive and the next gone," he said. "And then there was the fact that he and I argued so much. I wondered if somehow that had caused his death." He held up his hands. "Not that I did it. I wasn't anywhere near there, and I could never—do that. But is it possible that my anger was transferred to someone else? Or that I made him react to someone else?" He shook his head.

"I don't think so, Grant," I said.

"I hated him in the end. So much. I'm not sure I've ever hated someone like that before," Grant went on.

"In the end?" I had pulled into his driveway.

He put a hand on the door, but didn't open it. "You can come in," he said. His eyes were rimmed with red, but in other ways he seemed better, as if the weeping had restored him. Why didn't it ever work like that for me?

We sat in his living room while he fixed me some Postum. It had been a long time since I'd had Postum. It was something I'd grown up on, a hot, dark-colored drink made from very finely ground roasted barley. It looked like coffee in the cup but didn't taste much like it, unless you thought of coffee as burned and nasty, which I guess most Mormons did. But once you put a lot of cream and sugar in it, I suppose you could pretend it was almost anything.

Grant's living room was decorated with black leather arm chairs, the walls a deep teal. White lace curtains hung in the windows. Stenciling ran along the border of the ceiling, a nice floral. I puzzled over the different impulses at work and wondered if there had been a steady girlfriend in the past I didn't know about.

"Are you feeling guilty about your relationship with Carl?" I asked him when he rejoined me. "If you want to talk to Kurt,

I'm sure he would be glad to help you sort through your emotions. Tell you what process you need to go through to be good with God."

Mormons don't have anything so simple as a Catholic confession, where you say what you have done and are given a set penance for it. Usually you only go to confess to a Mormon bishop if you have committed a serious sin, like breaking your marriage vows or abusing your children. You could go to a bishop for counseling about smaller sins, but he wouldn't necessarily be able to absolve you of sin or even tell you what you needed to do for forgiveness. He could give advice or offer discipline if necessary.

"I don't think I'm ready to do that," said Grant. "And besides, Kurt isn't technically my bishop. My records are still in this ward." He waved to the houses around him.

"I know that. But this isn't an issue of church policy. It's an issue of conscience."

"I'll think about it." Grant sipped at the Postum.

"It isn't your fault he's dead, you know. Being angry with him didn't cause him to get killed. It doesn't work that way."

Grant didn't say anything.

I wanted him to keep talking to me, about anything. So I tried our last topic. "This girl, Jenny. You didn't feel any connection with her?"

"None," said Grant.

"But you are interested in dating? I'm just wondering if I should ask around and see if there's someone else I could set you up with. Any ideas about what kind of woman you would be interested in?" Not that I had any desire to meddle in love lives. There were plenty of online Mormon dating services already.

"I think one date this year is plenty for me." He didn't elaborate.

I raised my mug of Postum, inhaled deeply, and realized something. I stood up and headed toward the kitchen. "Just need a glass of water. Hope you don't mind!" I called out. I poked around in the kitchen, as if looking for a glass. When I opened the cupboard next to the stove and took out the Postum jar, I sniffed it deeply, and realized it was coffee. There was no sign of a freeze-dried coffee can anywhere here, but the Postum jar was pretty old and the wrapper around it was yellowing. He must constantly transfer the powder from one container to the other, and then go on lying to himself about what he was doing.

No wonder he'd had so many problems with the bishop of his assigned ward. I'd always thought they were philosophical. I dumped out my cup into the sink, and refilled it with water after swishing out any remaining coffee.

I could have finished the whole cup and told Kurt that I hadn't known what it was, that Grant had lied to me. It would have been a good excuse to drink coffee, which I seriously missed from my atheist period. But I would have known I was lying, and what point was there in that? I could have coffee any time I wanted. No one was stopping me except for me.

I had made a commitment to Mormonism before Kurt and I married. It wasn't the only church I thought had truth in it. I wasn't even sure it had the most truth. But it was my truth. It was the religion I had been brought up in, the religion whose rituals were most comforting to me. When I went back to God, Mormonism was the religion I went back to. And I was going to follow its rules, not because they made me more worthy or more wise, but because they were part and parcel of the rest of it. If I wasn't willing to do the small things, then there was no point in being in the religion at all.

On the other hand, I felt no need to chastise Grant about his choices. I knew there were plenty of Mormons who would have felt betrayed or even defiled by breaking the Word of Wisdom inadvertently, but I wasn't one of them. I didn't think it was purity from the substances themselves that mattered. It was your relationship to God, and that was completely individual.

"Carl Ashby and I were friends in college," Grant announced when I went back into the living room to sit down. "Did you know that?"

"No. I had no idea," I said. This was what I had come to hear about. This had to be why the police had questioned Grant, not because of his religious arguments with Carl.

"We were in the same department and hung out in the same common areas."

I felt like the world had turned upside down and I was trying to figure out how to rearrange it again into a coherent scene. Grant and Carl had been about the same age, though I hadn't thought of that before now. Late forties to early fifties. Carl had been thinner and in better shape, but they were both getting older.

"He was still Carla Thompson then?" I asked.

Grant stared into his coffee, swirling it around as if his whole past were in there, if only he squinted hard enough. He spoke as if he were in some kind of trance: "When we graduated, we lost touch for a long time. He got married and I—didn't." There was sorrow and longing in his voice, and I wondered if it was possible that Grant Rhodes had been in love with the Carla he'd known in college. It made a complicated wrinkle in the division between gay, bisexual, and heterosexual.

"But I saw him in the store one day a few years ago. I recognized him despite all the changes," said Grant

I could not imagine Carl as a woman. Had he walked differently? Interacted differently with others? Or had he always been masculine as a woman? How had Grant recognized him so easily, in a random location? Had he seen him from a distance? Had they literally bumped into each other? What a huge coincidence. Did Grant think it had been the hand of God at work?

Grant continued. "He didn't see me, but maybe he hadn't thought about me as much as I'd thought about him all those years later. I followed him out to his car and then drove behind him to his house, sure I was going to lose him just when I had found him again. But when he pulled into the driveway, and I realized how close he lived, I knew I could find out more about him. That was when I made excuses to leave my ward and started attending with you."

What he was describing was stalking. I was sure Kurt hadn't known anything about this, or he wouldn't have been so welcoming and understanding toward Grant in the first place. I should have been more creeped out—I knew stalking was a sign of fixation, one that could possibly lead to murder—but I was dying to know what else Grant would say. I could hardly leave now, even if I'd wanted to.

Grant set the coffee cup aside, and for a long moment I was afraid that the storytelling was over. Then he said, "Maybe I was crazy, but I really thought we would be friends again. I thought Carl would be glad to see me and we could talk. But he wasn't. He was busy with his own life and he didn't have time for me. And I was hurt."

"You knew he was a woman," I blurted. "All this time, and you never hinted at it." As soon as I spoke, I realized I was doing the same thing that Kurt, and Tom deRyke, and Detective Gore had done to Carl, which was to reduce him to his biology. I was ashamed of myself, but there was nothing I could do to take it back now.

"That he had been born into a woman's body, yes," said Grant. "But even before he converted to Mormonism, before he took up his new life, he was always one of the guys. We didn't think about things like surgery, but we called him 'Carl' most of the time, joked around about how male he was and how well he fit in with the rest of us."

This was why Grant Rhodes had called me to pick him up at the station, instead of Kurt or any of the members of the high priests quorum. He knew that they would be bothered by direct talk about Carl Ashby's transformation. And that I wouldn't.

"Did it surprise you that he was married with children?" I asked, watching him closely.

Grant shrugged. "I thought it was a good thing for him. It seemed right, you know? It fit him. Traditional. He always wanted the traditional stuff—as a husband, not a wife."

"Was he afraid you would expose him?" I asked. That might explain some of the underlying animosity between them in the ward. Carl had spent how many years safely in his life as a man? Then Grant shows up, coming to his home supposedly to argue gospel topics with him, every moment making it more likely that his past would be revealed.

"Maybe. But it still hurt me, the way he kept me at a distance," said Grant. "I called him repeatedly in the days before he died. I wanted to make things right between us. I asked—demanded really—that he meet me at a restaurant in Salt Lake City. In public, but not close to anyone here."

"And did he meet you?" I asked. If Carl had felt threatened by Grant's stalkerish behavior, surely he wouldn't have done that. Unless he felt that he couldn't refuse. What had really been going on in Carl's mind those last few days?

Grant nodded. He looked up at me for the first time, and I was surprised at how beseeching his expression was. "We spent hours together. We had to leave the restaurant eventually, and we went on a long walk through Temple Square. We talked about everything that we hadn't talked about in all the years I had been waiting for him and watching him. He told me about what had happened to him after college. Changing his name, changing his wardrobe. Cutting off his family and everyone who had known him in the past. Getting a job as Carl Ashby. Then meeting Emma and getting married. He told me about his children and how much he loved them."

Grant paused, then took a deep breath and spoke more rapidly, as if to get all the rest out at once. "We even talked about his worries that someone would find out about—his body. He talked about his marriage, and how it worked. The compromises he had made and that Emma had made." He shook his head, then leapt out of his chair and began pacing energetically. "I think we could have talked forever, but Emma called and he had to go home to the family. I thought we would have lots of time after that. I thought that everything would be perfect." Grant put his hand to his heart, and I could see him as he must have been in college, just a lost and heartbroken teenager. "And then I heard that he was dead, and it was like some part of me died too, a part of me that had just come alive again."

There was more emotion in Grant's stance and more

energy in his words than seemed appropriate, considering. What had really happened between the two of them that day? What else had Carl told Grant?

But Grant stood up. "I don't want to keep you. You should go and I'll talk to Kurt later, if I want to." He had become formal again, the emotion gone from his tone. "Thank you for bringing me home."

"Of course," I said, trying to leave the door open if there was more. "And anytime you need someone to talk to, I'm here. I want you to know I won't judge you."

I DROVE HOME, mulling over my unanswered questions from our conversation. Was Grant the murderer? Had he called Carl to meet him at the church? Had Carl told him that they couldn't meet again? Had Grant killed him for that? After watching the manic Grant pace, I could almost see him holding a scarf around Carl's throat. But the police had thought it was a woman from the outset. Had they simply been wrong or was there something else I was missing?

I tried praying to ask for help to understand all of this, but I didn't receive any inspiration. It was like there was a fog between me and God, and it made me angry that now, when I most needed guidance, I felt forsaken. What was I supposed to do? Keep this to myself? Tell Kurt? Tell Emma?

I didn't know.

CHAPTER 23

On Wednesday evening, Kurt came home from the church late, at nearly midnight. I was still awake, mostly because I had come down with a terrible migraine and the medication for it made it impossible for me to sleep. It was always a debate in my mind between no sleep and no migraine or fitful sleep and migraine. I'd chosen no sleep and no migraine this time and was upstairs rereading an old Agatha Christie favorite of mine, *Curtain: Poirot's Last Case*.

Kurt lay down on the bed next to me, on top of the blankets, still dressed in his full suit and tie. He closed his eyes and folded his arms across his chest as if he were a corpse in a coffin, only less peaceful.

"What is it?" I asked.

He took several even breaths, and I wondered if he had somehow fallen asleep that quickly. It had happened on a couple of occasions since Kurt had become bishop. He got a lot less sleep, and his body had learned to simply turn off when it had to.

"I don't think I should tell you," he said.

"Which means it's about Carl Ashby, I suppose," I said.

He let out another breath.

"You know it'll be worse if you don't tell me; my imagination will run amok with possibilities. Did the police come to the church to talk to you?"

"No," said Kurt.

"Then it has to be someone in the ward. Did the murderer come in and confess to you?"

Kurt didn't answer this time.

"Kurt, you have to tell the police if that's what happened. There's no sanctity of the confessional in Mormonism. The First Presidency of the church has made the rules very clear. Bishops have an obligation to relay information about serious crimes—"

"I know what the church instruction to bishops about criminal confessions is," said Kurt. He pulled at his neck and loosened his tie.

"Then what's the problem?" I asked. Was it someone I already suspected? Or someone else entirely?

"The problem is that I'm not sure if it has anything to do with the murder. But it might."

"So someone hinted at it? Or implied it? You should probably still go in and talk to the police."

Kurt hesitated for a long moment. He rubbed at the hair on his head, then rolled up to a sitting position. He would only tell me bits and pieces as he thought appropriate. "It was William Ashby," he said. "He came in for his interview. His birthday is next week. He'll be fifteen." Bishops were supposed to conduct interviews with every member of the youth group on a yearly basis.

"What did he say?" I asked.

Kurt shook his head. "I asked him about the crash in Grant Rhodes's car. He was very distant about it. He spoke almost as if someone else had been doing everything. Like he'd been watching himself."

"It might have felt like that," I said, thinking back to how confused he'd been as he'd hurled accusations at Grant.

"I wanted him to say that he was sorry, but he wouldn't. He was sorry that he hadn't gotten away with it, I think. And that was all."

Kurt was holding back. I could see it in the tenseness of his shoulders.

"That's not what's bothering you," I said. "Is it?"

Kurt sat up, took off his jacket, and threw it and his tie toward the dresser. He might have been aiming for the top, but they didn't make it. Then he lay back down and said nothing for a while.

"Do you think that William is the murderer, is that what you're saying? Even if he didn't confess to it specifically?" The pills I'd taken for my migraine were in full swing now. They tended to make me feel jittery at first, and then slowly just made me feel better, more energetic, more myself.

"He's fourteen, almost fifteen," said Kurt. "And I don't want to believe that a boy that age could kill his own father."

"I thought that Emma said that he was out with friends," I said.

Kurt pursed his lips as if to keep from saying anything more. Had William admitted to Kurt tonight that his alibi was a lie?

"Do you know what bothered me most?"

A brief pause, but I said nothing.

Kurt went on: "It seems like a stupid thing, and really not enough to call the police about. But I asked William if he loved his father. He wouldn't answer me."

"That could just be confusion about his father's gender identity," I said.

"But he doesn't know about that, does he? As far as I know, the police have kept that tightly under wraps. They haven't leaked it to the press, and I don't think Emma Ashby has told anyone. Have you?"

"No," I said, hoping that it was true. I had hinted at the truth to Anna, but she wouldn't have told William. Could William have guessed? Perhaps even before the murder? "Grant Rhodes knew," I said.

"What? You told him?"

"No. He already knew. He knew Carl in college, or that's what he told me yesterday when I picked him up from the police station." I explained what Grant had told me, then got up and went to my desk.

"What are you doing?" Kurt asked.

I opened up my computer and searched for University of Utah graduates from 1985 to 1995 and the names "Carla Thompson" and "Grant Rhodes." It didn't take long before I was staring at a photo of the two of them from back then. Could William Ashby have happened upon this image? It seemed unlikely he would guess his father's old name, but maybe he had come across something else that led him in that direction?

I could hardly turn away from the photo of Carla. It both was and wasn't the man that I knew as Carl Ashby. The photograph was strangely androgynous. Carla wore gigantic glasses that covered almost all of her face. The hair was very short, almost as short as Carl's, but there was a tiny curl at the top. I couldn't tell if it was natural. The neck was strong and the collar of the shirt bore an indistinct pattern, possibly dots. If I had seen this photo without knowing it was Carl, would I have recognized him?

"What is it?" asked Kurt, over my shoulder.

I moved to the side so he could see the two photos.

"Grant and Carl. Carla," said Kurt. "They look so young." He shook his head and made a sound deep in his throat.

Then I clicked through to another page that showed Carla and Grant holding hands, and moving into a kiss. The photograph captured them in the moment before their lips touched, and there was an innocence in the way they looked at each other, with perfect happiness and the expectation that there would never be anything else. What if William had seen this?

"Grant didn't tell me about that," I said. But clearly, my impression that he had been in love had been right.

"Do you think that the police have already seen this?" asked Kurt.

"Surely they've done an online search for Carla Thompson already," I said distantly. I was thinking of the letters that Emma had asked me to take away. What if they were old letters Carla had written to Grant?

I turned off the computer and tugged Kurt back toward the bed. He undressed at last, pulled back the covers and tucked himself in next to me, putting his cold feet on my legs. I didn't mind. I'd started asking him to do that when I was going through menopause and had hot flashes on a regular basis, and it had become a habit since then.

Old habits die hard, I thought to myself.

CHAPTER 24

It was early June, and on Friday that week, Samuel officially graduated from high school. He hadn't wanted to make a big fuss about it. In fact, he had begged Kurt to allow him to skip the ceremony and just stay home instead, since he had a rare Friday off work.

"It's not like it matters if I go. They'll just send me my diploma in the mail. And then I'll throw it away," said Samuel that morning.

"Why would you do that? It's taken you twelve years to finish this. Why don't you want to celebrate it?" asked Kurt.

I muted the television so I could listen to the conversation. I wondered how much of this was really about Samuel's coming out, rather than the graduation.

"Because it's high school. It's like graduating from preschool. Anyone can do it."

"Well, we celebrated you graduating from preschool, too," I put in. "You were adorable in that tiny black cap and gown." I might even still have the cap somewhere in a filing cabinet in the basement. I felt a little teary thinking about it. It was so long ago, but in many ways, Samuel was the same person he had been then. Intelligent, thoughtful, kind, easily hurt.

"Well, that's because I was too stupid to object. And besides, I bet preschool graduation took a lot less time and was a lot less boring."

There had definitely been more singing. But little Samuel had fidgeted through the whole thing. It had taken every ounce of his patience and mine to make it through. And I was still glad that we had gone. If nothing else, I had great photos of the moment that I could one day show to his— partner, I suppose, if he ended up marrying outside the temple someday.

"You really don't think that getting through high school in one piece is a significant hurdle?" said Kurt.

Samuel's motions were all angles that morning, even his shrugs. "What does a high school diploma get me? I'm going to college because that's going to actually be about my future. I'll finally get to choose what I study and the classes will be really hard," he said.

"What if they're not? What if you get to the end of college and think that's not a big deal, either? Because it's never hard once you've reached the end of the road, is it?"

Samuel stared at his father, and I wanted to shout at both of them to stop pretending. Samuel didn't want to go to graduation because he wasn't sure Kurt had accepted him yet. And Kurt was trying to tell him that appearances mattered, that traditions mattered. As if Samuel didn't already know that.

Samuel sighed and rubbed at his hair, a heartbreaking echo of one of Kurt's own habits—and something neither of them recognized. How alike they were, in prickly pride and goodness. But they were hurting each other even so.

"How about we make a deal?" Samuel proposed. "I

promise to go to college graduation and you let me off of high school graduation as a reward?"

Please, Kurt, listen to what he means, and not what he says. Tell him that you love him. Tell him that you are proud of him, no matter what. Tell him that there will be a place for him in the church, that you'll make sure of that.

But Kurt was taking this all literally. "I don't think so."

"Seriously, Dad. I'm going to be spending plenty of my life in boring meetings. Why do I have to start now?"

Please listen to me. I'm hurting. Why couldn't Kurt hear that?

"Practice?" said Kurt. "And you may be surprised at how many of those meetings are a lot less boring when you're in charge of them, and when you believe what happens in them matters."

You don't respect me or the choices I've made, Kurt was saying. But Samuel did. He just wasn't the same man as his father, however many similarities they shared.

"But this doesn't matter. I don't have to go to graduation. That's what I'm saying. It's just a boring bunch of name reading, self-congratulation, and stupid pranks." Samuel sounded bitter now, though he never had seemed bitter about high school before. He'd always had a lot of friends. But if he had come out to us, he had probably come out to them. And maybe it hadn't gone as well as he'd hoped.

I wanted to sit down and talk him through it all, but I didn't want to be a hovering mother. I didn't want him to think he couldn't handle his own life.

"What if I tell you that you're doing it for me and Mom?" Kurt said, gesturing to include me.

Samuel looked at me. I put up my hands. "Leave me out of this," I said.

"You don't care if he goes to graduation or not?" said Kurt.

"I care about what Samuel wants. If he wants a different kind of celebration, what's wrong with that? We can take him out to lunch someplace special."

"He'd be the only one of our five sons who didn't go."

"He's different from our other four," I said, as naturally as I could without embarrassing either one of them. They both stiffened in response.

"He's the same in every way that matters," said Kurt in a low tone. He looked away, as if he were speaking to the window to the backyard instead of to us.

I was pretty sure that Kurt was trying to show Samuel unconditional love, but he also seemed to be asking him to get back in line. Was it possible that Kurt thought Samuel was mistaken in some way, that he only thought he was gay? I thought of Ben Tookey again, and how impossible it had been for him to talk about his sexuality.

I spoke cautiously. "Kurt, haven't you always said that, as parents, we learn as much from our children as they learn from us?"

I prayed in that moment that God would soften Kurt's heart, that he would relent and let Samuel talk to us—really talk. Kurt could tell him that there was no pressure on him to go on a mission as the other boys had done, if he didn't feel called to it. He could let us have the conversation that was going on unheard and unspoken in our hearts.

"If you refuse to participate, then I suppose that's ultimately your choice. Even Satan and his followers ultimately had their own choice. No one is forced into heaven," said Kurt instead, and with that, he turned and stomped to his office, slamming the door behind him.

My heart throbbed. I loved Kurt and I loved Samuel. I knew they loved each other. So why were they hurting each other like this? And why couldn't I figure out some way to fix it all easily, with a kiss and a hug, like I managed to when Samuel was little?

"I'm so sorry," I said to Samuel, who was standing so upright and rigid that Kurt would have congratulated him on looking like a proper Eagle Scout. Which Samuel had been at age fourteen. Because he knew it mattered to his father and he wanted to honor the tradition of his brothers. But that had been four years ago and things were different now.

A part of me wanted to excuse my husband's behavior because, as bishop, he was overwhelmed with so many problems on all sides. He was supposed to be able to come up with spiritual answers for everyone in the ward, as well as in our family. Maybe Kurt was angry at God that he wasn't getting a pass on problems like this as a kind of blessing for his five-year commitment of service as bishop.

If only he didn't see Samuel's coming out to us as a problem.

"It's not your fault," said Samuel. One shoulder sagged then.

I went over and patted him gently. "I thought he was going to get it," I said. The Kurt I had always loved wasn't usually so bullheaded. Well, except when he was. And then he always apologized afterward. But I wasn't sure this was the kind of thing you could apologize for later and go on as usual.

"Do you really think I should go to graduation?" Samuel asked, only half looking at me.

I knew I was about to cry sloppy tears over this, and I didn't want Samuel to have to deal with that on top of everything else. But that he would ask me what I wanted—didn't that show he was the same thoughtful kid he'd always been? He wasn't being rebellious or trying to fight.

I took a deep breath and said, "I think it would make your father happy if you went. How much do you care about that?"

Samuel thought it over. "I'm never going to be who he wants me to be. I might as well accept it now."

"Samuel." I held his hand tightly and wouldn't let him squirm away. "He is proud of you. Don't doubt that. Whatever is going on with him right now, I don't understand it. But he'll get over it. Things will get better. I know they will. And this is not because he doesn't love you."

"Do you think we could just go out to eat instead then? Do what I want? Could he be okay with that?"

"Yes," I said, with more confidence than I felt. "I'll go talk to him. You think about where you want to go." I was going to make this happen. For Kurt, it would be a concession, but he needed to meet Samuel where he was.

I knocked on the door to Kurt's office, but didn't wait for him to tell me to come in. He was sitting at his desk, head in hands.

"Have I ruined everything?" Kurt asked. His eyes were red and he only lifted his head a couple of inches to look up at me. I wondered if he had been crying or praying—or perhaps both.

"Come out now and see. I told Samuel we'd take him out to eat wherever he wants to go."

Kurt hesitated a long moment. "Maybe you should take him without me."

"Kurt, that will only make him feel worse." But I was so relieved that he wasn't pressing the graduation ceremony issue anymore.

"I just don't know if he wants me to be there. It seems like he used to ask for my advice about everything. He used to want to be like me. And now—" Kurt turned away and took in a gasping breath. I could see him wipe at his eyes.

"I think he still wants to be like you, Kurt. He just has to find his own way to do that," I said.

We went to Chuck E. Cheese's as Samuel ironically suggested. It was where Samuel used to ask us to take him for birthdays when he was eight or nine years old.

When we arrived, it was almost entirely empty. We ordered pizza, and Samuel went off to play a few games before it came. Then he sat down and I felt a lump in my throat, thinking about how young he still was.

"So, what's happening with your apartment? Did everything go well signing the papers?" I asked.

"I'm moving in the first of July," Samuel said. "I want to get a head start on a job near campus and, you know, get acquainted with the area."

That soon?

I felt as if he were tearing me in half with those words. One part of me wanted to cheer him on as he moved forward in his life. The other part of me wanted to keep him at home forever.

I would miss his keen insights into people and world events, and the way he saw the best in everyone, including me. I would miss his laughter and his knack for guessing what was going to happen at the end of a TV show (though I always said I hated it). I would even miss him finishing off every baked good that I made, no matter how huge the quantity. I'd really have to work on cutting back my recipe sizes now.

And once he—my youngest boy—left the house, what

would happen to the identity I'd cultivated for the last twenty-five years as a full-time mother? I would have to look at my own life and figure out what more I wanted to do with it. Did I want to go back to school? Do more charity work? Get a job of some kind?

The world has no need for a drone, rang in my head whenever I thought of an empty nest. It was a line from an old Mormon hymn that described the way many people looked at those who were not contributing meaningfully to their communities. Even stay-at-home mothers of five grown sons.

"Well, you'll have to cover the costs of the apartment and your own food. You're not supposed to use your college fund unless you're taking classes," said Kurt.

"I know that, Dad," Samuel said irritably. "You don't have to worry about me coming to bug you for money. I've got a job."

"What about your mission money?" asked Kurt. When the boys were tiny, we taught them to pay 10 percent of any money they got to tithing, and another 40 percent to a mission savings account. They could only ever spend half of what they earned, though we'd always tried to give them a good allowance for chores so they didn't miss the other half much.

But when Joseph had decided to get married his freshman year instead of going on a mission, he'd used his mission fund for the deposit on a married student apartment, which was a lot more than sharing with five other guys. Kurt had been disappointed, but he'd gotten over it. Just as he would get over this.

Samuel was silent for a long time. Then he said, "I'd still like to go on a mission."

Kurt went very still. I could see his knuckles go white on the fork he was gripping. "You'd still like to go on a mission?"

Samuel stared at Kurt's hands, and I could see his own knuckles had gone white from being clenched so hard. "Do you think the church would want me? I mean, if I'm openly gay, would they still assign me to a real mission?"

Kurt let out a long breath. "Of course they'd want you. Why wouldn't they want you? You'd make a great missionary!"

"With me—like this?" said Samuel, nearly choking halfway through the sentence.

"Well, you'd need a missionary haircut," said Kurt after a moment. "And a lot of white shirts and ties."

"Yeah," Samuel said, his face reddening as Kurt leaned over and tousled his overlong hair. "I guess I would."

"You're already eighteen. You can turn in papers whenever you're ready," said Kurt. "You just have to have an interview with your bishop and get started on a medical exam."

I wanted to put my hands up and tell Kurt to slow down. He didn't need to push Samuel into this. The church now said that young men could go any time between the ages of eighteen and twenty-five.

"I think I'd like to finish at least a semester of college first," said Samuel. "You know, make sure I know what I'm getting into."

"You can get your papers in this summer, then. Just put your availability date as December or January, whenever you want after classes are over."

I'd sent three sons on missions already, and each time, it was hard to see them go. For two years, they were supposed to focus entirely on the work, which meant weekly emails or letters and no more than that. Two phone calls a year, for Mother's Day and Christmas. That was it. Parents were strongly discouraged from visiting their children in person, no matter how close they happened to be stationed to the family home, though it was usually some distance away.

If watching a child leave for college was painful, watching him leave for a mission was worse. I was angry, but was it because Kurt was pushing Samuel to go on a mission I felt he wasn't ready for? Or was it because I wanted to keep Samuel to myself? I wasn't sure. And the truth was, Kurt was right to have confidence in Samuel as a missionary. He was cheerful, understanding, and the kind of person everyone was drawn to. He wouldn't be pushy about his message. He'd just try to help people who wanted help.

The pizza came and we all dug in, no sounds but slurping and gasping from hot cheese burns for a while. When we were all finished and even the crumbs had been picked up by Samuel's licked fingers, there was a long silence.

Then Samuel said, "I'm scared. I've been terrified since the day I came out." His eyes were blazing, and in spite of his words, he was courageous enough to look at us squarely. Another reason he would make a good missionary. He didn't mince words, my Samuel.

"Afraid of what? That people will tell you you don't belong in the church? That God doesn't love you?" said Kurt, just as honestly.

I cringed, but I didn't interrupt.

Samuel's eyes filled with tears, and I could see his shoulders shaking. "Yes," he got out in a whisper.

"Well, some people will say things like that to you. Do you think you can handle that? From people in the church, as well as outside of it?" Kurt asked.

Samuel took a moment to think. "I don't need other

people to tell me what's right. Or if God loves me. You two always taught me to find out answers for myself. I've done that."

Kurt nodded shortly, then said, "Look, Samuel. I love you. I'm not going to say that I'm glad that you're gay. I wish your life were easier. I wish that you had a path that was laid out with fewer challenges. But I'm not God. I'm not the ideal father for you or anyone, which is why you have a perfect father in heaven who sees how strong you are and isn't afraid like I am that it will be too much for you to bear."

I reached for Samuel's hand. He pulled away to wipe at his face, but I reached over to hold it again. I was glad that even the handful of preschool-age children and parents had left now.

Kurt thumped Samuel firmly on the back. "I wish I could fix everything for you, but I can't anymore. Maybe I never could. It's a hard thing for a father to learn. But anything you need, just ask me. I'll do my best."

"You really don't think I'm wrong somehow, then?" asked Samuel, smiling with childish delight and surprise, as if he had just been given the present he'd asked Santa for and never thought he would see under the tree.

Kurt had tears on his face now, too. His voice was thick. "I love you. That's all I know. I'm afraid, too. But I think that if anyone can face this challenge and ace it, it's you, Samuel."

Samuel took a deep breath, then nodded. "Yeah."

So there it was, the beginning of something new.

We got back into the car, and Kurt drove us home in near silence. He and Samuel started belching about halfway home, some kind of bizarre contest between them. I rolled down the window and rolled my eyes, pretending to be more annoyed than I was.

As I went to bed that night, I wondered how long this fragile peace between them would last.

CHAPTER 25

The following Tuesday night, we had our weekly Relief Society meeting. For a long time, it had been called "Homemaking," and the classes were all on cooking, sewing, and cleaning. But as more women started to work and the General Relief Society Presidency of the worldwide church realized that unmarried or divorced women might be frustrated with a meeting that didn't focus on their needs, things changed. Sometimes we had a spiritual lesson. Sometimes holiday craft activities, or even a game night.

This time, we were having a dinner and a short presentation. One of the women in the ward, Yolanda Jones, had visited Egypt over the summer and had become involved with a charity group. She wanted to get us all involved too, and Kurt had approved it, despite the fact that fundraising in the church building is usually frowned upon.

I arrived a few minutes early and found myself helping Sheri Tate set up chairs. Emma Ashby arrived next, and she stared daggers at Sheri, who reacted by ignoring her. I had no idea what was going on between the two of them, but ended up sitting next to Emma out of sympathy. I wished Anna were here, but she didn't usually come to these meetings. She insisted they were optional, and that it was her prerogative to decide whether they were uplifting to her or not.

"How are you doing?" I said to Emma. "I am so impressed that you feel up to attending something like this tonight."

"I don't need to be coddled," said Emma, her chin high. "I'm not a child."

"Of course not." She was so different than she had been the last time I had seen her. It worried me, the way she swung back and forth. I wondered if she was entirely sane.

"I just meant that with your two children out of school for the summer, you must feel overwhelmed by everything going on in your life," I finished lamely, unable to bring up Carl's death so casually.

"My children are perfectly capable of managing by themselves for a couple of hours on a weeknight," said Emma. "They're teenagers, not infants."

"Of course. And with a cell phone, I'm sure that you can keep in touch with them if there's an emergency," I said soothingly.

Emma glanced at her cell phone as Sarah Andrews entered and sat on the other side of the room. Emma typed something in, looking up as another member, Erica Grange, came in, then typed some more. Her hands made jittery movements, and if I hadn't known it was strictly against the rules of the church, I would have thought she was high on something.

"Emma?" I said, trying to feel her out.

She looked up at me and her eyes seemed unnaturally bright. "Do you think she's prettier than I am?" she asked, nodding to Janel Eckerton, the frazzled young mother of twin boys who had moved into the old Helm house just weeks before.

I hesitated, confused by her question.

"Tell me," Emma insisted, her face flushed. "What do you think of her?"

"I don't know how to compare," I said cautiously. "She's so much younger, and she has a completely different body type." Janel was very thin and tall, and her build was more gangly and birdlike than graceful.

"You do think she's prettier, then," said Emma. She typed something else into her phone.

"What are you doing?" I asked.

"I'm giving each woman a score."

"What? That's terrible. Why would you do that?" It sounded like some adolescent game my sons might have made up, and which Kurt and I would have had to lecture them severely about to stop it from ever happening again.

"I'm trying to figure out who Carl was having an affair with," said Emma intensely. She was chewing at her lower lip, making it bleed again. "It has to be one of the women in the ward. I thought this was the best place to come and observe them all in action. One of them killed him, and she's not going to just step forward and admit it openly."

I gaped at her. "Emma, you can't—" I started to say.

But by then Donna Ringel, the chorister, was standing in the front of the room, and it was time to sing the opening hymn.

Emma didn't sing. She just kept craning her neck around and making notes on her phone. I think she was even scoring the elderly women in the ward, who were sorely unlikely to have had an affair with her husband, whether he was transgender or not.

I hadn't told her anything about Grant Rhodes, and I resolved I never would. Not if this was the way she reacted to jealousy.

But I instinctively found myself looking around the room myself and wondering how Emma was evaluating them. We didn't actually know who those letters were from. If the police were right and the killer was a woman, then it was most likely someone in the church who knew Carl. My skin crawled. How could I tell which ones were the most likely?

Tanya Marisco, who had a D-cup chest and didn't seem to wear temple garment clothing to cover it?

Debbie Levitski, who'd had a complete makeover about two months ago—hair, wardrobe, and makeup? She'd gone from rather homely looking to quite pretty. Was it for her husband's sake, for her own sake? Or for someone else? Her preschool-aged children hadn't liked it at all, I remembered. They still seemed to look at her as if she were a stranger.

Kristin Allison, who wore so much perfume that you could practically cut through the air around her with a knife?

Gretchen Torres, who looked bored, and kept playing a game on her phone during the lesson, even during the slideshow, when the light from her phone glowed noticeably in the dark room? Why had she come if she had no desire to be here? Had she wanted to get away from her husband and kids?

There was hardly a woman in the room I didn't suspect, now that Emma had planted the nasty thought in my head.

When it was time for refreshments, which were set up on two tables—one for cookies, the other for drinks Mormons could imbibe without breaking the Word of Wisdom, from sparkling punch to hot chocolate—Emma stood up and got ready to leave. I followed her as she walked outside. She hadn't brought a car this time, so she was walking home.

"Emma!" I called.

She didn't turn around until I was at her heels. "What is it?" she snapped, irritated.

I had jogged to catch up to her, so I was breathless when I said, "You can't let your jealousy eat you up." Relief Society was supposed to be a community of friends, not an arena for competition.

"I can't help it," Emma said, and in the harsh glare of the streetlights, I felt like I could see straight to the bones in her face. How much weight had she lost in the past month? She hadn't had any extra to begin with.

"Emma, if Carl was having an affair before he was killed, you need to let it go. Forgive him and move on with your life." I tried to keep my voice down, because I wasn't sure who might be listening through an open window. We weren't that far from the church, either, and on a night like this, our voices could carry all the way back to the parking lot.

"And forgive her, too, I suppose? Is that what you think I should do? Even if she has never asked for forgiveness? Never even admitted what she has done wrong?" Emma started walking again.

It seemed politic to go along with Emma at the moment. "That's for God to judge, surely, not us." Would quoting scripture at her bring her back to her senses? I was reluctant to make it sound like I was calling her to repentance.

Emma turned back to me, and I could see her whole body shaking as she took in long, shallow breaths. What had she taken? Had a doctor prescribed something to keep her functioning? Had she started drinking Red Bull? Or was all this natural? "Whoever it was, she killed him. You think she should get away with that?" she demanded.

I tried to put a hand on her, but she pulled away. In that

moment, I could feel the rhythm of her tremors in my bones. There was something very wrong here. She needed serious help, and she didn't realize it. "No, but you need to let the police deal with this," I said. Advice Kurt would probably very much appreciate that I follow myself.

She started walking again, and I had to move swiftly after her to hear what she said next. "The police are doing nothing. All this time, and all they say is that he wasn't—that he—" Her voice strained and broke, and she started pounding her fists into her legs. It had to hurt, but she didn't seem to even notice.

I paused, trying to think of what Kurt could do for her. Could he force her into psychiatric care? As bishop, probably not.

"Emma, you need to think about who Carl really was. Who you were together. You knew him better than they did. You knew what a good man he was," I said firmly, echoing Kurt's words.

"Yes. He was a good man." She let out a little gasp. "Which is why I have to find her. She's the one who lured him into it. He would never have done anything like that unless someone pressured him. It had to be her fault."

"Sometimes good men make mistakes," I said. I didn't really want to argue this with her. I just wanted her to accept that it wasn't all some other woman's fault. If there had even been another woman.

"Not Carl. Not my Carl," Emma said fiercely.

"I'm sure that if you look carefully at your marriage, you will see some areas that were flawed," I said.

Emma lunged toward me and slapped my face.

My ears rang. She had a strong arm, I realized. A dangerous woman in a temper.

"Don't you dare say that again. We had a perfect marriage and Carl was the perfect husband. If there was a problem, it was her fault. And I know who it was now. I came tonight just to be sure. I was being fair, considering the others. But it was always her, always." Emma was breathing as heavily as if she were running. She whirled and started walking again, and I was genuinely worried she might break down and collapse, so I trotted to keep up with her, my face stinging in the night breeze.

"Who, Emma? Tell me who it is you think did this." I figured Kurt needed to know this. We might need to warn the woman or protect her in some way.

"I don't see any reason why I shouldn't tell everyone. It was Sheri Tate." Her hands clenched again.

"What? Sheri Tate has been so good to you. Why would you—?"

"She's *pretended* to be good to me to cover her guilt. Can't you see that? She came over that first night when Carl died. How did she know he was dead?" She turned her head to look at me, though she kept walking.

"Kurt called her and asked her to check on you," I said, suppressing the urge to laugh at this.

But Emma wasn't laughing. I don't think she even heard me. She looked like she was wandering through some new world no one could see but herself. "She used that first night to search the whole house. She had the chance to hide whatever she wanted to. If those letters hadn't been locked away, she would have found them, too."

Could she hear herself? How crazy she sounded? She had swung from one paranoia to another. But she probably hadn't been getting much sleep. She was stressed about her children.

And she had to rethink her whole life, forward and backward. I wanted to feel sympathetic for her, but she was making it difficult.

"Emma, please. I know you're grieving. Let me help you." I wanted to put my arms around her and cry with her. But she hurried the last few steps up her own driveway and onto the porch. She opened her front door and slammed it behind her.

I walked back to the church, putting my hands on my face to feel the heat there. I was too embarrassed to go back inside the church building looking like I had just been in a fight, so I drove home, thinking furiously about what to do next.

Later that night, I called Sheri Tate. Emma needed help, and Sheri should know that as Relief Society president, but she also needed to know enough to protect herself. Gossip inside the Mormon church could move alarmingly fast, and it wasn't easily forgotten.

Sheri's voice was calm. "I already suspected something like that, based on the way she talked to me tonight. But thanks for the heads up."

"What are you going to do?" I asked.

"Pray," she said. "And I hope you pray, too. Pray for her, and pray for me."

I tried, but I felt no resonant chime from the other end, no sense that the phone had been answered.

CHAPTER 26

Within two days, it was obvious to the whole ward what Emma's crazy suspicions were. She began to spread rumors about Sheri Tate and her husband in every way she could. I was glad that Samuel seemed too busy packing up his whole room to pay attention to any of it. The Mormon church's close-knit network of members showed its flaws now.

Emma had the contact information of every woman in the ward: cell phone numbers, email addresses, and home addresses. I got a glimpse of the message she sent around, a rant about Sheri Tate's "looseness," along with several unflattering photographs that made it look as if she were about to undress.

One of them I recognized as a photograph that had been taken at our annual swim party at the Dimple Dell outdoor pool last August. Sheri had worn a modest suit that was a little old and too loose around the chest. The person with the camera had probably not intended to embarrass Sheri, but had put all of the photos online and sent a link around to ward members a couple of days afterward. In one "action shot" of Sheri, I rather liked the relaxed expression on her face, but the pose, with her breasts hanging half out of the suit, might be seen as provocative.

I didn't know where the other photos had come from. One was of Sheri appearing to take off her shirt, though she might not have been. Another was of Sheri kissing a man whom I assumed was her brother, or perhaps a close male friend.

A second email came to me later, with a request for everyone who had been a "victim of this hussy's machinations" to respond with their own complaints. I saw two additions from women in the ward who added fuel to the fire, one claiming that Sheri had spent an hour talking to one of the young men in the ward after expressing interest in hiring him for a lawn care job. The other said that Sheri had spent a long time staring at another woman's husband at the church Christmas party last year.

There were a few voices on the other side, trying to defend Sheri, but they were outshouted by everyone outraged with her. When I had been in my atheist phase, I had attended several sessions of an atheist support group that met on Sundays. I had hoped that it would fulfill my need to attend church meetings. One of the other atheists I had met claimed that the worst vices of humanity were given license in religion, and top on her list was "gossip that was sanctioned as a call to repentance." I had thought about that critique on numerous occasions, never more so than now.

I forwarded everything I saw about Sheri to Kurt, though I wondered what in the world he could do about it. Then I tried to call Emma, but she wouldn't answer the phone. Was she screening all her calls or just not answering me?

Verity deRyke called me before I had a chance to call Sheri. "Have you seen these photographs?" she asked.

I was a little surprised that at her age she was tracking emails so closely. "Yes, I've seen them." I sighed heavily.

"This is terrible," said Verity. "A woman in our ward. A Relief Society president."

"They don't mean anything," I said, frustrated that Verity was on the side giving gossip credence.

"Then why do they look so raunchy?" she asked.

"You can make anything look raunchy if you frame even innocent actions the wrong way," I said.

Verity sniffed. "I'm not sure I believe that's true."

"What do you think should be done, then?" I said, more impatiently than I intended.

"I think that Tom and Kurt need to get together to pray about whether Sheri Tate is worthy to continue in her calling."

"And if she is?" I asked.

Verity said nothing for a long moment. "Well, then, I suppose we will have to forgive her."

It was a kinder tone than many ward members had taken online, but it still infuriated me. Sheri had done nothing wrong!

"I'll talk to Kurt," I said, and hung up.

But first, I called Sheri. "I am so sorry about this, Sheri," I began, so she wouldn't have to wonder what page I was on.

"I've seen the emails," she said. "People have been sending them to me under the guise of keeping me informed. I don't really believe it's out of kindness."

I felt sick at her wounded tone. Sheri Tate was not easily hurt. "It's a madness of some kind, but you must see that there are some people on your side, too." That was the only excuse I could offer.

"This is the reward I get for being Relief Society president."

Her voice was clipped and angry. "After all the hours I have spent helping the women of this ward. I've had to stop all my other volunteer work. I quit my part-time job. And all because I thought that what I was doing with the women of the ward really mattered. The last three years of my life, I listened to them tell me their problems. I gave advice. I cleaned houses, wiped up vomit and poop and everything you can imagine. I answered the phone in the middle of the night to deal with emergencies. I held women who were weeping. I helped with every project imaginable. And this is the thanks they return to me."

"You can't look at it that way, Sheri," I said.

"I am looking at it that way. I'm asking Kurt for a release, effective today. I need some time off, some time to recover. To see what I want to do next. See what I'm capable of doing next."

Technically, Kurt couldn't release her until Sunday. "It would be a terrible loss to the ward if you go," I said. For all my problems with her tendency to take the strict view on everything, she had been the best, most conscientious, and most capable Relief Society president I had seen in all my years of church service.

Sheri let out a long breath. "As long as this rumor is circulating, I can't do any good with the women in the ward anyway. They wouldn't trust me in their homes or with their secrets."

"Sheri, if you ask to be released now, you have to see how that will look." It would look as if she were admitting that the rumors were true. And Emma Ashby's worst side would triumph.

"I can't think about how it will look. I have to think about practicalities. The ward needs someone who can actually do the job without all this back biting."

"And what are you going to let Emma force you to do next? Move to another ward?" I asked. "Sell your house? Move out of state so that the rumors don't follow you? You've got to deal with them now. You should send around your own email. Or call everyone in the ward and tell your own story." Surely that would get her defenders to start speaking up more loudly.

"I'm too tired for that," she said, and for the first time in my memory, she did sound tired. "And too disheartened. They're all so eager to believe the worst of me. I feel like I'm living in a reality TV show." I could hear the cracks in her voice now, the end of her strength.

We were supposed to help each other in Relief Society. We were supposed to prove that women could be friends, no matter what their differences. This had all gone so wrong.

"You have to fight back," I said. But I wasn't even sure that was the right thing to do. Weren't we supposed to be turning the other cheek?

"Fight against Emma Ashby? How can I do that when she's the one still suffering? She lost her husband. I can't make her the villain in this."

"That doesn't excuse her," I said.

"No, but I just can't find it in my heart to push back at her. She's lashing out because she's hurting."

I was silenced for a long moment by this graciousness despite all. Then I said, "You are the better woman here, Sheri." I wanted her to know that I knew that, even if no one else did.

"Thank you for that, Linda," she said, and hung up.

I called Kurt then and told him about my conversation with

Sheri. He had already seen the emails. "Can you get President Frost involved? Or the Stake Relief Society Presidency?" I asked.

He sounded very sad and very tired. "I will contact them, Linda, but I don't know what they can do, either. We can have a talk in our next stake conference on the subject of gossip, or even have one of our Sunday combined meetings about it."

I knew as well as he did that the next stake conference wasn't for three months. "If you wait until then, it will be too late. They will all think they have a right to pass this specific example of gossip along because they think it's true, and they're shaming her into repentance."

Kurt was silent for a long moment. "Maybe I can do something before then if I get a few key people moving in the right direction. Peer pressure can be useful at times," he said at last. "We use it all the time, to get boys to go on missions, to finish their Eagle Scout award, to marry in the temple. We get girls to be modest like their friends, to attend regular church meetings, to go to camp."

And Sheri Tate was going to end up giving up her calling and retreating before any of that worked. Fine. Kurt had had his chance to act in the best interests of the ward. "I'm going to go talk to Emma," I announced. "Right now."

"Linda, please, don't do that," said Kurt.

"Why not? You're not going to. Sheri isn't going to." And Emma was the only one who could really put an end to this.

"What good could possibly come out of it?"

"Well, it can hardly get any worse," I said.

"I'm not so sure about that, Linda. If I come home right now, will you promise me you will wait until I get there? Then we can go over and talk to Emma together?"

"You promise we will go talk to her? You'll tell her what you think of these baseless attacks of hers?"

"Linda, I will talk to her about what she's done. I'm not going to argue with her, though. I'm not going to browbeat her either."

At least he was offering to do something, and I had the feeling that he would get further with Emma than I would. She liked him. "Get home fast," I said. "I don't know if I can wait."

We hung up, and then I walked out the door, deciding not to wait for him after all. I had my cell phone with me, but I turned it off and walked faster and faster. It was mostly downhill to Emma's, and I was in better shape than ever after a year of almost daily walks with Anna.

I KNOCKED LOUDLY on Emma Ashby's door, buoyed by a sense of righteous indignation.

I could hear footsteps within, but the door remained closed. Emma was hiding inside her own house and I couldn't allow that.

I put a hand on doorknob, and it turned. Emma hadn't thought to lock it because she hadn't thought anyone would just walk right into her house. We were all so used to leaving our doors unlocked because we trusted the other people in our neighborhood.

"Emma!" I called out.

I heard movement in the kitchen. Emma was standing next to the refrigerator, almost hugging it.

"I don't want you here," she said to me, her words imperious, but her tone much less so. "Please leave."

"Sheri Tate hasn't done anything wrong. What you did to

her with those emails is reprehensible," I said. My whole body was tensed.

Emma's eyes were red rimmed and wide. "She deserved that and more. She took my husband from me. She is a murderer!" The words came at me with spittle.

I wiped at my face. "Sheri didn't murder anyone," I said. Emma seemed to have remade everything in her own imagination.

I moved closer to her and she stepped back defensively. "The police haven't found anyone else. It has to be Sheri Tate," she said.

"What makes you think that?" I asked, not sure I could reason with her at all. Was that why Kurt had wanted me to stay away? Because he realized Emma Ashby was unhinged and there was no point in talking to her anymore?

"She had so many meetings with Carl. And I saw the way she looked at him." Emma nodded at her own words, adamant.

"Sheri is a good woman. She would never kill anyone," I said. The only thing that could make a woman like Sheri kill, I thought to myself, would be a threat to her own children. I might kill if it came to that. But I considered that instinct a virtue of proper motherhood, not a flaw.

"I want those letters back! I want to put them where everyone can see them!" said Emma. "I think they were from Sheri, but others can judge the truth."

"The letters are gone," I said. "You asked me to burn them, don't you remember?" Which I hadn't, but I didn't say that.

"No! How could you do that?" Emma said wildly. She let out a huge, shaking sob and buried her head in her hands.

I remained focused on what I had come for. "Emma, you have to apologize to Sheri for this." I was close enough to Emma now that I could touch her. She was backed into the corner by the refrigerator.

"She should apologize to me and my children! And then she should go to prison for the rest of her life!" said Emma. Her jaw was tight, the words indistinct, but loud and fierce.

Emma Ashby had made such a mess of our ward. All the bonds that Relief Society was supposed to nourish had been destroyed. And willfully. I found that I was now trembling in anger as I looked at Emma's defiant face.

I slammed my fist into her mouth. I could feel the skin splitting against my knuckles, and the warm blood oozing out. As soon as that happened, I was ashamed of myself. What had I been thinking?

Emma groaned and fell to the floor.

I might have bent over and tried to help her, but before I had a chance to move, I felt myself pinned from behind.

"Linda, stop!" I heard Kurt's voice in my ear.

He dragged me out of the house and then locked me in his truck. I saw him go back inside. He was ashamed of me, and I was ashamed of myself, too. But I wasn't sure I had been entirely wrong.

Several long minutes later, Kurt returned and unlocked the truck and got in.

"I told you not to go to her house alone," he said, looking straight ahead, his voice stern. Now he was the parent and I was the child.

"She's dangerous," I said, knowing it was justification.

"Linda, she could make a statement to the police and send

you to jail for assault. You were trespassing on her property and she certainly has evidence of how you hurt her."

"I know," I said. "I have no excuse for doing that." But I hoped it would make her think twice about gossiping about another woman in the ward just the same.

CHAPTER 27

For the rest of the week, Emma told everyone who asked her that it was Sheri Tate who had accosted her. I meant to correct anyone who talked to me about it directly, but no one did. I admit, I didn't send out an email to the whole ward admitting my guilt because I thought it would be playing the same game. And also, Kurt asked me not to, at least not like that. Besides, it seemed Emma's ranting had become so outrageous that people had stopped believing her. Even Verity called and said she thought something had to be done to rein Emma in.

On Sunday, I stayed home from church, depressed about the whole situation. I hadn't cooked in a whole week, so I was in the kitchen, making myself hot chocolate with whipped cream and some fresh snickerdoodle cookies, when the doorbell rang.

I was afraid that it might be messengers Kurt had sent, ward members who were skipping a meeting to cheer me up. But it was Sheri Tate. And she wasn't dressed in church clothes any more than I was. I tried to remember a time I had seen her dressed in sweatpants and a torn T-shirt but couldn't think of one.

I opened the door and let her into the kitchen.

Before I asked her why she was here, I made her a cup of hot chocolate—the real stuff from milk and chocolate chips, not from the powder in a can. Whipped cream on top and a plate of fresh, hot cookies.

She didn't take more than a sip and a tiny bite, but I thought I could see her shoulders relax just a little. Sugar therapy. I should have tried it on Emma Ashby.

"They're releasing me today, but I couldn't go," said Sheri.

I felt a wave of anger like a hot flash, and had to breathe through it.

"I heard about what you did to Emma. I even saw the photos of her face that she posted online, though she said it was me who did it. I knew the truth. Thank you," she said.

I wondered who had told her. Kurt? Who else knew? "You're thanking me? Why are you thanking me? I made things a hundred times worse."

"They were already so horrible, I'm pretty sure they couldn't have gotten worse. And you let me feel the satisfaction of revenge without having to feel guilty about doing it myself." Sheri's lips twisted into a smirk.

She and I had never been particularly friendly, but I felt a companionable warmth toward her now, a fondness that comes from knowing someone well. "No, you are definitely not guilty for that." I was glad she'd come.

"Did it feel good?" she asked, her eyes alight.

I thought back. "For a moment, I suppose." I had felt like God's avenging angel, but the feeling had faded now.

Sheri spread out her hands on the countertop and stared at them. They were sunspotted, wrinkled—the hands of a woman whose life had not been easy. "I don't know what I'm going to do next. I can't imagine a future where we stay here, but I can't imagine leaving, either. Everyone and everything we know is here. But it's all changed now."

"What does Grayvon say?" I asked. Her children were all grown and out of the house now. Perdita had married last year, and she was the youngest. Sheri's husband—thin as a rail and nearly seven feet tall—was a quiet, almost painfully shy man. He worked for the city government as a surveyor. When Sheri was around, Grayvon tended to fade into the background. Even when she wasn't around, actually.

"He says that it's up to me. But I think he wants to go. I've embarrassed him too much."

Her hair was straggly and in her face, and I realized how much time she must have normally spent on it to make it look full and bouncy.

"I don't know when I will be able to go back to church," I said. "But since Kurt is bishop, I suppose I'll eventually have to." We were not going to be moving.

"Look at it this way: no one knows what you did," said Sheri.

"Hmm. Which is worse, people thinking that you did something you didn't? Or people not knowing you did something you did? Is it better to have dishonor but no guilt or guilt but no dishonor?"

Sheri shook her head. "That's the problem. You think I'm innocent. That's why I had to come over to see you today. This is what God insists that I do today—confess to you."

Confess? I stared at her face, which was gradually suffused with color. She should've been with the bishop, not the bishop's wife, if she truly had something to confess.

"I didn't have an affair with Carl Ashby, but I flirted with him. What Emma thought she saw between us wasn't nonexistent."

"You—and Carl Ashby?" I managed to say, spitting out the sip of hot chocolate I'd been about to swallow. At least I hadn't choked on it.

Carl had been loyal enough to Emma to share a marriage without sex, but he had let Sheri Tate flirt with him? Was it just an ego boost, or had he intended to follow through with it somehow?

Sheri looked at her hands for a long moment. "I touched his arm on several occasions. I hugged him twice. You know, in a way that might have looked too long to observers. And we had several meetings at the church that weren't about anything other than us sitting together, talking about our lives and sharing things that we shouldn't have been."

And that was what she felt guilty about? She thought that justified her being forced out of her home and humiliated in public?

I didn't understand any of this. If Carl had wanted something he couldn't get from Emma, wouldn't it have been sexual? Would his relationship with Sheri have led to that, eventually? Would she have wanted that? Was there something sexual missing in her marriage as well? Or was this just about them both enjoying the tiniest bit of the forbidden?

"I'm sure you think horribly of me now, and it's just what I deserve. Even the police treated me as a suspect for a while there." Sheri was gripping the cup so tightly that the handle broke off. Hot chocolate splashed everywhere and she cursed as she tried to mop it up with a towel. I was shocked at the cursing from Sheri Tate, by far the most Molly of all the Mormons I knew.

"Why would the police have treated you as a suspect?" I asked. But as soon as I considered it, I realized that Sheri would have had access to the church that night. She could have lured Carl there on some pretext or another.

She shook her head, the color in her face fading. "Carl and I had set up a time to meet and talk there that night, but I texted him at the last minute and told him I couldn't make it. But I guess he didn't get the text in time, because he went there anyway."

I took the dirty towel from her and bunched it up in a pile on the counter. "So you didn't go to the church?" I asked.

"No." Sheri brushed her sweats and put her hands on the counter, folded neatly like we were in Primary and she was demonstrating proper behavior for the youngest kids there, the Sunbeams.

"Where were you, then?" I asked, feeling ridiculous about asking. If I couldn't believe in Sheri Tate as an adulteress, how could I believe she was a murderer?

"Grayvon and I spent the night watching a movie on television," she said.

"The letters?" I blurted out, without thinking about how old they were, far too old for her recent flirting with Carl. But she might have been lying about all of that. "Did you write those, too?"

"What letters?" Sheri said, looking up at me, her head tilted.

"You never wrote Carl any love letters?"

"No. Of course not. That would have been stupid. You don't put down thoughts like that on paper. Someone might find them," said Sheri.

Someone *had* found those letters. Emma.

Sheri sighed. "I keep thinking, if I hadn't encouraged Carl—if I hadn't set up that meeting with him at the church—he might still be alive now. He was only there that night because of me. Whoever murdered him had the chance because of me. If it was a burglary, he was only killed because he happened to be there at the wrong time, when he should have been home with his family."

I pressed my hand on top of hers. She was right about that. I couldn't deny it. It didn't make her a murderer, but it made her guilty of something.

I could feel a slight shudder pass through Sheri. "After everything she's done to me, I have a hard time feeling sympathy for Emma, but I feel for those children. I wish I could do something for them, but I'm just running away now. I need to be alone and think about things." She stood up and I followed her.

At the door, I hugged Sheri tightly. "I'm so sorry for all of this."

"Are you? Even still?" she asked. There was a hollowness in her voice. Would she ever forgive herself for this?

"Even still. I have always admired you, Sheri. Even when we disagreed. This doesn't change that."

She began to sob, her body limp against mine in the embrace. "It does change it. It takes everything away. Any good I've ever done is gone."

"No, Sheri, it isn't," I said, as I wondered about my own good deeds and how much I had diminished them with what I had done to Emma.

CHAPTER 28

Anna called on Monday but I didn't answer my phone. I let myself lie in bed and eat soup and watch trashy old Cary Grant movies all day. I'd always hated *Suspicion*, but after watching Emma Ashby in real life, I found I was now fascinated by it and watched certain scenes over and over again, trying to catch the lies and the facial tics that gave everything away.

Samuel looked in on me a couple of times and brought me the raspberry hibiscus herbal tea he knew I loved, but he was busy putting his boxes in our storage room in the basement, just as our other sons had done with everything they'd wanted to keep safe after graduating from high school. It was a graveyard of childhood treasures, things that I knew they were unlikely ever to take with them in the future. But Kurt and I held onto them anyway. Inside those boxes was the physical evidence of all our years of parenting, for good or ill.

By Tuesday morning Samuel had moved nearly everything out, leaving Kurt and me truly alone in our big house. Anna called again and I made myself answer and set up a time for a walk.

"I got those terrible emails about Sheri Tate. I tried to counter them as best I could," said Anna as we started out on our usual walk around the neighborhood.

"I don't want to talk about them," I bit out.

"You always say that when you actually need to talk and don't know how to begin," Anna said, proving how well she knew me. Her long, gray hair was out of its normal ponytail so that it was dancing in the wind. She looked utterly carefree, and I was jealous of that.

"Then the truth is, I can't talk about it. It's not mine to share." It was a good excuse for avoiding Anna's judgment, at least, though I had shared plenty of other things with Anna I probably shouldn't have. Technically, Sheri Tate's confession to me had been personal, with no hint of church authority in it. If she had wanted guaranteed discretion, she should have gone to Kurt.

"Well, then," said Anna.

We walked in silence for a few minutes. I wasn't sure I was ready for the big hill yet, but here it was anyway.

"I will admit that I have something that's been weighing on me since before we met, and it's time that I tell you," Anna said.

I was surprised enough to stop in my tracks. "Is it a bad thing?" I asked.

She didn't answer, but motioned for me to keep walking with her. We were in silence for several blocks before Anna began again.

"When I read those emails," she said finally, "I thought about how devastating it would be to have all the truth come out like that. Even if Sheri Tate was guilty, and I have no reason to believe that she is, to have all her worst deeds thrown in her face. And then to have to look people in the eyes . . ."

I made a noncommittal sound. We had finally crested the hill and were right on the mountain. In the fall, it was colored red and gold, but now it was all shades of green and brown and gray, a combination unique to Utah.

"But I'm not talking about Sheri right now. I'm talking about me." She stopped walking and looked out over the lake, as if she were confessing to it, and not to me. "I've never told anyone this before, but a few years after we were married, I felt like Tobias was ignoring me. I realize now that he had his own worries, but at the time, I was hurt and angry and I told myself I had license to cheat on him. I wanted to hurt him, and I looked around for someone to hurt him with."

"You cheated on Tobias?" I said in a whisper. Anna? I would never have guessed it. Not in all the eternities.

"It was a short-lived thing, just a couple of weeks. I think we slept together four times all in all. It was just sex. Just his bits and my bits. It was mechanics, like a recipe in a book. You know?"

I felt sick for a moment.

It is terrible to violate marriage vows for anyone in any marriage, but especially in a marriage between Mormons, who believe that the procreative power is as close to godhood as we can ever get—so this news was shocking to me, even if Anna and Tobias had never had their marriage sealed forever in the temple.

Had she ever confessed her sin? Did she still have a temple recommend? Anna might say it was just about "bits," but this was enough for some people to be excommunicated. I loved Anna, and I feared for her soul.

Facing the wind, Anna spread her arms like wings for just a moment before letting them fall helplessly to her sides. "I can't make excuses for myself. What I discovered was that trying to hurt Tobias hurt me more than anything he could have done. I didn't enjoy any of it, not a moment. I was miserable."

There was a long silence as I tried to take this in. "Did Tobias know? Did you ever talk to a bishop?" I asked finally.

A car sped by below us, going down the hill loudly. She waited until it passed to speak, shaking her head sadly. "No. I never told a bishop or Tobias. I talked to God about it instead. I know that sounds heretical, but I was worried that a bishop's intervention would only make things worse."

I was sure Kurt would be furious about this if he knew. Forgiveness for a serious sin like this could only come through confessing to the proper authority according to Mormon doctrine. But why shouldn't Anna deal with it in her own way, talking to God herself, and making amends her own way? Was it because she was a woman that she had to have a man mediate her repentance?

"If I'd told Tobias," she said, "he would have had to work on forgiving me, which would have caused him so much pain. I know he would have eventually done it. He was too big a man with too big a heart not to. But it seemed unfair to place such a burden on him when the sin was mine."

If I had done the same to Kurt, could I believe he would have forgiven me, too?

He might have forgiven me, but it would have taken a long time. I could understand why Anna had never told Tobias, why she had chosen to carry the pain herself.

"Tobias would have felt I was telling him he was inadequate," Anna went on. "It would have haunted him. I don't think he would ever have recovered. And I couldn't do that to him." She shrugged. "So I never did. If I was ever angry that our marriage was based on lies for so long, I reminded myself it was all my fault."

It sounded to me like Anna had suffered plenty in her repentance, and that what she had done had been out of love for Tobias, not out of a desire to make herself look better. I couldn't give her any absolution, but I found that I loved her more than ever. How was that possible? Did we love people in spite of their flaws or because of them?

We started walking again, very slowly, down the hill. I let my hand brush against Anna's as our arms swayed back and forth in the same rhythm, then caught and held her fingers up to my cheek. Somehow it seemed to be the only way to show her how much I cared for her. I could feel the heat in her hand, her quickened pulse. She wasn't crying visibly, but the emotion was there, just the same.

"Sometimes I wish that you could be the one I confess to," said Anna. "Instead of Kurt. Women maybe need another woman who understands."

I thought of Sheri Tate, who'd done that very thing. But that wasn't my place as the bishop's wife. I had no official role and no priesthood power. Did that mean that I couldn't be inspired, as well?

"I wish you could put your hands on my head and give me a blessing right now," Anna said.

"Me?" I asked, confused. I'd always known Anna was a bit of an iconoclast, but this went beyond skipping Relief Society meetings during the week and talking about Ordain Women leader Kate Kelly with sympathy.

"In the temple, women put hands on women and bless them. I don't see why it's not the same outside the temple." She looked at me directly.

I was the one who flinched away. Because it wasn't the same. We both knew it wasn't. She was talking heresy now, the very thing likely to get someone excommunicated from the church—all temple sealings canceled, no longer allowed to speak to or serve the ward family.

"You're always talking about how women need to take more power within Mormonism," said Anna, her head tilted to the side so that it caught the light from the rising sun just so—it almost made me think of Eve in the temple film that was essentially the story of the Garden of Eden.

"I do talk about women taking power," I said. But I didn't mean giving priesthood blessings—did I?

Anna started walking again. Her tone was more confident now. "Women are the reason I have stayed in the Mormon church all this time. My connection with other women, and the way I feel that we are the same when we worship together. Isn't that true for you, too?"

I thought about it, and realized that I didn't know. I had come back to the Mormon church years ago because I wanted—something. And then I'd found Kurt. I guess that for me, my religion had been about family. But it wouldn't be the same for everyone.

Anna squeezed my arm. "You're always thinking about how to follow the rules, or how to twist them to fit a situation. But someone else's rules are never going to make you perfect."

We walked back to her house and I was left with a lot to think about.

CHAPTER 29

I called Detective Gore that Tuesday afternoon and told her about the letters that Emma had given me. After everything that had happened, and with my new doubts about Emma, I couldn't hold the letters back anymore.

Detective Gore came to pick up the letters herself, though I offered to bring them in to the precinct.

"Emma Ashby gave these to you?" she asked as she looked through them. We were sitting on the couch in the front room. She showed no sign of discomfort or embarrassment reading them, as I had. I suppose if you were a police officer and then a detective, you got used to much worse things than sitting on strangers' couches and looking through someone else's explicit correspondences.

"She asked me to burn them," I said.

"You don't think she gave them to you wanting you to give them to the police?" said Detective Gore.

I took a breath. That had been a possibility I had never considered. "I don't know," I said. Was Emma Ashby that calculating? Before the email campaign against Sheri Tate, I would have said no. Could she have written them all herself?

And planted them after the police had searched her house, looking for evidence against her? I suppose she might have done it to point the finger at someone else. And I had gone right along with it.

"Do you know Carl Ashby's handwriting?"

I shrugged. "A little bit. But I'm not an expert."

"Did she tell you where she had found these?" Her scrutiny made me squirm.

"In his drawers," I said.

Detective Gore shook her head. "We would have found them in the search. Tell me, what is your impression of her relationship with her husband? Do you think that she had any reason to doubt his fidelity before he was murdered?" She seemed so matter-of-fact.

"There was something wrong between them," I admitted. "I overheard a conversation when I was on the phone with Emma. At the time, I almost wondered if Carl was abusive. He was saying something about his rights and her duties to him." Was that right? I wasn't sure anymore.

"What if I were to tell you that Emma Ashby had moved a large sum of money out of their joint account and into her personal account a week before her husband was murdered?" she asked, watching me carefully.

I tried not to show my surprise at this. "How much?"

"More than two million dollars," said Detective Gore.

"What?" I was shocked.

"There was ten million dollars in various accounts, mostly under his name. I believe the money was from an invention he patented some twenty years ago. A medical device used by doctors during difficult childbirths."

I was surprised to hear the nature of Carl's invention. I

wondered if it had been inspired by his own experience. Of course he'd never told anyone the details.

The detective went on, her dark eyes boring into mine. "Carl Ashby's will was written some years ago, and it divides the money between his wife and his children. But his lawyer claims that Carl recently called about changing the will, about six weeks ago. Do you know anything about that?"

I shook my head. Carl wouldn't have cut Emma and the children out of his will himself on legal grounds, would he? That would have outed him as legally female himself.

"He apparently never got around to changing the will before he died. But the fact that he wanted to means something. I don't know what to think of these letters . . ." She held them up. "You Mormons hold things awfully close to the chest. You're the most forthcoming Mormon I've interviewed, and you're no open book."

I could hardly blame her for her disdainful tone, considering.

"And then there's the community interference. Everyone sticking their nose in, telling me how to do my job. I don't much like it." Detective Gore spoke slowly, choosing her words deliberately, watching me in a way that made me wonder if she was telling me this for my benefit or for her own. "The chief tells me I can't go after my prime suspect because she's an innocent housewife. He knows because a friend of his who is a fellow Mormon told him."

Was she trying to make me feel ashamed of my own religion? Well, it was working.

She went on. "Can't let out certain pieces of information to the press. Too inflammatory. And now I'm pushed into cleaning things up because there's a big mess. And it's all my fault, somehow, because I didn't do my job after I was told I couldn't do my job."

This was about President Frost. He was nervous about the fallout in our ward and the surrounding stake if the details of the case came to light. I hated to believe that Gore was right about Emma, but my doubts about her had been mounting for a while. Clearly, Gore was trying to get me to break rank and spill my community's secrets, to feel like I was doing the right thing by helping her when no one else would.

I guess I was another stonewalling Mormon, though, because I didn't say anything to her about Sheri Tate, or Grant Rhodes, or William Ashby. I felt like I should protect them all somehow. Why? Because they were members of the ward, and I was the bishop's wife.

"Well, thank you for these, in any case," she said. "If there's nothing else you want to tell me?" She waited for a long moment.

I shook my head. "I'm sorry," I said.

"I will talk to you again, I'm sure, Mrs. Wallheim," she said, and left.

CHAPTER 30

I didn't say anything to Kurt about what Detective Gore had implied about President Frost and the chief of police, but I did tell him about Emma's transferring money out of the accounts she shared with Carl.

"I'm sure there's a good reason for that," said Kurt, but he didn't suggest what one might be. I wondered if Detective Gore's problems with Mormon interference were from more than President Frost, and I stopped talking because I didn't want her to have to deal with more pressure about the subject of Emma Ashby.

On Wednesday, Samuel offered to come over and have lunch with me at home. It should have been lovely, but I expended all my energy trying not to cry over him. He seemed to be adjusting to his new apartment life just fine. He had been open with his roommates about being gay, and they were all welcoming, at least for now. He was going through mission papers with his new bishop instead of with Kurt, which I thought was a good idea, too. That way, he didn't have to talk about anything uncomfortable with his father—not that I thought he had anything he needed to confess. But just in case.

When he left again, I let myself cry noisily in my room. Afterward, I felt hollowed out and pitiful, sure this was the end of my life. Which was why I went back to poking around in the Carl Ashby murder.

THAT AFTERNOON, ALICE Ashby came to see me. It was as if God had been listening to me complain about Samuel being gone. I felt needed as soon as I opened the door. Alice looked too thin. Hungry. And that was one thing I knew how to fix. I asked her into the kitchen and offered her a fresh batch of my patented whole-wheat gingersnaps, made completely out of food storage supplies: molasses, whole wheat flour, oil, and a giant container of spices. In an apocalypse, not only would we not starve, we'd live well.

They were Samuel's favorites. If he were here, he would have eaten a whole dozen by himself. Maybe I could replace his hungry mouth with a few others, and keep going on as I had before. But Alice ate a few cookies, then put a hand to her stomach.

"What can I do for you, besides give you a stomachache?" I asked, though I could have guessed the answer.

"I just wanted someone to talk to. Someone who isn't—"

Her mom, I thought.

"—who isn't pushing me about a long list of things I should be doing when all I can think about is my dad being dead and my whole life making no sense at all." She looked at me with real confusion in her eyes.

Poor girl. "Well, maybe it's a good thing you have the summer off right now. So you can spend some time healing before school starts again."

"And then I'm supposed to care about school and grades

and stupid assignments and tests again?" said Alice. "What about right now? All my friends want to talk about is clothes and sleeping in and watching stupid YouTube videos. Or kissing boys. I can't stand to hear about them. It just makes me want to float away in some hot-air balloon where I can look down and see all the people like tiny ants below me." She raised a hand to the air.

That kind of detachment didn't sound good. "You can focus on one thing at a time," I suggested. That's the way I'd survived Georgia's death, with lists of concrete things I could do to get through each day. But she didn't have people depending on her in quite the same way I had. "Maybe you could study for the ACT and SAT for a little while each day."

"Why? To get into college? What's the point?" she said. "As soon as I'm twenty-one, I'll get all the money Dad left for us. It's not like I'm ever going to have to work. I can do whatever I want and Mom can't stop me. What kind of a job is going to earn me more than the interest I'll get from Dad's money?"

"So, do you want to live off your dad's money, or do you want to make your own life?" I asked bluntly. It was one thing to be in mourning. It was something else to ruin her future while she was doing that.

"My own life? Yeah, right. There are seven billion people on the planet. How can one more or less matter?" said Alice dully. She pushed the plate away and started tapping absently at the tabletop.

"One life can matter, if it's lived deliberately. If you live with an aim of making a difference in the world," I said.

"No one makes a real difference in the world," Alice said softly.

I looked at her, this sad girl with so much of her life in

disarray, whose own mother had nothing to offer her right now, no guidance or support. I tried not to think of Georgia, who never got to be Alice's age, but I said to Alice what I would have said to one of my own children. "Why don't you stop telling me about how most people don't matter and start thinking about your own choices? What are your dreams?"

Alice let out a long breath and shrugged elaborately. "Dad wanted me to become a doctor."

"I didn't ask what your dad wanted." Was she so used to being told how to think that she couldn't even tell me what she wanted? No wonder she thought her life insignificant.

"Mom thinks medical school is too hard, and besides, working a doctor's hours would mean I couldn't be a mother. She says maybe a nurse. But that's almost as hard to do, and the hours aren't great, either."

I had known several Mormon women who were doctors in my life, and they seemed to manage motherhood and a demanding job, as long as they had husbands and other family members who were understanding. Nursing was just as difficult as being a doctor, as far as I knew, but it paid less and got less cred.

"Do you like science?" I asked. "Do you like computers? Do you like working with people?"

Another shrug. "I don't know," she said. "I don't think I really like anything."

That distance again. I decided to try from another angle. "What subjects are you good at in school?" I asked.

"I get straight As in everything," said Alice.

"But what do you like? What do you get excited about doing?"

Instead of a shrug, she said, "I hate homework. All of it. But I do it, and then it's done."

"And what do you do after it's done?" I asked. There had to be something underneath all her lack of caring. Somewhere.

"I go shopping with Mom sometimes. Or call up friends. Or do my nails."

I didn't want to give her the impression that it wasn't enough to do those things. But I had the feeling there was more, suppressed inside her for some reason.

"What about William?" I tried. "What do you think he's going to do with his life?"

"Oh, he complains about everything. He hates school as much as I do."

"But what does he like?" I asked. "What do you think he would be really good at? I mean, if you could design a future life for him, what would you have him do?" Give someone the chance to pick out a present for someone else, and you learn a lot about them. I used to do this with Samuel, the only son of mine who refused to make a list of things he wanted for Christmas or birthdays. But he was happy to pick things out for his brothers. Somewhere in what he wanted for them, I could see what he wanted for himself.

"Well, if William listened to me at all, he would think about joining the Air Force. He has always wanted to fly airplanes. When he was little, you could see him just light up when he saw a jet overhead. When Dad went on a trip and we picked him up at the airport, it was like William forgot about everything else but the jets."

"So why doesn't he sign up for an ROTC program for the Air Force?" Hill Air Force Base was in Layton, and that was only about forty minutes north of here.

I got a full eye roll from Alice at that. "Mom wouldn't have it. It's too dangerous. She doesn't want to worry about him every moment for the rest of her life. She doesn't even like it when I go out driving. And now she says that William has forfeited his right to get a driver's license at sixteen. He has to wait until he's eighteen *and* he has to have his A1c below seven point five, which is even harder than the eight the doctors say."

I assumed this must have something to do with his diabetes, and the insulin levels a patient needed to maintain to drive safely without risking diabetic shock. "And you don't think that sounds sensible after what already happened?" I asked, not mentioning Grant Rhodes directly.

Alice waved her hands in the air, using up her own nervous energy. "William needs something exciting. He needs to push himself. Dad would try to play football with him to get out some of the energy, but now that he's gone, I can see William just blowing up at random things. He needs an outlet. But Mom thinks that every time he does something wrong, she should just punish him more."

Was William in danger? Maybe, but at the moment I really needed to get Alice to open up to me. I couldn't help her if I didn't know more.

"And what would William say that you wanted?" I asked.

"William? He doesn't know what I want. He doesn't pay attention to me. I'm just a girl," she said, as if this were a perfectly reasonable attitude for him to have.

Hadn't her father or mother ever taken William to task about it? I guessed not, after what I'd heard from Carl at the bishopric dinner. "Then what would your friends say you wanted?"

A shrug. "Clothes and makeup and maybe plastic surgery," she said.

Again, only things that related to her appearance. Because clothes and makeup were what she loved? Or because that was what she thought a woman had to be? Interesting, considering that her father had been the one to worry most about appearances. "Are you unhappy with how you look?" I asked.

A snort. "No one is happy with how they look. Not really."

Truer than I wished it was. "Maybe you should think about a career in fashion design. Or being a makeup artist," I said.

Alice made a face. "Helping people do things they shouldn't care about? Making life even more expensive for them?" She shook her head. "My mom would hate that."

"Oh? What else would your mom hate you doing?" I had the feeling I had almost hit the geyser here. It had taken long enough.

"Theater. Art. Anything that has to do with playacting. I guess she would also hate it if I did commercials or modeling or something like that."

With her body, Alice might make it as an actress. She was thin enough, and she had a beautiful face. But would it make her happy?

"Do you feel like your mom wouldn't be able to support your dream, then, if your dream was to be an actress?"

Another shrug. "She just wants to protect me, I think. She says that when I get married, what will matter are organizational skills and homemaking and money management."

Alice's tone sounded as if she was talking about sewage treatment.

I had always wanted a daughter. But what would I do if my daughter were like this, prickly and uncertain? She had described William as being in a prison, but she was in one, too. I wanted to give her wings to fly wherever she wanted to go. I wanted to give her what I would have given my own daughter.

"Do you want to take a break from your house? Live somewhere else for a while?" I asked. "You could come here. We have space, now that Samuel has moved out." My heart felt tight at the thought.

"What?" Alice said. "What are you talking about?"

"I just mean, if you need some space. I think I could help your mother understand." I really didn't think I could. But I thought I might make Kurt do the dirty work for me and go talk to Emma. What would Kurt say about me inviting the teen daughter of another ward member into our home, just days after our youngest son had moved out? Was I afraid of having my own life? Did I need to be a mother in order to feel like I had any value? Or had I just been doing this mothering thing so long it had become a habit I couldn't break?

"Move in here?" Suddenly, Alice was looking around the house as if evaluating it, and I noticed how shabby it was. We hadn't done any major home improvements since we moved in when Joseph was a baby. "But what about William?" she asked, shaking her head. "I couldn't leave him. Or Mom. She needs us."

Yes, but what did Alice and William need?

"Well, he could come, too," I said blithely. In for a penny, in for a pound, right? "Or you could go over every day for a few hours during the summer, or after school during the school year. Whatever you decided would work best for you."

Alice shook her head. "That would kill Mom. She lives for us."

Right. And I so much wanted to see myself as different from Emma Ashby, stronger and more independent. Was I?

"Well, you can come talk to me whenever you want, then. I hope you know that. You and William both," I said.

"Thank you," said Alice. "I'll think about it." She walked out of the house with her back a little straighter. I told myself that was all I wanted.

CHAPTER 31

Kurt came home very late on Thursday night. He often looked worn after his weekly interviews, but he was dragging his feet a little, as if he'd forgotten how heavy they were, and his eyes looked puffy with rubbing.

"Bad day?" I asked.

"Good and bad," said Kurt.

There had been a good part?

"President Frost got word today that we're not to redo any of Carl Ashby's priesthood ordinations, after all."

I leapt up from my seat. I'd have danced if I knew how to dance. "That *is* good news," I said. What kind of bad news had made Kurt droop in comparison to that?

"We spent hours making that list, but Tom and I never got around to calling people to set up appointments. It's confirmation that I can feel the Spirit sometimes, I suppose. I just felt wrong about the whole thing, from the moment President Frost insisted on it. I was trying not to show him I was dragging my feet, but I was."

I had never heard Kurt criticize one of his church leaders before. I wasn't sure this was even a criticism, the way that he put it. But it was skirting close to it.

"Tom and I had to explain Carl's birth gender to Brad, or else he would have been completely confused about the list we were making. You know, Brad never once got upset about it. He didn't seem to think it was anything to blink an eye at."

Good for Brad. And good for Kurt, too. He'd been almost respectful in mentioning Carl's past.

"So what's the bad news?" I asked after a moment, stroking Kurt's hair and wishing that we could just find a space to leave all of this behind and be a married couple again, without the whole congregation of the ward seeming to follow us around wherever we went.

Kurt shook his head and sat down, pulling away from me slightly. "It was after President Frost called. I'm still trying to figure out how I could have let it happen. I had a great spiritual moment of feeling God's approval, and then it was gone in an instant."

"I'm sure you did what you had to do," I said, trying to be reassuring.

Kurt snorted. "I had asked Grant Rhodes to come in at the end of all my other interviews. And after we'd been talking almost an hour, I told him what I thought of his choices, things you know about and some other things he told me." Kurt's voice was harsh. "I told him he was not to return to our ward. I told him to go back to his own ward or he would have to find someone else willing to take him in."

I was sure Grant Rhodes had done something to bring on Kurt's outburst. "What did he say to you?"

Kurt shook his head. "I don't know if I can tell you or not. I can't decide if it falls under my obligation to keep silent or not. He was so angry when I was finished, I had to get Brad Ferris to physically remove him from my office. He fought back, breaking the chair he was in and kicking in the wall. Brad ended up getting hurt as much as Grant did, I think."

This had certainly never happened to Kurt as bishop before. I rubbed his shoulders, feeling their tension under my hands. "Did you call the police?"

Kurt shook his head ruefully. "No, but I probably should have. I may regret that choice for months." His stomach grumbled and I decided maybe I should deal with that and leave the rest until he was ready to talk.

"Can I get you something to eat?" I said.

When Kurt didn't say no, I went and got him food anyway. He needed to get some calories in.

But before I got back, his cell phone was ringing.

I came in and set the cookies down as he answered it. "Oh, that's wonderful. Just wonderful," he said sarcastically. "Yes. Fine. I understand." He hung up.

"Who was that?" I said.

Kurt turned, smiling widely, a rictus grin.

"The police," he said. "Grant Rhodes went in to sign a petition against me." He emphasized the last word with outrage.

"But I thought you said it was Brad Ferris who made him leave." I didn't see any scrapes or bruises on Kurt at all.

"It was, but I'm not going to throw my new and very young second counselor to the wolves in his first month in the bishopric. He did what I asked him to do. I'm the one Grant is angry with, and I'm the one who should face the music." His jaw was set so tight that only a crowbar could've loosened it.

I put my hand on his shoulder. I wanted him to know that I was here with him, for him. "So what's going to happen now?"

"The police want to come interview me. Grant went to the hospital to have his injuries documented."

"But surely if they see the damage to the bishop's office, they'll realize it was all in self-defense," I said. "Not to mention Brad probably has injuries he could get documented, too."

"I suppose," said Kurt sourly. "But how do you think it will look to the rest of the ward if that's their introduction to the new member of the bishopric's handling interviews with the bishop?"

That was a good point.

NEAR MIDNIGHT, THE police came to our home to ask Kurt questions. There was no detective among them, just uniforms. Kurt lied valiantly to shield Brad Ferris, and I didn't contradict him, though I thought the lack of injury on Kurt's body might be brought up. Somehow, it wasn't. They didn't ask to see the physical evidence at the bishop's office, either. I didn't know what to make of that.

Kurt and I finally climbed into bed sometime past 2 A.M.

"Should we call President Frost?" I asked in the dark, my words like a cloud of breath between us.

I heard a choked bit of laughter from Kurt. "You know, President Frost advised me from the beginning to encourage Grant Rhodes to return to his home ward, and to make sure that he was not allowed to participate openly here. He said he had a feeling Grant was a troublemaker. I prayed about it and felt pity for the wardless man. Pity, can you imagine?" A strange, tight smile appeared again on his face as he reached for the light switch.

"Are you going to give me a hint about what Grant Rhodes told you?" I knew something specific had provoked Kurt to react the way he had.

Kurt sighed, and then said, as if it were still hard for him to get the words out, "Since he's not technically in our ward and I will probably have to tell the police anyway, I'll tell you. He admitted that he and Carl had resumed their love affair from college days. The last week of Carl's life, they were having sex at the church building and at Grant's house."

I thought about Sheri Tate's revelation that she had planned to meet Carl at the church that night. Apparently, Carl had made other plans. I began to see why Kurt had been driven past his normal limits. The discovery that his own counselor had been transgender and hiding the fact from his own family was shocking enough; but now Kurt had just learned that Carl Ashby had been defiling the church building with an extramarital sexual liaison, and with another man to boot. Or had it been a heterosexual affair, technically? Did it depend on what exactly they'd done? Had Grant told Kurt details like that?

"If Carl weren't dead, he would be facing a disciplinary council," said Kurt. "Breaking his temple covenants and his marriage vows, unrighteous priesthood use, lies and deceit, on and on. I told him I didn't think he should be wearing his temple garments anymore because he was unworthy and insisted that as soon as he was called up to a council, he'd be denied the privilege."

"And that's when he got violent?" I asked.

Kurt hesitated a moment, and then admitted, "I yanked the sleeve out of his shirt, to make a point, I suppose. So I touched him first. I didn't hit him first, though." His cheeks were now dotted with red. Who does the Mormon bishop confess to? Some people would say the stake president, but in this case, it seemed he confessed to his wife.

Kurt went into work that morning, but I could tell he was still worried about what would happen with the police and

Grant Rhodes. Then he called me and said that the police had asked him to turn himself in, because Grant was pressing charges. He asked me to call Brother Carrington, a lawyer in the ward, to come act as his counsel. I was humiliated for him, though he seemed to be pretty calm about it all.

After I hung up with Brother Carrington, who said that he would deal with Kurt as soon as he was booked, I called Brad Ferris, who had just arrived home after working a late shift at the airbag factory he supervised. He invited me over. I got to see Gwen for a moment before she left for her job as manager of a store in the mall. She gave me a hug, and I saw the tension and worry in her eyes. She and I had both testified at the Carrie Helm murder trial just a few weeks before. We'd never spoken of it outside of the courtroom, but it haunted both of us.

Gwen kissed Brad goodbye, and he and I were left alone.

"She doesn't know about last night," he told me. He looked better than I feared, but I wondered how much I wasn't seeing. His shirt was buttoned to the neck, but I could still see a couple of scratches on his face. How had he explained those to Gwen? "I didn't want to worry her."

I explained about Kurt turning himself in as I glanced around the front room, which had a futon instead of a couch. College student furniture mostly, cheap and easy to replace. Now that the church had closed the adoption arm of LDS Family Services, it was harder and much more expensive to adopt a baby, which I knew they were working toward, after years of infertility treatment. "There won't be any need for her to worry," I assured Brad. "Kurt will make sure of that."

I wondered if it was appropriate for me to be alone with

him, though I hadn't worried about the same thing with Grant Rhodes.

"Let's step outside, shall we?" I said.

We stepped out onto the front porch, which was enclosed in scrub oak and almost as private as indoors. But this was all about technicalities, so I didn't care.

I leaned against the railing and said, "I just wanted to hear your side of what happened last night."

Brad wiped his forehead. It was already in the nineties, and though I'd heard many people say that dry heat wasn't as bad as humid heat, Utah summers were still pretty bad. "I wasn't trying to hurt him, you know. I was just trying to make him leave," Brad explained. "He kept struggling and then he threw himself at me. I just used my hands to defend myself, and then to grab him again."

"Can you tell me about what Grant Rhodes did?" I asked. Brother Carrington might need this information.

Brad gazed out from his porch toward the mountain that filled the horizon. Kennecott, the world's biggest copper mining operation, had been hollowing it out for years, but despite the destruction the mountain had a strange, striped beauty.

"Brother Rhodes was shouting that the bishop didn't know what love was. He said it over and over again. That the bishop didn't understand what it was like, that it was the most important thing, that the bishop was trying to stop love." Brad played with his gold wedding band. "Of course, I know that's not true. The bishop is one of the most loving people I know. He loves you and his sons. He knows love." But Brad looked up at me, as if for confirmation.

"Yes, Kurt is a very loving man," I said. But maybe not the kind of love Grant Rhodes was talking about.

I had a sudden inspiration. "Listen, Brad, could you go over to the church this morning, before anything is moved or cleaned? Take a camera and make sure you take pictures of everything you can, so we can use them in court if we need to. I want to be able to prove that Grant Rhodes was the dangerous one. And take a couple of photos of your face, too? For Kurt's sake."

Brad agreed, and I felt a little relieved.

CHAPTER 32

B ut I went over to Grant Rhodes's house anyway. I knocked on the front door, and when there was no answer, I stepped inside. The door was unlocked.

I called out, "Grant? It's me, Linda Wallheim! I'm just here to talk to you."

I made my way through the rooms of his house until I found him upstairs in his bedroom. If I shouldn't have been in the living room with Brad, what was I doing here alone with Grant?

"What do you want?" Grant asked. There was no disguising the damage he had sustained in the fight with Brad Ferris the night before. His face was badly bruised, a bright reddish purple, his jawline obscured by swelling. One eye was nearly swollen shut. He was wearing only a garment top, so I could see that his arms had livid marks on them as well, from someone holding him with a great deal of strength.

"You think I haven't been through enough pain?" he murmured.

I held out my hands in a gesture of submission. "I promise I just want to talk."

"I got home at two A.M. last night from the hospital. I

haven't had enough sleep yet. I don't know that I can talk very cogently."

The fact that he could still use words like "cogently" indicated otherwise. And at this point, I needed the truth from him. All of it at once. If he didn't give it to me, I was going to call up Detective Gore and have a very frank talk with her. But first, I put on my solicitous nursemaid hat. "I'm sorry. Do you need any help with medications? With some food?"

Grant seemed to forget that I was Kurt's wife as I helped him into the bathroom, got him water, and looked through his medications to see which he needed to take now. Then I went downstairs and got some toast and "Postum" for him to dunk it in to make it soft enough for a sore jaw.

He nibbled at the toast and sipped at the coffee.

"Now, how are you feeling?" I asked, fluffing a pillow up behind him. I was a little jealous of the caffeine, and trying not to think about it, despite the glorious smell. At least it wasn't fresh roasted.

"A little better," he said, nodding warily at me.

"Good." I leaned in close. "I just want to make sure you know that it wasn't Kurt's fault, what happened to you last night."

Grant's eyes flashed and he put a hand up to ward me off. "I was the one who ended up in the hospital," he said.

I moved back, feeling defensive. "You threw things in his office. You damaged the walls. I think that whatever was done to you was only what you deserved."

Grant Rhodes flinched at that, and I immediately felt horrible for badgering him in his weak and vulnerable state. But what better time to get him to tell the truth—the whole truth?

"I know this is all because you are grieving about Carl, and you can't even tell anyone how you really feel." Because most Mormons would be offended at the very thought of his pain from a long-finished love affair with someone who was now a transgender male.

After a long moment, Grant said, "You don't know anything about Carl. Not really. You only knew the parts he was willing to show people."

"Tell me about the real Carl," I said. I prayed silently that whatever Grant told me, I would hear the truth in his meaning and his bearing. I needed to know if he was a killer or not.

Grant looked down at his hands, held firmly at his sides. "We loved each other," he said. "And there is nothing wrong with that."

In my reading, I'd learned that transgenderism and sexual orientation are not linked. Some transgender people are heterosexual, others homosexual. Some are even bisexual. Although Mormons might think that it was all the same thing, all about giving license to more and more depraved sexual urges, the studies seemed to show the opposite—that once they have transitioned, transgender people act out sexually less than the rest of the population.

"But Carl must have felt enormously guilty about his wife and children," I said. Did Grant feel a little guilty about that, as well?

"You have to understand how long Carl fought against who he was," Grant Rhodes said. "All those years. In college, he went through so many migraines, whole days he was unable to get out of bed, until he realized he had to match his body to his mind. It was only once he realized this that he was able to start living normally, facing the day." He touched his chest, a gesture I remembered from when he had first spoken to me about Carl.

"After that, all he wanted was for people to accept him as a normal man. He did everything the way he was supposed to."

"I understand that." Or I was trying to. "But once he married Emma and had children, surely he had made his choice."

Another flash of anger in Grant's eyes. "He never stopped loving me. Not even through that horrible pregnancy when he felt like his body had betrayed him. He insisted on giving her up for adoption. Do you have any idea how difficult that was for me? I told him I would be willing to raise the girl on my own, but he wouldn't have it. He didn't want any chance that she would find him, or that he would be drawn back into his old self."

Maybe Grant should have been emotional telling me this, but he sounded as if he was just tired of it all. He spoke almost in a monotone.

"So after she was born and all the papers were finally signed, he started on his transition. He had surgeries, started taking hormones. I thought that maybe he would let me stay with him, that somehow we could find a way to be together. I still loved him, no matter what his body looked like. I wanted so much for him to believe that. But his parents had already rejected him. They said that he was rejecting God's plan for him, and that he would never be able to go to the temple to be sealed forever to his own family."

So his parents *had* been Mormons, after all.

"He hated them. They'd already tried to send him to 'reparative therapy' when he was in his teens. They called him a lesbian, because of the way he talked and acted and wore his hair. He'd always put on men's clothing by choice, and they wanted him to go to church in dresses, to wear a gown to the prom." Grant shivered a little, as if this were unfathomable to him.

"Did he never have any contact with them after his transition?" I asked quietly.

Grant shook his head. "Not that I know of. His parents only live about thirty miles away, in Fruit Heights. But they never contacted him again, after his transition. Carl has a younger sister and a younger brother. He never saw them again, either. It was the price for becoming his true self. His parents thought this made him a bad influence, that he would lead his siblings astray in some way. As if a change like that is catching."

There are very few transgender people, less than 1 percent of the population. I had never thought through how difficult it would be to make the transition, and the cost of doing so. No wonder so few people undertook the process. I didn't know what Carl's reasons were for not having more than top surgery, but maybe it was simply too painful and too long of a process, once he had already married Emma and began living as a man.

"He didn't want any ties to his old life," Grant continued. "He even sent all the love letters I'd sent him back to me, and demanded I do the same. They were the only proof I had that he had loved me once."

Ah, so here was the answer to the letters. They had been Carl's, after all. Not Emma's invention. Not some other woman he'd had an affair with. But Emma must have known about them before the police came. She must have hidden them so they wouldn't be found until she wanted them to be.

"I tried to date other women, to fall in love with someone else. But it never worked." Grant Rhodes's fists were clenched, but that was the only emotion he showed. "They only reminded me of a shadow of Carla, and how perfect she had been. When I saw Carl for the first time after all those years, I could feel the connection between us still there. He was the same Carla I had always loved."

How interesting, that Grant had still loved Carl, and Carl had apparently still loved Grant, even after his transition to a new body and a new identity. Would I still love Kurt if he came to me and said that he wanted to live as a woman? I wasn't sure that I would. Maybe Grant was right on some level, that he understood a higher love than we did. Or maybe to Carl it wasn't eternal love, but rather a longing to be with someone who knew the full truth about him.

"But that night he died, Carl said it was over, didn't he?" I asked, watching Grant closely. He hadn't said this, but I guessed at it. Carl had wanted his life as a man too much.

"I tried to talk him out of it," Grant admitted. "But he was resolute. I told myself that he would be weak again, that he still loved me. I thought I just had to be patient. I didn't know that was going to be my last chance to talk to him, to touch him, to—" He broke off, and his hands seemed to spasm before he could control them again.

Was love really a choice, or wasn't it?

"Did you ever consider how selfish you were being? Did you think about the cost to Emma Ashby's happiness when you were having this affair?" I pressed, trying to get Grant to show some anger so I could evaluate it.

"Her happiness? What about my happiness?" He thumped his fists on the quilt. "I had Carl for one week. Four nights, that was all." His voice broke and he had to take in several breaths before continuing. "And she'd had him for twenty years. You call that selfish? That's barely survival. That's taking a drink after being thirsty for twenty years. That's one sliver of a lifetime."

But he'd had Carl far more fully than Emma ever had, I thought.

"Did you have any hint that Emma knew about you and Carl? She never saw you at the church, did she? Did Carl mention if she had seen any messages? Overheard anything on the phone?" I asked.

Grant shook his head. "Not as far as I know."

"I'll go, then. Grant, please remember all the good things Kurt has done for you. All right? You really don't want to see him in jail for this, do you?" I stood up.

"I do remember all the good things. That's why I can't bear it that he won't let me come back," said Grant softly. "I know I was wrong, but I need a place to belong. This ward is the only place I've ever felt at home."

I could no longer feel anger toward Grant Rhodes. I hated the thought of Kurt in jail, but I could also see that Grant Rhodes needed my help.

"What if I found another ward for you? If I talked to the other bishops in the stake and found one who would let you go to his ward? It wouldn't be too far out of the way for you to drive to, and you could meet new people. Start everything fresh. Wouldn't that be a good thing for you?"

"And what would you tell them about me?" asked Grant, his eyes slits of watchfulness.

"I promise that I will only say that you can be a pain in Sunday School because you think you know everything. And that you had personal issues with Kurt that are unlikely to ever come up again with someone else." I hoped that was true.

"Would you do that?" said Grant.

"I would," I said.

USING KURT'S OFFICE once I got home, I found the contact information for three bishops in our stake who lived within a mile of us.

I called the first one, Thomas Shaw, and introduced myself. I apologized for taking up his time while he was likely at work, but then said that Kurt was my husband, that he was the bishop of our ward, and that he had a member who needed to find a new ward. I explained about Grant's quirks and suggested that while he was difficult, he could also add to a ward's character.

"Then why isn't he staying in your ward?" asked the bishop.

"He and Kurt have had a personality conflict," I said. It wasn't false, but it wasn't the whole truth, either. I wondered how God would view this deception. I didn't feel the "burning in the bosom" from the Doctrine and Covenants that meant it was right, but I didn't feel the stupor that meant it was wrong, either.

Sometimes God expects us to take chances, I guess.

"I'll pray about it," said Bishop Shaw dubiously.

That wasn't good enough for me—or for Grant Rhodes—so I moved on to the next number. And the third. I ended up going out of our stake and into the next one, which Kurt also had a directory for, though perhaps he wasn't supposed to. I wondered if President Frost had already warned all the bishops in our stake about Grant Rhodes. But I finally got Andrew Shiner in the next stake over, still in Draper, and not that far away. Bishop Shiner actually seemed happy at the idea of

Grant Rhodes joining his ward. He said they were newly split and the adult Sunday School class was extremely thin because everyone who would have gone to it ordinarily was instead filling the other callings a ward needed to function.

So by 1 P.M., I was able to call Grant Rhodes and give him the name and number of his new bishop. "He's agreed to take you into the ward, no questions asked," I said, perhaps exaggerating the agreement slightly. "So, if you would call the police about Kurt, I would appreciate it greatly."

There was a long pause, and I wondered if I had made a bargain with the devil. But finally Grant said, "All right. I'll call them."

About an hour later, Kurt called to tell me that he was being released, after only a couple of hours in a cell. He hadn't even had to wait for Brother Carrington because Grant Rhodes had called and said he wasn't filing charges.

I called Samuel, just to hear his voice. But he sounded hurried.

"Maybe we could do something tonight, just the three of us," I proposed. "You and me and Dad?"

I could hear his genuine compassion when he said, "Sorry, Mom. I've got plans up in Salt Lake. The roommates and I are going to play Ultimate Frisbee and have a picnic afterward. Sort of a chance to bond before we all get too busy with other stuff."

"Okay, well, I—we'll miss you," I said.

"It's not like I'm dying," he said cheerfully.

Sure, *he* could be cheerful about it. But it felt like I was the one dying. The old mother I'd been was gone. I didn't know who would take her place.

"I love you. Call us if you need anything. Call us if you don't need anything, all right?" I said. I needed to hear from him more than from the other boys. He had always been my special one. My last one.

"I will!" he said. "Come on, Mom. Don't act like I've just cut off your arm."

No, it was much worse than that. But I worked up some enthusiasm in my voice. "I'm so proud of you. I love you. I want you to have a good life, all right?"

"As long as I'm really close to home so you can pop in on it now and again," said Samuel.

"Not at all. I want you to go far away from here. Mostly so you can tell everyone everywhere how great a mother I am."

"Oh, I'll do that," said Samuel. "All my roommates already know. They've heard legends of your cooking. So you can make us some cookie care packages. Hint, hint."

"I'll do that," I said, and with great reluctance, hung up.

CHAPTER 33

Church meetings on Sunday went smoothly enough. Relief Society was all abuzz about a new president: Donna Ringel, the former chorister. She spoke about her goal for her tenure of knitting the sisterhood into love and community service. She didn't specifically mention Carl Ashby's murder or what had happened between Emma Ashby and Sheri Tate, but we all knew the context. I thought it was a good idea for her to address the problem, however obliquely. We had all been involved in something that had sullied us and we all needed to feel clean again.

I wanted nothing more to do with the whole case. Detective Gore was going to have to bring her suspect to justice on her own. At least, that was what I thought, until Alice Ashby stopped by the house again on Monday just before noon.

"I have something I want to show you," she said.

I invited her into the kitchen again. There were no cookies today, unfortunately. I was working on a complicated recipe for lasagna that wouldn't be ready until dinner. But the smell of it was enough to make anyone salivate. I was pretty sure I'd eaten way too much of the cheese and sauce already, and I hadn't even started assembling yet.

"What is it?" I asked.

Alice poked around in her bag and brought out a flat manila envelope. She turned it upside down and a small piece of paper floated out. It landed facedown on the floor, and when I bent down to pick it up, I realized it wasn't regular paper at all. It was photo paper, and there was a young woman's picture printed on the back.

I stared at the girl, who bore a startling resemblance to the young Carla Thompson in the photo I'd found online, with the same dark eyes and luminous, androgynous features. Except that this young woman was dressed in much more modern clothes than Carla had worn when she was this age: a form-fitting floral shirt with a white jacket on top. I saw no resemblance to Grant Rhodes, but surely this had to be the daughter he and Carl had conceived, before Carl's transition.

"Who is this, do you know?" I asked. "Where did you get it?"

"I found it in the garage, on the shelves above the tools. I thought all that was in there were old toys that Mom wanted to keep for grandkids. But there was this."

Something else the police had missed, I thought.

On the back of the photo was written the name *Cristal*.

This, despite what Grant had said about Carl not wanting to have contact with his daughter after she was adopted. What a mess, I thought, feeling sick that I was being pulled into all of this again.

"Who do you think she is?" Alice asked me.

"I think you can guess, Alice," I said. If she hadn't had some inkling, she wouldn't have brought it to me. And I didn't like her playing stupid.

"I think she's Dad's daughter. From before he married Mom," she said.

I let out a breath. She had hit on a way of putting it that didn't bring out the complexities of her father's gender identity. Did this mean she still didn't know that part?

"But why would he hide her from us?" asked Alice. Her eyes were intense and fixed on the photo.

The young woman in the photograph wasn't a teenager anymore. She looked to me like she was in her early twenties, which fit with the time frame I'd assumed, considering Carl's age and the dates he was in college.

"You and William were adopted," I said. "And I think she was, too." Possibly by the same old LDS Family Services organization.

"But why wouldn't he tell us about her?" asked Alice.

"Maybe he was ashamed," I said. "You don't know how bad it used to be in the church. Having a baby without being married was seen as a terribly shameful thing."

Alice thought about this for only a moment. "I want to meet her," she said, her voice sounding less confident than her words. "Do you think I could find out more about her somehow? Her address? Her phone number? Maybe I could find her on Facebook or something, even if I only have her first name. Do you think she's in Utah?"

"I don't know, Alice. I don't know anything about her."

I felt heavy and slow. Did Detective Gore know about this child? Did Emma? Even Alice might be feigning surprise about this. It seemed I was fated to be involved in this case no matter how much I wanted to get out of it.

"Are you all right?" asked Alice.

I came back to myself enough to notice that I was staring at Alice, and turned away. "Fine," I said.

Alice chewed at her lower lip and twisted her hands together. "It's just—you looked kind of freaked out. Like you were going to faint or something. I've seen my mom faint before and that's how she looked."

"No, I'm fine. Really," I said, and tried to put on a blank face.

"Well, this girl," Alice continued, nodding at the photograph in my hand, "what if she was the one who met my dad at the church that night?"

I had never considered this possibility. Could a young woman like this be a murderer?

"I mean, if she's eighteen, can't she contact her birth parents and ask to meet with them?" asked Alice.

"I don't know the law. I think it depends on whether your father put himself on a list LDS Family Services kept. And if he decided he wanted to meet with her." Would Carl Ashby have said yes to a request from a daughter whose very existence would threaten his place in the world—and in the church?

I couldn't see it, but then again, I hadn't understood Carl well at all. Had he had feelings for this child who had come from his body, albeit a body whose female parts he had disassociated himself from? And of course, I'd never met this Cristal. Had she grown up in a good home? Or was she angry that she'd been put up for adoption and left to make her own way in the world?

I handed the photo back to Alice and wished that I felt some impression of the Spirit. But all I felt was confusion and a sense of sorrow that seemed to pervade everything about this story. Carl and Grant's lost love. The difficult marriage that Carl and Emma Ashby had lived in for twenty years. The loss of a father for William and Alice, and a mother for Cristal.

"Do you think my mom knew about her, too?" asked Alice.

And that was the most interesting question. If Emma

Ashby had found out about this adopted child, what might her reaction have been? After what I had seen her do to Sheri Tate, I could imagine almost anything. She could have threatened the girl not to contact her husband again. She could have threatened the girl not to contact her husband again. If she had begun to worry about the legality of her marriage and her children's adoptions, she might have been afraid that any mention of her might upend the other arrangements. I had thought before that if they were named in the will, Alice and William and Emma's right to Carl's assets couldn't be challenged. But I hadn't thought about a biological daughter coming out of nowhere to dispute the other claims. It might have made sense for Emma to demand Carl keep the girl's name out of the will. Or even send intimidating emails to Cristal's friends and adopted family. The more I found out about Emma Ashby, the more she frightened me.

"So who do you think the mother was? His high school sweetheart or something?" asked Alice, revealing what I wanted to know most without me having to ask.

"I don't know, but do you mind if I keep this photo?" I asked. "I'll see what I can find out about her for you, and then I'll get back to you."

Alice nodded slowly. "Thank you," she said.

Would she thank me later, if someone in her own family ended up in prison for her father's murder?

I walked Alice to the door. After she left, I held the photo for a long while. Kurt would tell me I should call Detective Gore. But I wasn't finished with my own part in this case.

CHAPTER 34

Monday evening, Kurt came home and we got ready to go out for dinner and possibly a movie—our own new version of Family Home Evening, now that Samuel was out of the house.

But a phone call interrupted us. "I'll turn it off," said Kurt. But when he looked at his phone, he said, "It's Emma Ashby," and answered it. "I'll be right there," Kurt said to her. He hung up the phone and turned to me. "I have to go."

Bishops are like firemen. They have to be ready to deal with emergencies at any hour.

"What is it?" I asked, as Kurt got into the truck. He turned the ignition, and I think if I hadn't pointed out that the garage door was closed, he would have driven right through it. And I'm not sure he would have noticed.

"Both William and Alice have disappeared this time. Emma says she thought that Alice was at the library today and that William was doing something for scouting, but they both lied to her. No one has seen them since before noon," said Kurt.

"Alice was here this morning," I admitted, wishing I'd said something earlier about it. "She brought me a photo of what might be Carl's biological daughter from before his transition."

Kurt's hands gripped harder on the steering wheel. "Why didn't you tell me this earlier?" he asked.

"I thought I had handled it."

Kurt shook his head.

"Maybe I should come with you to the Ashbys'. I might be able to help." I moved toward the passenger door.

Kurt hesitated a moment, then said, "Fine." He knew he couldn't stop me, and he might as well be able to keep track of me.

We drove over to the Ashby house and Kurt hurried inside. By the time I caught up, Kurt was sitting next to Emma on her couch, offering her a package of Kleenex as she wiped tears and mucus from her face. It had been almost two weeks, and she was mostly healed from the damage of our fight, with only a few spots of greenish-yellow bruising still to be seen. It hadn't occurred to me until I saw her how embarrassed I would be to face her again.

"How are you, Emma?" I asked.

She glanced up at me and flinched, but in such an exaggerated way I suspected it was staged. "I didn't know you would both come." She looked back and forth between us, but Kurt didn't offer an excuse.

I felt very cold at the sight of her. To my eye, she seemed psychotically imbalanced, and I wondered what I had been thinking when I sent Alice home to Emma a few days before. "Where Kurt goes, I go," I said.

"Emma, please. I have the feeling you know something else you need to tell us," Kurt said. His tone was tight, impatient. "For the sake of getting your children back."

"I don't know anything," Emma wept, leaning into Kurt's shoulder, then pulling away as she realized I was still standing uncomfortably at his side.

"Do they have their cell phones with them?" asked Kurt.

"I don't know," said Emma miserably.

Kurt got out his phone and called them himself. "No answer," he said. He pointed upstairs and gestured to Emma. "Can you go look in William's room to see if he took his diabetes kit with him?"

Emma turned and glanced at me for a moment too long, as if she didn't trust me. "All right," she said pointedly to Kurt.

When she was out of earshot, I sat back down and said to Kurt, "What do you think the chances are that she might be to blame for her children's disappearance herself?"

"That she's hurt her own children?" Kurt shook his head. "Whatever she's done with regard to Carl's money, I don't believe her capable of that."

"But if she killed Carl and they found out? Would she have felt she had to silence them?" I pressed him because of my own guilt. I wished more and more now that I had called Detective Gore and told her all I knew this morning. Somehow, I should have prevented all of this from happening.

"I know you got upset with her before, but Linda, she's just like you. You're both mothers who are trying to protect your children." He was still accepting the helpless image of Emma that she liked to present.

Emma came down the stairs just then, holding a small fanny pack that was labeled Medical Supplies.

"At least he has his pump on, but I can't check it to see when he last gave himself insulin or what his blood sugar is." She was shaking, and the pallor of her face under the bruises only increased the effect of her frailty.

I grimaced as Kurt stood up and led her back to the couch by her hands. He sat beside her, which left me on the opposite couch.

"Well, do you have a tracking app for their phones?"

Emma shook her head. "I'm afraid I wouldn't think to do anything like that. Carl did all the technical things."

Helpless again.

Kurt nodded sympathetically. "Then I should call the police. The more time they have for this kind of thing, the better chance there is of finding the children unharmed." He started to dial his phone, but Emma stopped him.

"What if William has stolen another car?" Emma asked Kurt. "Won't it be worse to get the police involved?"

I didn't believe for a second that was why she hadn't called the police yet.

"Is there some reason you think that's what he's done?" asked Kurt. "And that Alice has gone along with him?" He was still holding one of her hands in his own. Did he realize it?

I thought about texting Detective Gore right then, but decided to wait until I was able to give her my complete attention. I didn't want her to call me while I was here at Emma's.

"Alice seemed upset this past week," said Emma. "She wouldn't tell me what was wrong. And William—well, he is still very angry."

"But it was Brother Rhodes he was angry with, the last time I heard," Kurt said. "And his car is still being repaired. Is William angry at someone else? Whose car would he take? He doesn't even have a license, and I gave him a long talk about how he needs to treat his diabetes more carefully."

"Alice has a license," said Emma. "He sometimes talks her into things with him, when he's in a mood."

"All the more reason to call the police," said Kurt. He checked his phone for the time. It was a little after seven.

"No!" Emma exclaimed, snatching Kurt's phone away from him. Breathing heavily, she tucked it down her shirt. "I can't let you do that."

Of course she couldn't.

Kurt looked away from her chest area and frowned. Now he was suspicious of her, too. Good.

"If William is trying to drive a car, he's in danger. He could already be lying in a ditch somewhere." Kurt knew how to speak bluntly to the facts, but I shivered at the thought, and at how it seemed his mother had pushed him into that ditch. "Even if it's Alice driving, she's going to be distracted and worried. Those are the worst kind of circumstances for a teen accident."

"Promise me you won't call the police," Emma insisted, her hand clapped tightly to her chest. "Just promise me."

"All right," said Kurt, after a long sigh. "I promise I won't call the police."

It was one of his easy false promises. I knew the tone. Kurt had learned with our children that there were times when you lied because you had to. You did the best you could to make it sound genuine, and you told yourself it was in the best interest of your kids. Like the time when Samuel had made Kurt promise that he wouldn't let the doctors intubate him at the hospital when he was very ill. Kurt had promised, then held Samuel down. It had been months before Samuel trusted his father again. But it was what had to be done.

Emma tugged the phone out of her blouse and handed it to Kurt.

He held it gingerly, as if it had been infected with something, then wiped it on his legs. He looked up at me then, and by his pleading, worried eyes, I could tell he wanted me to make an excuse to leave and call the police. So did I. But I also wanted to hear what Emma had to say.

"William sent me a text this afternoon," Emma confessed suddenly with a new sob.

And she had held this back from us all this time? Purely to get sympathy from Kurt?

"What did it say?" asked Kurt.

In answer, Emma handed her own phone over to Kurt. He read it aloud for my sake.

"Mom, Alice and I aren't coming home until you let us see Cristal. You know who she is, and you must know where she is and how we can contact her."

So that was what this was about. No wonder Emma didn't want us to call the police.

I wanted to shake both William and Alice for further complicating the situation, but I could also see how they would have to do something extreme to get their mother to listen to them.

"Who is Cristal?" Kurt asked.

"She is Carl's love child. From before we married," said Emma faintly. Her lips were barely moving, as if she could hardly make them form those horrible words.

"How long have you known?" asked Kurt.

"About a year," Emma said, her voice strained. Well, that certainly would have triggered a reaction in their marriage. Was that the moment the snowball had begun to roll, gaining momentum through the year and ending with Carl's murder?

"How did you find out about her?" Kurt asked.

Emma put a hand to her throat, humiliated and distressed. "I found a letter she sent to Carl."

I wondered if Emma had always gone through her husband's mail—and other personal effects. How had she missed the truth about him being transgender? Or was that, too, a pretense?

"Did they meet?" asked Kurt. "This Cristal and Carl?"

Emma shook her head and looked away. "He never told me. I don't think so."

"Do you have her address or phone number?"

Emma shook her head.

"Do you know if she's a member of the church, or where she lives? With her full name, we might be able to find her that way," said Kurt. He had stood up so he was silhouetted by the sunlight from the window behind him, making his expression very difficult to read.

Emma shook her head again. "I don't know. I don't know anything about her."

"Have you texted William back?"

"Of course, I did that right away. I told him to come home. And then I begged him. I told him I would give him anything. But even if I had this Cristal's contact information, I wouldn't give that to him. She'd be poison to him, can't he see that?" She seemed desperate for Kurt's agreement.

"If we get the police involved, they could trace the text and find out where it was coming from," Kurt said. "Ask for records from the cellular service provider about pings to towers and such."

"No," said Emma again, this time breathlessly, as if she were about to collapse. "No police."

"You could call the service provider yourself then. You could explain the situation, that your children could be in danger, and that you need them to give you whatever information they have."

Emma shook her head. "I couldn't do that. I don't want to talk to anyone else about this. And who knows what information the phone people might put out in public? It could show up on William's record when he applies to colleges."

It was a thin excuse, but all of Emma's words seemed thin to me now.

"Have you tried contacting Alice separately?" Kurt asked.

"No. She's clearly not in charge," said Emma, holding the phone closely and seeming to shrink down into the couch. "She's just doing whatever William tells her to do. That's the way it has always been between them."

I didn't see Alice that way at all. Did Emma think that was the only way to be a woman?

"I'll tell William to come to my house and make sure he gets what he wants," said Kurt, as he typed the words into his own phone.

"But I don't want—"

"If this is the only way to get your children back safely, are you going to stop me?" Kurt hit SEND and I could see wariness in all of his actions.

After a minute, there was the sound of an incoming text from Kurt's phone, and he nodded to me. He showed me the message from William, agreeing to the meeting in two hours' time.

While still in the driveway, I finally texted Detective Gore.

I waited for a response for several minutes, but there was nothing. I made sure she had the information about where we were meeting and when. I hoped Emma would be forced to confess. If she did it in front of Gore, that would end this whole thing.

"I guess I'll just have to hope she shows up eventually," I said.

Then Kurt pulled out, but instead of heading home immediately, he said, "If we want to know about Cristal at this point, I think her father is the best resource."

"Grant," I breathed. "Of course." Grant Rhodes hadn't admitted to contact with his daughter, but it wouldn't be the first time he had been less than fully transparent.

CHAPTER 35

In front of Grant Rhodes's house, Kurt decided it would be best for him to stay in the truck, after what had happened at the church and the legal issues still to be dealt with there. But he gave me a thirty-minute deadline before he came in to "rescue" me. We needed to be home when Alice and William got there, not to mention Emma and Detective Gore.

"Say a prayer. A quick one," I told Kurt and gave him a kiss. I closed the door, then walked briskly to the porch and rang the bell. Lights were already on inside, and eventually, Grant came to the door.

"What do you want now?" he asked. He looked a lot worse than when I'd last seen him, one eye nearly swollen shut and his words slurring. It struck me then that Kurt and I were causing quite the little circle of pain in our ward.

"William and Alice Ashby have run away and are demanding to see Cristal before they come home. I came to see if you know any of her contact information," I said, not mincing words.

His reaction to the name "Cristal" was immediate. He tensed and his eyes gleamed. He looked out, saw Kurt in the truck, and motioned me inside. He closed the door behind him and sat gingerly on his couch.

"Did Cristal ever ask to see her siblings that you know of?" I asked.

"She might have," said Grant, admitting tacitly that he had had contact with her.

"I'm guessing Carl refused," I said.

Grant didn't contradict me. He just shrugged.

"Then here is a chance for you to give her what she's asked for," I said. "Alice and William are refusing to come home until they meet her, and while I think they're acting like idiots, I also think they deserve to have more truth about their father than they have been given so far."

"What's in it for Cristal?" asked Grant. Of course, he would be thinking more about her than about Carl's adopted children from his marriage with Emma. He'd already shown how little he cared for William.

I smiled and tried to sound like a parent speaking to another knowing parent. "Surely she would want to hear memories of her biological mother—er, her other biological father, that is. She must be hurting, too, if she knows he's gone." I waited and Grant didn't say anything. I didn't want to let on how afraid I was that he was going to deny my request. He had all the power here and I had none.

He was silent for a long time. Then he said cautiously, "Cristal only met Carl a couple of times. There were tensions between them."

I was surprised by this. Why? Had Carl been as hard on her as he had been on Emma?

Grant put his hands together, almost as if he were praying. "The adoptive parents sent Carl letters and photos every year at an anonymous P.O. box. But it stopped when Cristal was about eleven because Carl asked not to be contacted again.

He was afraid of what would happen if Cristal learned about his transition.

"So when Cristal turned eighteen some years ago, I was the only contact she had, and I asked Carl to meet with her." Grant took a deep breath, then unfolded his arms and rubbed his hands on his pants.

I did some math in my head and figured that if Cristal had been eleven years old when Carl had adopted William, she must be about twenty-five or twenty-six now. That fit with the photo I'd seen.

"It took several years for me to convince Carl. But when Cristal came back into our lives at last, it brought us closer again. For one thing, she asked to talk to Carl's parents. Carla Thompson's parents, that is. Carl tried to talk her out of it, but she was so insistent, and she was so beautiful and so winning that I think he believed she might be able to fix things between them, even after all this time."

He went stiff, then shook himself. "It didn't go well. They refused to acknowledge her. They'd told everyone that Carla was dead, and maybe they were afraid of being revealed as the bigots they really were." His tone was dark and bitter. "They literally pushed her out of the house and threatened her safety if she ever came back. She was shaking when she came here, and Carl and I had to calm her down. Once she was gone, we were so angry. Carl couldn't go home."

A long breath. "And that was where the trouble began. We started talking about the past, what might have been. If we'd gotten married. If, if, if." He twisted his legs and moved to the side, as if trying to protect himself from my gaze—or perhaps from my judgment.

I checked my watch and realized I had only ten minutes

before Kurt was going to come in. And only an hour and a half before William and Alice were going to show up at our house, expecting Cristal to be there. "Grant, I think you want to see this happen, too. You know it's what Carl would have wanted. It's the last gift you can give to him, now that he's gone. You can see his children all together and know that they are honoring him the way he should be honored."

"I didn't kill him," said Grant. His eyes were wet with tears, and I thought I could see new lines of anguish on his forehead and cheeks.

I put a hand on his. "I believe you, Grant. You wouldn't have done that. You loved Carl. And we can make things come out right; we just need to be able to talk to Cristal."

Grant sighed. "You're right. This is about Carl. And what he would have wanted." He stood up from the couch and walked away.

I was left there for a long minute, wondering what would happen next.

When Grant came back, he had a piece of paper with an address and a phone number on it. "She's a student at the University of Utah," he said.

Just like Samuel.

"Thank you," I said. Had Kurt had some inkling of how close by she was when he'd told William and Alice to show up in two hours? Or were we just lucky that people tended to stay in Utah because of the influence of the Mormon church and the desire to stay within the safety bubble of other church members?

I called Cristal as Grant watched me. It felt very odd to introduce myself to her as the wife of the bishop in Carl Ashby's ward, but I kept to the cold facts.

"He's dead," she said, her tone flat. Not "she," I thought. Even though Carl had been her biological mother.

"I know that. But he has two other children who would like very much to meet you. Their names are William and Alice."

"Carl told me about them a little, the one time we met," said Cristal. She sounded shy, her voice as high-pitched as Emma's.

"Well, they disappeared today and we're very concerned about their health and safety. William is diabetic and he shouldn't be away from home for so long. But they're very upset and they won't come home unless they can talk to you." I paused, but she said nothing, so I went on. "William is just barely fifteen and Alice is seventeen. Their father's death has really run them through the wringer. All the secrets he had keep coming out. I think they need to talk to someone who can tell them the truth about him."

"I'm not sure I can tell them much of any value," said Cristal.

"Please, I don't know what they will do if you don't agree to come see them. I promise, I won't leave you alone with them. Grant will be at our home, as well." I glanced at him to make sure he agreed to that.

He hesitated, then nodded.

"I've got a test tomorrow morning," said Cristal. "I was hoping to study. And then to get some actual sleep."

She was older than many college students. I wondered if she was working and paying her way through school. Or maybe she started after going on a Mormon mission. I didn't know anything about her.

"I know college is important, but so is family," I said. Family was a guilt trigger for any Mormon, and I was using it shamelessly.

"All right, I'll come," she said finally. "What time do I need to be there?"

"Thank you." I could feel tears dripping from my chin to my shirt. "Come as soon as possible. I told them you would be there in an hour and a half." I gave her the address to our house. "Do you have a car?" I asked. I would have to look up the schedule for Trax, but I could go pick her up at the station if I had to. Or drive to her dorm and get her from there.

"I can borrow one," she said.

Grant promised he would come over to our house soon, too, and I left his front porch just in time to stop Kurt from coming in. We got back home and waited tensely for everyone to arrive.

CHAPTER 36

Just after ten P.M., Grant Rhodes was standing in our kitchen uncomfortably while I madly baked cookies, not because I thought anyone wanted to eat them, but because it helped me feel calmer. Emma Ashby was watching me, giving me "helpful" hints about baking soda versus baking powder.

I still hadn't received any word back from Detective Gore, though I'd tried twice to call her and been sent straight to voice mail. Apparently, she had more important things to do than to tie up a murder case where she'd known the identity of the killer for weeks. I hoped that my word and Kurt's about what Emma would say tonight would be enough for the prosecution.

The doorbell rang and Kurt went to the door.

From the kitchen, I heard that same high-pitched, floating voice from the phone. Cristal, I assumed. She sounded nervous and I sent a prayer up to heaven for her. Coming here was a great sacrifice for her.

Kurt brought her into the kitchen. I admit, I was stunned again by how much she reminded me of Carl. The same dark hair, though longer and curlier; the same eyes; the same nose and strong chin. Even some of her body language echoed his, which was surprising, since she hadn't met him until too late in life for him to influence her mannerisms. Could they be hereditary?

I wanted to fold her into a hug, but I resisted and kept working on the cookies. Everything was too strained at the moment.

Grant hugged her instead, and she stayed by his side. She called him by his first name, "Grant," not "Dad." Hearing that made me a little sad. Grant had lost so much in all of this.

"Kurt Wallheim," said Kurt, holding out a firm hand to shake. Then he nodded to me. "My wife, Linda, is the one you spoke to on the phone."

I came forward, wiping my hands on my apron, and shook her hand. It was a limp, sweaty handshake, betraying her anxiety.

It wasn't until Emma cleared her throat that I remembered she was there, and that I hadn't introduced her.

"This is Emma. Emma Ashby," I said. I stumbled over the right pronouns and then gave up. "Your—his—Carl's wife."

"Glad to meet you," said Emma coldly. She didn't offer a hand.

Cristal ducked her head toward Grant, and I thought how very young she seemed. Maybe everyone seemed young to me now, but she seemed completely vulnerable.

When Grant nudged her, she held out her hand with a polite smile and said, "Good to meet you, Emma. Carl talked so much about you."

"Oh? What did he say?" said Emma. She was chewing her lip, her nervous tell.

"How pretty you were—are," said Cristal, stuttering a bit.

"I'm so glad he was happy with you, after everything he went through. I think—he deserved happiness."

I took a breath as Emma relaxed enough to let go of her lip.

Cristal held Emma's gaze, and I decided the young woman had strength despite her shy words. It made me think well of her adoptive parents.

Emma stepped back, but the two of them were still locked eye-to-eye. "What did he say to you about the money?" she asked bluntly.

"Money?" said Cristal, looking around the room with a confused expression, hoping for assistance from someone. Grant patted her shoulder and whispered something in her ear, and she relaxed. "Oh, Carl's money," she said, shaking her head. "We didn't ever talk about that. We only met a couple of times and that was a long time ago."

"But you kept trying to contact him," said Emma. "Because you believed that you deserved all of his money since you were his biological daughter."

"What? I never asked for that. Why would I?" Cristal looked wounded.

"And then you wanted to make sure that he put you into the will, so that if he died, you would inherit everything, didn't you?" Emma's tone was vicious, but there was an underlying fear in it, like a cornered dog whining.

"My parents paid for college. I'm not in debt. And I have a job of my own. I don't need any of Carl's money," said Cristal. She sounded less innocent now, and justifiably more defensive.

"Of course you don't," said Grant, patting her shoulder. "Emma, Cristal came here of her own free will to help you with your children. If you keep at her like this, I'll take her right out the door."

"What does she expect to get out of this if not money?" Emma demanded. With some enormous effort, she was holding herself rigid, and I frankly worried she was going to give herself an aneurysm.

"Let's have some cookies," I said, trying to cut the tension.

But just then the doorbell rang.

Emma started, and she was trembling and twitching again.

"I'll get it," said Kurt.

"They're my children," Emma said, and followed him. I let out a long breath as she left.

Cristal shuddered. I ate a cookie while I had the chance.

After a few muted words in the foyer, Kurt led William and Alice into the kitchen. Emma was busy chastising them. Grant and Cristal had taken seats at the counter. I handed them each a small plate of cookies, which were completely ignored.

"Do you have any idea how frightened I've been?" Emma asked shrilly. When no one answered, she went on. "I was imagining that car of Grant's, but with both of you inside of it, burning alive. Is that what you wanted? For me to suffer? Well, I've suffered."

William, obviously avoiding Grant, sat at the kitchen table. Alice, on the other hand, stepped right up to Cristal.

"I'm Alice," she said, holding out a hand.

"Oh. Oh," said Cristal. She ignored Alice's hand and hopped off her chair, hugging Alice tentatively instead. "I was worried about you." She glanced at William. "About both of you."

I brought William a plate of cookies, and Emma warned him, "Check your blood sugar first."

He deliberately ignored her and ate three cookies in a row.

"Have you bolused today at all?" demanded Emma.

William seemed to look reflexively at his pump, but stopped himself. "I'm fine," he said. "You don't always have to fuss over me. I'm not going to die when you're not there to watch over me."

I wondered at what age most children took control of their own diabetes care. He was fifteen now, but it seemed like Emma thought he was very irresponsible.

"Well, I'm not so sure of that," said Emma. "Let's get you home to bed."

"We're not going home yet," said Alice, facing her mother squarely with hands on hips. "We just got here. I want to talk to Cristal. That was the point of all of this. Wasn't it, William?"

William didn't say anything. But his eyes were taking everything about Cristal in. I could tell he was noticing how much she was like Carl, and it hurt him. He seemed to hunch down into himself.

Emma dismissed Cristal with a wave. "You've met her. What else do you want to do? You can go to the movies together some other time. We've all had a long day. I think it's time to end it."

"Emma, let's give them some time. Why don't you come with me and we can discuss Carl's funeral," Kurt suggested, putting a hand on her shoulder.

She shook him off impatiently.

"Maybe you should check your numbers and do your insulin—and stuff," said Cristal to William. She glanced up at Emma, as if for approval. She didn't get it. Emma only glared at her.

"I want to know what he said to you," said William. His voice cracked.

"Your father loved you so much," Cristal replied wistfully.

"He talked about you every minute I was with him. He thought you were going to save the world."

"From what?" William's tone was flat, feigning disinterest, but his eyes were alert.

Cristal smiled, and I could have kissed her for the way she seemed to make William feel important. He needed that so much. "From everything. He told me that you were the smartest person he ever met," she said to William. "Scary smart. He said you figured out you were smarter than he was when you were about nine years old."

William grinned at that, if only briefly

"And you . . ." Cristal turned to Alice.

"What about me?" said Alice.

"He thought you were beautiful and smart. He was afraid it would be so easy for you to get boyfriends to do things for you that you might never realize how capable you were yourself. He said that you had always shown William that he'd better listen to you. A natural leader of men, he called you."

If Cristal was faking all of this, she had to be the best actress in the world.

"He really said that?" asked Alice, her hand to her throat.

I glanced at Emma, who looked upset. Couldn't she see how therapeutic this was for her children? Or was she too far gone?

Cristal nodded. "I admit, I felt a little jealous when he talked about you two. I wondered what my life would have been like if—" She stopped. "I mean, I have the best parents in the world. I'm in no danger of forgetting that. But Carl was so passionate. It was like he loved you twice as much as any parent."

As much as a father and a mother combined, I thought.

"Sometimes that was hard," said Alice, her hand still at her throat. "It felt—heavy. Like this weight was on me, wherever I went. Like he was watching me."

"Yeah. I feel like that, too. My parents have high expectations," said Cristal, shrugging. "I think good parents are always like that."

My phone buzzed and I glanced down to see a message from Detective Gore:

Keep everyone calm and whatever you do, don't let Emma get Cristal alone. She may be in danger. I will be there as soon as I can. Ten minutes if I use the siren.

Did I want her to use the siren or not? I wanted her here right now, but I was afraid of what Emma would do once she realized that this gathering wasn't just for William and Alice. I still needed her to confess. How was I going to manage that?

Grant began to tell a story about Carl/Carla saying goodbye to baby Cristal for the last time, and the three young people leaned in to listen to it. Soon there were wet eyes. Cristal ducked her head and stepped away from Grant. Kurt motioned for me to come stand by him. I thought to myself that we were going to make it through this. I just needed to get Emma in the right mood to talk about the night of Carl's murder.

She had conveniently forgotten so many things. Maybe she had forgotten the moment of Carl's death, too. But if I could just get her to admit she had been at the church, that she had been furious with Carl, then—then what? Well, it would be a start, anyway. Would Detective Gore be able to arrest her at last? Would President Frost step out of the way?

I was thinking too much instead of watching Emma. And that was when she acted. In one swift movement, she grabbed the butcher knife from the block on the side of the counter and held it to Cristal's throat. "She's coming with me. No one else would deal with her, so now I have to. It's for the sake of my children. They need me to protect them from her."

Cristal's face went white with terror and her hands fluttered at her side. "Kurt!" I let out.

It was so easy to think of Emma Ashby as petite and thin, helpless as she liked to pretend to be, but now her muscles were taut in her arms, and her face was a rictus of anger.

"Emma, let Cristal go," said Kurt calmly.

"I won't," she said. "I'm the only one who knows what has to be done." And at that, she sliced the knife shallowly across Cristal's throat. My heart stopped for a moment, but Cristal only whimpered as blood welled up along the poor girl's throat and made a dark, red smiling line under her chin.

Emma seemed thrilled at her sense of power, and I had an image of what she might have looked like when she was strangling Carl: intent, satisfied, and with a measure of righteousness.

"Emma, stop!" Kurt shouted.

It was enough to get Emma to move, but she didn't let go of Cristal. Instead, she grabbed the young woman's arm, knife pointed at her chest, and pulled her along the tiled floor of the kitchen, toward the front door. I stood there, frozen.

"Emma, you don't want to do this," Kurt said in something between a horrified shout and a hoarse plea.

"I'm going to save my family!" screeched Emma. Her whole body was trembling, but she didn't loosen her grip on Cristal.

As Emma fumbled with the door, Cristal's eyes met mine, and God forgive me, I motioned for her to stay quiet and go along with this. I was thinking that Emma would let go, that Cristal would have a chance to break free, that Detective Gore would be here any moment. That someone was going to step in and stop the worst from happening.

But Emma didn't let go of Cristal. She used her elbow to knock the door open, then lurched her way onto the porch. I could see the veins on her neck popping out as she hustled Cristal at knifepoint toward her car.

"Linda!" Kurt called as I ran after them both.

The porch lights were on so that I could watch Emma fling open the back door of her SUV. Cristal's eyes rolled back in her head as Emma shoved her in and slammed the door. I ran to the car and thumped on the locked door, but Emma had already reached the driver's side and jammed the key in the ignition. The engine revved to life.

"Emma!" I shrieked as Kurt hurtled past me, throwing himself against the hood of the car. But the SUV was already moving, and he tumbled as it pulled out of our driveway.

I hesitated for a moment, and then I knew what I had to do.

Kurt moaned something to me as I rushed toward my car, still parked on the street. I felt for keys and found they were still in my pocket.

I was racked with guilt for having put Cristal in harm's way. I had cajoled her to come here tonight, exposed her to the wrath of this deranged woman, failed to protect her in her moment of need.

I roared down the street after Emma's car. I could just see the dark SUV ahead of me. I had to keep it in sight. I had to catch it.

And then what?

I had no idea. I just had to trust that I'd get some kind of inspiration in the moment, though I felt completely unworthy of asking for it. God must love Cristal, I thought to myself, even if He had His doubts at the moment about me and Emma.

CHAPTER 37

What in God's name was I doing?

I asked myself this again and again as I swerved after Emma Ashby's zigzagging SUV. Whenever she made a right turn, I could see Cristal's face pressed against the back passenger window. Emma seemed to be purposely taking corners fast so that Cristal wouldn't have the chance to jump out of the car. But I wasn't sure Cristal was conscious at all.

Emma veered down the mountain toward I-15. I had a brief hope that a traffic cop would see her and stop her. Or at least chase after her so I wouldn't have to anymore. The drive down the mountain was the biggest speed trap in the history of speed traps. I'd gotten two tickets there in the first two years we'd lived in that house. But no cops stopped her, and no cops stopped me as I flew down after her.

There was a light at the bottom of the hill, and I could see that it was glowing green against the dark sky. I prayed that it would change to red, and it did. It seemed an answer to my prayers. God had finally heard me!

But if He had, it didn't matter, because Emma ran the light.

Then it was up to me to decide what to do. I couldn't see traffic going across. It was about just past 11 P.M. on a Monday in a small Mormon city in Utah, where most people had long since gone to bed after a dutiful Family Home Evening.

I ended up running the light just like Emma did, although I don't know if she closed her eyes like I did. Yes, it was a stupid move, but I did it anyway. I figured if I was going to die, closing my eyes wouldn't make much of a difference.

I kept hoping that I would hear a siren behind me, that Detective Gore would ride to my rescue. But I wasn't going to wait for her. I had done sensible things all my life, and I had never changed the world. I didn't need to make a difference in the world right now, but I needed to make a difference in my ward.

I had told myself for a long time that men were the reason that women were so powerless. I had blamed problems in marriages on the husband again and again. I had assumed that Emma was being abused after the bishopric dinner. I had been so eager to see that narrative that I had been blind to her true character for so long. But not any longer.

I turned onto the highway and sped up. I was driving my little compact. She was driving an SUV. I got great gas mileage. But Emma had power.

She pulled ahead of me and yanked her steering wheel to the left to pull into the HOV lane. I guess when you've kidnapped someone, that counts as having a carpool. I kept behind her, thinking furiously about what I would do if I caught up to her, trying to imagine what she was planning to do when she arrived wherever it was she was headed. What was going on in that broken mind?

Squinting in the darkness, I watched as Emma got herself caught behind a block of cars driving at exactly the speed limit. God bless the obliviousness of Utah drivers at any time of day or night. Emma was tailgating and no one cared.

I pulled into the lane next to Emma and got a glimpse of Cristal's terrified face under the freeway lights above, eyes now open wide. I'm not sure if I could actually see the dark trail of blood on her neck, or if I just knew it was there. She must be in pretty bad shape, but she wasn't just lying back and accepting it.

"Help me!" she mouthed. Or at least, I assume that's what she was trying to say to me.

"Stop her!" I mouthed back, taking a hand off the steering wheel to point and mime an exaggerated *STOP* like a kinder-garten crossing guard.

Emma was so laser focused on the road that she didn't even look over at us.

Cristal's face was desperate. "How?" she mouthed.

I shouted the only thing I could think of: "Emergency brake!" I pantomimed pressing down and hauling a lever backward, hoping she understood me. She'd have to reach around Emma in the front seat to manage it, but at least Emma wasn't holding the butcher knife anymore. I didn't know where it was now, dropped on the driveway back at my house or on the floor of the car.

Emma sped up and I lost my view of Cristal. The SUV pulled in front of me and then moved around the car that had been blocking her in the HOV lane. I hoped to see the SUV lurch to a halt, but Cristal must not have been able to get to the emer-gency brake, or maybe it hadn't worked to stop it at this speed.

I was behind a semitruck and couldn't follow. I lost Emma's SUV then for several precious minutes, suppressing my feel-ings of panic as I kept pace with the traffic, waiting for a break in which to catch another glimpse of it. Finally, I was able to move left into the HOV lane, even though I had to cross a set of double white lines. I prayed, again, that God would forgive me.

Where was Emma? Had she gotten off the freeway at some point? Was Cristal all right?

What should I do? *God, tell me what to do. Give me a revelation.*

And it came to me. Like a fist to the head. I felt enormous pain, a flash of something that was either a light or just so much sensation it overwhelmed me. I might have crashed, but my arms were still steady on the wheel, as if someone else were holding them there.

Stay! I heard a voice say to me. It sounded like Carl's ghost voice, low and smooth and absolutely convincing.

I stayed, right there in the HOV lane. And then I saw Emma's SUV ahead of me again. Good. That was good.

Only, what did I do now? I'd never been in a car chase before, only seen them in movies. If this were a movie, I would drive her off the road by ramming her car with mine. But in a movie car chase, there wouldn't be dozens of other cars on the road, innocent citizens who might be harmed too if we ended up crashing. I also wouldn't be driving my dinky little car, which would be wrecked instantly if I tried anything like that. God had given me one wonderful revelation, but there wasn't another one to follow. Was I too distracted to hear the Spirit speaking to me? Or did God trust that I was going to do the right thing now? How could He trust me, if I didn't?

I saw the SUV's back window go down on Cristal's side. Was she trying to talk to someone else on the road?

No.

She was throwing things out of the SUV. I thought I saw a book crash onto the highway pavement. Then a backpack. And a bunch of papers.

What was Cristal doing? She could end up wrecking a bunch of other cars, if only by startling them. Luckily, nothing was too heavy. Was it possible that God was inspiring Cristal to do all this?

Around me, cars were honking on all sides. The drivers were also picking up cell phones, presumably to call Utah Highway Patrol about the debris falling around them and the dangerous SUV.

In less than two minutes, I heard two UHP cars coming up fast on the left.

The desire to be a hero had faded, leaving me exhausted and feeling ridiculous. I pulled out of the HOV lane and let the patrol cars zoom past me.

One of them sped ahead and pulled in front of Emma's car. The other one pinched her in on the right. The sirens were blinking red and blue, but Emma kept going, trying to outmaneuver the police cars.

In one breathless, heart-stopping moment, I saw Emma's SUV crash over the median barriers and land in the strip of grass between the two sides of the freeway. The front of the SUV was crushed. Only momentum kept it moving forward, and then it eased slowly to a stop.

I pulled right and stopped my car. The chase was over, though I still felt my blood galloping in my veins.

My head pounding so hard I could hardly see straight, I ran across the freeway in time to see Cristal limping out of the SUV. She didn't get far before Emma tackled her from behind.

I lunged forward, but one of the UHP troopers stopped me from getting any closer.

"Does she have a weapon?" he asked me. We were standing about twenty feet away from the vehicle.

"She had a knife before," I said, as Emma got to her feet and swayed.

"You stay here, all right?" said the trooper. He pulled out a gun and moved closer.

I could hear cars rushing by behind us on the freeway only a few feet away. My phone was buzzing in my pocket. I only looked down at it after I saw Detective Gore step out of one of cars I'd assumed had pulled over to rubberneck.

"Let me handle this," she said, holding up her badge to the UHP trooper. "She's a murder suspect and I need to take her into custody." Detective Gore gestured to Emma Ashby.

"I'll back you up," said the trooper.

Detective Gore flashed a glance at me. "You keep out of this now. I should never have gotten a civilian involved." She looked nervous. Did she think that I was going to tell her superiors about when she'd come to the house and admitted to me she knew who the murderer was and asked for my help?

But my righteous anger deflated as I realized she hadn't asked me to do any of this. She'd specifically told me not to do this. But at least there were dozens of witnesses who could now testify in court against Emma. She would be under arrest for kidnapping and reckless driving, along with a dozen other minor charges, just for what happened tonight.

I watched as Detective Gore took out her gun and slowly approached Emma, who was now staring at her bloody hands and at what looked, from the angle of the bone, like a broken arm.

As for Cristal, as soon as Emma had let her go, she had come to life again and crouched toward the far side of the upturned SUV. She kept glancing up at Emma to time her final flight properly. I could see the coiled energy in her back, hands pushing against the ground to give her a good head start, once she had decided to move.

Detective Gore stood with feet spread and gun trained on Emma. "Stop, Emma. It's all over now."

Emma glanced up at her and I saw no sign of recognition in her eyes. Was she going to throw herself at Detective Gore and end up being shot? My whole body was tightly clenched. I wanted her to stand trial for her husband's murder, not be killed in front of my eyes.

"We know you killed your husband. Your fingerprints were all over that classroom."

So why hadn't they arrested her before now? Because of President Frost, of course.

"You had an argument with Carl, didn't you? What was the argument about?" asked Gore.

Emma took another step forward and I winced. *Please, God*, I prayed, *save Emma*. She was a murderer and maybe worse, but she was also a mother. Her children deserved to see her again, even if it was in prison.

"We never argued," said Emma, stumbling slightly. "Carl was the perfect husband." She kept repeating this to herself.

"You found out about his affair. You were furious. How could he do this to you after more than twenty years of marriage? How could he betray you and your children?" Gore prompted.

How much of what Gore was saying was backed by proof, and how much was guesswork?

"He was a wonderful father. He was always there for William. He would never have done anything to harm his son," said Emma. "Never." She was shaking her head. Who was she trying to convince?

"And then you found out that your marriage wasn't legal, nor were your children's adoptions. All that money you had assumed you would have was in jeopardy. Cristal might get it all if he changed his will." Gore was egging her on, but Emma's expression seemed oddly blank, as if she wasn't hearing it.

My eyes moved to the side for a moment as I saw Cristal sneaking her way around the other end of the car, and into the arms of the UHP trooper. As soon as he had hold of her, he hustled her inside the car.

Cristal was going to be all right, I thought. No thanks to me. And all this time, I'd thought that Emma hadn't known Carl was transgender. But she must have found it out, perhaps recently. Maybe some part of her mind had still been refusing to accept it, while the rest of her plotted against him. I did not understand her at all.

"I never cared about the money. Carl knew that. He knew that I loved him for him. Our marriage was based on respect and affection. It was as good as any of the other marriages we saw around us," said Emma defensively.

"Emma, you strangled your husband. You brought that pink scarf with you from your house. Any jury will see intent in that," Gore said. "We have proof of where you bought it. The receipt was in your house for a set of three scarves, and the charge is on your credit card statement from only two days before Carl's death. You went to the church building that night to kill him. And then you walked home and waited for someone to find him. But when no one did after a few hours, you panicked and called the Wallheims."

Was that all that Kurt and I had been to Emma? A convenient way to get someone else to find the body so she wouldn't look as guilty? Well, at least it hadn't worked, since the police had suspected her from the first moment.

Why had she left the scarf there, though? Was it just a hysterical woman's mistake?

"I bought that scarf to show to Carl. He liked that color on me. There was no other reason," said Emma. But it seemed to me that she wasn't as foggy minded as she had been. Her eyes were narrowing sharply at Detective Gore.

"Did he fight you at all? As you wrapped that scarf around his neck, did you tell him why you were killing him? Did he think he deserved it?" asked Gore.

The detective was crying, and I thought that of all the people who had been involved in this case, she was the one who had understood Carl Ashby the best. I didn't know why. I didn't know much about her at all. She wasn't Mormon, but somehow she was in Carl's heart.

I could absolutely see the scene as she described it, Carl submitting to Emma's punishment because, even after all these years, he still didn't think he was really a man.

"He had a devil inside of him. I had to get it out. I had no choice," said Emma. She leaned over and vomited, and I wasn't sure if that was because she was remembering or just reacting physically to the trauma of the accident. Did she need medical attention? Did she have brain damage? A concussion? Was she in imminent danger?

"Tell me about that night. Tell me what you said to Carl as he died," said Detective Gore. She was close enough now to

Emma that she could have reached out and grabbed her. Instead, her gun was still steady, because Gore understood Emma as well.

"He said that she deserved some of his money. He said that she was his daughter, born of his body. He said he'd die before he'd let her be abandoned by him, like he'd been abandoned by his parents."

I found myself choking at this. Carl had needed to give his daughter up for adoption so he could live the life he imagined for himself, give himself a real future. But at some point, he must have reconsidered that choice. We all reach an age when we begin to wonder how much we are like our parents, and it haunts us.

"He begged me to understand, because he said that I was a mother. But I wasn't her mother. I needed to protect my own children. And our children needed that money. All of it. They needed to know that their father was their father. That he had been rightly sealed in the temple." There was the mother in her again, the fiercely protective spirit that I had connected with from the beginning. Was I looking into a mirror image of myself? Could I become this?

"Those kids are lucky to have you," said Gore, without a hint of irony in her voice. She glanced back at me.

Gore handcuffed the unresisting Emma and led her away from the SUV. I moved toward Cristal in the UHP vehicle, and asked to speak to her before she was taken to the hospital to be checked over. She had a line of dried blood on her neck, but it didn't look too bad. She was in better shape than Emma, in fact.

Once the door was opened, Cristal flung herself into my arms as if I were her own mother.

"I am so, so sorry," I said. "I didn't mean for any of this to happen to you."

I owed her more than an apology. Kurt and I would do everything in our power, I vowed silently, to make sure that she got the money that Carl had intended for her to have. Carl had died to give it to her, and it seemed the last thing that Kurt and I could do for our friend.

Cristal sobbed into my shoulder, shaking violently for a long time. Then she took a deep breath and said, "I have a test tomorrow. I need to study."

I almost laughed at that interjection of the mundane into this heightened reality. Instead, I said, "Tell me your professor's name. I'll write and make sure you're excused from this test." It turned out I could do this one small thing for her, after all.

I called the professor while we waited for an ambulance. I watched as Emma, handcuffed despite her broken arm, was bundled into another.

CHAPTER 38

Since I was sitting next to Cristal and she was clinging fiercely to me, the EMTs assumed I was her mother. I didn't bother to correct them.

"Come, get in and we'll make sure your car is transported," said an EMT with the most exaggerated unibrow I had ever seen, gesturing to the back of the ambulance.

I got in and continued holding Cristal's hand. They said her blood pressure was very low, and they gave her oxygen as a standard procedure, but they didn't seem to think her life was in danger.

Thank God.

I texted Kurt to tell him that Cristal was safe and that Emma was in custody with Detective Gore, who had found us on the freeway. I didn't trust my voice on the phone, and I wasn't eager to have Kurt yell at me and force me to admit that he had been right and I had been wrong.

Cristal and I rode to LDS Hospital, where she was given a blood transfusion and stitches to her neck. Since I wasn't, in fact, her mother, I had to stand outside, and I got to see Emma being led in to have her broken arm set with Detective Gore at her side.

The troopers came and took a statement from me. They said they'd get one from Cristal when she was out of danger.

When I saw Cristal being wheeled to another room and talking to someone on the phone, I finally called Kurt. "I'm at the hospital with Cristal, but we're both fine," I got out before he could start yelling.

"My knees are not, however," said Kurt, whose voice was surprisingly calm.

"What?"

"I've been on them since you left, praying for you to be safe. Since I couldn't pray for you to be sane." His voice was thin, and I honestly couldn't tell if he was angry.

"Well, it worked," I said. Was that the reason I'd received the spiritual help I knew I hadn't deserved?

I started crying messily, mucus everywhere, which was stupid since everything was over now. I wanted to tell Kurt that I was sorry for leaving him behind on the driveway and for making him so worried about me. I wanted to tell him that I wouldn't do this again, not ever. And that he was a good man, a good husband and father, and a good bishop. But that seemed too much like what Emma had said repeatedly about Carl, and besides, it was the kind of thing to tell someone privately, not on the phone in the hospital hallway with random strangers passing by.

"What about William and Alice?" I asked.

"Alice was nearly hysterical after her mother disappeared like that. William helped me calm her down. I took them home after your text message. I just got back a few minutes ago."

"Are you sure that's a good idea?" Emma Ashby's presence was all over that house.

"Linda, they need some rest. Best that it's in their own

familiar beds. In the morning, we'll think what to do next. I'll call a couple of foster families in the ward and see if they would be willing to take them in officially. Then I'll ask Alice and William what they want."

Well, we would see, wouldn't we? "What about Grant?" I asked.

"He's fine. He went home when I took the kids back to their house," said Kurt.

"I just wondered if he looked all right to you. Do you think he feels guilty about all of this?"

"He should feel guilty. His affair with Carl was—" Kurt searched for the words.

Wrong? Was that what he meant? "They loved each other. Can't you accept that?" I asked.

"I think I have accepted it. But they still violated marriage covenants," said Kurt tartly. "If you think I'm going to crawl on my knees and ask Grant to come back to the ward, you're wrong." Then I heard a yawn through the line. Poor Kurt. He lost enough sleep as it was, just from being a bishop. Now he was losing even more because he was my husband.

"You know I love you," Kurt said.

"Even still?" I asked, embarrassed at the wavering in my voice.

"Do you remember what you used to say when the boys were naughty and you punished them? They would wait in their rooms for you to come in and say it. Until then, they wouldn't come out."

"I remember," I said, feeling relieved that he wasn't angry, after all.

"I love you now and always, including all the things you did wrong. But that won't stop me from trying to help you get better. All right?"

He even sounded like me when he said that, and it felt strange to hear the sentiment echoed back at me. It could have been patronizing, but somehow it wasn't. It was quaint, and very honest.

I hung up and saw a very short woman with blonde hair carefully coiffured, makeup to the nines. She was wearing jeans and high heels. After her came a man in a suit. They looked like the perfect Mormon couple. I guessed these were Cristal's parents and I watched as they were led to her room.

THE EMTs HAD brought my car to the hospital, as they'd promised. I drove home and found Kurt was still waiting up for me, the light on in our room.

I undressed in silence, and then reached for the light.

"Would you like me to hold you?" he asked.

Why did he think that, after all of this, he had to ask?

CHAPTER 39

That Sunday, we had our July family dinner. This time, I'd asked all five of my sons to come alone, without wives. I didn't explain why, but I needed some privacy for what I'd planned.

I had put a pot roast in the Crock-Pot before church started, and had the rest of dinner going within twenty minutes of church getting out.

Kurt came home about thirty minutes later, put on one of my frilly aprons over his white shirt and tie, and asked me what he could do to help. I looked him over and gave him a little nod of approval. Our family wasn't perfect yet, and Kurt and Samuel still had healing to do in their relationship, but we were doing some things right if Kurt could don a frilly apron without a wince.

So I assigned him the task of peeling potatoes and chopping the other vegetables that I had set out by the cutting board. I had them in the order I needed them. The last ones were for the salad, which I insisted on making for every family meal. The boys called it rabbit food, but the salad always somehow got finished.

"Are you unhappy about what happened with Emma?" asked Kurt.

She'd had a court date on Friday, but it had ended with her being declared mentally incompetent to stand trial, and she was remanded to the custody of the state until such time as she was competent. At least the world was safe from her.

"I still worry about William and Alice." They'd been officially placed with a foster family outside of our ward, the Frenches. Kurt had been to see them a couple of times, making sure they were doing okay with the readjustments. At the moment, no one was talking about the legality of the adoption, though that might happen in the future.

"They'd hear about her trial no matter what. It isn't as if they can just move out of state," said Kurt.

"I know."

"But you want to fix everything."

"No. That's you. You want to fix things. I want to comfort. I want to mother everyone," I said.

"Because you missed the chance to mother our daughter," said Kurt.

I looked up at him, my hands going lax, completely forgetting about the gravy I had been stirring. Was that why I had jumped into the car after Cristal? Because I was trying to save Georgia once more?

Kurt put a hand on mine, but before we had a chance to say any more, life went on. The doorbell rang and Kurt went to answer it. I went back to stirring the gravy in a futile attempt to dissolve the lumps. I always had lumpy gravy. Cookies were a lot more forgiving when it came to a momentary lapse of attention. They were still good even if they were a bit overdone.

Soon all five of our sons had arrived.

Kurt sat at the head of the table and I sat at the foot. This used to have a more practical function, back when sitting together would have meant having two fewer sides from which to supervise the kids. By sitting apart, we could separate the boys more and make sure that one of us was always close enough to deal with a problem immediately.

We'd done the same thing at church while sitting on those long, padded pews that seemed designed to encourage young boys to bounce on them like a trampoline. We'd also done it when we took the boys out to restaurants (rare in the early days) and movies (also rare).

I had spent years enviously watching the older couples who would sit together quietly on the shorter pews on the side of the chapel, but even now that the boys were gone, Kurt and I couldn't do that for other reasons—he was always on the stand, conducting as bishop, and I was below him in the cheap seats.

"Kenneth, will you pray?" asked Kurt.

I had lowered my head, but I glanced up at that. Why would Kurt ask Kenneth, of all the boys?

Kenneth opened his mouth and I was sure he was going to tell Kurt no. But then he simply bowed his head and said one of the simplest prayers of gratitude I had ever heard.

"Thank you, Lord, for this food. Thank you for the hands that made it. Thank you for the love of family around us. Amen."

It was not at all a standard Mormon prayer, but it was a good prayer even so.

I noticed that Kurt caught Samuel's eye for a moment, and then Samuel's gaze slid away. What did that mean? Were things really okay between them now?

We passed the food around the table and heaped our plates high. I had lost a little weight over the summer with all the walking I had been doing with Anna Torstensen, so I ate without much guilt, as much as any of my boys. One of the hazards of raising sons is that no one eats delicately.

As I digested too much food, I thought about the changing family I had to deal with now. When Adam had gone off to college for the first time, I had felt a long period of sadness. No one had warned me, while I was struggling with all my boys at home at once, that soon enough they would be leaving and I'd have to face the loneliness that came with that. It was a severing of bonds, and no matter how much Kurt reminded me that Adam was bound to me by the sealing ordinances of the temple, it didn't lessen the sorrow of that earthly severing. And then it happened again with Joseph, Zachary, Kenneth, and Samuel.

To have them all back like this, as if they were still mine and belonged here, was a gift. It almost tempted me to ignore the important information I needed to share with them tonight.

But no.

I looked at Kurt on the other end of the table. It was covered with half-full platters, serving bowls, dirty plates and silverware.

I stood up. "I have something I need to say to all of you," I announced.

"This sounds bad," said Zachary. "Is it about your birthday this year? Because I agree we gave you crap presents last year. We should definitely do better for Christmas."

He got some laughs, and then Joseph nudged Zachary. "She's really serious, you jerk."

"Why am I always the jerk?"

"I don't know, why are you?" said Samuel. He already knew what I was about to say.

There was silence after that.

"I need to tell you something about my past," I said finally. "I never meant to keep this secret, but somehow it never came up. And now it has come up, and I have to explain it all to you."

Samuel had done this much more gracefully, I thought. And he hadn't waited for nearly as many years to do it.

Zachary said, "Maybe she's finally going to admit she's an alien from another planet. And we're all half-alien, too."

There were no laughs this time. Probably because of my steely expression. And Kurt's.

I didn't want to do this, but I had to. Might as well get it over with.

"I was married before I met your father," I said bluntly.

Now Zachary was speechless, which happened rarely. It was too bad I couldn't enjoy it much with the way my stomach pressed against the waistline of my pants and my heart pressed into my throat.

"His name was Benjamin Tookey. I married him when I was twenty and we divorced when I was twenty-one. We were only married for eighteen months," I added breathlessly.

"What did he do to you?" asked Joseph. Of course, Joseph was the one to assume something terrible had happened. I was conscious of the fact that I had asked him to leave his very pregnant wife at home this time. He hadn't batted an eyelid at the request. He had become gentle of late.

"I've always believed that he was gay," I said as delicately as I could manage. "He felt obligated to marry, I suppose. The church didn't have any tolerance for being gay back then. It was considered a choice, a lifestyle, and wrong. But in any case, it isn't his fault that I never told you the truth about my past. I'm sorry I kept it from you for so long, but if you have any questions now, I'll be happy to answer them."

More silence.

"Why did you marry him?" asked Kenneth eventually.

"I loved him. Maybe a part of me will always love him. He was the first man I ever loved." I glanced at Kurt to see if he was hurt by this, but he didn't seem to be.

"Well, I think he was an idiot," said Joseph. "And I'm glad that you found Dad."

"Because if you hadn't, none of us would exist," said Zachary. "And we sort of couldn't be in favor of that."

I waited for more pressing questions, something painful from the boys, accusations about me lying to them. But nothing came. Maybe there was something good about having all boys, after all.

Being a mother is a big job with a lot of power. God is the craziest of all parents. He gives us enormous power, then steps back and watches what we do with it. It is up to us to prove that we have done something good, and on a very deep level, I believe that the most important thing I'll ever do with my life is be a mother. That is the greatest power of all.

We had my favorite dessert, chocolate trifle, and then the boys finished up with the dishes.

Samuel was the last one to leave. "I'd like to meet him sometime," he said to me. "This Ben Tookey. If you don't mind."

"Sure. If you want. If he agrees to it. And if he's around."

"Do you have a phone number?"

"I'll try to find it for you," I said.

At that, Kurt gave Samuel a firm couple of thumps on the

back as he hugged him goodbye, and I could see the love stretch between them. That was a good thing. Love was what kept families together.

It was Carl's love for all his children which had ultimately led to his death. He hadn't been willing to cut himself off from love. He had done a lot of things differently than I would have done, but for that, I admired him. And hoped I was a little like him.

AUTHOR'S NOTE

This book came out of a journey that our family has followed along with our dear friends Neca Allgood and David Moore. My husband, Matt, and I met Neca and David when we were at Princeton for my graduate school from 1991–1994 and became close friends. When Neca was pregnant with her oldest child, Kale, and was two weeks overdue, we learned to play bridge every night to keep her sane. After grad school, our paths diverged and we didn't know if we would ever end up living close to one another again. But David eventually finagled a job in Utah and then hired Matt to work for him. Our infrequent visits became weekly bridge nights. It wasn't always easy to get our kids to play together, but we became closer than friends, family in every way but blood.

In 2010, Neca and David's son Grayson came out as transgender and we were privileged to be some of the first people he shared his new identity and name with. We transitioned along with him, to seeing the struggling LGBT community within the Mormon church very differently. Grayson wasn't leaving Mormonism, though it would have been easy for him to do so. His father was an atheist and suggested that if Grayson didn't feel welcome in the Mormon church, he could try other religions—or none. But Grayson and the whole family became huge advocates of embracing difference within Mormonism. They invited our family to join them on pride marches, to walk with "Mormons Building Bridges," and to "Hug a Mormon." Carl Ashby is not Grayson Moore, because Carl was born at an earlier time, but my understanding of Carl's situation comes from my love of Grayson and his family, and those within Mormonism who are working to show true Christian love.

If you are interested in Grayson's story, there are many videos of him online. Perhaps the best one is here: http://www.reelboyproductions.com/project/we-are-utah-grayson-moore/

For those who are LDS and who are concerned about those within the church who are struggling with sexual orientation or gender identity, the Family Acceptance Project (http://familyproject.sfsu.edu/) is an excellent resource for anyone who is trying to figure out how to show love and help family members. There is a specific LDS booklet available that will answer questions and give advice (http://familyproject.sfsu.edu/LDS-booklet) and new videos on the project are frequently posted (http://familyproject.sfsu.edu/family-videos). This is for conservative and liberal Mormons alike.

ACKNOWLEDGMENTS

I had no idea when I first signed with Soho in 2012 how amazing everyone at the company was, or how incredible their list of authors was. It came to me in flashes of brilliance, as I saw what could happen when everyone worked together to get my book the kind of attention I'd never experienced before. And then, as I met Soho author after Soho author, both kind and brilliant in turns, I began to be humbled. And tearful. And exhilarated. So this is what is meant when you find a "tribe," or perhaps even better, a "family," in the world of publishing. I have honestly spent most of my writing life a little perplexed by acknowledgments pages. I am a very solitary person by nature. I don't have readers beyond my editors, the literarily bloodthirsty Juliet Grames, who I met years ago and was fast friends with before I ever wrote anything she might be able to publish, and then Annette Lyon, who makes sure I don't make too many mistakes with regard to Mormon stuff. I don't often think about people who help me in my process, except for a few close family members (thank you, Sage, who reads almost everything I write!). I research my books, but in my own way, online or poking through old musty books, or just observing those around me.

I've always thought it odd that writers have become celebrities who speak to large groups of people, or who are expected to spend hours greeting fans and signing books. It's not that I dislike doing this on occasion, but it's not a skill that I expected to need to learn. Writers are people who naturally like to be by themselves, in a very quiet room, for hours on end, talking to no one other than the people in their own imaginations. We are introverts, and the idea of doing interviews, book tours, or meeting with strangers regularly once terrified me. Until Soho came along to prod me, encourage me, and show me how it's done. It began at BEA in 2014, months before *The Bishop's Wife* came out officially. I walked onto the floor, saw an enormous poster with my face and book cover on it (created by the keen-eyed Janine Agro), was half thrilled and half terrified. Then I came to the booth and was enthusiastically greeted by Dan Ehrenhaft, Meredith Barnes, Abby Koski, Paul Oliver, Amara Hoshijo, Rachel Kowal, and Rudy Martinez. I ducked my head and tried to take it in and be gracious. Then publisher Bronwen Hruska squired me around to everyone she deemed important. The fact that these smart, savvy people were interested in me was an overwhelming compliment, far beyond any accolades *The Bishop's Wife* got in the press. After that came the dinners with other Soho authors: Dylan Landis and Robert Repino that first ALA. And later, Stuart Neville, Kwei Quartey, Tim Hallinan, Stephanie Barron, Cara Black, Lisa Brackmann, Ruth Galm, Matt Bell, Shannon Grogan, Martin Limón, Ed Lin, Justine Larbalestier, and Fuminori Nakamura. I read their books often after the fact, and then wished I had been able to talk to them about the books, but realized I would have been fangirling at them more than being collegial. And there are the authors whose books I have read whom I haven't met, but whom I am honored to share a list with: Lene Kaaberbøl, Agnete Friis, Gary Corby, Cynthia Weil, James Benn, Margaux Froley, Elizabeth Kiem, Andromeda Romano-Lax, and Colin McAdam.

I would say that being a Soho author is a dream come true except that I never had a dream like this. Introverts tend to have rather boring dreams, of days spent by lakes alone, or about food. As a triathlete, I also dream about running, cycling, and swimming—the same motions over and over again. But in this case, reality exceeded any dream I might have had. I didn't know publishing houses like this existed, peopled by real-life book royalty who are really rooting for you.

Thank you, all those at Soho who have championed me and my "little" book. Thank you, all you authors, for being so welcoming to me. But more than that, thank you for writing the books that you write. Thank you for being true to whatever this thing inside of us is that demands that we write, that we bleed into our books every color of the rainbow. Thank you for being on this journey with me, and for finding Soho and making it your home. You are my family.

Continue reading for a preview from the
next Linda Wallheim mystery

FOR TIME
AND ALL
ETERNITIES

My son Kenneth pulled up in the driveway as I was cleaning up the breakfast dishes one morning, just after Kurt had left for work. A surprise, considering Kurt and I hadn't seen much of him lately.

"Mom? You home?" I heard Kenneth call out, not bothering to knock on the door.

"In the kitchen!" I answered. I loved that my sons felt like they could come and go as they pleased. As far as I was concerned, this was still their home as much as mine.

Kenneth came over and gave me a big hug. "I love you, Mom," he said. "You know that, don't you?"

He smelled just slightly, like he'd been sweating on the drive up. "What's up?" I asked cautiously. His coming over unannounced like this had to mean something was wrong, and he was clearly nervous to tell me about it.

"I'm getting married," he said simply.

"What? How? To whom?" Why hadn't he said anything about dating someone seriously? Why wasn't he announcing this at a family dinner with everyone there—his father in particular? If he was already ready to commit to marriage, why hadn't we met her before now? And why did he look like he was waiting for me to get mad at him?

"Her name is Naomi Carter," Kenneth said.

"That's a lovely name," I said, trying to reassure him that he didn't have to be nervous about this. If he loved her, I was sure the whole family would love her.

"She's great, Mom. I'm a lucky guy."

"You'd better say that!" I said, shaking a finger at him, but not seriously. "Oh, Kenneth, I'm so happy for you." I hugged him again, but could feel stiffness in his back. He was still holding something back. "So?" I said, when I released him.

"So what?" said Kenneth.

"Sweetheart, there's obviously something wrong or you would have told us about this two weeks ago at the family dinner. Does she have two heads or something? Is she a felon?"

He sighed and then looked around the kitchen as if to make sure Kurt wasn't there. I wondered if he'd waited down the hill until his father's truck had passed before coming in to see me.

"Spit it out," I said. Now I was really starting to wonder. Why hadn't he brought her with him? Wasn't that the traditional thing, to show off the ring to the family?

"Naomi's part of—well, her family is only kind of Mormon," Kenneth said.

"Kind of Mormon? What does that mean? Isn't that like being kind of pregnant?" I was going for a teasing tone, though clearly this was a big deal to Kenneth. I figured he meant that she was from an inactive family of some kind, and that made sense to me, given Kenneth's own inactivity since he returned from his mission four years ago.

It also made sense that he hadn't wanted to tell Kurt first. He was going to want me to act as an intermediary. I wasn't worried, though—I was sure eventually everyone would get over it. Most Mormons were inactive at one point in their lives for various reasons. It wasn't the end of the world—or the end of an eternal family.

Kenneth sighed again, and rubbed at his head in a way that made him look just like Kurt, if Kurt had had more hair. "I guess there's no easy way to say it, Mom. Her family is polygamous."

I was so shocked I had to gather my thoughts. Of all my sons, Kenneth was the last one I would have expected to be interested in a polygamous branch of Mormonism. I really was not sure how I was going to handle it if Kenneth were about to tell me he'd be having multiple wives, if that was what he planned for the future with this Naomi Carter. My youngest son Samuel's being gay might be problematic in the church, but polygamy felt just plain wrong to me, legal or not. I'd never really accepted the polygamous past of the Mormon church and had always assumed I'd never have to. I thought I'd raised Kenneth to think the same way.

"Are they FLDS?" I asked slowly. The Fundamentalist Church of Latter-Day Saints was the most infamous polygamist branch of Mormonism, led by the now-jailed "prophet" Warren Jeffs, who had been indicted for statutory rape after he married dozens of barely teenage girls, some of whom were also his close blood relatives. Just the idea of Kenneth sitting down for Sunday dinner with men who did that made me sick. I suddenly wished that Kurt were here, after all.

"Not the FLDS, Mom," Kenneth said. "Her family is independent. And very modern. Her dad is an OB/GYN at Salt Lake

Regional. One of the wives is an investment broker and another is an artist. Naomi is in med school, too. She wants to be an OB/GYN like her father." He held my gaze and it was as if he was begging me not to judge him just yet.

I struggled not to make a remark about it being a lot cheaper to have a lot of babies if you were a baby doctor yourself.

"Okay," I said slowly, hoping I knew my son as well as I thought I did. "Are you two planning to be polygamous?"

He snorted at that. "Of course not. Mom, I'm just trying to make sure you understand her history. So when you meet her parents—her father and her mothers—you aren't caught by surprise."

I felt an enormous wave of relief. Mormons hadn't been polygamous since the late 1800s, when the prophet and president Wilford Woodruff had ended the practice. Sometimes I heard older Mormons say that God was polygamous or that polygamy was still going to be required in heaven, but it wasn't a topic I'd heard mentioned in General Conference and I figured that was clear evidence that it wasn't part of the modern church anymore.

"How did you meet her?" I asked, glad to get to the more normal part of being a nosy mother.

There was a long pause and I realized we weren't done with the difficult part of the conversation. "If you must know, Mom, we met at a former Mormons group. We call it Mormons Anonymous."

I felt a twinge of pain at that phrase. Mormons Anonymous—like Alcoholics Anonymous or Gamblers Anonymous? They were talking about Mormonism as if it were some kind of addictive behavior that you had to recover from.

"I knew you were having trouble with the church," I said, waiting for him to explain.

"Mom, the final straw was the exclusion policy."

I felt a gut punch at this and found myself holding onto the kitchen counter to keep from sinking to the floor. This was the one thing I couldn't defend the church I loved on.

If Kenneth had said any other issue had been his breaking point, I could have talked him around it. Or I thought I could have. The church was full of flawed people, even the prophets and apostles, and we couldn't expect that there would be no mistakes made. But deliberately punishing children for the choices of their parents—that was not only cruel but directly against Mormon doctrine, which said we believed that God judged us as individuals and not because of some inherited sin from our parents.

I'd always loved the church's feminist reinterpretation of the Garden of Eden story, the emphasis on education being the way to divinity, the close-knit Relief Society and the way Mormons looked after each other. I loved The Book of Mormon and eternal families and the idea of a Heavenly Mother. It hurt that Kenneth was throwing all of that away because of this one thing. And yet, I understood it.

"You weren't one of the people who went to that mass resignation event, were you?" I asked Kenneth. It had been all over the news. Ten days after the policy on "same-sex attraction" was leaked back in November, thousands of people had lined up in City Creek Park in Salt Lake City to have their names struck from the Mormon church's register in protest against it. Things had been tense between Kurt and me as well. We had had one epic argument back in November about how the policy would affect Samuel's future, and it had gotten so ugly that Kurt had left the house and slept at his office that night.

I hadn't thought about resigning from the church myself, but I hadn't known how to go to church the next week, or the week after that. The only thing that had saved me had been joining a private Facebook group called "Mama Dragons," a group of Mormon women who were fierce in defending their LGBT kids. I could say anything I wanted to them and no one else (including Kurt) would see it. Some of them had left the church, but others were trying to stay like I was.

"No, we didn't go to the mass resignation," Kenneth said. "Actually, Naomi and I hadn't met yet in November. And I didn't want to do anything rash that would affect the rest of my life and my relationship with all of you. But ultimately, I felt sick about having my name connected to the church in any way. So I looked for a support group and started going to the meetings. Naomi was there, too."

"You've officially had your name removed, then?" I had to ask. It would hurt Kurt deeply, and even though I understood Kenneth's choice, it hurt me, too. It meant our eternal family now had a Kenneth-sized hole in it.

"I know you were busy getting Samuel on his mission, Mom, and I didn't really want to open it up for family discussion. But yeah, I went to see a lawyer who said he'd file the letter officially, so I didn't have to go through the harassment and the waiting period the church wanted to set. It was official in March." His words were clipped and sounded almost rehearsed.

"Oh," I said softly.

Then Kenneth started apologizing. "Mom, I know I should have told you about all this before now. I kept telling myself

I should bring it up at family dinner, let it all hang out. But I guess I was a bit of a coward. I knew how disappointed you and Dad would be."

"I love you, Kenneth. I will always love you." That was the most I could manage.

Kenneth sat on one of the stools and after a little silence said, "I've never told you this before, but one of my companions during my mission, Elder Ellison, was gay. He told me in confidence, and I'd been told so many times that gay people were pedophiles and perverts that I believed it. I was scared of him. I called the mission president and outed Ellison to him." Kenneth looked ill and tense.

"What happened?" I asked, feeling a well of sympathy for the poor gay elder who must have felt so alone in the world.

"The mission president immediately came to interview him, and Ellison was transferred to the mission office, directly to the Prez instead of another missionary." He took a shuddering breath and couldn't seem to look at me.

"And then, two months later, I heard Ellison was sent home because of 'emotional problems.'" There were air quotes around those two words. "He committed suicide the day before I was released from my mission. He was only twenty-one." He looked at me, and then looked away.

I'd never known any of this backstory, and I could see now why Kenneth hadn't told me. I thought of Samuel, who could be hurt by a companion who treated him like this. At least Samuel wasn't in the closet, but there had to be hundreds of other missionaries who were. I was glad Kenneth was ashamed of himself. I felt a bit of shame, as well, that I had raised a son who could do this.

But sadly, it made sense of so many things. No wonder

Kenneth had refused to go back to church for weeks after coming home from his mission. No wonder he hadn't done the typical post-mission talk in church, telling all about his converts and funny stories about companions.

Kenneth rubbed at his face, and his hand lingered there, half-obscuring his eyes. "Mom, I've been in agony about this every day of my life since then. I've tried to think of some way I could make it up to Ellison, but I never will. The only thing I can do is to figure out how to prove to myself that I'm not the person I was then, that I'm never going to be like that again. I'm not going to be part of making more gay Mormons commit suicide. I'm doing everything I can to make sure they know I'm not like that, that I understand them."

I reached for Kenneth's arm and patted it, but he pulled away, as if he didn't believe he deserved my sympathy.

"The truth is that Ellison was the best companion I ever had," Kenneth added, talking more to himself than to me, I think. "He was a really good person. He wanted to help others. And he believed in God. Really believed that every prayer he said was being heard and answered in some way. And still, I did that to him because I was afraid of—I don't even know what." He clenched a fist and then looked back at me, his eyes bare and bleeding emotion.

"Whenever I think about Samuel on a mission," he said, his voice almost testimonial, "I can't help but think of Ellison, and how things turned out. I really hope Samuel never has a companion like me. But the way the Mormon church talks about gay people, I don't know if the average church member is any more enlightened now than they were when I was a missionary. Or maybe they are worse if they think that their prejudices have been justified by the new policy."

I thought about Elder Ellison and wished that I had at least gone to his funeral and heard a little more about him. I felt some kind of spiritual debt to him, through Kenneth. I should have raised my son better. I should have talked to him directly about gay people and how I felt they should be treated. Instead, I had covered up the fact that I had previously been married to a gay man. I hadn't admitted that to my sons until after Samuel came out to them. What kind of a person did that make me? A flawed, Mormon one.

Kenneth sighed deeply. "I had planned to tell you after I resigned, but it was harder than I thought it would be. I mean, I probably hadn't gone to a church meeting in my own ward for a year. But that Sunday, I felt horribly guilty. I couldn't sleep for fear that God would punish me somehow."

"Punish you? You mean about Ellison?"

"I don't know if it was about anything specific. But maybe. You grow up believing that God protects the people who are righteous and obey Him, and that everyone else has to deal with hurricanes and droughts and stuff. And yeah, even if you're trying to give it up, it can be hard to stop thinking about God that way, as someone who punishes."

I wanted to ask him if he'd given up belief in God entirely or if he was thinking of joining another church, but it seemed too invasive of his privacy somehow, even if I was his mother.

"I was so jittery I started buying some pretty hard liquor to try to combat it. And maybe to flip off the church's rules. But I realized that was stupid. I didn't want to get drunk to numb myself. I needed to figure out how to deal with the change. So I called up Naomi, who I'd met in Mormons Anonymous, and talked to her about everything, and well, we got closer and closer after that."

"I'm so sorry you went through all that alone, Kenneth." I wish he'd told me. But it was so tricky now, with Kurt as bishop. Even with my own son, maybe I couldn't be completely honest about my feelings for the church anymore.

Kenneth shook his head, "No, Mom. Samuel is the one who needed your attention the most. Going on a mission was a big deal for him, especially in those circumstances. I really hope that being open the way that he is, he can change minds. Make things turn out differently than they did with Ellison. But I just needed to explain to you what was going on at the time so you'd understand how much Naomi means to me. And why we're not getting married in the temple. Or even in the church."

I let out a long breath. "If Naomi was from a polygamous family, did she even have to have her name removed from the records like you did?"

"It's complicated." Kenneth sighed. "Her parents were married in the Salt Lake Temple, and they weren't polygamous until much later. So, yes, her name is on the records of the mainstream church."

"And did she leave for the same reason you did?" I asked. "The new policy?"

Kenneth's mouth twisted. "Partly that, and partly other things," he said.

"Such as?" I prompted

"Well, to be honest, she couldn't stand the way the mainstream church covers up so much about polygamy in the past and makes it sound like Joseph Smith and Brigham Young are these heroes who never did anything wrong."

"But the new essays on Joseph Smith and polygamy admit he married a fourteen year-old girl," I pointed out. There was a new series of "Gospel Topics" essays on the church website, even if they weren't that easy to find if you didn't know about them. Kurt still had people in church complaining when they were taught because they didn't believe they were official.

"They admit it but don't condemn it. Naomi thinks that's even worse. It's okay to take a fourteen-year-old bride if you're the prophet?"

That was definitely a problem in my book, as well. But how could the church condemn Joseph Smith's polygamy without disavowing the other things he had done, like translating The Book of Mormon and restoring the sacred temple rites and proper priesthood power? If that was all gone, we'd just be the same as most other Christian churches, not the "one true Church."

"I'm confused. If her family is polygamist, wouldn't they all have been excommunicated?"

Kenneth seemed almost amused. I guess now that he was out of the church, this wasn't his problem anymore. "The bishop of her family's ward excommunicated her father, but thinks the wives and children aren't culpable. Naomi thinks it's all hypocritical. A wink and a nod kind of thing."

I mulled this over, hoping that I would like Naomi as much as it seemed that I would based on her views of polygamy. "So if Naomi resigned from the church because of polygamy, does she still have any contact with her family?" Kenneth had said that he was telling me about her family as if he expected me to meet them in the near future.

Kenneth drummed his fingers on the countertop. "Some contact. She's trying to figure out how to negotiate things."

I heard the same uncertainty in my son's voice. He didn't

know how he was going to negotiate things with his family, either. This was all such a mess.

"Will they be attending the wedding?" I asked, because it was easier to focus on the particulars than on the emotions behind them.

"She wants to talk to you about all that herself. I'm hoping that you and Dad will come to dinner with us next week. We can meet in Salt Lake whenever is convenient for you two."

He wanted to know if I could smooth everything over with Kurt by then?

"I'll do my best," I said. I could make sure Kurt was there, and try to make sure that he kept his judgments to himself. I didn't know if I could manage anything more than that.

That night I made a special dinner, Kurt's favorite pot roast and mashed potatoes with peas. Homemade rolls were just coming out of the oven when I heard the garage door open, and I tensed, worried that the conversation I would have to initiate about Kenneth would lead to another big argument between us. Kenneth had left this for me because he thought I could deliver the message to Kurt better than he could, but I wasn't sure it was true.

Kurt stepped into the kitchen through the garage door but stopped on the threshold. "Are we having guests tonight?" he asked.

"No, just us," I said.

He loosened his tie. "Did I forget something?" he asked. I could see he was going through the list of occasions in his head. It wasn't our anniversary. It wasn't my birthday or his.

"Kenneth came over this morning and told me some things we should talk over," I said.

Kurt nodded. "Let me get changed, all right?"

"Do you have any church appointments I'm not thinking of?" I asked, because I wanted to make sure we had plenty of time to talk this through. It wasn't something he could start and then leave off while he went to do interviews at the church.

"No, nothing tonight," he said. Right then, his phone chirped.

"Go ahead, check for messages," I said. If there was a ward emergency, I'd get to eat this lovely meal by myself. Or maybe I could pack it up and send it to a ward family who would enjoy it more than I would.

Kurt looked at his phone. "It's fine," he said. "Nothing important."

"Do you want to go answer it and then come back?" I asked, trying to be understanding.

He considered, then nodded. "I promise I'll be back in just one second," he said, and headed into his office.

It was actually about five minutes before he came back, but luckily, by then, the rolls had cooled just enough for me to put them on a plate and set the table with the nice china that I never got to use for family occasions since we only had four settings. I'd put down the lace tablecloth Marie had given us for Christmas last year.

"This looks delicious," said Kurt stiffly. "Thank you."

I passed him the roast and then the potatoes. I had already eaten one of the rolls fresh out of the oven, so I wasn't as hungry as I might normally have been. I watched Kurt. He was clearly nervous, and kept glancing up at me as if he were afraid of me.

"I need to talk to you about Kenneth," I said.

"Right," he said. "Kenneth." He swallowed hard and then put his fork down, waiting.

"I don't know how to put this," I said, hesitating.

"Just get it out, Linda. I'm a grown man. I know bad things sometimes happen."

But it wasn't as if Kenneth had a terminal cancer diagnosis. That, of course, would have been terrible, but at least Kenneth would be part of our eternal family still. He would be in the celestial kingdom, the highest part of heaven, if he was a baptized and endowed Mormon and died without sin. But resigning from the church would mean no matter how good Kenneth was, he could never be with us in heaven. He had rejected the truth and denied his temple covenants. That was worse, much worse, than never being a Mormon in the first place.

"Kenneth resigned his membership in March," I said. After I got it out, I expected to feel relief, but it didn't come. I waited for Kurt to respond. It wasn't as if I thought he'd throw things, but I also knew he wasn't going to just accept this.

"He resigned without even talking to me?" said Kurt in a pained near-whisper.

"It was because of the policy change," I said. Maybe it was selfish of me to say that, because I was using Kenneth to prove my own point, that the policy change was a big deal, that it wasn't just an extension of everything the church already taught, as Kurt had argued with me before.

"I see," said Kurt.

There was a long silence. I had more on my mind, but I wanted Kurt to react to this first. When he didn't, I said, "Don't you have anything to say?"

"I don't see that what I have to say matters. Kenneth has already done this. He clearly didn't want my opinion."

That was true. Kenneth hadn't asked either of us. A part of me wanted to defend him and mention his mission companion, Elder Ellison. But I didn't want to hear Kurt's dismissal of a young gay man's suicide as his own problem and not the church's, so I left it unsaid.

"I think we need to make sure Kenneth sees that we treat him exactly the same as before and show him our love for him will never change, no matter what."

Kurt shook his head and put down his fork. "Linda, I will love Kenneth with every part of my being for all of eternity, but that doesn't mean I will treat him the same. I can't just pretend he hasn't done this."

It was about what I should have expected from Kurt. I started to tear apart one of the rolls I'd buttered, which was entirely unfair to the long strands of beautiful gluten I'd worked so hard to create with my kneading. "He's just as much our son as he ever was. He's a good person."

"Yes, he is," said Kurt mildly. "But God is a god of order. There are rules in heaven, as there are in any place of order."

Again, I didn't want to argue this point with him. So instead, I said, "Kenneth also came to tell me that he's engaged."

Kurt's eyes widened. "To get married?"

I smiled for the first time in this conversation. "Yes, to get married. Her name is Naomi Carter. She's also resigned from the church."

"Ah," said Kurt.

Was he going to ask anything about her? I could only tell him what Kenneth had told me. I hadn't even seen a photograph of her.

"She's in med school," I said. "She wants to be an OB/GYN." I was deliberately avoiding her family's polygamy for the moment. It wasn't like me to do that, especially to Kurt, but everything had changed between us in the last few months. None of our old marriage habits worked anymore. We weren't strangers, but there was now an unspoken contract for how we interacted and avoided conflict. We both followed the rules because we still loved each other and wanted to keep from inflicting pain. So all the pain got held inside.

"Well, that sounds good for both of them. She'll have a steady career if they stay in Utah. Are they planning to stay in Utah, do you know?"

This was like the kind of stilted, polite conversation I had with my parents on the occasions when I called them on the phone dutifully to make sure they were still healthy and alive. The night before Mother's Day, the night before Father's Day, and Christmas Eve, so that the actual days were unspoiled by the bad taste in my mouth my extended family left with me. We were all politeness now, no recriminations about the past and how they had treated me after my divorce, more than thirty years in the past.

"I don't know," I said. "I didn't ask him that." Kenneth hadn't said anything about leaving Utah, but there were a lot of ex-Mormons who were happy to get away from a state where Mormonism was so much a part of the culture and politics.

"Well, I hope they are very happy," said Kurt. There was clearly part of that wish left unsaid.

"But . . . ?"

He shook his head. "But nothing. I hope they are happy."

"You hope they're happy, but you think it's unlikely if they both have left the church."

Kurt looked down at his plate, took a long drink of water, and then set down his glass deliberately.

I said nothing.

Finally, he offered, "I just mean that I don't know how a marriage will work if the two people in it can't depend on each other absolutely for commitment."

It was hard for me not to feel that this was an indictment of me, being disloyal to the church, as well. But I took a breath and focused on our son and his marriage again. "What do you mean by commitment?" I asked. Was Kurt going to say that he thought only Mormons could have good marriages? Because that was demonstrably false. Our divorce statistics were not that different from the rest of America's.

"Well, when someone has been baptized and has made certain promises to a church, and then they turned their back on those promises . . ." He didn't finish. He didn't have to.

"Kenneth was eight when he was baptized. Do you really think that's old enough to make a promise for the rest of his life?" I asked.

"He said he was ready. He was very certain about it," Kurt said.

I wanted to roll my eyes at him. At eight, most children just wanted to please their parents. It was one of the reasons I didn't like it when children bore their testimonies in Sacrament Meeting. They were just too young to do any more than repeat what they'd been told. They hadn't had spiritual experiences of their own. But in Mormonism, eight was supposed to be the "age of accountability."

"People can change their minds, you know," I said instead.

"Yes, they can. But it doesn't bode well for marriage."

Was this about Kurt regretting he'd married me because I'd been divorced? Was I a covenant-breaker, too? "She's from a polygamous family," I blurted out, to direct the focus elsewhere.

"What?"

"Not the FLDS," I said. "I guess they're an independent group. Kenneth said that her father was excommunicated, but it sounds like the children and the wives are still active members of the Mormon church." Sort of.

Kurt muttered something to himself that I decided I didn't want to ask him to repeat.

"He wants us to go meet her for dinner in Salt Lake City if we can find an evening that works."

"Fine. I can do that," said Kurt. "Any evening that week. Except for Tuesday and Wednesday because I have bishopric stuff then."

I waited for him to add a few other days as he thought about it, but he didn't.

He stood up. "Thanks for the lovely dinner. It was delicious."

He'd barely touched it, but he was scraping the plate and putting it in the dishwasher before I said anything else.

"I'm going to spend some time reading scriptures and praying in my office," he added as he walked out of the kitchen.

I suspected he'd be praying for Kenneth and Naomi. And me, too.

Fine, let him. God wasn't going to change who I was. That was a fundamental principle of Mormonism that I loved. We all had free agency. It was the reason that Christ had made the Atonement, so we could all choose and learn from our mistakes instead of being forced to do everything right, which had been the other plan, the wrong one. I didn't know if Kenneth was making a mistake or not, but I was going to honor his choices and not try to pray them away.

I cleaned up the kitchen, packing the leftovers into containers for Kurt to take to work the rest of the week. He often forgot to eat if I didn't pack him a lunch. Despite all our problems since November, I'd packed him a lunch every day. It was easier to do things like that, and not just because it was a habit. It was a concrete expression of love that didn't imply I agreed with him in any way. If only Kurt could figure out something equivalent to do for Kenneth.

An hour later, I passed by his office on the way to putting away my coat and stopped by the door. The sound of weeping was clear, even through the door.

My heart clenched and I thought about going inside to comfort him. I could hold him, at the very least, and tell him that I loved him. I should have done it. If I were a better, more Christ-like person, I would have done it. I wouldn't have thought about my own pride or about him thinking I was admitting I was wrong. I would have cared only about showing my husband that I loved him.

I went to bed alone instead and thought for a long time about how long an eternal marriage could really be. Forever. Eternity. That's how long Kurt and I were supposed to be bound together. And I had always, through every disagreement we'd had before, felt comforted by this idea, buoyed by the thought that we would work everything out eventually. But things had changed.

We should have been celebrating our son's decision to marry, but at the moment I wondered if our own marriage would survive. And if I wanted it to. Forever was a long time to be sealed to someone you thought was profoundly, deeply wrong, about the nature of God, about the workings of the leadership of the Mormon church, and about marriage itself.

Martin Limón cont.
Buddha's Money
The Door to Bitterness
The Wandering Ghost
G.I. Bones
Mr. Kill
The Joy Brigade
Nightmare Range
The Iron Sickle
The Ville Rat
Ping-Pong Heart

Ed Lin
(Taiwan)
Ghost Month
Incensed

Peter Lovesey
(England)
The Circle
The Headhunters
False Inspector Dew
Rough Cider
On the Edge
The Reaper

(Bath, England)
The Last Detective
Diamond Solitaire
The Summons
Bloodhounds
Upon a Dark Night
The Vault
Diamond Dust
The House Sitter
The Secret Hangman
Skeleton Hill
Stagestruck
Cop to Corpse
The Tooth Tattoo
The Stone Wife
Down Among the Dead Men
Another One Goes Tonight

(London, England)
Wobble to Death
The Detective Wore Silk Drawers
Abracadaver
Mad Hatter's Holiday
The Tick of Death
A Case of Spirits
Swing, Swing Together
Waxwork

Jassy Mackenzie
(South Africa)
Random Violence
Stolen Lives
The Fallen
Pale Horses

Francine Mathews
(Nantucket)
Death in the Off-Season
Death in Rough Water
Death in a Mood Indigo
Death in a Cold Hard Light

Seichō Matsumoto
(Japan)
Inspector Imanishi Investigates

Magdalen Nabb
(Italy)
Death of an Englishman
Death of a Dutchman
Death in Springtime
Death in Autumn
The Marshal and the Murderer
The Marshal and the Madwoman
The Marshal's Own Case
The Marshal Makes His Report
The Marshal at the Villa Torrini
Property of Blood
Some Bitter Taste
The Innocent
Vita Nuova
The Monster of Florence

Fuminori Nakamura
(Japan)
The Thief
Evil and the Mask
Last Winter, We Parted
The Kingdom

Stuart Neville
(Northern Ireland)
The Ghosts of Belfast
Collusion
Stolen Souls
The Final Silence
Those We Left Behind
So Say the Fallen

(Dublin)
Ratlines

Rebecca Pawel
(1930s Spain)
Death of a Nationalist
Law of Return
The Watcher in the Pine
The Summer Snow

Kwei Quartey
(Ghana)
Murder at Cape Three Points
Gold of Our Fathers

Qiu Xiaolong
(China)
Death of a Red Heroine

Qiu Xiaolong cont.
A Loyal Character Dancer
When Red Is Black

John Straley
(Alaska)
The Woman Who Married a Bear
The Curious Eat Themselves
The Big Both Ways
Cold Storage, Alaska

Akimitsu Takagi
(Japan)
The Tattoo Murder Case
Honeymoon to Nowhere
The Informer

Helene Tursten
(Sweden)
Detective Inspector Huss
The Torso
The Glass Devil
Night Rounds
The Golden Calf
The Fire Dance
The Beige Man
The Treacherous Net
Who Watcheth

Janwillem van de Wetering
(Holland)
Outsider in Amsterdam
Tumbleweed
The Corpse on the Dike
Death of a Hawker
The Japanese Corpse
The Blond Baboon
The Maine Massacre
The Mind-Murders
The Streetbird
The Rattle-Rat
Hard Rain
Just a Corpse at Twilight
Hollow-Eyed Angel
The Perfidious Parrot
The Sergeant's Cat: Collected Stories

Timothy Williams
(Guadeloupe)
Another Sun
The Honest Folk of Guadeloupe

(Italy)
Converging Parallels
The Puppeteer
Persona Non Grata
Black August
Big Italy

Jacqueline Winspear
(1920s England)
Maisie Dobbs
Birds of a Feather